Hidden Truth & Secrets

Book 1 of the Hidden Series

Cora Janzen

Copyright © 2020 by Cora Janzen/Phoenix Publishing.

All rights reserved. Reproducing, uploading, and/or distribution of this book, in part or its entirety, in any printed or electronic form without permission is theft of the author's intellectual property. Thank you for your support of the author's rights.

This is a book of fiction. Names, places, characters, and events are the product of the author's imagination or are used fictitiously.

ISBN: 978-1-9992263-0-5 (trade paperback)
ISBN: 978-1-9992263-1-2 (ebook)

Cover design by Maria Spada
Book edited by Cara Lockwood and Abbie Nicole
Book proofread by Claerie Kavanaugh
Book formatted by Desiree Scott

To Rod, Gunnar & Ava,

You believed in me and without you, I would never have started This journey. Thank you for supporting and honouring the process.

Grab The Hidden Dossier, the companion document for the Hidden series. This provides readers with some unique insight into the characters, the books, along with other interesting tidbits to illuminate bringing the story to life.

Get your FREE copy at www.corajanzenwrites.com

Acknowledgement

This might be the hardest part of the book that I have written as there are so many people who provided me with support, unyielding excitement, and enthusiasm.

Thank you to Terri, who on a fateful evening in January 2017, insisted we get her sister over to talk about this idea of a book that I just blurted out. I'm still not sure what made me do it but it kickstarted this journey! Cue, Jennifer Sparks, my #booksherpa, who gently nudged me along to consider doing this and then "made" me declare at her *Your Words Your Way Writing, Marketing & Publishing Retreat* in November 2017 that yes, I am going to do this, and yes dammit, I am a writer. She wanted author but I wasn't ready to be that bold. Jennifer, you've challenged and helped me learn so, so much. You have been invaluable.

Thank you to my Beta Readers, who read an unpolished version of this story. Your feedback has made the final product better and picked out those nuances that I miss because the story is so familiar to me.

To all my technical peeps. Wow, this would not have been possible without you. Maria, for your amazing abilities at cover designs and your patience for walking me through the process and revisions to get the final cover. To my editors, Cara and Abbie, for your keen eyes and knowledgeable minds. To Claerie, for not only providing a final proofread of the book, but for going above and beyond. And to Desiree, thank you for allowing me to avoid the need of demystifying the art and science of book formatting.

To all the people from where I grew up. The love and excitement that comes from you warms my heart.

To my colleagues. I'm blessed to have such wonderful, passionate people in my world. The genuine interest and support for each other's personal lives, struggles and triumphs is unparalleled.

To my friends, my cheerleaders through every step of the process. Providing ideas, names of characters that came to you or sending me a small message to tell me you are proud of me. Thank you feels so inadequate.

To my kitties, Caster and Houston (you know I couldn't resist them). You two have been the most annoying supporters, but oh so heartwarming. Whether you are trying to lay across my keyboard or perching your butts stubbornly on the table beside the laptop (and giving me the "No human, a blanket for me to sit on will NOT do" stare), your presence is loved.

My family. To my aunts, uncles, cousins and all those who eagerly and willingly show me so much love. To all my parents and siblings - birth, step and in-laws - I am filled with gratitude for your belief and the words you encourage me with. To my nieces and nephews, may you dream big and never set limits on what you want to achieve.

And finally, my inner core. To Rod, for the emotional, mental and financial encouragement for this. To Gunnar and Ava, for you being the whole reason why I decided to do this. After years of denial, disbelief and doubt, it was being your mom, and wanting to role model to you to never be afraid to step out of your comfort zone to try something new and, that we fail only if we stop trying, that made me leap on this journey. Your excitement throughout this all has lit my fire.

I am humbled and blessed.

Chapter 1

Severyn held the door for a small, elderly woman before slipping into the ladies' restroom off the food court. She breathed a sigh of relief that there wasn't a long wait, the facial prosthetic adhesive was beginning to aggravate her.

Once safely in the stall, she removed a small vial from her inner pocket. The faint odour of the liquid made her nose wrinkle. She applied half the liquid to her short brown wig and dumped the rest on her black jacket. While that diffused through the fibres, she worked quickly on her facial structure. She didn't have the adhesive remover with her, it was safer not to be caught with it. So, she focused only on her chin and jawline, as she had applied those prosthetics with a less binding adhesive.

With those removed, it sufficiently changed her appearance. If anyone was watching and waiting for her, she'd be long gone before they figured it out.

She stepped out of the bathroom stall and smiled at a young girl who pranced, anxious to use the facilities, with her harried-looking mother.

The image of her own mother, tightly holding her hand in a big mall like this, flashed in her mind. She had grown up in a remote community and the city was as overwhelming for her mother as it was for herself as a young girl.

Still to this day, she preferred quiet locales. Ones with small, locally owned businesses rather than big, mainstream ones.

A voice clicked in over her tiny hidden earpiece. "There is no other presence in the surveillance system; ours are the only eyes. And it is clear behind you."

Another voice clicked in. "You're golden, kid. Time for your exit."

She washed her hands, watching herself in the mirror. A young woman with a white jacket and short blonde hair looked back at her. The squareness of her chin was gone, replaced with the natural curve of her jawline.

Satisfied with the revised disguise, she grabbed her bag and left the restroom. Her eyes swept the food court, quickly scanning the people who relaxed, laughed, and ate before they continued their evening shopping.

"Make your way to the extraction point."

Severyn did as the voice in her ear instructed, her confident, long strides carrying her toward the exit.

"Well done." A dark-blonde man smiled at her when she climbed the few steps into the turbo prop aircraft. Zane Andrews sat in the captain's seat and finished his take-off procedure as the door sealed behind her.

"I didn't notice a tail."

"Me neither on the CCTV cameras. We are clear." A Japanese man sat in the co-pilot seat working on a small laptop, his black hair tousled. Kotan Luo possessed a dash of genius for anything electronic and all things computer, there weren't many systems he couldn't hack.

Severyn slipped into the seat behind the two men, cinching the belt tight around her hips. She swallowed, annoyed by the apprehension brewing in her gut.

Kotan gave her a small smile and a nod of understanding.

"It's bumpier than the Gulfstream, but I'll minimize that as much as I can." Zane gave her a knowing smile, crinkling the corners of his amber-coloured eyes.

Both Zane and Kotan were in their early fifties, but were aging gracefully. She snorted, as much in response to Zane and Kotan's read on her as to her thoughts about their aging process.

She wasn't afraid of flying. It was something she was slowly becoming accustomed to. The turbo prop aircraft wasn't a tin can with wings and a propeller. But Zane was right, his private Gulfstream G550 was much smoother which made it easier to distract herself from the fact that they were hurtling through the air at alarming altitudes.

She sighed, settled back into the seat, and focused on her breathing rather than the rapidly disappearing ground as they took flight.

"Welcome home, my girl."

Three hours later, a tiny woman bustled toward her, heels clicking against the tile floor of the foyer as Severyn, Zane, and Kotan entered the large, sprawling house.

"It's good to be home, Nessa." She bent to return her fierce hug, hoping the woman who had become like her second mother didn't notice the slight stumble over the word home.

Nessa held Severyn at arms-length, dark brown eyes assessing her for any sign of injury. The sharpness of Nessa's cheekbones added to the beauty of the Chippewa-Cree woman.

"There were no blips in the op. Kotan and Zane would've let you know." Severyn bit back a smile as Nessa marched around her to shrewdly inspect all angles. "This isn't necessary."

Nessa stood back in front of Severyn, a smile on her beautiful face, as she reached up to touch her cheek. "I know. But a mother needs to see for herself. You may not be born of my blood, Severyn Andrews, but you most certainly are of my heart."

Warm eyes glistened up at her, making Severyn's heart clench.

Not for misgivings about what Nessa had said, but the ache in her heart for her absent family. All that they had lost. All that they were being made to endure.

"Always second fiddle, my lovely wife." Kotan placed the bags of equipment on the entrance floor and scowled but his onyx eyes danced. "My Alinessa."

"Always, my warrior husband." Nessa gave Kotan a sly wink, quick to embrace him with gusto. Nessa was small but she did everything with a enormous passion.

"Zane, your turn." Nessa whirled to him.

Zane dipped his head low and kissed his dear friend's cheek.

"It's good to be home. Everything went smoothly. Our girl here executed the op flawlessly. No broken bones or stitches for you to tend to."

Nessa was a retired physician and surgeon. Retired, not for her age, but because she no longer practiced in a public way. She spent time stitching up operatives from the covert missions Zane and Kotan ran, and making regular visits to her home community in Montana to assist there.

"That is a blessed relief. I rather like that my skills are not needed. Now—" She clapped her hands. "— go clean up and I'll bring supper to the battle room."

"It's my night to cook, Nessa."

"Nonsense. I'm happy to trade, Severyn. Go finish taking everything off your face. Your frequent nose scrunching tells me you're near your breaking point."

"Like Sabrina the teenage witch?" Zane laughed.

"Watch it," Severyn scowled. "I'll turn you into a toad."

Severyn tossed her jacket on her bed, looking longingly at the comfortable surface, but stalking to her bathroom instead. Nessa was right, her face itched to be free of all the adhesive, prosthetics, and make-up added to alter her appearance. At least her persona for this op didn't require a change in skin colour. She lacked the energy to scrub that off her whole body tonight.

On the plane, she had taken off the wig and skull cap. She shook her hair out again now, relishing its freedom before tying it back to work on her face. As her natural face slowly emerged, she mentally worked to keep her mind occupied. It served her better to do so after an op rather than letting it wander into dangerous territory. Dangerous territory, like her family.

Instead, she contemplated Zane and Kotan.

Zane was a self-made millionaire many times over, and a successful business tycoon in the technology and security sector, heading up Gādo Technologies. Kotan led the Research and Development arm as the technical expert partner. Unknown to almost everyone though, Zane and Kotan also developed security technology that was not for market use.

Yet.

They eventually took the products to market, but not before creating something new and improved to replace it. They kept all the new and advanced devices for the covert ops and missions they ran, to always have a leg up over the competition.

Not solely in terms of the business competition, but the competition they encountered in their off-the-books operations. Having the upper hand in the latest hacking, tracking, listening and transmitting devices, had saved their lives countless times.

Kotan and Zane have been doing covert work for years. They stumbled into it in their early twenties when trying to bring the murderer of Kotan's sister to justice and never looked back. They right injustices that have been dismissed, ones that are unknown or authorities aren't pursuing. People get the closure they need, and the perpetrators get the consequences they deserve.

Severyn's case, so to speak, was the key one they have been working on for close to two years.

She grimaced as her face stung from the powerful adhesive remover. Maari was working on a less harsh formula.

Maari, Kotan and Nessa's only child, was a chemistry and computer science genius, as well as a theatrical make-up wizard. Her skills and knowledge were a key contributor to the ops Severyn did.

Maari's ability for altering appearances was a product of her own ever-changing looks growing up. Many would think it was an eccentric teenage girl trying out new things to be different, but Severyn had come to discover it was the by-product of low self-esteem and Maari hiding herself away.

Hiding herself was something she could relate to, Severyn thought as she watched her reflection in the mirror and let her long, wavy hair down again. It was the colour of rich caramel, with high and low-lights of browns, reds and blonde.

Growing up, her hair had been the bane of her existence and it had only begun to develop the rich diversity of colours. As a teen, she would do anything to blend in, to avoid standing out, to allow herself to be as unnoticed as possible. She had worn coloured contacts to hide the rare grey colour of her eyes and used her hair as a prop to hide as much of her face as possible. As soon as she had turned thirteen, she started colouring her hair a flat black and loved the normalness of it, much to her mother's dismay.

Tears sprung forth to hover on the edge of her eyes. Her mind hit on the dangerous territory she was trying to avoid.

She braced her hands on the counter fighting the emotion that washed over her. It was always more intense after an op.

How she missed the feel of her mother's strong arms, the reassuring tone of her voice. The way her dad affectionately ruffled her hair when he came home from work. She missed them all. Especially her little sister. Sweet, little Fi.

She huffed at her reflection. "Not helping."

Severyn lifted her shirt, grinding her teeth at the ache in her right shoulder. It was from an injury almost two years ago. She'd gotten it during an incident she was lucky to escape alive. When her and Zane's paths converged to change her life forever. Zane coined it her 'death scape'.

The hot cascade of the shower washed the grime of the op away, and helped ease the ache in her heart caused by thoughts of the family that was lost to her.

She braced her hands against the cool tile wall, letting the water rush over her taut body to splash around her feet, and swirl around the drain. Whenever she thought of her family, she stood at a crossroads. This time, like all the others before, she would not let it defeat her. She would focus her heartache to fuel her commitment to keep pushing forward.

Fulfilling her goal and completing the mission was all that mattered.

Chapter 2

Severyn walked silently down the hallway, the plush carpet squishing between the toes of her bare feet. The hallway led to the room they'd all coined 'the battle room.' It was one of many rooms in the massive, sprawling house, and where Zane and Kotan planned the various ops to complete their missions.

Computer and surveillance equipment filled a large portion of the room to allow them to plan, oversee, and direct ops. Unless the situation warranted them to be in close proximity, like if they thought she may need some emergency assistance to get out of a jam; then they would accompany her. Which was becoming more and more the case lately.

The battle room was next to Nessa's den of magic: the medic unit. It was where Severyn had spent her first weeks at the estate almost two years ago. It was, understandably, her least favourite room in the beautiful house.

The medic unit and battle room were at a point of transition in the house, beyond them lay the Luo's family living quarters.

Kotan was Japanese and Nessa was Chippewa-Cree, and their living quarters proudly displayed vibrant elements of their heritages. As Severyn made her way along the hallway, the artwork and energy of the space changed.

Severyn traced the outline of the bronze dragonfly pendant she wore, then tucked it safely under her oversized sweater. A treasure from Nessa before her first op, she wore it whenever she wasn't on an op. The dragonfly was a powerful symbol for Nessa, as her Cree family felt it symbolized change in the perspective of self-realization and resiliency.

Severyn needed both.

The smell of steak, double-stuffed potatoes, and green beans greeted her as she walked into the expansive room.

Zane smiled at her groan, pulled out a chair, and motioned for her to join them at the table they used for eating. Food and dirty fingers were kept far away from computer equipment and touchscreens. "Food before debrief."

"Can we multitask? I feel sleep hunting me down."

"We eat, then talk. It will be a quick debrief." Kotan gracefully forked a piece of steak into his mouth.

Her stomach growled watching him, clueing her into how hungry she actually was.

"This is amazing, Nessa. I'm so glad I didn't cook tonight," Severyn managed around mouthfuls.

"Us too," Kotan said softly, and Nessa and Zane howled.

Severyn shrugged, taking no offense. "Homemade macaroni and cheese is my go-to dish but I do have more on my repertoire of menu selections. Which, by the way—" She pointed her fork in Kotan's direction. "—I pull out when it's my night to cook."

"And for that we are most grateful."

Money was no object, but the rule was they all took turns with cooking, meal prep, and other household tasks. Maari and Severyn had begun to stay at their own places in Boston, but insisted they be kept in the rotation as they still spent a good deal of time at the estate. The estate technically belonged to Zane. However, he never made any of them feel that they were guests. It was their home, as much as it was his.

"I reserve my mac and cheese for those that truly appreciate it. Maari and Lok know good cuisine."

"Lok loves his comfort food, doesn't he? I miss him raiding the kitchen." Nessa laughed, referring to Severyn's friend and international electronic music DJ.

"Did I hear my name along with Ryn's mac and cheese? Yes, please." A tall lithe woman glided into the room, graced with her parents' striking features while fully embracing her own uniqueness. As she swung a magenta wool wrap off her shoulders, the tattoos up her neck were displayed and the diamonds of her facial piercings glittered.

Severyn was the name that Zane and Kotan selected for her deep cover identity as Zane's niece when she came to live with them after her death scape, but Maari quickly gave her the nickname Ryn.

Maari was a perfect blend of her mother and father. Tall and long-limbed like Kotan, with his onyx eyes, Maari also had Nessa's razor-sharp cheekbones and poker straight hair. Maari's swung like long sheets of black around her, whereas her mother wore hers in a chin length bob.

Graduating two years ago from Harvard University with high honours in double degrees of Chemistry and Computer Science, Maari immediately went to work in the Research and Development arm of Gādo Technologies. As for the other part of the 'family business' she was reluctantly initiated by her father to be involved in the covert work. Maari and Kotan even had a fully outfitted workspace at the estate, where Maari created tools like the dye and colour changing solutions used on Ryn's jacket and wig today.

Maari swept into the chair that Ryn pulled out for her. "Ryn, you can make me mac and cheese later when we stay up late and you tell me all about the op."

Zane hid his smile while Kotan furrowed his brow at his beloved daughter. "You have work in the morning."

"Oh, I know, Daddy, but Ryn and I are young. We have the youth of our twenties on our side. Besides, she only sleeps four hours a night anyway."

That deepened the furrow of Kotan's brow further even though her sleeping problems weren't a secret among them. Most nights, four hours was the magic number before her nightmares caught up and tormented her.

"Now tell me, how did my creations hold up in the field?" Maari munched on the green bean held delicately in her graceful fingers.

"The facial anti-detection cream worked well." Zane leaned back, intertwining his fingers over his stomach. "But we had worked the kinks out of that one already."

Maari nodded and pushed her long hair over her shoulder. "Yes, but it's good to know it's holding up with all sorts of imaging equipment."

"The solution for changing the colour of my wig and jacket worked out well. It turned quickly; under a minute, I'd say. And no smoking this time." Ryn snatched a bean from Maari's plate, grinning. "The taser had some kinks though and didn't communicate well with the master device."

"Shit. Sorry, Papa." Maari flashed an apologetic glance at her father. "I told you not to take that, Ryn."

"I know. I didn't really need it when I used it; I was testing it." Ryn shrugged. "If it worked, it would've been an added bonus."

"Yes, ah, well, he wouldn't have seen it that way." Zane chuckled low.

"The low-life had it coming. Like I said, I didn't need it. This way though, we have a field test and can refine from that. It's a win-win. I resorted to a good kick in the ball-sack instead for the piece of crap." Kotan and Zane's handsome features scrunched up with empathetic pain. Nessa and Maari grinned.

"Grow a pair of tits, they're tougher than balls." Maari winked at Ryn and her mom while Kotan choked on his water.

"I know the man would have had it coming; Ryn isn't vindictive or mean for sport."

"You're right, Nessa." Zane, still chuckling, finished the last of his red wine. "He did have it coming. And he most definitely was a low-life."

"I hate to break this up, but can we debrief, then clean up? I have to hit the sack in a serious way."

"No mac and cheese?" Maari pouted.

Ryn stifled a yawn. "No mac and cheese tonight."

Kotan patted his daughter's arm in an amused, conciliatory fashion. "I uploaded the stick you were able to get from the taskforce, Severyn. It should be almost finished. I will get a search running through it for our key items of interest to see if there are any connections. But from the initial run I did before you came in for supper, there weren't any."

Ryn closed her grey eyes, fighting to dispel the flash of disappointment. Were they ever going to catch a break, or even a thread, on this without it being another dead end?

"Eliminating what it is not, *is* progress, Severyn." Zane understood her silence.

Her chest rose and fell with her sigh. "I just thought this would be over by now, not still at the beginning stages. I thought I would have been able to accomplish more."

"I know it feels like forever. You have to remember though, you spent many weeks healing from your injuries." Nessa clasped her small hand over Ryn's. "Getting your memory back, coming to terms with what happened, and then training to get ready to do this. In that regard, two years is not that long."

The memory of laying in pain from the physical injuries to her shoulder, ribs, back, and face was still vivid. As was the mental distress caused by her complete memory loss, followed by guilt, devastation, and terror once her memory finally returned.

"You're right, Nessa. But, being occupied doesn't make the time easier."

It didn't lessen the implications either. The implications that, for almost two years, her family had been separated from her. Believing her dead.

Almost twenty-four months of them grieving, healing, coping, and trying to move on.

She pushed away from the table and started to pace because sitting still, with the wave of sorrow and guilt that came, would surely crush her.

"I'm certain Kotan's search through the Taskforce's information will confirm what was gleaned through your little chat with Webb Rodent, aka The Rat. But we will run through the data diligently," Zane reassured her.

"Such an unfortunate nickname for a guy working with connections to organized crime. The Rat. Sheesh." Maari shook her head.

"We identified that Monahague Bay by my home is, or was, a location of some significance. We eliminated that it was drugs being run through the area and now, almost certainly, that it was not money running or laundering. There wasn't or hasn't been much for missing persons, so what was happening there two years ago?"

Ryn stopped pacing and didn't finish her frustrated rant. What was so big, so significant, or so important it got Vlad, her childhood friend and Zane's nephew, killed?

Had gotten her killed? Or so everyone thought.

"Unfortunately, there are many more criminal intentions besides the three big ones you mentioned. But Zane is right, eliminating what it is not is still progress."

"I know, Kotan. I'm sorry if I'm coming across as a complainer. And I know we've circled around this many times before." She massaged her temples roughly.

"Not in the least. This is the hardest on you. Our commitment has not wavered, we will do whatever is needed to stand by you and figure this out together." Kotan stood and kissed his daughter's head and then hers. "Zane and I will clean this up. You head to bed to get what rest you can."

"Zane has to go back to running his business empire and you

back to leading Research and Development. You guys coming on site with me for ops is a challenge for you." Guilt plagued Ryn while sleep tugged ruthlessly at her. "I only have to touch base with a few clients later in the morning, you guys head to bed, I can clean up."

"Nonsense," Kotan and Zane said in unison.

Ryn smiled. Two lifelong friends who had fought and struggled to right justices for decades, forging a security and tech company worth millions in the process. Two extremely different men but yet, so similar.

"I can see the headache brewing behind your eyes. Can I give you something? It won't have a sedative in it, I promise." Nessa's shrewd eyes missed little.

"No, I'm fine. Honest, I am," Ryn added quickly when Nessa was about to press it further. "I have the peppermint solution you gave me last time. Thank you though."

Strong, slender fingers gripped her hand and yanked. "Come on, when have they ever insisted we ditch clean up? Night Mama, Papa, and Uncle Zane."

She let Maari pull her out of the room and down the hallway toward her room. They walked in comfortable silence. Maari was a few years older than Ryn, but the age difference didn't prevent the strong friendship that had formed over the past two years.

At first, it took a lot for Ryn to let the spirited and vivacious young woman close to her. Not only because of her current situation, but because she had a long history of keeping people at bay and not showing her true self to others. Ryn didn't have many friends growing up, specifically because she never wanted them. Or to be around groups of people for long periods of time. It might have been a product of growing up as one of five children, or how she was engineered.

Maari knew the whole story of who Severyn Andrews really was, how she had come to live at the estate, the covert ops she did, and her mission. That had deeply unnerved Ryn at first. Many nights she had woken up covered in sweat, having a panic attack worrying that one of these four people would inadvertently, or purposefully, put her family in the crossfire once again.

But slowly the trust seeped in, the panic attacks subsided, and Ryn allowed herself to have a friend in Maari.

"I know you're frustrated, but are you okay?" Similar in height, Maari looked directly into Ryn's grey eyes with concern.

"Sorry, I'm cranky with my impatience. And impotence and inability to perform." A very unladylike snort emitted from her companion. "To get the job done, you know."

The hallway walls around them fell away as they crossed the walkway that spanned over the floor down below. Large windows on the second floor surrounded the walkway and the ceiling opened up to skylights that showcased the twinkling stars. When sleep eluded her, Ryn would sometimes come here, lay on the walkway, and look up at the sky.

It reminded her of watching the sky while lying in the forest that surrounded her childhood home. Sometimes with Vlad, sometimes with one of her three brothers, or her favourite, with her young, small sister.

"Speaking of impotence. You're still going to New York to meet up with Lok, right?"

Ryn sputtered, choking on her laugh. "What? Speaking of impotence and then you bring up Lok? Oh my God, he'll kill you, Maari."

Maari turned to her, red with laughter. "I know. But really, it's quite the opposite. Well, I'm assuming, anyway."

Maari reached back and grabbed her hand to pull her along again. "It would probably be best not to mention the impotence comment to him. I would hate for him to have a damaged ego."

Lok Bello was an international electronic dance music wizard that Ryn had met over a year ago when he, along with his friend and music executive Antonio Demeanus, had discovered her talent for music and songwriting. Both men had been relentless in trying to convince her to pursue her musical talent, and Zane, Kotan, Nessa, and Maari had surprisingly agreed with them. Eventually they all wore her down and Ryn had acquiesced, but only as a songwriter. Over the course of the year, she'd had tremendous success with her clients. Along the way, while working closely with him, she'd lowered her guard a bit and found another good friend in Lok.

"He's totally into you." Maari laughed at the panicked look on her face. "Not in a romantic way. A guy like that has lots of people around him, but he's picky about who's in his inner circle. He values you as a friend. But seriously, you guys have never bumped uglies? Not even once?"

Heat warmed Ryn's cheeks. "No. We've never bumped uglies. Or anything else for that matter. He likes the songs I write for him that make him the big bucks."

"That's so cynical." Maari's laugh vibrated off the walls around them. They had reached the door to Ryn's bedroom and Maari tugged her arm to get her to stop when Ryn kept walking. "You don't need your studio now. You need some sleep."

"When did you become my mother hen? It's very unbecoming." Ryn grinned at Maari's sour look. "You're supposed to be my fun, mad-scientist friend."

"I'm kinda like a mad-scientist, aren't I? But you'll thank me when the black bags are gone from under your eyes."

"It adds to my sparkling personality."

That warranted another snort from her friend. "You're lucky I love you so much. But honestly, get some sleep. All you do is train and exercise. Mind you, you do have the body of a svelte Olympian."

"I do more than that." Ryn scoffed.

"Ah, yes, between training and exercise, you do ops, write music, and now you have taken on mentoring young music students at Annelou's Fine Arts school. All work and no play." Maari walked backwards away from her, toward her own room. "Promise me you won't ditch out on Lok and New York. Promise?"

"Promise."

Chapter 3

"Let me down, Vlad. You're being a jerk; you know I don't like heights."

Vlad's freckled face came into view through the trap door of the treehouse that led to the ground. The ground where her feet could embrace the cold, hard earth beneath her sneakers.

On the verge of puberty, Vlad had all the awkwardness and gawkiness the challenging transition offered. His dark hair stood up in tufts, like someone had jammed their hands through it repeatedly to make it permanently that way.

"Right this way, chicken shit."

Her feet finally hit the earth and she opened her tightly squeezed eyes.

No longer in the trees where Vlad's treehouse had stood, but now overlooking a crest of rocky land that sloped majestically down to the valley below. They were nestled in the edge of the Rocky Mountains, outside the town where they grew up, along the west coast in Canada.

Turning to look at her companion, Vlad's pre-pubescent gawkiness was replaced with the face of the man he would become. His height and girth, however, had yet to get the memo that puberty was coming to a close. His dark hair still stood up in tufts and he affectionately called it his bed head look. He claimed it was part of his sex appeal, but she had never witnessed any drawn in or allured by it.

This dream of her childhood friend was always the same. Even in her unconscious state she recognized the dream for what it was.

And knew the journey it would take.

She could feel the rising dread wrap its nasty tendrils around her heart as the fog and mist started to rise from the valley below.

Like watching a movie in fast forward, stuck in a time warp, memories flashed by of her childhood, with Vlad never far from her side.

Not all the memories were happy ones though. Close to graduation Vlad turned moody and vicious, and there were many fights between the two who had been inseparable most of their childhood. During that time, they went weeks without speaking. And then without explanation, Vlad was back.

Her angst grew as the feeling of dread escalated. She felt herself falling through the darkness, not seeing, but feeling herself spiral down, down, down until finally she laid still. The cold, hard earth beneath her like the steel slab of a coroner table. She knew what she would find when she turned her head. But in this dream, she had never once been able to stop or change the dreaded outcome.

Slowly, unwillingly, her head turned, her eyes compelled to stay open to prevent blocking out the sight. Blocking out the pain. A soundless scream, filled with horror and agony, gripped her throat of what was always beside her.

The lifeless, vacant, hazel eyes of her childhood friend staring back at her.

Forever unseeing.

Forever uncaring of her sobbing pleas for him to come back.

Forever gone even as she begged him not to leave her.

She shot up in her bed fully awake, trembling, and choked back a sob.

Always. It was always the same. She could never wake herself up from this dream and break the cycle. Forever doomed to relive the painful memory of finding Vlad dead, over and over again. Instead of sleep being an activity that rejuvenated her body and mind, it was a nightly cycle of torment and despair for her soul.

Shaking and sweating, Ryn rammed her hands through the tangled mess of her hair. The contact with the solid floor grounded her when she swung her lean legs over the edge of the bed. Her heaving gut, racing heart, and tense muscles started to dissipate.

Two years ago, she was a normal, quiet girl who graduated high school along with her friend.

She was the oldest in her class with her late-in-the-year birthday, but even with that, she was always mature for her age compared to her peers. A bit of a social recluse and extremely introverted, she spent most of her social time only with Vlad.

He never hammered her with a thousand questions like the girls she grew up with. His mother wasn't especially stable and Ryn always assumed that he, too, appreciated the lack of questions or having to explain situations or any of the whys.

They had been inseparable.

Then he was gone.

Local authorities said it was an accident. No foul play. A tragic accident with a faulty electrical system.

Grieving the loss of her friend, she accepted that. Accepted that and sought to find a way to move on.

Until they came for her too.

Ryn loved the feel of the earth under her long, steady strides and her breath coming deep from within her chest.

The large sprawling house faded behind her as she sprinted across the field. She smiled when the grazing horses pranced toward her. They quickly realized she brought no treats and Kenzo, the big black and white paint, nipped at her bouncing braid before leading the other two horses back to grazing.

She settled into a brisk pace, breathed deeply, and closed her eyes as she entered the woods beyond the field. Within a few strides, it was a completely different world. One with a muted hush, yet the sounds of the birds chirping and snapping twigs were crisp and magnified.

The trail was soft with the mulch of dead vegetation, pine needles, and dirt. Large tree trunks, felled years ago, had moss and small treelings sprouting on top of them. A decomposing ecosystem that fed a new generation of life.

One large trunk bisected the trail, but instead of removing it, the previous landowners had cut an opening to minimize the disturbance to the ecosystem around it.

The myriad of greens cast a soothing picture for both her eyes and mind as she ran deeper into the trees. She felt more and more like she was coming home. Here, she could almost imagine she was racing through the forest of her childhood home.

Vibrant green-yellow colours accented deep emerald-green, mixed with rich browns and the cascades of bright purple wildflowers. Thoughts and sounds of her childhood filtered through her mind and mingled with the present around her. The chirping of birds echoed, reminding her of cool early morning walks as a young girl holding her father's large hand. Of jumping over fallen trees, the burning in her legs when she had chased after her brothers up the rugged slopes.

Gentle tears slid from her eyes, but she didn't wipe them, or her memories, away. Bittersweet, they made her heart ache terribly. But they kept her loved ones alive and vivid for her. They renewed her resolve.

Allowing the nature around her to be a comforting hug, she ran on through the trees, and let her mind wander. It settled on one of the many conversations around her decision to pursue music. She hesitated to call it a career. That sounded forward-looking and long-term.

Antonio and Lok were persistent, stubborn, and could not fathom the reason for her resistance.

Those who did know the reason for her resistance - Zane, Kotan, Nessa, and Maari - surprisingly stood aligned with Antonio and Lok's case for trying the music business. Only Ryn stood on the opposing side.

They all stood united, but for different reasons.

Antonio and Lok saw her talent and huge potential.

The others knew Ryn was uncomfortable and obstinate about doing any tasks that were not directly related to her mission. Knew how hard it was for her to pause and focus on anything else. But they also knew how that wore on her since she had limited outlets to emotionally decompress.

It was hard to believe it had been over a year since they had converged on her, working to make her see exploring the songwriting path would be an asset to her and the mission.

"It's happiness, Severyn. It has been a long time since you have had cause for that in your life. In your heart. Let it settle back in there and you'll feel more at ease." Nessa's luminous, brown eyes had shone with motherly support.

"You'll be surprised what can happen, the things you may remember, the ideas to help with your mission, when you remove the pressure from your subconscious." Zane was the ever-practical mentor, but the reasoning rang true and similar to what her own mother used to tell her when she had been stuck with a big problem growing up.

"Sometimes another path leads us to what we need."

"You are right, Maari." Kotan had picked up where his daughter left off. "Severyn, you feel this is a side journey that distracts you from your main goal. This does not mean you are giving up. It does not mean that you are closing your heart to your family. Instead of closing a door on finding a way back to them, you are opening yourself up and giving your mind a break to think of other things to aid in that goal."

What they all said resonated with her and she knew they were right. Writing and playing music did give her body, mind, and psyche the reprieve it needed. It provided her constantly working brain the ability to percolate the random info gathered from the ops, to make sense and connections out of it. And it provided her a measure of contentment and peace, even if it was temporary.

As if sensing her openness to considering it, Zane added, "And regarding your concern about anyone recognizing you from your past, there is little chance of that. With the facial reconstruction, and the other physical changes you have gone through, coupled with your solid cover identity and background, it's nil according to our analysis. And you'll choose how public you go with this."

She had finally relented to use this as a strategy to destress, cope, and be better prepared for her ops and mission. Anything that would help her achieve her core foundational goal, her current reason for living, couldn't be bad.

She smiled now, remembering Lok and Antonio's dismay, when she would only commit to focusing on songwriting. She could control her time commitment better this way. But most of all, being a performer, coming out as a musician, would shove her too firmly in the public eye.

Of course, Lok and Antonio didn't know this was her reason. And not much had stopped them from trying to find ways for her to perform in front of a crowd.

Snapping back to the present, she realized where she was along the path, where her body and subconscious naturally steered her. She broke into an all-out run to the clearing.

Relishing the burning feeling in her thighs and the force it took to breathe in adequate air to feed her strong leg muscles, she pushed herself harder. The strength of her body surged her forward to her destination. A gentle stream curved and ran alongside the trail, gurgling happily as she sped by like a bird in flight.

The wind off the ocean blew across her face in welcome when she burst into the clearing high above the water. She took deep gulps of the sea salted air and closed her eyes, loving the roar of the rough ocean waves hitting the rock face below. Imagining the power in each square inch of water. By itself, each droplet was powerless. Together, with its collective power, the water could destroy ships.

She loved racing through the trees and coming here. The sights, the sounds, the smells. Maari called it her Zen space; her small sliver of the universe that provided her unquestioning calm, peace and tranquility.

The ocean, the trees. So much like her home.

Kotan had brought her to the woods behind the estate once she was physically healed enough from her death scape for short walks. He introduced her to the practice of Shinrin-yoku - a Japanese healing practice of Forest Therapy. It involved taking an extremely slow journey, focusing on the sounds, the smells, and all the intricacies of the life that bloomed at all levels in the treed area.

Although her preference now was to run through the trees, she still enjoyed heading out with Kotan for the slow, mindful walks. They were, in fact, what started her healing journey when she had come to them memory-deprived, battered, and grief-stricken.

Thinking of Kotan, she realized what time it was. She cast a wistful look out at the water wishing she could linger longer but she had learned the hard way of being tardy for her training sessions with her Sensei and mentor.

That was a dirty one." Ryn doubled over from the vicious jab Kotan laid on her ribs under her raised arm.

Kotan nimbly moved on the balls of his feet out of her reach. "I told you, your elbow is flaring out and to keep it in. A novice mistake."

"So self-righteous." Ryn moved fast and low to sweep Kotan's feet out from under him. He reacted quickly, but not quick enough to avoid landing hard on his back. "You're favouring your left foot.

Not a stable base," she said between breaths as she offered a hand to help her Sensei up.

Kotan graciously accepted it. It didn't matter who was the student and who was the teacher, Kotan said there was no room for ego during training, or in the field.

"Well done," he said with appreciation. "Knowing your weaknesses is key. Knowing your opponent's weaknesses is survival."

"You've taught me well."

"You are an apt pupil."

She wiped the sweat from her face and neck, tossing the towel on the counter before chugging her water. "Obsessed pupil, more likely."

Kotan nodded, his tousled hair swaying with the movement. "There certainly was, or is, an element of that. But that does not negate your quick aptitude for learning these new skills. And others." Kotan swept his hand around the large room and indicated the training area, along with the music studio, that they had set up for her when she decided to pursue songwriting on a formal level. She loved this room and spent the majority of her time here when she was at the estate.

The room boasted a high vaulted ceiling with hardwood rafters and floor to ceiling windows along the outside wall to showcase the fields in the back of the house to the trees beyond.

The training space held everything she needed: weights, mats, full-size punching bags, chin-up bars, ropes and ladders hung suspended from the high ceiling. It had a treadmill and rower, for days the weather didn't cooperate, and even parkour half-walls bisected the room. Everything she needed to incorporate endurance, power, stability, and flexibility into her training.

The deeper half of the room housed her piano, keyboard, and other music equipment that allowed her to compose her music. Shortly after she had made the decision to pursue songwriting, she had come home to find this beloved room had these surprise additions. Maari knew how much she loved being in this room and had slightly redesigned the space, so it could pull double duty for her.

She remembered the sudden self-doubt in Maari's dark eyes, worried that she had overstepped her bounds, and Ryn would be upset she had tampered with the space. But the emotion that had hit her like a tidal wave wasn't anger. It was awe and appreciation that they would do this for her. People who were invested in her and who knew, even before she did, how this would feed her soul. And they supported that. Like family.

"You love this space."

Ryn's eyes were dark grey with the memory and swung to Kotan's gentle ones. "It's what it represents."

He nodded in understanding. "Come, we are not finished."

Kotan continued to push her through a gruelling session for the next hour demanding and taking every ounce of her strength and endurance while he did so. He worked all her large muscle groups, but was a master for eliciting movements that strengthened her internal core to give her power and stability.

"Keep your legs straight and torso upright. Good, push up with your arms, and lift your buttocks and legs off the ground."

Sweat dripped into her eye, she blinked it away and ignored the distraction.

"Slower now. Slow and controlled, do not let momentum or the larger muscles help. Pike at the waist, keep the legs straight, and avoid touching the ground."

"I'm not a gymnast training for the Olympics for Christ's sake." Ryn's arm muscles and tiny stabilizing core muscles trembled as she pulled her legs through her arms into a backward pike position and up into a handstand. Which Kotan ruthlessly made her hold for a full minute.

"Perfect," Kotan clapped his hands, and she sprung onto her

feet. "And yes, I know you are not training for the Olympics, you are much too old." He gave her shoulder a soft jab, but his onyx eyes turned serious. "Give no quarter to your body when training. In the field, none will be given to you."

He was right. In the field, she wasn't sparring with opponents that were competing for a gold medal.

"Now, it is time for you to shower the lovely smell off you and head to New York to meet Lok."

"You sound like your daughter. You guys reading out the same manual?"

"If it is the manual of how to prevent you from burning out, then yes. It is on the second rendition. Now get. If I see you here in an hour, I am pulling out the back bender and headstand bench so we can train more."

For once Ryn did as she was told, when she was instructed to go have fun, and bolted from the room like the hounds of hell were nipping at her heels.

Chapter 4

Ryn sat back in the molded black leather seats of the Porsche 911 GT3, as the driver made the engine purr like a kitten. She knew that Antonio liked to drive fast and aggressive. She also knew he was an extremely good driver. But she had trust issues.

On top of driving like an Indy 500 pro-racer, Antonio chirped away like a TV talk host. In classic Antonio-style, he was a non-stop stream of chatter and commentary about the result of their short time together spent on meet and greets with new potential clients for her to work with.

Most guys can't multitask, but leave it to Antonio to defy the stereotype she thought, as he zipped along New York streets, dodging taxis and slower moving vehicles, talking continuously. She kept her features relaxed even though she was bracing inward. "I believe the building will still be standing if we arrive ten minutes late. Lok is there all night, you know, and it's not like you have to be there early to score a good seat."

Her hand shot out to clutch the 'oh shit handle' as a pedestrian made a rash decision to dart out. "Fuck, Antonio."

"Ooh, that was a bit close." Antonio flashed his trademark smile, showcasing stellar white teeth, making his Hispanic heritage more evident.

"You better cool your jets, Romeo, you don't want Miguel to think you're overzealous."

"Overzealous? What, are you a 16th century poet? Taking your songwriting into new territory maybe? Hmm, me likes." He winked and his chocolate brown eyes danced in delight.

"You're such a tool." She laughed. Time spent with Antonio was never dull. Being a successful music executive at Classic Vibe Recordings, Antonio could very well be a stuck up, pain-in-the-ass or an egotistical ass. Fortunately, he was neither.

"A tool? I feel like I'm back in high school. Well, you, *mi amor*, are a dolt. But have I ever told you that your beautiful, sexy, cat-like eyes are the exact colour as the metallic chrome of my beauty here?"

It was always a game of keeping up with Antonio to track the insane tangents of conversations with him.

"I think you're trying to distract me from the topic of Miguel and how you swoon when he's mentioned."

"Swoon? Pfft. I'm cool as a cucumber, and you know it. But really, when I was picking out the colour, white is hell to keep clean - and you know how I'm with things being just so - everyone and their Chihuahua has black, and red is such a cliché overstatement. When I saw the chrome one and how it shifted in the light to change right before your eyes, I said, this is Severyn, our sweet, sexy Ryn. And that's why I picked this colour."

"Oh my gawd," she drawled, "you're so full of bullshit, Antonio."

"No, *mi amor*, my sweet, I'm telling the truth." He swung into a fortuitous parking spot. "You've never seen a better park job, right?"

"You're a tool. The biggest one."

"Why, thank you. It's always gratifying to have my manly parts appraised so positively."

Antonio narrowly missed a bike messenger whizzing by before he raced around in chivalrous fashion to open her door.

"Rather late for a bike messenger, isn't it?"

Antonio gripped her hand to help her out of the low-slung seats. "This is a city that never sleeps. And lawyers, and others that don't like to live and spend the money they earn, are probably slogging it out at the office and demanding others do the same. The poor bugger is probably headed to see one of the dickheads in my office."

She pulled her long sweater tighter around her, against the June evening breeze, as she got out of the metallic Porsche. The faint smell of saltwater mixed with car exhaust and street vendors' wares contributed to the eclectic atmosphere. It wasn't unpleasant, only different from the coastal sea breeze she was accustomed to.

"You're rather different than the majority of people I've met in your office and industry."

"Unique as a rare gemstone, right my beauty?"

"Absolutely." She couldn't help but laugh when he dipped low with a dramatic flair to kiss her hand.

On cue, Miguel opened the side door of the club as they approached. A sharp glare from the large burly man, who easily looked like he played linebacker for the Giants, was all that was needed to halt other potential patrons from slipping in with them.

"Good to see you again, Ryn." Miguel latched the door. "You too, Antonio." A smile cracked his dark features. A stark contrast to his ominous countenance, but he didn't become the head of security for one of the most popular clubs in New York by being a teddy bear.

A definite undercurrent of attraction filled the narrow hallway. Neither men were openly homosexual but there was definitely chemistry brewing. One short and stocky, trendy professional, and the other a tall brick shithouse, jeans and t-shirt kinda guy. It was an interesting pairing.

She noted a healing gash on Miguel's large bicep as she moved past him.

"A risk of the job. Some dope thought a knife would convince my staff to let him in."

"Not a well thought out plan." She wondered how the guy fared after swiping a blade through Miguel's corded bicep.

Miguel smiled deeply. "Not well thought out at all."

The narrow hallway spilled into the main part of the club. A large circular room with two upper mezzanines that formed rings around the main floor. Patrons on the upper two floors had a grand view of the large stage at the front.

It was early evening, but people were steadily filing in. The local talent was well into her set, successfully ramping up the energy levels to entertain the early arrivals.

They moved along the outer perimeter, Ryn's white sneakers looked like a bright beacon in the black lights that strobed all around. Antonio confidently led the way to the door, tucked off the side of the stage. Being a close friend of Lok, he was no stranger to the club where Lok held his residency. She strongly suspected the music executive had started frequenting the club even when Lok wasn't playing here.

A smaller version of Miguel opened the door, and they climbed a flight of stairs to a large sitting room with sofas, chairs, and a bar off to the side.

Standing at the bar, mixing a drink, Lok beamed when he saw her. He rushed over to grip her in a tight hug. His dark hair tightly cropped, dressed in black leather pants and a black t-shirt with "Mama's Boy" splashed across the front, his blue eyes were electric as he pushed back to look at her.

"I'm so happy you came. It's been way too long since I've seen you."

She laughed, her eyes a light grey with the ease she felt in his presence. "It's only been a few days."

"Videoconferencing doesn't count." He ruffled her hair.

As internationally famous as Lok Bello was, he was no diva superstar. He always made people feel welcome in his presence, rather than that they should feel honoured to be in his. His authenticity, and down to earth nature, was what sealed the friendship for her.

"Did Antonio squeeze some work in with you?"

"Of course." She smiled and waved at Pauline and Belinda, two of Lok's friends and wives of his crew members.

"They're a good match." Lok smiled at Antonio who gave him a friendly salute before returning to his conversation with Miguel. Lok pulled her back over to the bar to finish his drink and mix her a vodka soda with lime.

In the music business, it seemed like non-heterosexuality was a bit more readily accepted, but it was nice to see Lok fully accept his friend.

"For Antonio and attraction, he isn't restricted to the gender identity," Lok explained. "It's about the attraction to the individual, not the equipment they have. He is quite sexually fluid."

"Good qualities for you both."

Lok arched a dark eyebrow over his crystal blue eyes ringed with dark navy.

"He honours what's true to him, without the weight of societal norms, and you for being an open-minded, accepting friend." Ryn clinked her glass to Lok's.

"I suspect his successful status plays a part in allowing him to easily do that, but his, 'go fuck yourself I will live my life how I want' attitude definitely is a big factor."

Pauline and Belinda were impatiently waving her over. "I guess I have to share you." Lok sighed reluctantly.

Lok ran his DJ empire as a close-knit business. They were his lifelong friends who had found their careers alongside, and within, his. There were no employer-employee vibes; this was a family.

There was Peter and Carlo, who grew up with Lok back in Italy, who worked their magic for stage design, construction, set up, lights, and ambience, along with their wives, Pauline and Belinda. Gio also grew up with Lok, Peter, and Carlo, and was the videographer. Doyle, Lok's manager and supreme organizer all rolled into one, was newest to their group.

Ryn wouldn't consider herself as exceptionally tall, but next to the crew from Italy, with the exception of Lok, she felt like a lumbering giant. Ringing in at just under six feet, Lok wasn't exactly tall by North American standards, but he did have a good six to seven inches on his childhood friends.

"Ryn, it's so great to see you again." Peter gave her a jovial hug. His small round belly jiggled slightly when he laughed, reminding her of a younger, slimmer version of Santa Claus. She had liked him on first sight.

"Every time I see you, I'm surprised by your hair colourings." Pauline's compliment referred to Ryn's unique hair that was the colour of melted caramel with a mixture of blonde, brown, and red hues. "It never changes so I know it must be natural. It's beautiful."

Never one to be comfortable receiving compliments she blushed lightly. "Yours as well." Pauline boasted baby-soft and curly strawberry blonde hair.

"You came solo tonight? Again," Belinda joked accusingly.

"I didn't."

"Antonio doesn't count." Belinda's large breasts bounced as she gave a hearty laugh. "One day soon, some fella will catch your eye and ravage you."

Ryn choked slightly on her drink and Lok clapped her on the back, laughing.

"Doyle, you remember Severyn Andrews, or Ryn, as we like to call her?" Lok made space for his manager to join them.

"Of course, it's been a while since I've seen you, I hope you're doing well." Doyle extended her hand and her short spiky red hair shone in the overhead light. "Lok incorporated a lot of your pieces into his sets the last two weeks and they've been well received by the crowd. I'm sure they will be tonight as well. Especially when you play your newest one."

"Pardon?" Her stomach flipped, then dropped, and she looked suspiciously at Lok.

"Doyle, I hadn't gotten around to giving Ryn the good news." Lok looked sheepishly at his flashy red sneakers.

"What'd I miss?" Antonio wedged himself between them and wrapped his arms around their shoulders. Being the shortest of the three of them, it would be an uncomfortable position, but Antonio loved to be in the thick of things.

"Lok, it seems, is going to bring Ryn up to speed about his big, grand plan for tonight," Doyle quipped as she crossed her arms across her ample chest. She had a full frame and was very attractive. Her hair was fun and, rather than conflict, it complemented and balanced out the no-nonsense vibe she emitted.

"Oh, you really stepped in a steaming pile, Lok," Antonio ribbed as Belinda and Pauline stepped discretely away.

"You aren't helping," Lok glared at Antonio before he looked sheepishly again at her. "When promoting tonight's show, I may have alluded, okay I promised, that you would be joining me on stage for a song or two."

"Our deal is songwriting and compilation. You know how I feel about the public thing." Panic brewed in the pit of her stomach.

"It's the new one we were working on via videoconferencing. You can play it in your sleep. And the way you pitch and deliver the lyrics… I know it hasn't been polished yet, but it's real."

"The idea wasn't that I was the singer. We were deciding who would be best." She ground her teeth and relaxed her grip on her glass when she noticed her fingertips going white.

"And that would be you, *mi amor*." Antonio squeezed her rigid frame to his side.

"Jesus, you guys. And you spring this on me here, in front of everyone, after you made a public announcement I would be doing this?"

"When you put it that way, it sounds so—"

"Underhanded? Manipulative?"

Lok flinched at her accusatory tone. "You wouldn't have said yes otherwise."

"And that would have been my prerogative to do so."

"He's trying to nudge you out of your comfort zone. To try something we all know you wouldn't push yourself to do," Antonio said quietly.

"It's only one song, Ryn." Gio sidled up beside her. His silky white blonde hair swung over his eyes. "It will give me an opportunity to get some pics and footage of you in action."

"I just—" She paused, biting down her panic. "I hadn't reconciled myself to the idea of being a performing musician. I write the words, the music."

"This is a safe environment to see if it's something you want. To make an informed decision." Lok smiled softly at her. "Just the one song. Please."

"Why is this so important to you?"

"You're important to me. You have an amazing talent. Why wouldn't you want to try?"

In an industry where people fought and scraped by trying to make it, she was being offered an opportunity on a proverbial silver platter. They could not understand her hesitation.

They had no idea of the conflict she had with anything that distracted her from her focus. No idea of the panic of becoming more public and somehow being recognized, even though Zane and Kotan reassured her constantly there was no risk.

How can I get out of this without divulging my true reasons why?

Her mind zipped from one possibility to the next, discarding them all.

Resigned, she scowled. "One song."

Chapter 5

Ryn looked out over the sea of bodies moving enthusiastically to Lok's music. The three-story building was packed. She studied the elaborate ceiling, pillars, and grand marble staircases, that hinted at the history of the building, to take her mind off the crowd and what she was about to do.

They watched Lok play from the side of the stage. Privileged to witness him live his dream and the effect he had on the crowd.

It also provided her with a view of all the exits and what was happening in the club. Having an exit plan, and having more than one exit option, had become second nature to her. She swallowed hard, struggling to ignore the urge get the hell out of there.

"You ready?" Antonio gave her a small nudge. Miguel glanced down and gave her a brief smile of encouragement.

She looked down at her casual jogger pants, black tee, and white sneakers. "I'm not dressed to impress."

"You are a non-HMO. Your style is 'I'm dressed for myself' and along with your gorgeous face, and this hair—" Antonio ran his hands through it and let the waves fall over his hands before she could react. "—you're more than perfect."

"A non-HMO?" Gio asked, as he pushed his silky white blonde hair out of his eyes.

"A non-high-maintenance-organization," Antonio supplied.

"Love it, I'm gonna use that one." Gio swung the camera around to zero in for a close-up of Ryn. "You really should have seen this week's crowd response to your collabs with Lok. It'll be epic to get you playing together and debuting the new little beaut. I'm gonna have my vid equipment rollin' the whole time."

They all smiled, except her. She felt like puking her guts out.

"Gio is a wizard, you won't even know he's there." Belinda piped in. "Lurking. Filming in the shadows. Kinda like a creepy, stalker guy."

"Hey, you do what feeds your soul and bliss-ometer."

Out on stage, Lok gave her a big smile followed by two thumbs up. He was a kid in a candy store. She laughed, but the anxiety level rose another notch as her stomach did a few flip-flops. That was the signal he was transitioning to the part of his set where she was to join him.

Lok jumped up on the side of his console, his bright red sneakers a blur as he bounced up and down, yelling and amping up the crowd. Gio moved nimbly around the stage, working his magic and capturing the moment and all its electricity.

"I made a promise for tonight. How many of you are here because of that promise?"

The crowd roared their response.

"She can own the keyboard better than anyone I've ever encountered. Powerhouse vocals on top of that. Who wants Severyn out here to perform our newest song?"

The stage vibrated from the noise and stomping.

Lok jumped down off the console, and as she shyly stepped forward, the roar escalated. Her collaborations with Lok had become massive hits, and she had earned notoriety as a songwriter for a growing list of headlining musicians and bands. The crowd was impatient to hear her perform live.

Swallowing her trepidation, she took her place at the piano and electronic keyboards by Lok's console. His natural exuberance on the stage shone through as he prolonged the intro, allowing her to get settled. He bounced and moved while layering the sounds to ramp up the intensity. She watched for the signal the drop was coming and where she would join in.

She closed her eyes, swallowed hard, and began to play. It was a complicated, mixed tempo piece, and she focused on the fluid movement of her fingers.

The crowd was wild, the bass pounded in her chest, and she released a pent-up breath she didn't realize she was holding. She allowed the excitement in and the last sliver of hesitation shattered. With it, she felt an emotional release - contentment, peace, and bliss - wash over her like a wave. This happened each time she played but being on stage, playing with Lok, made it more potent. It was a drug and she let it take hold of her.

Lok kept her on stage for two more songs before she waved him off with a vigorous shake of her head. The old building vibrated with the crowd's roar of appreciation as she took her bow.

"I'm so happy I got to witness that; it was incredible. I do wish you would play more with Lok." Pauline hugged her so tight the apple scent of her strawberry blonde curls filled her nostrils.

"You were outstanding." Doyle, Lok's efficient manager was always a bit reserved, but her smile was as bubbly as the champagne she pressed into Ryn's hand.

Gio had his video camera trained on her but moved back to filming Lok after she put up a hand to ward him off. He came close to peck her on the cheek. "You were amaze-balls. Loved every sec of it."

She smiled watching Lok play to the crowd, his love and enjoyment plastered on his attractive face.

Ryn observed and scanned the crowd. Hands flailed in the air, a sea of bodies moved in unison to the rise and fall of the music.

She backtracked her gaze toward the main floor bar. The vigilant observation skills Kotan had worked her tirelessly to hone kicked into overdrive as she quickly took in the tall, broad-shouldered man leaning against one of the pillars.

Close-cropped hair accentuated his widow peak. The black leather jacket, snug charcoal shirt, and jeans paired well with his intensity. He had a strong, square jaw and kept his face neutral with a slight smile on his full lips. Regardless of the smile, there was a brooding nature about him that stood out to her.

The intensity in his slow sweeping gaze certainly warranted him a second look, but there was something else that had grabbed Ryn's immediate attention.

She had seen this guy before.

Her sharp mind ran through the files in her memory, like a computer scanning for the presence of the search word.

Zane's hotel. The one he purchased from a proprietor in New York who wanted to retire but cringed at the thought of the hotel being absorbed by a chain. That was where she had seen him before.

It was a little more than a year ago. The same day she had the chance encounter with Lok and Antonio, she realized with a small jolt. She had accompanied Zane to New York and was sitting in the park across the street waiting for him, feeding the birds, and killing time. She had watched Zane slip out of the hotel side door and meet briefly with the very guy who was leaning against the pillar, as well as two others. At the time, she thought the meeting had secretive undertones given the side door exit and that the meeting had lasted less than a minute.

And now?

She quickly scanned the club, but she didn't see the stranger's companions anywhere. That didn't mean they weren't here or close by.

Her mind processed the connections to assess the potential threat level. He obviously knew Zane. But the nature of their relationship - good or bad, friendly or foe - she couldn't say. She slipped her hand into her pocket to quickly type a message to Zane but hesitated to hit send. He obviously knew the guy, as evidenced by the New York encounter, but Zane had never mentioned him. Or warned her about him.

She smiled nonchalantly and responded to a comment Belinda made, careful to ensure her face and body language didn't portray the emotions and rapid analysis that were raging internally.

The man didn't appear to be paying any attention to her and briefly chatted with a variety of people. It was very possible that he just happened to be here. That it had nothing to do with her or any connection to the covert ops that were a secret part of Severyn Andrew's life.

She deleted the message to Zane but, as coincidental as the guy's presence may be, she kept herself ready for any sudden defensive action she might need to take.

By the time Lok's show was over, she was tired from being on high alert and appearing nonchalant, but Lok was reluctant to let her leave.

"I haven't really gotten a chance to see you and we need to celebrate. That was sick having you on stage with me."

"Pouting isn't becoming of you, Mama's Boy." She punched his shoulder lightly. "It's pushing two in the morning and I have a training session with Nero in a few hours."

Nero was a long-time friend of Kotan's, and a world-renowned fighter who trained both professional and upcoming fighters. It was a legitimate reason, she argued with herself, stamping down her guilt for not staying longer with Lok.

"I need to go if I don't want to get my butt beaten black and blue because I'm slow and sluggish."

"Okay, I get it." The dampness of his back pressed into her palms when Lok pulled her in for a tight hug. "Thanks so much for tonight. Being here. Playing with me. Words can't express my feelings at having you on stage with me. It was stupendous."

She laughed. "Stupendous?"

"Yeah, you heard me. Stupendous. And you loved it too." He

swiped a hand through his wet black hair and his eyes shone.

"I want a turn." Antonio swung in to give her a bone-crushing hug. "It was a marvellous show, Lok. And you." Antonio looked at her with pride. "*Mi amor*. They. Loved. You. I'm so proud of myself for reeling you in after stumbling on you playing the piano in the park. I pat myself on the back every night before bed."

"The ever-humble music exec." She chuckled and gave him a wink. "Enjoy yourself tonight."

"Oh, I will." He kissed her full on the mouth before she could respond and was off, leaving her shaking her head at his whirlwind personality and antics.

"You're sure about leaving?" At her nod, Lok continued, "I'll call Ted to take you back to your hotel. No, stop right there, I'm insisting. Ted would have my ass in a cast if I sent you home in a cab this late."

Lok used Ted, a retired police officer, exclusively as his driver whenever he was in New York. Ted was cool and efficient and knew how to keep his patrons safe and unbothered.

She relented, and once Ted arrived, Lok gave her another giant squeeze before she quickly slipped into the limo.

"Tomorrow." Lok stated firmly, pointing a finger at her while he walked backwards toward the club's side door.

"Tomorrow." She promised.

Fully exhausted, she leaned her head back against the seat, closing her eyes. But she opened them again when all she saw was the intense, brooding eyes of the stranger in the club.

She couldn't get rid of the feeling that this wasn't the last time she would see those eyes.

The handler clicked in over the tiny hidden earpiece of the man watching Severyn Andrews. "She is on the move."

The darkened building across the street offered an unobstructed view of the club's side door and provided him with both cover and time to wait. A sleek, black limo pulled up and on cue, the side door of the club swung open as the driver quickly opened the back door for his passenger. The woman he watched play with the DJ tonight tucked her long hair over one shoulder, pushing it impatiently out of her eyes as the wind gusted around her.

Her sweater was pulled tight around her lean frame. From his vantage point, he watched the streetlights brush over the skin of her face and slender neck, making it glisten like pixie dust had been sprinkled over her.

He meticulously removed any signs of his presence in the darkened building, slipped out the door and into a black Audi RS 5. He wasn't in a hurry to follow the limo, the handler on the other end of the earpiece would keep him apprised if the destination changed.

He knew who was in the limo. Any number of people knew her by now. She had blasted onto the scene and her success as a songwriter for several famous musicians, and her own musical talent, had rocketed her into orbit. And rightly so, he decided, after watching her play tonight.

Yet, he wondered why he was sent to watch over her tonight and for what end goal. If there was a concern for her safety, why didn't she have bodyguards?

But he wasn't paid to ask those questions. And the mission seemed innocuous enough without violating his code of ethics or boundaries, so he didn't press it.

"She is still en route to the hotel. If that changes, I will keep you apprised."

The destination was Zane's hotel and he took a shortcut but listened intently for any updates if the limo changed course. He arrived before the limo did and settled into place to observe it pull up to the hotel lobby.

The driver walked with military rigid posture, but that didn't hinder him as he smiled generously at the striking girl when she graciously thanked him.

Momentarily transfixed, he admired the myriad of colour in her wavy hair from the illumination the of hotel lobby lights. Her body movements were sure and smooth. Like a wild cat.

When she had left the club, his keen eyes noticed her casual glance to take in her surroundings. She did so again when she got out of the limo, and again before she entered the hotel.

It was subtle, but he knew the practice. Scan and observe your surroundings for any threats. Take note of key details that could be critical later.

He was surprised to observe the practice from a songwriter, especially from an individual that was quite young.

Interesting. Maybe more than a songwriter and musician after all, he thought.

"Safe and sound," he quietly reported.

"Thanks, Alpha, for your service tonight. We will be in touch soon."

The click in his ear indicated the transmission had been cut off and finalized the end of his work for the evening. Watching her stride into the hotel, Tag wondered, "Who are you, Severyn Andrews?"

Chapter 6

Taking in the sights on the cab ride to meet Nero Gareth, Ryn was always amazed how the feel of the city changed from one section to another.

Growing up in a small community that lived a fairly remote existence, the vastness of a city like New York could overwhelm, especially the traffic. Her cab driver, Theo, a chatty guy who was content to double as tour guide, preoccupied her mind during the ride to the Bronx and she relaxed, immersed in his animation of the city.

"Did you know the Bronx is one of the most densely populated counties? And almost a quarter of the area is open space? Can you believe it? Just unused space, no buildings or nothing."

"I'm sure it's well used. Are those parks?"

"Parks, cemeteries, you name it. Even a zoo. But the city is a zoo so why they have that there, I'll never know." Theo's cackle was cut short to dodge another driver that had slammed on his brakes. Fists and curses flew everywhere as he sped by.

Thankful to arrive with her limbs intact, she assured Theo that Nero's Hell Den was the destination she wanted.

"I hear Nero is a stand-up guy, but there sure are some ruffians around here. You're sure, miss?"

"I am. Now scram."

Pulling open the heavy door to Nero's fiefdom, she was greeted immediately with a pungent smell and the thud of fists and feet meeting punching bags or opponents' flesh. The street-side windows of the gym were not transparent and on her first visit, Ryn discovered it was a thin film of material, not dirt and grime. Nero kept a meticulously clean gym.

A short and stocky bald man strode up to vigorously pump her hand in greeting before crushing her in a bear hug.

Never being one that was comfortable with people invading her personal space, she was inadvertently surrounding herself with those that did.

"Severyn, the wolf in sheep's clothing. It's a pleasure to have you back in my world." His gruff, gravelly voice perfectly matched his rough outer countenance.

"I'm never a hundred percent sure if that's a compliment."

"One hundred and ten percent. Come." He gripped her elbow and led her toward the mats. "Tell me, how is my friend, Kotan? Is he still telling you lies?"

Ryn waved at Sven Andres, known by all as Tank, when he grinned at her while stalking his prey around the ring. "By telling me that he has the lead in TKO's between you two, then yes."

The gym was a variety of training areas with mats, rings, caged-in rings, as well as areas with large and small punching bags, and all the training equipment you would expect in a place that bred strength and agility. Anyone not engrossed with their opponent bowed respectfully to their master trainer as he walked by.

Nero turned to bark form corrections at one of the two females grappling. The cauliflower ear perfectly matched his bald head, crooked nose and gruff demeanour, all souvenirs from his years of boxing, wrestling, and grappling.

"She's going to be the next great MMA fighter, I'm damn sure of it. You need to get on the ground with her, I think you could teach each other a thing or two. She's a Pitbull, just like you." Nero laughed, his barrel chest rumbling.

Regardless of who's tally of TKO's was right, Kotan respected and honoured the trainer Nero was. Early in her training, Kotan insisted she meet with Nero; she now had regular sessions with him. Kotan's style leans more to the technique executed precisely whereas Nero is as scrappy and cutthroat as they come. The diversity of instruction had served her well.

"You ready, butterfly? Or do you need some calisthenics to warm you up?"

"You ask the same thing every time I'm here." She tossed her sweater to the side and kicked off her shoes. "And the answer's always the same."

She had tightly braided and wrapped her hair, so it could not be used against her, and stepped onto the mat. Warming up was wise when it came to muscle and joint health however, in the field, her opponent was not going to clean their nails while she did a proper warm-up.

Nero had never taken the passive trainer role with her. He cracked his knuckles, rolled his thick shoulders and got ready for action.

She bounced on the balls of her feet to reacquaint herself with quick, agile movements and jog her muscle memory for executing rapid, powerful moves. Without hesitation, Nero came at her with a fast jab, punch, hook combo to assess her actual readiness.

Her reaction was immediate and swift. Hours of relentless training made it look as if she was born with the swift reflexes. She deftly dodged the jab, blocked the punch, and cushioned the hook to her ribcage.

"Nice. Let's see what you have to show old Nero."

He was unforgiving in his offensive attack, but she skillfully blocked most of the punches and kicks from his onslaught. What she didn't block, she did her best to minimize their impact.

Nero had come to know a few of her tell-signs, a drawback for training with someone frequently, but she took him by surprise with a spinning back fist that landed in the soft section between his ribs and hipbone. If she was in the field, the fist would have been aimed for the head to disable her opponent, but she refused to fight to maim with Nero.

He fell to his right knee and was back up on his feet in the blink of an eye, but it was enough to give her the offensive advantage and she pressed forward. He might have been an older man, but he fought like he was twenty. Only with years of learning and wisdom to hone both his offensive and defensive moves. She had learned the hard way to stay out of range of his hands as much as she possibly could and used front kicks to keep a perimeter of safety. However, he was fast and still took her to the mat in a chokehold, which she maneuvered out of quickly.

In the end, they both were sweaty and laboured to catch their breath. "You've been working on finding your opponent's weaknesses in their lower body."

Ryn swiped at the sweat dripping in her eyes. "The knee is the natural one, so people try to protect it. But there are many others that can be as debilitating, even if it's only momentarily."

Nero nodded approvingly. "I have to agree. Those would-be assailants won't know what hit them if they ever make the mistake of you being an easy target. Come, I'll save my MMA future prospect from you for now. You seem extra fiery today."

She laughed. But thinking that Nero thought she was a threat to his prized newcomer gave her a small jolt of satisfaction.

"But I know Tank was hoping to have another chance with you in the ring."

The first time she had come to train with Nero, after he had experienced firsthand what she could do, he paired her in an extreme height and weight disadvantage. She literally could have shit her pants when she watched the one they affectionately called Tank stalk toward her. It was not one of those oxymoron nicknames where they called a short man Giant.

"I'm never one to shy away from a challenge." She grinned.

Lok ducked quickly into the old warehouse that had been re-outfitted into the infamous training den of Nero Gareth. Removing the dark ball cap and glasses he wore, he let his eyes adjust to the interior lighting. Square windows lined the front of the building with a flimsy material to hinder people spying, but still allowed some light in.

The clank of weights, the sound of padded gloves hitting the bags and flesh, greeted him as he took in the room with the sections of weight training, dojo mats, and what looked like the cages from MMA pay-per-view fights. The cage in the middle of the gym had a large gathering around it to watch the fight within.

Ryn insisted she would meet him at the restaurant so he could sleep and avoid the trek across the city. But he had grown up watching and idolizing Nero Gareth, a legend in his time. So, he decided that sleep and time could be sacrificed so he didn't miss this opportunity of finally being in the city when Ryn was working with his idol.

Not seeing her, he paused to look around while he waited for their lunch date.

Well, he wouldn't call it a date. She had always been very firm on that. He chuckled thinking about the time shortly after they had met that he shot her the question, "Should we kiss?"

He thought it was completely logical that two attractive people might be attracted to each other, but she had sat up so quickly and rigidly he expected her to sprint out of the room. He never had to chase his love interests before. However, he never got that kind of vibe from Ryn and he was happy with the uncomplicated closeness that had been developing. But maybe there was something there, he had explained to her, and they had just overlooked it.

After some convincing, she had agreed to give it a try - he suspected so that he would drop it - and they both leaned in. But as their lips neared, they both burst out laughing. Shock registered on both their faces followed by more gut-busting laughter.

At least they knew it was the friend zone for them and wouldn't be plagued with any *what ifs*. They both appreciated that the pull they felt toward each other was that of friendship, nothing more.

His wandering attention was brought back to the gym and he glanced around again but still no sign of Ryn. Taking notice of the cheering crowd around the MMA cage in the middle of the gym, he made his way over there. The crowd bristled with excitement. He pushed his way a little closer to see what epic fight was taking place that would make so many disregard their own training to watch.

"Holy fuck."

Those were the only words that Lok's stunned brain could manage as it struggled to explain what he was seeing.

Inside the cage stood a beast of a man, sweat glistening as he blocked an assault from the vixen in the ring - a snapping front kick followed by powerful sidekick with the opposite leg and a backhand punch. Ryn turned to face her significantly over-sized opponent and reset into a ready stance.

"She's kicking your ass, Tank!" Tank's fellow training mates jeered.

"Again," added another.

A man that size might not take the beating or the ribbing all that well, but this Tank fella grinned good-naturedly at his opponent and the crowd. "She's good. No shame in that!"

Lok recognized Nero pacing back and forth outside the cage, coaching both Ryn and Tank.

"She's a rocket." The guy beside Lok vibrated, and his short, blue Mohawk bounced as he jumped.

Agile and quick, she was able to avoid most of Tank's offensive moves and when his side was exposed, she moved in like the rocket the Mohawk guy had called her. She got off two fierce rapid hooks to Tank's left kidney area, followed by a quick uppercut to the underside of his jaw.

Winded and in pain, the guy hunched forward and Ryn quickly moved backwards. But not quite fast enough out of the long reach of Tank's arms that snaked out.

Grabbing her shoulder, he spun her around and slammed her back against his front with his arm firmly clamped around her neck in a chokehold.

Not a millimetre of space between the two, Ryn was locked tightly in place. She looked so small against the mammoth man who was clamping off her airway. Looking around to see who the hell was going to intervene before things went too far, Lok stood rigid. Surely Nero would step in soon.

To his shock, he realized Ryn wasn't trying to remove the vise grip from her neck. Or panicking at the cut off air, even though her face was turning an alarming shade of red. Instead, she leaned forward slightly to move her body off-centre to the left, which would increase the pressure on her windpipe. Lok held his breath, thinking her last maneuver would render her unconscious; he expected her to go limp any second.

Instead, he watched in fascination as she hitched up her right knee to savagely stomp down on the guy's foot. Tank would be lucky if he didn't have a good part of his skin ripped off or if his foot bones weren't cracked.

Just as soon as she had finished her attempt at crushing the guy's foot, she honoured him with a vicious right elbow jam to the gut. The combo sent Tank doubling over and Ryn used the momentum to crouch down and ram her body and shoulder back against Tank before she launched forward to flip the beast-man over her body. Ryn didn't resist the flip and Lok watched amazed as she tumbled over as well.

Lok did his best to stay out of altercations as they often involved crazed, fanatic fans that you had no way of predicting if they were looking to stick a knife in your side. But he had been in enough fights to know it was wise Ryn didn't resist the flip.

Otherwise her neck would have been severely torqued, or possibly snapped, since Tank hadn't relinquished his vise grip.

Ryn took advantage of her weight winding Tank to do a backward left shoulder roll and get out of arm's reach.

The crowd was momentarily stunned before it erupted with mad cheering. Lok finally released his pent-up breath and joined in the rivalry, still not quite sure if he truly witnessed what he thought he did.

Tank worked visibly to get his breath, kneeling on one knee in front of where Ryn was slowly rising to her feet. "I asked you the first time I met you and I'll ask you again. Marry me."

Throwing her head back and exposing her slender neck with an angry red band across it, she laughed heartily and reached out a hand to Tank to help him to his feet. She winced slightly as he pulled on her arm but continued to smile.

"You couldn't handle that much woman, Tank," the scrawny guy beside the blue Mohawk guy yelled out, pleased with the chorus of laughter that followed.

Nero pulled his two fighters aside to provide a critique of their bout while the crowd dispersed to go back to their own training. Lok watched, fascinated that his childhood idol was not only standing ten feet from him, but was mentoring his friend. His friend who surprised the hell out of him with her fierce ability.

She obviously had trained to use physics, levers, biomechanics, and the law of gravity to her advantage. Otherwise, how could someone smaller, albeit muscular, best someone so large?

His curiosity was piqued. Where had she learned to fight and move like that? To take on someone so large? And why?

Ryn looked in his direction, her grey eyes meeting his crystal blue ones. A faint look of dismay crossed her face. She bit her lower lip, then gave a smile and waved him over. Her initial reaction was so fleeting he thought he must have imagined it.

"Nero, Tank, this is my friend Lok Bello. He's a long-time fan of yours, Nero."

"Nice to meet you, boy," Nero rumbled in a gravelly voice. "A long-time fan, it's always great to meet those." He had a strong grip and a vigorous handshake.

"I honestly can't believe that I'm getting the opportunity to meet you. It's an honour, sir."

"Lok Bello? No shittin way." Tank's large hand gripped his tightly. "Great to meet you. I'm a big fan of yours."

"Nice to meet you too. And nice to know I'm not the only one that has to work hard to keep up with this one." Lok thumbed in her direction.

Tank let out a big laugh. "I hear ya, man. But here, you gotta check your ego at the door, otherwise you don't improve. And if you aren't coming here to improve, then why bother coming here. That's my motto."

Lok liked Tank immediately. Guys that big often had egos as large as their biceps. Lok was familiar with the type. He employed a few of them as his bodyguards during shows and festivals. But they, unlike Tank, wouldn't take lightly to a smaller opponent, add to that a female, flipping them on their ass.

"I caught you by surprise. I often get underestimated because of my size."

Tank grinned and gave her a playful jab in the side.

"You caught the sparring then? Nice you didn't miss our little fireball here." Nero nodded in approval.

Nero was the shortest of the group, yet Lok felt he was looking up at his legend. "I didn't catch the whole thing, just the grand finale. Remind me not to get on your bad side." He winked at Ryn.

Nero's laughed reverberated around them as he ran a hand over his bald head.

"Anytime I can get a rematch, Severyn, I'm game. I think you're the type to always have a trick or two up your sleeve when you're in a tight jam. You're wily. I like that." Tank rammed her tightly to his side. "And it was awesome to meet you, man." He shook Lok's hand again and then bowed respectfully to Nero.

Nero looked at Lok. "Why don't I show you around while Severyn hits the showers. You can tell me a bit about how you became a long-time fan of mine."

A smile spilt Lok's face and Ryn laughed. "A kid on Christmas."

Ryn showered quickly, wrapped her wet hair in a messy bun, threw on jean capris and a white linen tunic top before rejoining Nero and Lok in the gym. She was finally able to pry Lok from Nero's side and he beamed when Nero told him to stop by anytime he was in New York.

"I will see you soon," Nero told her sternly. "I need to tighten up where Kotan is getting sloppy." He slapped his knee and coughed with his hearty laugh.

The corners of her mouth twitched. "I'll be sure to pass your sentiments on. But seriously, it has been an honour, as always." She bowed respectfully to him.

They stepped into the sunshine on the Bronx sidewalk, squinting and sidestepping the crowd of teenage boys that sized them up. Seeing that they had exited from Nero's Hell Den, the teens gave them brusque nods and a few cocky smiles.

Ted stood ready to intervene if needed and Ryn smiled in greeting as her phone went off.

"It's Zane," she told Lok with an apologetic smile. "I have to take this."

"Of course." Lok moved to chat with Ted, watching the street life.

"Hello, Zane." Her phone, along with Zane, Kotan, Nessa, and Maari's all had the highest level of security and encryption out there. Well, the encryption program wasn't exactly out there, not yet anyway.

"You have finished with Nero."

"I have. Lok's here and we're about to head for lunch."

"Lok's there? At Nero's? Interesting."

"Not overly," she said tersely. "It was a surprise. What's up?" Ryn smiled at a young girl staring up at her as she clutched her grandmother's hand.

"I hate to do this, but we need you to come back earlier than planned. Captain Vega will be waiting for you at the airport in an hour. I can give you an hour and a half if absolutely needed to wrap things up, but no more."

Shit.

Lok flashed her a smile, his blue eyes bright in the sun.

"Code?" she asked quietly.

"Yellow."

Not the highest level of emergency then.

"I'll be there to pick you up."

Zane hated leaving vehicles unattended in public spaces if they weren't secure and monitored. He must be able to give up some precious time devoted to the task at hand. This helped frame the situation in her mind even without the context or details. Important, something is brewing, but not immediate implementation.

"See you in about two and a half hours." She clicked off.

This was increasingly becoming a habit. A bad one. How many times would Lok be okay with her sudden need to leave? So far, she had successfully avoided telling him an outright lie, but it was getting more difficult.

Guilt ate at her while her mind quickly raced through, analyzing and discarding possibilities as she joined Lok and Ted at the car.

"You have to leave," Lok stated matter of fact.

Letting someone close enough that they start to know you well, had its definite drawbacks.

"I'm sorry."

Lok rubbed his forehead, his long, tapered fingers pressed into the skin, his eyes never leaving hers. She could see the disappointment and questions that lingered in them and braced herself for the questions he deserved to ask. That she, in truth, even now, did not know how she would answer.

"Me too. Antonio is going to be pissed. Anytime he can carve out time with you is a top priority. I'll break it to him gently." Lok leaned down slightly to kiss the top of her head. "And make unrealistic and obscene promises on your behalf. You remember your promise to me?"

The last time she had to leave suddenly, he refused to pry. Instead, he made her promise that she would take care of herself.

She nodded, a lump in her throat. "I really am sorry."

"I know. You always are."

Chapter 7

Ryn sat heavily in the comfortable seat on Zane's Gulfstream G550. She ran through her mental checklist to ensure nothing had been forgotten in her mad rush to the airport.

She knew it was an exercise to keep her mind occupied during the take-off. She was becoming less uneasy about flying, but the take-offs and landings still made her queasy.

The uneasy feeling wasn't only for the flight.

She hated not being completely open with Lok. It was easier with Antonio as it was business first, personal second. He wore his professionalism like one of his expensive Armani suits. He'd understand that Ryn needed to get back and would assume that her sudden departure was related to one of her clients. Antonio would make assumptions on his own, and that was okay with her at this point.

Lok was different. He preferred the personal time with her, the professional portion was more an added bonus. It wasn't often that he had much down time and she was loath to give up the leisure time with him as well. She wouldn't lie to him and tell him she needed to get back for some sort of client emergency. But she also couldn't tell him the truth.

She rubbed her hands roughly over her face and sighed. Her temples got a rough massage, and then she brought down the neck and upper shoulder massage attachment on the seat to hold off the headache brewing at the base of her skull. She relaxed under the heat, and the rough kneading motions on her shoulders and neck.

No longer needing to be hypervigilant of her surroundings, she felt the pull of sleep tugging her gently into its comforting embrace. With the added effect of the massage, she drifted.

Floating in the clouds like a majestic bird that sliced through the wisps of cloud. Looking down below, the clouds broke and the rocky, treeline coast of her childhood home opened before her. Sailing through the wind, the salt scented air brushing over her.

In the dream, she was a child again, standing on the beach. Remembering.

Her love to breathe the ocean air deep into her lungs as it rushed over the water and hit land.

The boisterous laughter and jeers of her three older brothers that rang through the trees as they bet who could ascend the steep hill first. Each one of them doing whatever it took to sabotage the others to ensure their own victory.

Their mother calling them in for supper.

The rumble of her father's work truck coming home for the evening.

Her young sister, Fiala, sweet little Fi, asking her to play in the surf or read a stack of books while they cuddled in front of the fire.

Suddenly. the replay of her memories halted; her oldest brother, Reg, was by her side on the beach.

"You coming home?"

Reginald. Advisor. Wise counsel.

He looked at her with serious grey eyes, just like her own. All that his name stood for was represented in that look.

She ached to touch his cheek.

She sadly shook her head at his inquiring look. As she floated away, she tried to reach her hand out to touch him.

One more time.

One more time to feel the warmth and strength of his hand, as if it could carry her over the deep gulf and reunite her with her lost family.

But he had gone now and there was only her, alone, in the swirling pearl white of the clouds.

After a turbulent landing, Ryn was happy to be on solid ground.

"Sorry about the rough ride coming in, Miss Andrews."

Smartly dressed, her sable hair pulled back into a tight bun, Ryn had yet to get a good read on Captain Vega. A long-time and trusted employee of Zane's, she was the poster child of professionalism with the perfect mix of cool aloofness and discretion.

"You maneuvered it smoothly, Captain Vega. As always. Thank you for the safe arrival as well as for taking the time to come to New York to pick me up."

Captain Vega gave her a curt nod but her full mouth spread into a genuine smile. "My pleasure, Miss Andrews."

Zane stood leaning against the side of his favourite ride chatting with the airport baggage attendee on the tarmac where the private planes landed and went through the arrival protocol. The black Aston Martin DB11 gleamed in the sunlight. Both men made a move toward her, but she wove them off. "I travel light, this is all I have." She indicated her solo bag.

A smile creased Zane's face, accentuating the deep laugh lines around his amber-coloured eyes, as he thanked Captain Vega before opening the door of the Aston Martin for her. The June sun highlighted the white streaks developing in his dark blonde hair.

They sat in companionable silence, Zane navigating them through traffic toward the coastal highway that would carry them home to the estate.

She sat back to enjoy the cool air and the scent of the ocean. They zipped along the scenic route, the lush green fields on her right, the ocean waving its welcome on her left.

"Any updates on the situation and what's unfolding?"

Zane shook his head. "Rather than get it piece by piece, Kotan will lay it all out when we get home and highlight the developments so far. I'd like to give it to you fresh and complete to get your gut-read and initial take on it."

Ryn nodded. She had expected as much as she had learned how Kotan and Zane liked to operate.

"Lok is well, I trust. I understand you played with him on stage last night."

She pulled her black sweater closed, over her white linen tunic shirt, against the cool afternoon air. "He is, and I did. You had someone watching me last night."

Zane cast her a sidelong look before refocusing on the winding road in front of him. "Kotan's continuous online search for you let us know that you had. Which is fine. When you decided to go into the music industry, we knew that you would eventually take a more public role. You're too good not to."

Her cheeks warmed slightly with his compliment and she silently cursed herself with annoyance. She wasn't seeking approval. Even if Zane had morphed into a quasi-father figure.

"And your cover identity is strong, as is your physical identity, based on our analysis." Zane added.

She touched her cheekbone and forehead unconsciously, thinking about the alterations her physical appearance had now compared to two years ago.

"That's not what I meant." Ryn shifted to watch his reaction carefully. "You had someone watching me last night."

Zane's face registered a moment of shock before he deftly maneuvered to avoid an oncoming car. The driver, going too fast, had drifted over when they zipped around the curve. The embankment of the rocky hill rose up and gravel flew behind them when Zane swerved to avoid a sideswipe. "Bastards, watch where you're driving. I guess that was karma."

"Well, don't let your bad karma take me out." She crossed her arms over her chest, her heart hammering lightly against her ribcage.

"And, yes, we did. I'm both thoroughly surprised and genuinely proud. Although Taggert won't be, he's one of the best."

"Well, Taggert can stick his bruised ego up his ass. And why? I spoke with Kotan prior to the show, nothing was said about any concerns or a situation." Her shoulders were rigidly set against the back of the seat.

"It makes me rest a bit easier that you're so capable. I know that, and so does Kotan, but it's nice to get those independent validations."

"So, this was a test? A way to see if I'm worthy of your praise. Your pride?" she asked tightly.

"No, absolutely not." Zane's handsome features registered his distress at her thoughts. "We like to make sure you're safe and unharmed. You're capable and skilled as I have said, but it gives us peace of mind that you have an additional layer of protection."

"Is there an active concern that I'm unaware of? And if there was a concern, then you don't think I should have been brought in on that? Am I part of the team, Zane, or just someone that has to be watched over like some vulnerable victim?"

"I understand that you're feeling disgruntled."

She gave an unladylike grunt, but he pressed on.

"And yes, you're part of the team. A very important part. I'm sorry we never mentioned it. But there wasn't any purpose in doing so. Taggert was only there as a precaution and he wasn't to approach you. I'm curious how you got onto him. Like I said, he is one of the best, if not the best, that I've worked with."

They were approaching the estate. The density of the trees increased and provided a scenic, bordered highway, but the trade-off was the shoreline was less visible. Ryn felt an urge to race through the trees to watch and listen to the waves pound against the rocky Massachusetts shore.

Zane was methodical and purposeful. Everything he did fed into a bigger picture. And so much of what he had done these past two years had been for her.

Her flare of anger subsided, but mild resentment at his behind-the-scenes actions lingered.

"I've seen him before. With you."

Zane wasn't quite able to limit his shocked reaction before it registered fully on his face. "Oh? And where was that?"

Zane sounded a bit too casual and Ryn wondered if she had made a mistake in telling him. She had always been painfully honest with Zane, so she never quite understood her hesitation to bring up the observed chance encounter.

"In New York, the day that I met Lok and Antonio. I was killing time in the park across from the hotel. This Taggert guy and his two buddies were walking down the street and grabbed my attention and then I saw you talk briefly with them outside your hotel."

"You never mentioned it."

She shrugged. "You're a businessman. You have several branches and fingers in your empire. Not to mention the covert stuff you do. I imagine you meet and talk to a variety of people."

"And yet, you not only picked out three men walking down the street as points of interest, but remembered one of them a year later, even though you would've been well over two hundred feet away. I'm impressed." He smiled, and slowly turned down the lane leading to the sprawling house.

Zane was as outgoing and friendly as he was successful, but he took their privacy to the next level. And between him and Kotan's knowledgeable skills and creativity in the tech and security field, the next level was outside the scope of many people's imagination.

Throughout the four hundred acres of property, as well as the perimeter, undetectable devices with visual, motion, heat, and auditory capabilities were set both at and below ground level and monitored from above. This, coupled with a detection radar that could pick up frequencies from ten kilometres away, security signals, and a computer system that could not be hacked or jammed, made the property a nearly impenetrable fortress. A beautiful, peaceful, and protected sanctuary.

Ryn thought about Zane and Kotan, as they drove slowly along the lane leading to the house. The level of technology and devices they kept for themselves, rather than immediately mass marketing them, all for the purpose of protecting their home and to have an advantage for their covert operations.

Zane had built Gādo Technologies over the years with his silent partner and friend, all while operating behind the scenes to right wrongs and bring those who had successfully avoided justice, to their knees.

The beautiful two-storey mansion came into view as they rounded a bend, gloriously set with the sun dancing off the white pillars to cast the entrance in a soft, golden glow. Framed in the backdrop with the towering trees that separated the house and field from the ocean, the house looked picturesque, warm, and welcoming.

Ryn inhaled deeply as she got out of the car, smelling the fresh cut grass mingled with roses that Nessa loved to tend. The front entrance, and the gentle slope that rounded to the side of the house, were filled with every colour of rose imaginable.

The wind shifted, ruffling her hair and carrying the ocean breeze that came off the Atlantic beyond the tree line. She longed for a long pounding run across the field and through the woods beyond. There, she would find the stream to follow it as it meandered through the property to where she loved overlooking the ocean from the cliff high above.

Zane smiled at her, reading her thoughts, but beckoned her to follow him into the house with a nod of his head.

She sighed softly. That would have to wait until tomorrow, unfortunately. Or longer, if she needed to leave in the morning for whatever op Kotan and Zane were unfolding.

"Nessa and Maari aren't back yet from the city, but I'm sure they'll be soon. Kotan will have his face buried deep into his computers, no doubt. If it's alright with you, I'd like to get right to the briefing with Kotan."

"As long as there is food involved, I'm game."

She adjusted her bag on her shoulder in the welcoming front foyer. Her gaze took in the sweeping grandeur as it greeted her into the warm home.

The entrance tile transitioned into wide knotted hardwood floors and to the right of the foyer, large windows showcased the back of the property and French doors led to the long patio and pool. A sunken space sat off to the side, occupied by a long comfortable table and matching sideboard. Kotan could be found there most mornings drinking his green tea. Off to the left of the foyer lay the two-storey room which was a large den and library with shelves upon shelves of books, and a spiral staircase leading to the loft level. Panelled with dark wood, sofas, and an abundance of wing chairs, it was a favourite room for all of them.

The sweeping staircase was straight ahead. A table Nessa had made was in the centre of the larger foyer, in perfect position to showcase its beauty. The base was smooth black legs that wound and interlocked, giving a stable base for the large, flat stone. The stone had come from a riverbank near Nessa's childhood home. It was one she had sat on for hours as a child. Reading, fishing, or laying on her back to watch the clouds slowly float by. The riverbank area was being commercialized and they had rescued the stone and brought it to a new home. The underbelly was rough, but the top was smooth and flat from laying exposed to the elements for centuries. It currently held a crystal vase that exploded with Nessa's prized roses.

Running her hand over the stone, she felt its energy welcome her home. The wild scent of the roses added another layer of comfort.

"Take your time." Zane gave her a small smile. "Things like a welcome home shouldn't be rushed."

She nodded, but quickly hid her face to hide the unbidden tears that sprung to her eyes. "I'll put my bag away and meet you in the battle room."

Zane started to walk deeper into the house, shoes and socks in hand. Ryn couldn't repress a smile. The powerful business tycoon would go barefoot any chance he got. He looked a bit sheepish at her grin, knowing her line of thinking.

"Nessa put on her mouth-watering stew. I will get us some, with fresh rolls, and meet you up there."

"Make sure the socks aren't by my plate."

She nimbly ducked the shoe that flew her way.

The suitcase got tossed onto her bed. Throwing the thick burgundy brocade drapes open, she relished the cool glass as she leaned her forehead against it.

In a house that boasted no shortage of beautiful features, the floor to ceiling windows found in almost every room was one she appreciated most. The manicured grass sloped gracefully away from the back of the house until it met the finely trimmed hedges. A white fence beyond the hedges kept the horses from encroaching on places they weren't wanted, but still gave them ample space to run in the fields.

Moving to her bathroom, mourning her lack of freedom to go for a run, she splashed water over her face instead. She watched the water droplets drip off the end of her nose in the mirror.

Some days, it felt like a stranger stared back at her. Nothing about her was the same as it was two years ago.

She continued to stare at her reflection. "If you're being honest with yourself, you're more yourself now than you have been the past seven years."

Back then, she did everything to fall into the shadows and go unnoticed.

She had been a late bloomer and had only begun to morph into her womanly curves and slimmer adult face two years ago, when everything happened to change her life forever.

Along with the late physical changes that her family never had the privilege of witnessing, she had finally stopped hiding any physical attributes - particularly her hair and eyes - as well as personality traits and talents that made her stand out.

Now, after the physical changes that followed her late maturity, leaving her hair and eyes unchanged along with some facial reconstructive surgery for shattered bones in her forehead and cheekbones, Severyn Andrews was living unhidden, undisguised. And no one from her past suspected or recognized her.

She was hiding in plain sight.

Living a life full of hidden truth and secrets.

Her tangled hair fell in waves to her mid-back after she released her bun, and her scalp screamed in protest as her fingers pulled through the knots. The colour of the strands that ran through her fingers looked like the caramel filling of a Christmas chocolate, swirled with light and darker colours.

Her mother would love that she was no longer colouring her hair a muted black. However, in the seven years since her mom had seen her true hair colour, even she would not believe the variety of colour that had taken root.

Ryn's mind scrambled to change her line of thinking from thoughts of her mom.

She wondered if her young sister's hair was starting to change characteristics.

But that line of thinking was a mistake too. Images of her tiny, sweet sister, Fi, twisted her gut.

Her breath hitched and her fingers clenched the vanity counter as she regained control of her emotions.

I am Severyn Andrews. For now, she reminded the reflection staring back at her.

Her eyes grew hard as steel with resolve before she turned to march toward the next steps in her journey back to her family.

Chapter 8

The door to the battle room was ajar and Kotan typed vigorously at one of his many keyboards, before zipping on his wheeled stool to pound the keys of a different one. A grey tabby cat sat on the console, supervising, but out of Kotan's way. The cat gave her a steady-eyed stare before jumping down to wind through her legs, purring happily as she gave him some love.

Ryn had found and rescued Cletus as a bedraggled kitten. She had discovered him in the woods behind the estate, right after her memory had returned. She often wondered though, who had rescued whom.

Sensing her attention shift, Cletus jumped back up on the console where Kotan worked like a wild man on the verge of a breakthrough, ready to spread anarchy.

Without looking up, he welcomed Ryn home then continued on his keyboards. "I am….oh, you sly little bastard. Sorry, this firewall is giving me more hassle than I expected. It looked sloppy and elementary at the start. Let me get this to work and then I will be right with you."

She peered over Kotan's shoulder and scratched Cletus under the chin. "Hack it or Sack it. Creative name for the new diagnostic-code-breaker-hacker-algorithm thingy."

Zane walked in with a full tray and Ryn's stomach rumbled at the heavenly scent of Nessa's stew, fresh rolls, cheeses, and fruit. The scent caught Cletus' attention and he jumped down to greet Zane.

Ryn smiled, watching Cletus snatch up the chunk of meat Zane tossed him. "Hmmm, fresh rolls from Mr. Kotter's Bakery."

"A welcome home treat from Maari." Zane handed her a plate.

She dove in, savouring each bite, as Kotan festered away, continually muttering he'd take a break in a minute. Well on the way to being fully sedated, she felt a tinge of guilt that Kotan had yet to pause. "Is there anything I can do to help?"

"With the computers? God, no, child."

Okay, she wasn't *that* inept with the stupid things.

Kotan gave a few hard pokes on the keyboard and turned with a flourish to bound out of his chair and load up his plate. He was amped up and quickly swallowed a chunk of bun before he began.

"Alright, let me lay out what we have so far. We have pieces of information, but none fill in the full picture." While Kotan paced like a caged cat, he talked and his wizard algorithm worked in the cyber world behind him.

"From our past intel gatherings, we know it has something to do with shipping; a large boat, or cargo ship." Zane kicked his feet up on the desk and entwined his fingers behind his head with Cletus curled on his lap.

"That's what you two concluded based on the intel you intercepted right before my death scape almost two years ago." Ryn paced as well. Kotan's nervous energy was contagious and the movement helped her think.

Kotan turned his attention to the monitor that started to beep and typed in a few quick keystrokes. "Yes, I still stand by that being the most logical inference thus far. We will keep that as the working theory foundation."

"Originally, we examined if it had to do with a drug run route in the Monahague Bay area. But Kotan and I weren't convinced due to the inconvenience of the land routes to and from there as well as the unpredictable waters between the mainland and islands. Since it wasn't a straight exit out to the open water, it didn't provide very reliable escape options if that need arose. And any criminal worth their salt wouldn't needlessly cut off any options for a rapid exit."

"There also was not any chatter or data that we could find from the Canadian Drug Enforcement Unit about Monahague Bay being a drug run route. New or established," Kotan added. "And on your first op, Severyn, you eliminated the last shred of doubt with that line. While, at the same time, helping to end the career of some significant drug dealers in that area."

After Vlad's death, his murderers came searching for something, then came after her and her family. When she couldn't give up what they were hunting for, not because she didn't want to, but because she had no idea what they were after, they rigged an accident on the mountainside that would surely kill her. Zane and Kotan had intercepted and miraculously prevented her demise, but she suffered severe physical injuries and full memory loss in the process.

Once her memory had returned, and after many weeks of physically healing from her death scape, Ryn delved obsessively into training. It had taken time for her to be deemed capable for ops. However, she was adamant that she be involved in removing the threat that hung over her family. Zane and Kotan had other operatives they worked with, but she refused to pull in strangers when her family's lives hung in the balance.

On her first op, she had scouted, planted bugs, and worked over some smaller dealers to find out the bigger source of supply for the area. That intel had added to what Kotan had gathered electronically. Together, it was a serious piece of work about the supply source and the leaders and dealers in the area, but it wasn't related to their mission.

Even though it didn't help them, and they couldn't deviate from their own agenda, they did their due diligence to make the information 'findable' by the Canadian Drug Enforcement Unit and the RCMP. This led to a successful shutdown of that problem.

Ryn's attention was pulled back to the present.

"Shipping illegal items then. Stolen art, artifacts, exotic animals? That field wouldn't necessarily have a need for a rapid getaway as the clientele isn't as volatile or ruthless."

"There are cutthroats in every line of work, Severyn." Zane swung his feet down and nabbed a piece of cheese.

"Why go to such extremes in this case? We know that Vlad was murdered, they came after me, threatened me to give up only Lord knows what. And then they blew up my dad's work truck and almost killed my little sister. Not to mention they think they successfully took me out."

Kotan stopped his pacing and gave her a deep look. She had spoken unemotionally, even though she spoke about the murder of her childhood friend, the traumatic threat to her vulnerable young sister and family, as well as her own perceived death. Being okay with what he saw, he continued pacing. "You are right, that does raise it up there on the overreaction scale."

"What about people? Human trafficking?" Ryn felt sick to her stomach mentioning it again for them to reconsider as the motive for the mystery they were trying to solve.

Zane ran his hands through his thick dark blonde hair and rubbed his eyes. "It would match the intensity of their actions."

"However, no one went missing from your hometown. We expanded our search to a larger catchment area back around that time. Police reports and files within a substantial radius only showed deaths from natural causes, some overdoses, a fatal vehicle accident, and a ten-year-old girl who went missing but was found shortly after," Kotan reminded them.

"And that leads us back to the roads and water routes in the area. Unpredictable, inconvenient, slow, but we have links to shipping something out." It was Zane's turn to pace as Kotan crossed his arms and leaned his tall frame against the computer console.

"Okay, so where the hell are we at then? And why did you pull me home on a code yellow when I was coming home in less than twenty-four hours?" Frustrated, she planted her palms on the smooth black surface of the long table.

"We caught a nugget from Virginia."

"Was she sacrificing baby puppies or leading lambs to their slaughter today?"

Zane shot her a sharp look.

"Sorry, that was uncalled for."

"She makes hard calls to do what's necessary."

Virginia Ruthley was a long-time friend, previous lover, of Zane's, and also happened to be the Director of the CIA. Virginia was one of the few people that knew all of Zane's business and workings.

Ryn sighed softly and bit down the discomfort the woman made her feel. "I'm not ungrateful even though I sounded like a shit. What did Virginia have today?"

Zane gave her a small smile. "On its own, it has some twinges of interest, but add it to what else we've unearthed along the way...Well, I'm tugging on some threads right now to weave it together. I plan for us to have an action plan for implementation tomorrow."

Kotan tugged gently on the high collar of his black shirt. They were all getting a bit antsy. "Do you recall the op you did right before you had your music debut?"

Antonio had insisted that to launch her as a legit songwriter, she needed fanfare while showcasing her own music. She had vehemently protested that she only wanted to share her songs with other artists for them to sing and perform, but Antonio would not back down.

A few days before the debut, Kotan deployed her on an op that couldn't wait, as their window of opportunity was small. Antonio almost had a stroke that she needed to leave out of town unexpectedly."

"The one with the fire that was a dismal failure. The only thing I could recover was a piece of a ship manifest with a small piece of a signature for the port clearance authority. No names of people, company, or of the ship or cargo."

Zane walked over to the bar and poured himself a cognac. "Virginia was able to access a brief clip of satellite recordings."

Alarmed, Ryn tensed. "I thought she couldn't access those files without being detected. Is there a risk that someone is going to start looking into this and link back to us?"

"She had authorization to go into those recordings for another case and she was able to pull a brief clip for the date of interest and within a good radius from our point of interest."

"The clip was encoded, and it has taken some time to work around that since we could not exactly view it on one of their computers. The decoding program I have written to break the encryption—"

"Oh, that won't sit well with Virginia," Ryn said warily.

Zane shrugged, tossing back the last of his cognac. "She's come to expect as much from us. I have to hand over the program after we're done so they can refine their encryption based on the weaknesses that Kotan exploited."

A brief look of annoyance crossed Kotan's features. "Yes, well...As I was saying, after some trial and error, I am happy to say it has been cracked. There were several ship names we could see on the recording. I have been working to track down and cross-reference any of them with the minimal details from the piece of ship manifest that you were able to save."

By track down and cross-reference, Ryn knew that meant hacking, secretly and illegally, into the company's servers.

He tossed his thumb over his shoulder at one of the computer monitors that rapidly ran numbers on its screen. "I have narrowed it down to a few companies and have been perusing their databases to pull up any info they have on their servers regarding that port. All benign, so far, with nothing of interest. Except a particular one has been a nasty little egg to crack. That is the one I am running *Hack it or Sack it* on right now."

"You suspect that having security and firewalls that hard to crack means they're hiding something of interest."

"Or they're trying to protect themselves from their competitors in the market and have someone good with hacking prevention on their payroll." Zane played the devil's advocate and thought like the businessman he was.

On cue, the computer sang out its success and Fenn Industries popped up on the screens. Kotan shoved up his sleeves to get to work.

Normally, he hated people looking over his shoulder as he busted through whatever barriers were preventing him in his cyber world quests. But he didn't notice, or care, tonight.

Screens opened and closed as the search scoured the files on Fenn Industries servers and Kotan clicked and scanned snippets of information himself. How the man could process that much information that fast, she would never know. The continuous flashing of screens thankfully stopped and Kotan pulled one to display onto the large blank wall.

"Here's what we are looking for."

Not really comprehending what Kotan thought was so significant at first, she soon realized it was the full manifest of the piece she was able to recover from the fire. Looking at the port clearance authority signature, she thought there had to be some mistake.

"Senator William Hanelson. Why would a senator provide port clearance authorization?" she mused out loud. "Are they even allowed to do that?"

"And why would the Senator of Florida provide authorization for a port in Washington State? Let's see what we can dig up on

Senator Hanelson." Zane pulled out a chair for her. All hands on deck for this deep dive.

Zane touched her shoulder and she jerked awake. Digging up everything they could on Senator William Hanelson was starting to drain her energy stores. She didn't find computer work nearly as titillating as Zane and Kotan. Add that to the gruelling schedule that she had worked the past few days, and she was pushing the exhaustion line.

If it was physical work, she'd be fine. But hunched over a computer digging down endless rabbit holes was draining.

Given the type of work she had been doing recently and that it was mostly 'peopling', added another layer to the exhaustion. She would take physical over peopling any day.

"Go to bed. We got this." Zane insisted when she started to protest. "You'll be heading out in the field on this soon enough and you need to bring your A-game."

She didn't argue and mumbled good night. Walking silently along the plush carpeted hallway, the silk wall hangings featuring Japanese and Cree symbols turned to smooth wall panels as she drew closer to her room.

When she had first come to the estate, she was afraid, battered, and without any memory of who she was or where she was from. Being immersed in a home that honoured the inhabitant's origins, even if she knew it wasn't her own heritage or upbringing, brought comfort. It was a lifeline to peace for her ravaged soul then as well as when her memory returned, and she realized the full gravity of the situation. The full realization of the danger her family was in.

"Christ, you're shuffling your feet, Ryn. Those computers really do suck every nanobyte of life from you, don't they?" Maari's tall, lithe frame glided toward her. "The wardens finally cut you lose?"

Nessa and Maari had returned earlier in the evening, with treats, of course. The sundae bar provided much needed fuel for the investigation into Senator Hanelson and she decided she could go for another one. If she had the energy to get down to the kitchen.

"Look that good, huh? I thought you were heading back to your place in the city. How come you're still here?"

"Mama and I got distracted talking and it's really coming down out there now." Maari's laugh tinkled through the hallways. "You did know it was raining out, right?"

"No." She shrugged. "Now leave me in peace."

"Are you going to be okay?" Concern replaced laughter on Maari's beautiful face, as her facial piercings glittered beneath the hallway lights. "You really do look like shit."

Ryn snorted. "You know how to make your friends feel like a hundred bucks."

"I think the saying is a million bucks." Maari tossed up her hands in mock defence at Ryn's scowl. "But I get your drift. When you get this tired—" Maari bit her lip. "I can stay in your room tonight."

"The nightmares come regardless. I'll be fine. Honest." She gave her friend's hand a squeeze and then shoved Maari down the hallway toward the Luo's part of the house.

"Rest easy, my friend." Black eyes stared into dark grey ones. Her friend's attempt to banish any dream demons, and then Maari was gone.

Chapter 9

The fog, so thick, weighed her down under its heavy blanket, blocking out any sight, any sound. It felt toxic, deep in her lungs, making her struggle to catch her breath, but she continued to push forward.

Arms reached out to feel the nothingness in front of her. Panic, coupled with urgency, rose in her chest to make her heart pound painfully against its constraining ribcage.

The feeling of forever and nothing loomed on until finally, the fog began to lift, revealing the shimmering outline of a large building. Her heart renewed its rapid beating in response, her breath came in gasps as panic gripped her again. She willed her legs to move faster when the hospital came into clearer view, but frustratingly slow movements were all they could muster. It was like they were slowly being paralyzed.

Gusts of wind howled around her, pushing and pulling her relentlessly from all angles, her knees screamed in agony as she fell to the ground again and again. When the wind brought the cries of a young girl's terror and pain, she yelled in anguish, the echo of it matching what coursed through her very own soul.

Rallying to her feet against the crushing wind, tears of frustration and torment burned down her cheeks until finally she reached the hospital.

Desperate to get to the young girl that laid within, she raced endlessly through sterile white hallways until she finally reached the room. But reaching her destination did not assuage the panic and anguish that had been escalating. It doubled it, making her knees buckle and she crashed to the floor.

Bloody. Bruised. Cut. The small, delicate face hardly recognizable. She was certain her heart would be ripped clean from her chest as she rose trembling to walk to the bed.

The tiny girl turned her battered face. A sad look of betrayal seared its image into her heart, making her collapse one more time, begging.

"Please forgive me. Fi, please forgive me," she whispered, broken.

The wind howled through the sterile halls growing to a roar until it finally reached the small room. The young girl swirled in the wind and Ryn clutched at the air, frantic to stop the young girl from leaving her.

But Fi was gone. They all were. And she was alone once again.

Fully awake now, Ryn clutched her pillow to her chest as the tears dried on her cheeks. Rather than rationalize and dispel her emotions, she let them wash over her.

The dream was a mix of past real events mingled with fragments twisted by guilt and regret. Her sweet, innocent young sister had lain in a hospital bed bruised, bloody, and lucky to be alive. But it was Ryn's emotions that twisted the dream to include Fi's betrayed look. It was her own heart that used her guilt and regret, twisting it into shame, to bastardize her memories to be something to haunt her.

Ryn clenched and unclenched her hand in her pillow, a powerful desire to touch and hug Fi. To hear her laugh. To cuddle with her while she dozed off to sleep. To assure her young sister that her big sister never abandoned her. That Fi's sadness could end, and her big sister was there, safe and sound.

Fully emotionally spent, Ryn tossed the blankets aside.

When she first came to the estate, she had no memory of her family or what had happened to her. Once her memories had returned, the emotional turmoil began. She lived but everyone, except for the four people she currently lived with at the estate, believed her to be dead.

She could secretly let her family know that she lived, that she was working to resolve the threat, and would return to them as soon as it was possible. It was a thought that crossed her mind a thousand times before.

And it was one she knew she had to discard a thousand and one times.

Letting her family know, even secretly, would only serve to renew the danger to them. And if she died in the process of her mission, her family's grief would be doubled with guilt to add to its burden.

No, she had reconciled herself with the decision that she had chosen the right path. To live secretly as Severyn Andrews, have Zane and Kotan train her for this mission, and to use all their resources was the only path forward.

But that did not make it any easier.

"Good morning, dear."

Ryn startled when she came out of her room. "Were you lying in wait for me to get up, Nessa? I'm sure you have much better things to do."

Nessa, still dressed in beautiful, bright blue silk pajamas, looked as elegant and put together as ever. The tiny woman gave her a squeeze before guiding her toward the staircase.

"No lurking, I promise. Good timing only. I noticed you had overslept past your usual wake-up time and wanted to check on you."

"I can't win," Ryn said with a small smile as she went down the stairs with Nessa by her side. "Damned if I don't sleep enough, damned if I do."

Nessa's laugh added to the brightness of the foyer from the early morning June sun streaming in the windows, spilling over everything in its path. Over the large rock surface table piled high with Nessa's fragrant roses and the knotted hardwood floor that led to the sunken space with the long comfortable table and matching sideboard.

Kotan sat at the table now, drinking his green tea and looking as content as the cat basking in the sunbeams, lapping up milk.

"Kotan's spoiling you as always, isn't he, Cletus?"

The grey tabby purred and arched his back into her hand.

Nessa gave Kotan an affectionate kiss before stealing a sip of his tea. Ryn took a moment to observe the two of them. Kotan, graceful and regal in his slacks and polo shirt, black hair slightly tousled. The tiny fireball by his side, just as graceful in her pajamas, wore her matching black hair straight, swinging against her sharp jawline. Him tall and lean, calm and analytical. Her small and petite, spirited and constantly moving.

"Can I get you some tea, Severyn? Or I brewed a pot of coffee if you'd rather."

Kotan started to rise but Ryn waved him off and went to the sideboard. "These are beautiful mugs. Are they from your trip home, Nessa?" Ryn carefully handled the pottery mug hand-painted with beautiful Indigenous artwork.

"They are," Nessa replied proudly. "The youth made them. It's turning into a successful social enterprise for them. They're getting orders from all over."

"Can you pour me one of those, Ryn? Coffee though, please."

Maari bustled down the stairs. Ducks were all over her pajamas and matching robe, plush duck slippers adorned her feet.

"Well, aren't you just ducky this morning. It looks like the ducks may have nested in your hair." Ryn laughed, watching Maari finger comb the tangles out of her long black locks.

"I wanted to get up early and show you this. You were too tired to appreciate it last night, so I saved it for this morning." Maari swung her duck-clad feet up on the end of the table.

Ryn regarded the dark brown bump nestled safely in what looked like a small earring case. "It looks like a mole."

"Precisely, Sherlock." Maari swung her feet down and popped up to stand beside her. Like her mother, she had boundless energy, anytime of the day.

"What does it do or is it more for disguises?"

Maari held out her fingertip where she placed the mole, inviting her to feel it.

"It has the texture and feel of a real mole. This model has the ability to be undetected by devices scanning to detect bugs or transmitting devices. And the best thing?" Maari's onyx eyes glistened with excitement. "It collects electronic data that is transmitted around it."

Ryn shook her head in wonderment at Zane, Kotan, and Maari's collective genius.

"It's programmed to collect electronic data – texts, emails, other electronic messaging, computer data – and uploads it to our server right before the battery life is drained. That way, if there are any transmitter detectors out there, that ours isn't superior too, there's only that one instant of when it can be detected."

"That's fantasy movie-grade spy gadgetry, guys." Ryn nodded in approval.

"It looks like a mole, or we can dye it to be the exact colour of your skin. I'm still perfecting the adhesive to be more long-lasting though. Right now, it will last two hours, tops, when it's on the skin because the skin oils make it unstable. And the transfer spot cannot be skin.

"It looks so fragile; I'm stressed thinking of handling it."

"You'll be fine handling it. As I mentioned, it has limited transfer abilities, so you have to be sure it's on the spot you want it. Both on you and on the transfer site," Maari stressed. "But I see daddy has a thick file beside him, so I'll let you two chat about all the boring op details. I'm off to do my more exciting part of the job." Maari winked, looping her arm through Nessa's as they left.

Ryn stole a glance at the file Kotan placed on the table. She had been tired last night, but she was sure it wasn't that full when she left for bed. "Busy beaver."

"As is our senator. Zane had to tend to a video conference, but he asked me to get you up to speed as soon as you woke." Kotan passed her a few documents from the file. "On the surface, the Senator appears squeaky clean. But too squeaky. And things are different when you examine them with a different lens or have other information that changes the colour of the picture. But he is well guarded electronically, and I can't break through."

"How is that possible with you are the helm? Or the keyboard? Or whatever."

"I could break in, but I can't do it undetected. We are going to have to gather intel on sight."

"Enter the mole little thingy. Good timing."

Kotan chuckled. "Maari has been frustrated trying to figure out the adhesive stability and life but fortune is on our side."

"Who and what are the how and where?" Ryn topped up her tea waiting for the caffeine to kick in.

"We should have that within the hour. In the meantime, you up for a sparring session or would you rather go for that long run you have been wishing for since you returned home last night?"

"And miss out on punishing you? Never, Sensei." She gave a respectful bow. "And it will give me a chance to tell you all the ways that Nero thinks you're getting sloppy." She grinned, but wisely darted out.

Kotan was waiting in her studio after she changed.

"Regardless of my old friend's disparaging view of my training abilities," Kotan gave her a wink, "Nero spoke highly of you once again."

As she approached on the mat, she smoothly dodged a vicious snapping, front kick meant to whip her head right off her neck. If the powerful blow had connected, she would have been out for more than this training session.

"That's how you repay pride in my actions? I would hate to see if I disappoint you."

She crouched down low and, like a cat, sprung up and over Kotan when he ducked low in an attempt to sweep out her feet. "Good deeds do not warrant mercy."

After that there were no more words from Sensei or student. The intensity of their attacks and counterattacks rose. Kotan had trained her hard for months, holding nothing back once she developed a proficiency at protecting herself. Today was no different, as he showed her no quarter. Like a sponge, she absorbed all he threw at her, using it to learn, improve, and hone her abilities.

"Your hand is tracking down slightly." To prove his point, his fist glanced off her jaw.

She ignored the pain that snaked up her temple and gave him a vicious rib shot. "And you left your side exposed, ever so slightly, when you transferred your weight to do that kick."

"Well done," he grunted, and then signalled the end of the session. "You are keeping aware of your opponent's weaknesses and patterns. Good. I am very pleased to see that you have not been sluffing off."

She arched her eyebrow at his word choice. Kotan's vocabulary choice was often as articulate as his appearance.

"Shower and then meet in the battle room for a full debrief and op instructions. Breakfast will be available there."

Chapter 10

Ryn took long, deep breaths - breathe in calm, breathe out tension - as the plane started its take-off. She turned to look out the window as the city of Boston disappeared quickly below. Captain Vega was a long-time pilot of Zane's and had thousands of hours of flying under her cap, she reminded herself.

Annoyed at her lingering discomfort for flying, she focused on the op. They had no specific knowledge of what Senator William Hanelson was up to, or how he tied into this. If, he did indeed tie into it.

But the Senator did appear to have his sticky fingers in odd places, such as providing port authority clearance in a state across the country from his own. He also had sophisticated enough technology that Kotan couldn't break in without being detected. Granted, the Senator would have sensitive information that the government wouldn't want public. However, for the home network to be so secure that even Kotan couldn't breach it, even though he easily accessed a variety of government databases undetected quite frequently, did raise some flags of interest.

No, they could not disregard or underestimate the long-time political wrangler.

The wild card in the scenario wasn't the Senator though. It happened to be Chedrick William Bartholomew Hanelson. With a name like that, she could understand why the son of a powerful, uptight father wouldn't tow the family political pristine image.

In his late twenties, Ched was the poster child for rich party boys, according to the intel they gathered on him.

Any chance to throw mud in good ole dad's face was his trademark motto. And that worked well in their favour this weekend with Ched hosting a wee gathering, of five hundred or so, at the family home in Miami, before dear dad arrived. Not only did it give her an opportunity to access the Senator's study but, according to his travel itinerary they absconded, he would be working from home the next few days from that study.

The perfect opportunity to plant the mole device and collect some electronic and digital information.

It really was awfully considerate for the Senator and his son to cooperate in such a willing manner, she thought sardonically.

Her grin faltered though when she thought about her role in the op. Using her femininity to charm her way made her feel sick but with all the dead ends so far in removing the threat to her family's safety, it was the lesser of the two evils.

Nessa felt the same way, concern etched on her face when she stopped by Ryn's bedroom before she left.

"Don't let it go too far," Nessa's dark brown eyes were worried. "I have every faith in your ability to control a weasel like this, Chedrick. But if you are incapacitated somehow...I shudder just thinking about it. Kotan and Zane assured me they have an extraction plan. Be safe and come back unscathed, my dragonfly."

That was Nessa's standard send-off before an op. One that always clenched her heart and kicked her in the gut.

The dragonfly was a treasured symbol to the Luo family, it was the first tattoo Maari ever got to symbolize her triumph through a dark path of self-destructive behaviours in her teen years. Ryn thought of the bronze dragonfly pendant Nessa had given her before her very first op and how deeply moved she was.

Ryn could never wear it on ops even though it brought her comfort. Something as innocuous as a pendant could be linked back to her persona of Severyn Andrews. And she would never put another family at risk because of her.

At the sidewalk café, she had an unobstructed view of the patio across the street where Ched and his entourage were indulging in a liquid lunch. The intel pictures they gathered on Ched didn't lie, and she had watched him press his good looks to his advantage at every opportunity over the past forty hours.

Golden hair with bleached blonde streaks accentuated his tanned complexion and blue eyes. A toned body completed the package of someone who made hanging out at the beach and clubs his profession.

From her surveillance, as well as their online investigation, Ched definitely had a type that he liked to hang with. Attractive beach bunnies and dudes, but he made sure that none were more attractive than him.

Interestingly, though, the type of female that he sought out to share his bed weren't the bleach blonde airheads that followed him around like he was a Greek Adonis reincarnate. They were dark, both in physical looks and outlook. Not the bubbly party girls but more the anti-establishment type with a flair for risk-taking.

She pushed a tight curl of hair securely behind her ear. It was fiery red today and her scalp begged to be itched under the skull cap that secured her own hair firmly under the wig. The wig and skull cap in the scorching Miami early summer heat, coupled with the long hours of wear, made her want to rip it all off and scratch her head until it bled.

Instead, she calmly paid cash for her bill, then sauntered away from Ched and his cronies, confident she had what she needed to meet Ched.

Chapter 11

The limo brought her to the beachfront mansion, and heads turned to take in the long lean expanse of her legs when she slipped out of the sleek, black car. She used a semi-washable ink to tattoo her muscular quadriceps and the words earth and fire moved as she strutted with model confidence and cool aloofness.

She recognized two of Ched's buddies when the blonde beach boys shoved each other as she sauntered toward the burly security guard at the front door. She flicked her gaze away uninterested.

Beach Boy Number One got the door for her, nodding at the security guard. "She's with me."

Not to be outdone, Beach Boy Number Two squeezed in close. "I love your tits. I mean, tats."

"Classy, Scoad." Beach Boy Number One elbowed Scoad out of the way and swept the door open for her into the lavish foyer that was overrun with bodies in various states of dress.

She wasn't sure if Scoad was his last name, nickname, or a sarcastic reference to the slang term for belly button lint. Either way, she disliked the dickhead on sight. She sensed Scoad moving to grab her ass, in predictable dickhead fashion, and whirled to twist his arm painfully behind his back before shoving him face first into the doorframe.

"Okay, okay. I get it. No touchy." Scoad whined, as she gave his arm a nasty push higher before whipping him around to face her.

She squeezed his jaw tightly, looking into his bloodshot pale blue eyes, her own blue eyes flat and cool. "Fuck off."

Scoad's friend snickered gleefully.

"Please let me rescue such a beautiful woman from two dregs of society."

Scoad's scowl turned to a pout as he glanced over her shoulder. She followed Scoad's line of sight, taking in Ched standing close and openly checking her out. Her skin crawled under the scrutiny of his look.

Barefoot in a white linen suit with a teal shirt open to reveal his golden hairless chest. Others might look like they stepped out of the 1980s, but Ched pulled it off without looking like a complete cheeseball. Still, she felt the urge to unleash a sharp laugh but covered it with a smile.

"Toad—" Ched and Beach Boy Number One burst out laughing and Scoad's scowl returned. "—was finding elsewhere to be. But thank you, Ched. I'm honoured the host would intervene on my behalf."

Ched smiled, pleased. "You know who I am, but I'm not blessed with the same privilege. And that, I must rectify at once. Come, my sweet, let's get you a drink and find out more about you."

He clasped her hand as they wove through the throng of people that spilled out to the pool and deck area overlooking the glistening aquamarine waters of Biscayne Bay. He nodded, smiled, and smoothly addressed the many people who vied for his attention. He acted more like a politician then he probably realized, she mused.

He interlinked his fingers with hers in an intimate hold and flashed a charming grin at her over his shoulder. She was surprised that her disguise had worked to grab Ched's attention so fast. Alarm bells went off in her head, that he had somehow been aware of who she was and her intent, but Zane's communication through her tiny earpiece indicated nothing was amiss.

She knew she stood out from most of the other females at the party. That was the whole point. Instead of traipsing around in a skimpy bikini or a barely-there dress, she wore an asymmetrical off one shoulder white dress that fit her curves well and ended mid-thigh. The material wrapped around her body, leaving her left hip and lower side exposed. Her right shoulder and arm were bare, to showcase the myriad of tattoos she had placed on her skin.

Her dark hair and severely blunt bangs complemented her eyes, made blue by the contacts she wore. She had carefully applied the facial prosthetics, as Maari had taught her, to make them undetectable and give her face a fuller look. The full body spray she used to make her complexion darker, along with the dark hair, altered nose and cheekbones, she looked Mediterranean and exotic.

The standard issue that Ched liked to take to bed. And she was banking on that to gain access to the areas that were restricted for the guests.

Ched wrapped a hand around her waist and his fingers caressed the bare skin of the exposed crest of her hip. She suppressed the urge to break every one of his fingers. Instead, she continued to play cool, detached, and vaguely uninterested. "I'll take a gin and tonic with cucumber."

"You know, I still don't know your name. I've rescued you."

Oh, please.

"I've held your hand. Now know what you like to drink. But have yet to learn your name."

He pulled her into a corner beside the bar that was set up in the beautiful ornate family room. The cleaners would have their work cut out for them to put this place back together before daddy arrived home.

"Interesting." She took a small sip of her drink but let the fluid flow back into the glass when Ched was busy extracting a gorgeous blonde, with voluptuous cleavage spilling from her string bikini, from his arm. Regardless of being on an op, at a party like this, she wouldn't put it past anyone here to drug the drinks.

"Sorry about that. Now, where were we?" He pressed closer toward her and she turned her shoulder so it bumped into his chest, and looked at the people in the family room. "Ah, yes, your name. I must know your name. And, however did you come to be here?"

"Do you know every person here and personally invite each one?"

"Well, no…"

"Hmmm." She responded coyly but decided to throw the guy a bone. The mole device adhesive wasn't going to last forever.

"I'm in town visiting my cousin. Good luck and timing. She scored an invite from her modelling agency but got a severe flu. Poor dreadful thing." Wicked sarcasm dripped from her voice.

"The poor thing. I do hope she recovers quickly." Ched smiled just as wickedly. He leaned in to breathe against her neck. "And your name? If you were to disappear on me, how could I find you?"

"Desperation doesn't suit a man such as you, Ched. I truly hate to be the cause of it."

"I'm sure you do."

She sidestepped the hips that leaned in to grind against hers.

"Demetria Xeno."

"Demetria." He brought her hand to his lips. "The pleasure is all mine. How fortuitous that fate destined our paths to cross. If Scoad would have scared you away, I would have thrashed him to a pulp."

"I'm used to toads and don't scare easily." She lowered the hand holding her drink and secretly sloshed some of the contents into the plant that shared the cramped space with them in the corner. "But I've been here over ten minutes already and I haven't made it past the first room. I don't want to monopolize the host's attention."

It was a risky gamble that he might take her up on her offer to excuse himself, but she was acutely aware of the mole device adhesive life length on her skin. If Ched wasn't going to factor into the plan of getting into his father's study, it was better to determine that now.

He spun her to face him and planted his palms on the wall, on either side of her. "Demetria, please, I beg of you, monopolize and hijack my attention. Hijack me. There is no way I'm letting you leave my side."

The possessive tone of his voice raised her annoyance but none of that showed on her features.

He wasn't much taller than she was and he lowered his head slightly to graze his lips over her bare shoulder. She couldn't suppress the shudder, but from the look in his eyes he misread it as one of pleasure and anticipation.

"Come, let me show you around my humble abode. And some of my favourite places where I like to… relax." He pulled her out of the corner with a wink.

The crowd of people thinned as they moved deeper into the house and away from the pool area. Bouncers waited at the foot of the elaborate staircase, but it appeared guests could make their way upstairs for a price. She didn't even want to fathom a guess at what the cleaners would need to do in the rooms upstairs.

Two mountains of men nodded at them and she felt their leering gazes sear right into her ass as she ascended the stairs with Ched, the white dress hugging her curves.

At the end of a long hallway, Ched opened the door with a flourish, but she stopped before stepping over the threshold. "What's this?"

The large bedroom beyond the doors showcased a poster bed along with an heirloom bedroom set. Formally decorated and pristinely neat.

"I was pretty sure I didn't misread your interest. My apologies." No remorse accompanied the sly look on his face.

"Really? You brought me to your parents' bedroom?" She scoffed.

Ched's tanned cheeks turned slightly pink. "I thought it would be a good way to flip my dad the bird. And kinda kinky."

Jesus, is he fourteen?

"Look, if you want to screw someplace that symbolizes 'Go fuck yourself hard, dad' then I'm game. But not here."

A shit-eating grin split his face; his golden head shook with laughter. "I've got the perfect place."

He pulled her back down the hallway, turning to hurry down another one, and pulled out a key from his white linen pants as he clutched her hand. Fumbling slightly with the lock, he nudged her inside, closing the dark wooden doors of the study to block out the sounds of rivalry and mayhem down below.

The study was a stereotypical man space that had the Senator stamped all over it. Pictures of him with titans of industry, world leaders, including presidents from over the years, were tactfully placed around the room to be gazed upon from his seat of power behind the large oak desk.

In public, the Senator strives to come across as a wholesome family man. But there was not one picture of his family that could be seen in the space. Not even a single one of his son when he was younger, or his wife of over forty years. For her, this further refined the type of man he really was.

"Dad would kill me if he knew that I had a key made for this room. And he would flay my balls if he knew what I'm going to do to you on that fucking desk." He ran his hand over the worn smooth top.

"Did you know that this was Thomas Jefferson's? Supposedly, anyway. My father loves this desk more than any of us. With the exception of himself, of course."

Ched swung back to face her with a devilish glint in his eyes. As she stood by the sofa, he reminded her of a snake eyeing its dinner as he walked over to her.

"I know exactly what to do with that desk."

She deftly rolled out of his grip, as he clutched her hips, and walked over to the bar.

"Scotch?" She held the crystal glass filled with amber liquid out to him.

"I like how you don't rush things and want to prolong the game."

She smiled at Ched, passing him the glass. She needed to be by the computer when the door to the study burst open.

She walked slowly backwards toward the large oak desk and crooked her finger, beckoning him. The computer sat on the corner of the desk to her left. The mole device behind her left ear.

The computer hard drive would be the best spot for the device to capture any electronic information sent or received by the computer or any mobile devices within close enough range. The only drawback was that verbal conversations would be missed. However, within two weeks, once the short-term battery life was done and the data dump to their servers happened, they would, hopefully, have some hard threads to pull on.

Seeing the look in Ched's eyes, she deeply hoped the plan was keeping to the timeline they had plotted. In the soundproof room, she had no indication if that was the case.

"Less than sixty seconds." Zane reported quietly in her ear, like he had read her thoughts.

It may prove to be the longest sixty seconds of her life.

Ched downed his scotch before moving to press into her. Evidence of his readiness pressed hard into her thigh. She couldn't retreat any further because of the damn desk. He ran his hands down her arms again and the tip of his tongue ran over his lower lip.

"I'm so fucking hard and I haven't even touched you yet."

He dipped his hand lower and tried to work his hand between her smooth, firm thighs. She pasted a breathless look of anticipation on her face and pushed his shirt further apart to run her hands across his chest. Effectively putting a little bit of space between them and preventing him from getting any higher between her thighs.

"I bet you say that to all the girls. Especially the ones you bring in here."

"You're the first. That I have brought in here, that is."

"A virgin then." She smiled.

"Let's pop the cherry." He ground his mouth hard on hers and thrust his tongue in her mouth so fast she fought the urge to gag.

Where the hell is the intervention?

She pulled her mouth away from his and bit the side of his neck. He groaned deeply and tilted his head to give her better access. His hands began to kick up their intensity in roving over her - arms, neck, breasts. Dipping low again to slip up her dress. She could feel her heart accelerate. And not because of pleasure or anticipation of Ched's next move.

She bit his earlobe, hoping the pain might pause his overzealous exploration, when the door of the study flew open so hard it bounced off the bookshelf that lined the wall.

"Demetria," the man roared.

Ched swung around, stunned.

She took the moment of distraction and surprise to slip the mole device from behind her ear and place it on the computer hard drive. It only took a split second, and the colour of the device blended perfectly with the black of the hard drive.

"Who the fuck are you?" Ched said, clearly annoyed his sexual gratification had been interrupted.

Decked out in designer clothes, with a shirt that stretched over a paunch belly, and slicked back black hair, the scowling man looked like a rich socialite that wasn't aging well.

"Who the fuck are you? And what the fuck are you doing with my fiancé?" The man looked like he was going to pounce on Ched, and his fists kept clenching by his sides.

"Fuck you, Cyril. I'm not your fiancé." She moved a few steps closer to Ched, away from the desk, and touched his arm. "I am not his fiancé. Anymore." She sneered at the Cyril and his face turned a deeper shade of red.

"Like fuck you aren't. You think the empty ring box on the bed table before you took all your things, including the five-carat bling I gave you, makes you not my fiancé. And then you're here, with this fuckface."

"If you cleaned the earwax from your goddamn ears, you would have heard me loud and clear when I told you it was over, Cyril."

"Look, I don't know what's going on here. But I think we could easily straighten this out. Cyril, why don't you close the door and we can both have a go at this sweet thang." Ched slapped her ass.

Cyril was right, Ched was a fuckface and she dearly wanted to throat punch the sonofabitch. But they might need him as an asset in the future so, unfortunately, she restrained herself.

She turned to Ched and leaned into him. "It would be fun, if he could get it to stay up."

Cyril looked like he was going to have a fit. She held up a hand to signal him to stay where he was. "I'll go and not cause more of a scene here." She turned to Ched. "You enjoy your party and if you're interested, we can meet again sometime in the future."

Ched sneered at Cyril. "Plan, babe."

She kissed her fingertip and pressed it to his lips before he could grind his mouth into hers again. "Here's my number."

She swung around and stomped past Cyril. "You're such a fucking cock-sucking bastard, you know that? You think you goddamn own me. Think again, you twat."

They continued to rage at each other until Cyril spun the tires of the Ferrari away from the beachfront mansion.

"Car is free of any device including listening, tracking, or jamming but follow protocol," Zane affirmed in their earpieces.

At that signal, Ryn fell quiet and still, Cyril's face showed his shock with the sudden change. "Just like that, the switch is flipped." He offered her his hand. "Nice to meet you."

"Thanks for the intervention and extraction." She shook his

hand as he maneuvered them swiftly away from the Miami home.

"And in the nick of time." Cyril winked at her. "It looked like young Ched was chompin' at the bit to get on you."

"He's a horny fucker, full of shit swagger. I would have loved to twist his balls off."

Her driver paled visibly. "Sadist."

"Better it ended on good terms. Leaves it open if I ever need him in the future."

"A planner. I like that. You work with the old boys on a regular basis?"

An indignant noise came through over the earpieces and Zane gave a small warning which the guy playing Cyril shrugged at. "A guy's gotta try."

"Always digging," Zane replied.

"That's why you employ me, is it not?"

She quickly checked her appearance in the mirror to ensure all was still in place as they got closer to the hotel. In the event that anyone followed, or Ched was inclined to get the hotel footage, they kept up the angry, argumentative charade on the way to the room.

She caught knowing looks sent Cyril's way from a few older gentlemen. A feisty younger woman bent on making her sugar daddy pay for some transgression. She flipped them the bird as the elevator door closed.

She stomped behind Cyril toward the room and once they were safely ensconced inside, the arguing sizzled out immediately. The guy playing Cyril locked the door before offering her hand. "Nexin, my lady. Nice to meet you." Nexin gave her a chivalrous bow. "And you are?"

The choice of persona had obviously been left to her by Zane. "Let's stay with Demetria."

Zane hadn't given her many details of the man who was to play the part of Cyril. Only that he assured her repeatedly that both he and Kotan trusted him implicitly.

The guy who played Cyril had looked vaguely familiar to Ryn when he burst into the study, and when she walked into the hotel room from the short hallway, it all clicked into place.

The large king size bed was pushed off to the side, replaced with large video monitors that showcased the street leading to the hotel, the entrance, as well as all the hotel service entrances.

Two men were diligently watching the screens. One was extremely tall and large, with light brown eyes under high arched eyebrows, a broad nose that indicated some African ancestry and his long dark hair pulled into a man bun. He wore black army cargos and a black t-shirt that pulled tight across his impressive chest and arms. He gave her a brief nod before turning back to the monitors.

As she took in the third companion in the room, Ryn worked to keep her face neutral. He had slightly more facial hair growth in the few days since she had spied him at Lok's residence club in New York.

More formally dressed today, in tailored black dress pants with a crisp white dress shirt that wasn't fully buttoned up. She quickly removed her gaze from the expanse of muscular chest and chiselled abs peeking through his undone shirt.

These were the three men she saw Zane meet briefly outside his hotel, over a year ago.

Cyril, or Nexin, rather, would be the shorter one of the three of them from that day. The one with the angular face and flirtatious pearly whites. Today, he looked older, his nose was different, he had darker hair, and he was thicker in the chest and middle than she remembered.

Zane and Kotan were suspiciously quiet on their end of the communication.

"Come on in, Demetria. They're harmless. They sent in the real guns for the party. The big guy is Rolf and the pretty boy is Tag."

Nexin walked over to the bed and took off his shirt to reveal the high-quality body padding he wore to bulk up his lean frame, and started the process of peeling off the facial attachments that made his nose broader with an added hump at the top.

"I didn't realize this was a group affair." Her voice sounded tighter than she would have liked. But the presence of the three of them, being blindsided by Zane and Kotan, along with the look Tag was giving her while he buttoned his shirt, robbed her momentarily of her flat emotional control.

"We're one big happy fam-fam. Even though we're engaged, I'm assuming you'd rather change in private." Nexin gave her a playful wink. "The bathroom is right through there."

She quickly took her exit, as Nexin didn't have any qualms about changing in front of her.

Zane chimed in on her earpiece, "I know you're used to working solo in the field. In this case you knew that a team was being brought in. It makes sense to keep our footprint small at the hotel."

She glanced at the three men in the room as she turned to close the bathroom door. They didn't respond or react to Zane's comment so he must have used a different channel.

"Trying to improve my rating of 'Doesn't play well with others?'"

Zane laughed on the other end. "Something like that. You got the rest of the plan set?"

"A heads up wouldn't have killed you." She gritted her teeth slapping the wig on the counter. "Not only about their presence in the room, but who they are," she hissed.

She wished the dreadful skull cap could come off with the wig so she could shake out her hot, humid hair. She whipped the zipper open on the bag that had been placed in the Ferrari and rammed the long and curly blonde wig on her head.

"I suppose it wouldn't have, yes. But you aren't an amateur, you can, and should, respond to unknowns effortlessly."

"We can talk about your little tests later."

She fell silent, stewing and calming down at the same time. After ensuring the blonde wig was firmly attached, she took off the nose prosthetic but left the cheekbone ones. She quickly added a few more and her chin became square, with an added cleft beneath her lower lip.

The white wrap dress was shoved into the bag to be exchanged with a mauve jumper and jean jacket, which covered the tattooed marks on her arms and legs.

Kotan's voice popped into her ear as she entered back into the room. "All clear from my end."

Both Rolf and Tag nodded as they continued to watch from their monitors. "All clear here too. It doesn't look like anyone followed them back. And if Ched, or anyone, does seek out the hotel footage for whatever reason, the performance was solid."

Tag turned to her and she felt a jolt travel up her spine as her still-blue eyes met his. His eyes were as intense as she remembered from the club. Up closer now, she could tell they were a colour that was more golden-brown than chocolate. It was hard to pull her gaze away from his as he silently regarded her.

His crisp white shirt was fully buttoned, now topped with a double-breasted vest with burgundy and gold silk trim. A burgundy bow tie finished it off. She recognized the outfit as the hotel staff uniform she'd seen during her and Nexin's parade through the lobby.

Tag slid white gloves on, then flipped up the burgundy cloth draped over the room service food cart.

"You're flexible, I presume?" He hitched an eyebrow at her and a small smile tugged on one side of his mouth. His lower lip was fuller than his upper one.

She snatched her eyes quickly away from his mouth. "One would hope."

Nexin unfolded his lean frame from the chair, now natural and younger looking. "In our line of work, we don't dare rely on hope.

Now, come give me a kiss, fiancé."

"How about a handshake? We did break up, remember?"

"So cold, Demetria."

She crammed into the space beneath the table top of the food service cart. "Good thing I'm not as tall as the big guy over there."

Rolf snorted. "Or as big. Poor Tag would get a hernia trying to push the cart." He had a heavy German accent.

Nexin leaned down to blow her a kiss, before inspecting all angles to ensure she or her bag were not visible once the cover was in place. Tag rolled the cart toward the elevator.

The space was cramped, she was thankful it wasn't going to be an extended journey. The first elevator that arrived had people in it and Tag politely responded with a slight Texan accent that he would catch the next one.

The next elevator was empty, and she clutched the bag with Demetria's gear in it, so it didn't plop out, as Tag navigated the cart over the opening of the elevator.

Kotan clicked in when they started to descend, "Control of elevator cameras is coming online. Floor four is clear and video is jammed in three, two, one."

The cloth flipped back on one. A white gloved hand hovered to assist her, and she noticed the scar on his wrist, the ends of it disappearing under the cuff of his shirt and band of the glove. She hesitated a fraction of a second before grabbing Tag's hand to haul herself from the tight quarters underneath the cart. And regretted it immediately.

At the touch, even with the gloves, she felt a jolt even stronger than when she had looked into Tag's eyes. She quickly extracted her hand from his larger one, her fingers tingled, and she fought the urge to rub them. She stepped further away from Tag.

"Wait. My control of jamming the video camera feed is slipping." Kotan strung a series of Japanese curses.

"What does that mean for action?" She demanded.

"If anyone accesses the feed, you won't be there entering the elevator, but suddenly appear. It creates a situation for someone to ask questions and do a closer investigation. It leaves a loose end that potentially could unravel." Zane explained.

Ryn watched the numbers descend on the screen. Far too slowly for her liking to get to the fourth floor before the cameras came back online.

"I can get off early."

"We've locked the elevator."

"It won't work." Kotan agreed with Zane and cursed again.

"If we had a logical explanation that may lead people to believe that there was a semi-innocent reason why she would have snuck on the elevator in the cart?" Tag asked.

"I'm losing control over it, in four, three…"

"That could work." Zane responded quickly to Tag's question.

Floor eleven, then ten displayed on the screen.

"One. Their video is coming back on line in two seconds."

Tag grabbed her arms, whirling her back into the corner, and his lips found hers before she had a chance to process the plan.

Electricity surged through her, igniting every cell in her body, as she placed her hands on his chest trying in vain to push him away.

"Go with it," he whispered huskily against her mouth, before his lips reclaimed hers making every single rational thought fly out of her head.

There was only the feel of her body slowly starting to burn. Only the feel of his lips feeding relentlessly on hers, both hard and soft at the same time.

Only the feel of the hard contours of his body pressing tightly against hers. His hands holding her head, traveling down her arms, wrapping around her back to bring her closer to him.

Only the feel of the hard plane of his chest under the palms of her hungry hands. The feel of his muscular shoulders and back as she wrapped her arms around him, holding him as tight to her as he was holding her to him.

"That provides a nice cover story explanation. Forbidden love between a hotel guest and a worker. I do love a secretive love tryst in an elevator. Um, guys?"

Nexin's voice slowly worked through her senses and the elevator signalled the arrival to the fourth floor. Tag dragged his lips away from hers reluctantly, his heavy breath matched her own laboured breath. He rested his forehead against hers and she prayed his head hid her shocked face from the recording camera.

Tag kept his forehead pressed to hers, lightly holding her arms looking into her eyes.

"You okay on your own?"

"I've been flying solo since I started."

She broke away from his intoxicating presence, and slipped through the doors, just before they began to close.

Chapter 12

Ryn paced in front of the computer monitors and consoles in the battle room and picked absently at a healing scrape on her palm that she had incurred in her training with Kotan.

"Pacing in here is not going to change anything. I do love the company, but your actions are not productive." Kotan's tousled black head bent low as he continued working on his code for whatever new device he had dreamt up. "I came home from the lab to work quietly. And in peace."

Kotan's not-so-subtle point was not lost but Ryn threw up her hands instead of leaving him in peace. "How do we know it's even working? And that at the end of the battery lifecycle that it does what it's supposed to? This is driving me crazy. There could be conversations and communications that we're missing that would tell us key information. What if we never get those?"

Zane thrust a glass of water into her hands. Caffeine was the last thing she needed. Ryn slugged the water back and narrowed her eyes, her gaze swinging from one man to another.

"You." She pointed her finger accusingly at Zane. "You have the same worryings, the same questions."

"Technically, worryings is not a word." Zane popped a grape into his mouth.

"Oh, shut it," she snapped. "Admit it."

"Doing so only gives you validity. More fuel to grow your 'worryings.' It accomplishes nothing." Zane's tone softened, watching her rigid back when she stared morosely out the window.

"We've field tested this line of device previously. But even if the device doesn't work as expected, this was not a last-ditch effort. Remember that."

Ryn pulled the charcoal cardigan tightly around her, slumping her shoulder against the pane of glass.

"When do you leave for Panama with Lok?"

"For the tenth time, I am not going to Panama." She whirled to Zane; her brow pinched in annoyance. "You conspired with Lok when I was returning home from Miami, that doesn't mean I would comply. The Miami op was filled with your conspiring actions."

Zane wasn't taken aback by her accusation. They had had it out as soon as she returned to the estate, about his blindsiding her with the team.

Kotan's fingers paused over his keyboard, giving her an empathetic look. "Some down time to decompress, and to use as a distraction, is not time wasted."

"You're worried I'll pester you all day."

"This—" Kotan resumed typing. "—is true."

She pushed away from the window. "I promise I'll keep out of your hair. Now, please, leave it be about the Panama thing. I'm working on managing Lok at this stage."

"Easier just to give in." Zane popped another grape into his mouth.

"And when have I ever chosen the easy road?"

The video screen in her studio at the estate housed a larger than life version of Lok. Tall, dark hair, and blue eyes, currently frustrated, filled the screen.

"Be reasonable, Ryn. Why would you not come to Panama?"

"I told you, I have client deadlines that I need to meet. The A in A-list band does not mean awesome in Brimming Full's case. They're high maintenance divas and I have to manage them along with my other clients. Plus, finish the piece we're collaborating on."

"And, if you didn't run off who knows where, to meet who knows who, every second day, that would help you." Lok looked peevish. But he was right.

"I know, and I am sorry for that. Next time, okay?"

Panama was a frequent jaunt that Lok and his gang liked to get away too when they had a little down time. Lok's mom and brother often would meet him there. Any time he had with them, especially without his father having to be present, was cherished time. She felt honoured he was upset that she wasn't going with him, but that was a double-edged sword.

Lok finally relaxed on the screen and reclined back on his sofa, looping his arms over the back. "You met someone."

"What? No, that's not what this is about," she sputtered.

Lok picked at the nails of his long, tapered fingers. "Maybe not. But you still did."

Ryn grabbed a soda from her fridge in the studio. "I meet lots of new people. As do you."

"You'll tell me when you're ready, I suppose. I do hate your lack of full disclosure with me. However, I will go on."

"That's a bit dramatic, don't you think? I thought Antonio was the one with dramatic flair."

"You're an imp. That song better be amaze-balls when I get back."

She gave him a snappy salute. "As you command."

Lok tossed his dark head back with a laugh. "I hardly think so. Take care of you."

She wanted to keep her promise to Kotan about not bothering him, and she hadn't lied to Lok about deadlines for clients, so she decided to work out of her city studio.

Given the security measures of the estate and the sensitivities to their privacy, Lok and periodically Antonio, were the only people from her music world that frequented the estate. Maari, along with Zane, had surprised her by finding the perfect space in Boston to work freely with clients. Having her own place gave her some much needed private space as well.

Her city studio was along the river in an older warehouse district that was slowly being revitalized. Filled with low- and mid-rise brick buildings, the area was home to apartments populated mainly by college students and young adults newly in the workforce, restaurants, a bodega, and a variety of shops. They were fortunate to snatch her small building up before any big developers could. It had good bones and was easy to fit it to her needs. A music studio and training space on the first two levels and living quarters on the last two.

Complete with all the newest security measures that Kotan and Zane could install, of course.

One of the best things about her place in Boston was the restaurant, Near the Mason, that was right next door. Neara and Mason, an eclectic couple, quickly made it their mission to ensure she was well fed.

Her mind was preoccupied on the drive along the coastal scenic highway into the city. She still wasn't fully satisfied with her conversation with Zane about being ambushed by the unplanned and forced encounter with the other team. Zane had been prepared for her when she got home that night, still dressed in his suit, but without socks or shoes, and in his study, cognac in hand.

"You're not a puppeteer, Zane, nor am I your puppet. Am I, or am I not, a valuable part of this team?" She had blazed on without letting him edge in a word. "And if I am a valuable part of this team, then why the hell am I getting ambushed in the field by my own leaders? What purpose does that serve? Besides throwing me for a loop."

"You don't warm up to others quickly and you trust minimally."

Zane stated reasonably, making her want to act irrationally and chuck the crystal bowl on the edge of his desk at his head.

"And you think this is the solution to my trust issues?"

He held up a hand to ward her off. "You would've been distracted by that *minor* detail and we needed you one hundred percent focused. Ched may appear to be a harmless, partying playboy, but if he had caught even a sniff that he was being played…He has some dark contacts and the bankroll to foot the bill."

"And we couldn't risk fucking up this chance." She shoved her hands through her hair, thankful to have that damn skull cap and wig off. "Okay, I get it," her anger diminished. "Let's keep this to the past and not repeat in the future."

"You cannot do every op all on your own. It's okay to rely on others." Zane walked to her to squeeze her shoulders. "Both Kotan and I trust these guys and have trusted them with our lives. More than once."

Zane refilled his cognac, but she declined his offer. "When we decided to retire from the field, and not because we were getting too old," Zane quickly pointed out, "mostly because we're more valuable working the ops from behind the scenes. These guys have been our regular hands and feet on the ground in many missions. They're efficient, effective, and loyal. And we would never put you into play with operatives we did not trust implicitly."

She didn't doubt Zane's words or distrust him. It was the method that didn't sit well with her. And it didn't sit well to add even more people into her life that she needed to keep secrets from. Who could be a liability to her family, and who could potentially be at risk because of her true identity.

"Move on already," she said in annoyance, as much with herself, as with the car straddling the lane in front of her. She huffed out a relieved breath when she turned onto the quiet street where her studio was and parked the Range Rover she borrowed from the estate's stock of vehicles.

Thinking about her to do list and those deadlines, Ryn decided she would pop in to say hi to Neara and Mason closer to supper. She unlocked the bronze lock to swing open one of the big red wooden doors of the four-storey building, shutting out the street noises.

She disarmed the security system and engaged the outside system to monitor her vehicle and building parameter. She ran her hand along the narrow hallway that opened to the rest of the first floor, a large, open space that housed her music studio and training area. On the street side of the building, there were few windows, but the back side made up for it, showcasing the beautiful slow-moving river and riverbank.

The building was most recently a small department store and one of the most charming aspects was the second level opened up to feature a comfy loft. The old hardwood floors gleamed, and the rails on the staircase and loft were made from old pipe.

It was her very first place and she moved in six months ago.

Oddly enough, she got a rock bottom price as the elderly owner loved it wasn't going to a developer. Zane insisted that he pay for the security renos but that was all she would compromise on, insisting on a payment schedule to repay Zane for everything else. Zane and Kotan insisted on compensating her generously for the ops, as they would for any operatives they contracted. It was ridiculous, she argued, since the whole damn mission was based on her. For her. But the two stubborn men wouldn't be swayed.

That money had stayed untouched except for her regular donations to charities. And along with her income from her songwriting sales and royalties, she sat extremely comfortably. Whatever sense of accomplishment she felt though, was tempered with guilt and sadness.

This space, this opportunity was only available to her because of her life intersecting with Zane's and because of the tragic course of events that had steered her to where she was today. If she thought the cost of this place was for her family to forfeit their happiness, she would drive herself mad.

Maari sensed that in her the first time she had brought her to see the building. "You, in no way, traded your family and their happiness so you could have this, Ryn. This is the end result of a series of real shit events that landed you with an opportunity that's offering you a chance to grow. There's no shame in that. Would you trade this to turn back the hands of time to prevent the threat to you and your family?"

"In a heartbeat."

"Then that, my friend, is the answer your heart needs to accept."

Maari's words from that day echoed in the quiet space surrounding her now, giving her a bit of comfort.

A gentle knock broke through her reverie and she hurried to the door when she saw Neara on the security camera.

"What a nice surprise." Ryn swung the door open and relieved her visitor of the package she carried. "I was going to pop over in a bit."

The short portly woman in her sixties embraced her warmly. "I know you're busy," she said with a faint Australian accent. "I spied you coming in and brought you some fuel to work."

Ryn led them into the studio area to unpack the bag Neara had brought over and laughed heartily. "I'm not socking in for the winter."

"You're much too skinny. And I know you haven't been here for a few days, so I wasn't sure what groceries you had. This will keep you well charged while you work for today, at least. Here, this is also for you."

Ryn groaned in delight when Neara pushed the cup of coffee into her hand. Tea was her first choice, unless it was Neara's brewed coffee. All their coffees and teas were fair traded and the first time she went into their restaurant, Neara had selected the brew and method for her, Roma Aero Pressed.

"This still is the best I've ever tasted."

Neara's face, framed by the tiny grey curls that escaped the tight bun, beamed proudly. "As I told you, the light roasts are often higher concentrations of caffeine and the aero press method really steeps the coffee rather brews."

"Will you join me?" Ryn indicated the array of sandwiches, soup, and pastries.

"Goodness, no. I have to get back to the restaurant. Petro is training two new staff today." Neara slipped on the glasses that hung from her neck, and her light green eyes smiled as she looked at Ryn. "Come for supper. Mason is making his Australian meat pies."

"How can I say no?"

"You can't."

Chapter 13

Ryn worked as many hours in a day and night as her body and mind would allow. Not only to keep out of Kotan's hair, but to keep her promise to Lok that their song would be finished. As well as working to meet her many deadlines between clients, which kept Antonio happy and out of her hair, and prepping pieces to mentor the music students at Annelou's School of Fine Arts. Not to mention the training regimens to keep her fitness, power and flexibility at the highest level.

She was pleased with her progress and was especially pleased she had finally wrapped up her song contract with the band, Brimming Full. She had very little patience for people who thought they were above others. It didn't matter how much fame you had, you were still flesh and blood like the rest. Human, with a history and baggage.

Antonio preferred video chat, as opposed to a phone call, and her cheek stung from biting it to keep the smile off her face. He looked like he was in the throes of a heart attack when she expressed her ruminations of no longer working with clients like Brimming Full.

"Brimming full of shit and ego, that's what they are."

"That's the nature of the industry. To not have a diva is a rare find."

"Maybe I'm in the wrong industry then."

His face contorted, turning redder, his brown eyes widening in horror. The crisp white shirt and light brown Armani suit accentuated his Hispanic heritage; his dramatic reaction accentuated the passionate characteristic of his Hispanic heritage.

"*Ay, Dios mío*! You're never to utter those words again. Promise me. Promise me, *mi amor*," he insisted.

"Okay, breathe there, big guy." She laughed. "I promise. For now," she muttered.

"I heard that, you sly minx." His handsome face returned to its normal disposition and colour. "Now, how is the collab piece going with Lok?"

"I work better under pressure." She groaned, pulling at the two buns of hair that peeked from under her ball cap.

If she stilted Lok on finishing the song, the same way she stilted their plans, she wasn't sure how much longer she'd be privileged to call him a friend.

"Leave me in peace so I can focus on that."

"Bullshit, you're going to go for a run, then stop over at the school to check in on the music students." His eyes narrowed.

"It's a process, Antonio. You're always happy with my results."

"Yes, but the grey hairs you're giving me, I'm certainly not happy about."

"Say hi to Miguel for me."

Grey hairs forgotten, Antonio gave her a ball busting grin, "I most certainly will."

She did a modified version of what Antonio accused her of and called Annelou to check in on the students. She promised she would be there in the next couple of days. The music students worked with a technical coach and Ryn helped them find their creative potential, so it wasn't critical she was there on a daily basis.

Knowing time wasn't on her side, she headed out along the river and fell into a sprint pace for her run before dark. The run helped, as it always did, when she felt stuck and uninspired with the music.

Once she got back, she quickly savoured supper from Neara

and Mason before settling into work again. She worked through the night, grasping, pulling and weaving sounds and words that came to her. Finally, it meshed with the piece Lok had created prior to his Panama R&R trip. She played it through a few more times and, pleased with the result, allowed herself to be seduced by the thought of sleep.

Her shoulder ached, her tailbone screamed from sitting so long and her legs wouldn't carry her up the stairs, so she flopped on the sofa beside her piano. Only to be woken up what felt like seconds later by her phone.

Seeing Kotan's number she snapped fully awake. "What's wrong?" Her mind raced frantically, thinking of Maari, Nessa and Zane.

"Nothing, I am sorry to startle you. Were you still sleeping? I thought you would be up by now, as it is past seven."

Ryn scrubbed her face. "Late night working." Her mind finally cleared. "Something happened to the device?"

They had expected it to take close to two weeks before the device uploaded its information to their server, but it had only been a week.

"The battery life did not last as long as we factored in. The data is starting to come in, but I wanted to let you know as soon as it did. Get some more rest and then we will proceed."

"See you in an hour."

A sigh emitted on the other end of the line. "Drive safe."

Nessa greeted her at the door, reaching up to kiss her cheek. Dressed in slacks with a beautiful crimson red blouse that matched the woman's feisty personality, Nessa looked ready to take control of the day.

"That's a beautiful colour on you."

"Why thank you, my dear." Nessa tenderly picked a stray thread off Ryn's green sweater she wore over her tank. "You look as though you've been burning the candle at both ends." Nessa took her hand to lead her into the house, her heels clicking on the hardwood floor. "But lovely still, as always."

Ryn gave a gentle tug on her hand but Nessa held tight. "You will eat. The data only started coming in and still needs to be combed through. There is time." Nessa insisted gently when she made a move to protest.

"And Zane?"

"He's wrapping up his meetings in Tampa and will be arriving back early this afternoon."

Ryn looked at the back of the estate through the French doors seeing an older gentleman riding the mower along the manicured lawn. "I had forgotten it was Friday."

"Yes, Ned and Martha are here today, as per usual. Martha had to run to check on a neighbour but she did bring you and Maari her maple chocolate chip cookies."

Ned and Martha were the couple that Zane had employed for years to help manage his homes. They didn't live at the estate but came out once a week to tend to the yard and household. Everyone that lived in the house was responsible for their share of cleaning and tasks to run the home, Martha and Ned only came to put the final touches on things. Zane paid them as full-time employees to ensure they were well compensated and cared for and insisted on setting them up comfortably in a home of their choice. She suspected Ned and Martha played a parental-like role in young Zane's life after he had left his abusive home all those years ago.

Ryn breathed in the smell of fresh cut grass that blew in the open window breeze. "I'll have my portion of cookies for breakfast. With milk, of course."

"We will have omelettes first, then you can stuff yourself full of as many cookies as you can manage."

When Nessa was satisfied she had filled her belly enough, Ryn was free to head to the battle room, her grey tabby sidekick happily leading the way. Kotan chuckled as she strode in.

She pointed an accusing finger at him. "You sent Nessa to intercept me to give you more time free of me."

Kotan snatched a piece of her last cookie when he walked by to get the computer printouts, crumbs falling on his white polo shirt.

Cletus looked expectantly between the two of them but, sensing no milk was coming his way, he curled up on the console to clean himself.

"Both Nessa and I knew you would not have taken the time to eat. And you and I both know there is no use arguing with the hurricane we know and love as Alinessa Luo. I am happy you took the time to shower though."

Ryn snorted her response and refreshed her tea from the beverage area in the corner of the room. Caving in, she put a small bowl of cream on the floor and Cletus darted over.

"Alright, I'm fed, the cat's fed. Spill it." She stalked over to the console. "What have you found? Can you trace any of the emails or texts back to the senders? And why do you think the battery lifecycle didn't last as long as expected? Is Maari coming in, or is she at R&D?"

Kotan put his hands up in mock self-defence. "They use different burner cells each time and the IP addresses bounce. Maari is in the city at R&D, she is miffed and will work on the battery piece when she can. The lifecycle issues could be due to a few things. Over expectations of the battery, the electronic security parameters in the room, the amount of information it captured. Maari and I will analyze it further, but it may come down to field experimentation and trial by fire."

"Tell me what you have so far."

Kotan dragged his hand through his black hair. She knew he hated debriefing halfway through.

"Just a quick summary. Then you point me in the direction of where you want me to work and—" She made a zipper motion over her lips.

"Our senator is a busy man and not everything has to do with his political job. Or on the up and up either. Side stuff like a mistress, which by the way, I do not want you going through. Shoot any of those chunks over to me," he demanded. "So far, most of it is sickening."

The data was organized by day and Kotan pointed her to which day file to start on. "Remember, any mistress stuff, chunk it out and send it in this program to me. It will catalogue it with dates and cross-reference back to the original file, so we do not lose that level and organization."

She perched herself comfortably on the stool and got to work. According to the texts to and from his wife, the loving couple was nowhere near loving out of the public eye. As promised, she sent any mistress communications to Kotan, part of her happy not to go through those. Ryn suspected the Senator would have loose lips with the mistress, but she was confident Kotan would ferret any of those details out.

After a while, Zane appeared in the doorway and she looked up, shocked. "You're back early."

Zane's eyes swung from her to Kotan, understanding and concern intermingled in them. "I'm back on time. When was the last time you two took a break?"

Zane strode over to the consoles. He had changed from his business attire into khaki pants and a golf shirt the colour of his eyes. She didn't think the man owned a pair of jeans. And he was in his favourite footwear. Bare feet.

Ryn started when she looked at Kotan. "Holy shit, Kotan," she blurted and then winced. His black hair was a mess and his onyx eyes stood out vividly from the bloodshot whites of his eyes. She felt a stab of guilt and her gut clenched. He was doing this for her.

"You need a break."

Cletus raised a sleepy head from his perch on the console beside her, displeased with the noise disturbing his slumber.

Zane patted the cat's head, then smoothed back her hair. "As do you."

She winced again when she rose and caught her reflection in the mirror. Her hair was pulled back into a ponytail but the front of it stuck up all over.

"You two should take a breather." Zane sighed as neither of them made a move to concede. "At least take a break from the screens. Why don't you run through the gist of what you've come across so far?"

"Let me put the final touches on this. I have been summarizing what we found under a few themes or streams of intel." Kotan hammered on his keyboard.

"Severyn, come take a break while he's doing that. I brought food. Nessa had to run into the clinic and suspected you two wouldn't take time. Proving that lady right only emboldens her."

Ryn chuckled, knowing Zane spoke the truth. She did have a vague memory of Nessa saying she had to go to the clinic where she volunteered.

Her stomach rumbled, taking in the savoury smell of curry chicken rice soup. "You stopped at Neara and Mason's on your way here."

"I knew you would absolutely take a break to eat something from there."

"If you were there, then—"

Zane's smile cracked his handsome face, reaching into the bag to pull out a travel mug.

Kotan reached high to stretch his long body. "That does smell good." Balancing the bowl Zane offered him on his palm, Kotan ran through the data so far. "Our senator isn't as squeaky clean as he would like people to believe. But he is successful in keeping that well hidden from the public eye. First, there's his young mistress on the side. No biggie there."

Kotan paused reconsidering his choice of words. "I mean, no surprise there. White, rich, extremely privileged his whole upbringing - many stray this way. Our Zane is an exception."

"It helps that I'm not married. And I certainly did not have a privileged upbringing." Zane shrugged his shoulders and smiled. "I don't think Caucasian-ness owns infidelity, but I do get what you're saying."

"True." Kotan nodded in deference to his friend. "He spends a lot of time communicating electronically - text mainly - with the mistress. From the messages we intercepted, they are into some repugnant stuff and I instructed Severyn not to go through any of those communiques."

She didn't need to be protected from the perversions in the world, but she felt a spike of gratitude that Kotan felt so strongly to do so.

"Is there a search algorithm to slug through that instead?" Zane scooped Ryn another serving of soup.

"I started there, yes. But without knowing any key code words, we could miss critical things. And if there is something in there that's relevant to us, it could be in code, or more nuanced. It's better to do it manually."

"I didn't get any indication that the wife knows. You?" She asked Kotan.

"Nothing in their communications. He is either well-versed in keeping things in the shadow, or she does not care."

"Interesting about the wife." Zane reclined on the leather sofa, propped his bare foot up on his knee, and welcomed the cat. "He definitely is both capable and well-versed in keeping his affairs private. There have never been any whispers about this anytime throughout his career. But there are people out there who know about this. People he has quieted through money, favours, or blackmail to keep their mouths shut. We can explore that, especially regarding the wife, if needed, to get what we require from the Senator."

Exploiting weaknesses was something his friend, Virginia Ruthley, would do. Her stomach clenched, but she remained silent.

Fingers empty and clean, Kotan pulled up images of Ched.

"Moving onto the next stream. Ched has gotten himself into a smidge of trouble again. Partying, driving impaired, some allegations of inappropriate and aggravated conduct. The Senator is working his channels and greasing palms to make it all go away."

Rich, entitled, and no consequences for actions. On either Ched or his father's side. She really was sorry she didn't throat punch the asshole when she had the chance.

Ryn set her empty bowl on the tray and summarized what she had gathered. "There is very little love between father and son from what I deduced. Daddy does his best to keep him on a tight leash, demoralizes him every opportunity, berates him for no motivation except partying. Ched responds as you'd expect someone who doesn't cower or toe the line. It gets quite aggressive, but beyond a tense parent-child relationship, I didn't find anything illuminating."

"But it could come into play in the future. For our advantage or to help give context to something." Zane steepled his fingers under his chin, contemplating.

"Lastly, there are the communications with a lobbyist or lobby group. Severyn, were you able to find much on your search?"

"Very little. Either there's little action or they operate off the radar. I wasn't able to get too far with my basic searches."

Zane tossed a peeved Cletus a few cat treats for disturbing him, before settling into one of the stations. "What's the name? I can start digging on my end now. There's a bit of work stuff I need to wrap up, but I can multitask."

"Pallium. It's Latin for cloak. I found that much out at least," she said wryly.

She watched the two men studiously working at the computer

consoles. Neither had been raised with technology but they were exceptionally comfortable and capable. She was deeply thankful they were too. She was still figuring out all the features of her encrypted phone.

"I didn't find anything in my transmissions that alluded to the nature of why the Senator was in touch with them. It seemed well guarded over their emails, so maybe that's telling. One big cat and mouse game." She watched Cletus resume his nap on the leather sofa and shrugged the tension from her shoulders. "In his role as Senator, would it be common to have contact with lobbyists or is that not allowed?"

Kotan rubbed his chin. "I am certain that it happens more than the general public would ever imagine. I got the sense from the communications that this was a longstanding relationship, but the issue of interest was new. That is what I was diving deeper into when you came in, Zane."

Ryn watched Kotan pinch the bridge of his nose, saw the tired lines around his eyes. "You're working so hard on this for me. I regret that my urgency and inability to put it aside, for even a short time, is emanating onto you. We have to be diligent about this, so we don't miss details." Ryn braced her hands on the console, looking at Kotan, and then Zane. "If that means slowing it down, then that's what we need to do. All of us, me included."

A gasp sounded at the door, followed by a tiny lady stomping across the room. "You haven't stopped yet or taken a break have you." Nessa's eyes snapped with accusation. "Left to your own devices you would work yourselves into the ground."

Hands on hips, eyes flaring, Nessa may be small in stature, but she was a force of nature not to be reckoned with.

"Severyn was just saying the exact thing and Kotan's agreeance was on the tip of his tongue."

"Don't you protect him, Zane Andrews." But like a wave washing over the sand, Nessa turned soothing and compassionate.

"I understand the urgency, but you all have to look at the long game here. Burnt out and worn out, makes for mistakes. And those can be costly."

Kotan rose to his full height hugging Nessa to his side. "As Zane mentioned, Severyn said the very same thing." He smiled tenderly at Ryn. "The student becomes the teacher. I know that there is something here this time. This is not a dead end."

She felt a wave of hope fill her.

"But you are absolutely right, my dear. We have to take the time to be diligent and thorough."

Zane clapped his friend and partner on the back. "Now, take your wife and go do something else for a while. Take a nap, a walk, or whatever you're so inclined to do." Zane gave a suggestive wink. "And Severyn—"

"Yes, I know the drill. I'll go hit and pound on something."

Chapter 14

"That fucking son of a bitch." Ryn jumped from her chair, listening to Zane report on the secrets he had unearthed through his deep dive into Pallium and Senator William Hanelson.

She threw the sweaty towel onto the seat she abandoned; her strong long legs ate up the floor while she paced. At Zane's summons, she had bolted from her studio mid-workout.

Nessa pressed a cool glass of mango infused water into her hands, refusing to let go until Ryn took the glass.

Kotan looked as equally outraged. The walk in the woods with Nessa earlier had hit his reset button, but the relaxed look had vanished.

"I wish I could say I'm intrigued by the Senator's ability to operate so fluidly off the radar." Zane rubbed his eyes. "But this is disturbing, if, of course, I didn't piece it together out of context."

Ryn scrutinized the screen that had the snapshots of information and snippets of conversations from transmissions both him and Kotan were able to find.

"You organized in chronological order, as best you could. Some pieces are innocent on their own, but all together…"

"They paint a disturbing picture." Kotan finished for her.

"Pallium aren't like any other lobbyists and definitely are embracing the Latin translation of cloak. Cloak and dagger style." Ryn narrowed her eyes examining the screen. "It's like they aren't lobbyists at all. A shell lobbyist company if there's such a thing."

Zane nodded in agreement. "They're registered and

incorporated but their activity in the public realm feels fabricated. And from what we unearthed, they look to be a broker of illegal deals. Maybe legitimate organizations run illegal deals through Pallium, but these wouldn't be found in the public activities of the company."

"Outside the scope of the law and well outside any ethical means of dealing." She ground her teeth.

"And they're planning to hijack an education reform bill? But to what end?" Nessa's finely shaped eyebrows pulled together studying the details on the screen.

"They are going to kill it because that benefits Senator Hanelson." Kotan's disgust matched what Ryn felt.

"If they're successful in voting the reform bill down, there's a loophole they plan to exploit? The money that would be given to the education system will find its way to the Hillside project?"

"That's right, Severyn." Zane nodded, moving closer to study the wall screen. "From here I'm making two conclusions. First that Pallium is connected to the contractor that will be awarded the contract. Second, that they plan to somehow divert a chunk of the money for their own use. Maybe they plan to run it through Pallium; clean it somehow. But the Senator is most certainly one of the intended recipients."

Kotan's tall frame was held tight as a bowstring and Zane rubbed the stubble on his jaw. Both men had encountered corruption like this many times in their past and had righted it to ensure the guilty parties were brought to justice. Not always the legal system's justice, but justice all the same.

"I'm afraid it is out of our hands," Zane said quietly, turning to her.

"What? Just because it doesn't apply directly to our case?" Ryn swung around to face him, stunned. Her eyes hardened to steel when she saw the stubborn resolve on his face. Her eyes cut sharply over to Kotan. "Back me up here."

"I am afraid I cannot, Severyn."

Nessa stood silent, taking in the growing tension.

Ryn looked fiercely between the men. "And why the hell not? We're going to let this, this, entitled pig take millions away from children to continue to pad his pockets? Why would we let that happen? How can you both sit there and tell me that you are okay with that? After everything that you both have done for years to stop shit like this."

With each sentence, her voice got louder. She knew she was letting her emotions escalate, but in the safety of this house, in their company, she could do that.

"Think about the big picture, Severyn." Zane said calmly, and held his hands out in her direction, seeming to know that physical contact at this time would not serve the situation well.

She stood stock-still, processing Zane's words. "We're letting this go because of me?" Horror and denial rose like bile in her throat.

"No, not because of you. Or for you," Kotan added quickly. "We have to play the big picture. There is no other evidence that this backdoor scheming is happening, except what we have unearthed. Illegally and, many would say, unethically. The authorities are not going to act on it. Even if we slid it into the hands of the powers that be, there is no validity to the information because there is no other corroborating evidence."

"We risk overplaying our hand and raising the Senator's suspicion of how the information was obtained," Nessa concluded.

All in the room worked hard to ignore the flash of betrayal Ryn shot in Nessa's direction.

"Based on what we've started to pull out in the data, we're going to need him in play and to continue in his position of power," Zane added.

She felt like she was going to be sick. The cool, crisp pane of glass pressed tightly against her forehead, and her soul, felt black compared to the late afternoon sky.

"The devil's in the details, Severyn, and unfortunately, sometimes we have to leave the devil in play to achieve the bigger goal. I know this doesn't sit well with you. It doesn't for any of us, trust me. The best I can do is alert Virginia to the situation."

Ryn leaned her back against the window. "What can the CIA do on homeland soil and intervening in matters of legislature?"

"Nothing, but she can use her contacts to alert the pro-side to start digging deep to rally the pro-votes for the bill so that it actually does not get defeated. If it passes, then it's a win-win. Education gets the money it sorely needs, and the Senator and Pallium's plans are sullied. That's the best I can do."

"Zane, earlier you said that you may have found a needle in the haystack?" Kotan squeezed her shoulder, passing her a piece of lemon meringue pie.

She accepted the bribe. She knew that Kotan's change in direction of conversation was to allow her to process the decision that had just been made. But she pushed away both the pie and mango-infused water as it felt like liquid cement in her swirling gut.

"I tweaked into a term, *hacer señas*, that was referenced a few times. I recognize it as one related to a port from years ago in Mexico."

Zane pulled up a map shot of the port in question. "It wasn't the port's official name in Manzanillo but was what the locals referred to it as. I can't recall the full phrase but one fisherman explained that the beautiful ladies of land called them home while the beautiful lady of the sea beckoned them to go back out. In the Senator's messages, *hacer señas* wasn't used directly in reference to a port. However, when I re-read those messages with that context, the communication started to make sense."

"Like a coded puzzle."

Zane nodded at Nessa. "Exactly. From my interpretations, the messages are referring to cargo and that port by Manzanillo.

Unfortunately, there's nothing that alludes to the cargo type, where it's coming from or going to, or who the end receiver is."

Kotan bounced on the balls of his feet and continued to study the screens while Ryn pulled a chair up to a console to scroll through it herself. She went back to the segments of conversation with the unknown source, that Zane had highlighted, and let her eyes scan.

Nothing without me

She shot it to the wall screen. "It appears the Senator wormed himself into a bit of hot jam in the convo about the port, beautiful ladies beckoning them and all that crap."

"Thanks, Severyn, that was the second piece I wanted to bring forth. Whoever is on the other end of the communication is not happy with him."

"A flash of conscience?" Ryn scoffed. "Cold feet? Risk outweighing the benefits?"

You like to sit in your ivory tower and turtle the minute there's a bit of risk that might splash back on you…remember you're just a facilitator and can be replaced

The sender's tone was decidedly hostile.

And remember dear ol' Sen, who we're ultimately dealing with and what they do when they're disappointed

"They definitely want to ensure the Senator follows through on his part, whatever that is. Nothing about the who, what, when, or where. But we know that there's both an intermediate and a bigger fish in play." Zane surmised.

"We know he's dirty on various levels." She felt a bit of hope that they might change their mind on bringing that bastard to justice sooner rather than later.

"And he has a lot to lose. His power, position, freedom, and maybe his life, if he is in bed with people as ominous as they sound in that text. We will keep digging here and see if we can pull out more." Kotan turned her away from the screens. "Why don't you go decompress for a bit."

Normally she would have protested but she needed to get out of the confines of the room. Away from the endless words that pointed to a powerful man's corruption to benefit only himself. And that they were currently turning a blind eye.

The thought of a swim in the cool water and serene environment of the indoor pool pulled her to the bottom floor. When she walked into the pool room, she knew it was the right call.

The soft sounds of tropical birds greeted her; the humidity pulled at the soft tendrils of her hair. The rich browns and greens of the room comforted her, and faint rays of daylight peeked through the large windows at the top of the room. She glanced at the hot water pool area that featured a tall wall structure at the back with water cascading down. The area was peaceful, complete with a rock arch spraying water down where the hot water section was separated from the cooler waters of the long pool.

Right after she slipped into a one-piece swim suit, her phone rang and she contemplated ignoring it, but guilt got the better of her. She had been quasi-avoiding Maari, as she didn't need any more ribbing or reminders about Tag and their kiss on her last op.

"Thought you were going to ditch me again."

"That transparent, am I?"

Maari's pleasant laugh rang in her ear. "Sooo very much. How's everything going? Bad news the battery lifecycle didn't last as long as anticipated, which limits the data, but at least you're starting to get some data. I don't imagine you and daddy have taken much of a break and are suffering mama's anger."

"I hear very little sympathy in your voice." Ryn dipped her toes into the cool water.

"I've been on the receiving end of that wrath-stick too many times. You don't purposefully peeve that woman off. But honestly, how's it going?"

"We've categorized and themed most of the data and unearthed some corrupt bullshit. Some actionable, some not." The bitter taste still lingered thinking the Senator wouldn't be held accountable for his role in trying to hijack the education reform bill.

"Having to keep the bigger picture in view?" Maari clued in right away to the dilemma she was battling to come to terms with. "Sorry, Ryn."

"I'll get there."

"In the meantime, you can relive that elevator kiss. Unfortunately, daddy didn't record the loop for replay. With a name like Tag, the guy sounds stacked and hot as fuck."

"Jesus, Maari. Drop it already."

"I'm living vicariously through you. With my line of work, it's too exhausting thinking about getting involved with someone and having to keep half of my life away from them." Maari stopped abruptly. "Fuck, shit, I'm sorry, I didn't mean that was because of you. I was destined to be involved in the family business before you, you know that. And you're in the same boat, aren't you?"

"My feelings aren't hurt. But it's nice to know we're companions in misery."

"That we are. We'll hit the town soon," Maari gave a wicked laugh. "Find us some hotties, have a whole lot of fun, then ditch them in the morning light."

"You've never struck me as the one-night stand kinda girl."

"See what they're turning us into?"

Ryn felt lighter, laughing with Maari.

"Well, I'll let you go for your swim."

"How did you know that?" Ryn looked around, suspicious.

"I can hear the waterfall. You looked around for a hidden camera, didn't you? You're off your game, get some sleep tonight. Got it?" Maari demanded.

She promised Maari she would before hanging up, and felt the dregs of sleep pulling at her. She would probably drown if she started in the hot water area of the pool, so she slipped into the cool water instead. Pushing powerfully from the wall she broke the surface with smooth, long strokes. Falling into a rhythm, she focused on her breathing, letting her mind ease into a quiet zone.

When she swam it was hypnotic regardless of how tired she was. Often memories of her family would surface. And these were rare times those memories brought her contentment rather than guilt or sorrow.

Other times when she swam, things that her consciousness refused to see, would shimmer into crystal clear focus.

"The memory is a fascinating thing. Things that we have no ability to know that we even know, will suddenly appear. It may be the result of a dream. Or you may be seeing a completely innocent and separate thing and it makes that connection in your mind."

Her mom's wisdom and advice echoed, guiding her tonight.

Images swam in her mind, as her body cut through the cool water in that calm, trance-like state. Words flashing on screens, boats, cargo containers. All intermingling and surrounded by dark edges. Something was there, she just needed to get out of her mind's way.

After an hour, Ryn kicked harder with her legs as the old injury in her right shoulder started to burn. She'd have to quit soon, or it would spasm. It was a lingering pain in her ass, but it was her reminder that she survived a death that should have surely claimed her.

A death that surely would have claimed her had it not been for Zane and Kotan. It was fate, or whatever a person chose to believe, that brought her path across theirs.

She never had any inkling that her childhood friend had an uncle. She wasn't even sure that Vlad had known.

An uncle that was estranged from his sister and nephew, his only living relatives. One that kept an eye on his nephew from afar. One that came to investigate when his nephew suddenly died. One that had resources and skills most would never think about.

Layers.

All their lives were filled with layers.

Even their personalities were layered, as no one expressed the sum of their experiences or the essence of who they were, in their entirety, all of the time. And, in the case of her and Zane, one essential layer had overlapped and started another cascade of layers to her life.

To her.

Because the devastated girl that clung to her dead friend, the terrified girl who had sat paralyzed watching her tiny sister's still body in the hospital bed, had grown.

She had grown and developed new layers to make her a fierce, determined, strong woman.

Layers.

Strata.

"Holy shit." She shot out of the water.

Chapter 15

Ryn changed into dry clothes with lightning speed before racing back to the battle room. The scent of lemon roasted potatoes and grilled fish made her groan with both appetite and guilt.

"It was my night to cook, wasn't it?"

Nessa reached up and gave her a small peck on the cheek. "My pleasure. Now eat."

"Cletus isn't here begging for fish?" She moved quickly to the console.

"He is out mousing. Now, come eat." Nessa gave her a pointed look.

"You guys dish up, I want to pull something up."

"You look like you clued into something." Zane gave Nessa a gentle push toward the table.

"Yeah, yeah, I know. Take a break from the thing you're most intent on and the answers come to you when you focus on something else. No need to rub it in."

Nessa, Kotan, and Zane exchanged an amused look while she muttered under her breath.

"There. In the communication with the Senator and the threatening person, the one that said nothing without me." Ryn transferred the screen to display on the wall screen. "There was a mention of strada and I took that to be a spelling error and that strata was meant."

"Within the context of that sentence, strata, aka layers, makes sense." Kotan agreed.

"Yes, see, it says 'The various strada of the foundation are intact.' But I think they were talking in code. Why talk in code for that sentence when none of the others are coded?" Ryn glanced at them before turning back to the screen. "And then there's this."

She had a file open from one of their first investigations. A few clicks and the port papers they had discovered flipped up on the wall screen.

"I'll be damned." Zane paused his fork midair.

On the port papers from Fenn Industries, one of the companies listed as having cargo on the ship was Strada Indonesian.

"How ever did you remember that minuscule detail, Ryn?" Nessa asked in wonder.

"The mind is an amazing thing, if I can get out of its way." She shifted uncomfortably at the proud look on their faces.

"That is tremendous work." Kotan rose for a closer look. "Whoever the Senator was communicating with, this Strada Indonesian is important."

"Especially since he signed the port clearance authorization for the ship carrying their cargo." Zane reminded them.

Kotan nodded in agreement. "That one sentence does seem to be loosely coded. To refer to Strada Indonesian, but also to something else. Maybe referring to the various functions of Strada Indonesian are secure?"

"For Gādo Technologies, you guys have many divisions or subsidiaries or whatever you call them. But they aren't all housed in one location. What if they're talking about the different sites of the company?"

"Good thinking, Severyn, I'll start a search run." Zane wiped his hands clean on the napkin before working at one of the stations. "If they're openly listed on a port document, they'll have at least a few legit sites, but I'll dig deep. Kotan, you may want to add a fancy digging code to get us to where they don't want people to go."

"Would they possibly have sites that they're keeping off the radar? Sort of like black sites or sleeper sites?" Nessa wondered.

"A possibility," Kotan agreed while he set up the advanced infiltrating search tools.

"You've more than earned your supper tonight kid." Zane patted her shoulder. "Now, let's eat."

They worked well into the night, digging into Strada Indonesian. A legitimate shipping company that shipped everything from vehicle tires to priceless art. But Kotan, being the fanatic electronic whiz that he was, ferreted out details that were well buried off the radar.

"They have a number of 'on-the-books' facilities. But then there are these."

Her tired grey eyes burned, making her remember she had worked through the night on her music and had less than two hours of sleep this morning. She narrowed her eyes to focus on the map that Kotan had put on the wall screen, dotted with green pin marks, along with a few red ones.

"The green markers are the 'on-the-book' facilities and the red are the ones they do not want anybody to know about."

Two of the red markers fell in Washington State and Manzanillo, not too far inland. And close to two seaports that had come up through their earlier investigations. Others were scattered around the world in various places such as Portugal, Pakistan, and Nigeria, all of them close to port areas.

"Are you able to access any details about the two facilities closest to us?" Zane stifled a yawn.

"Now that I have found their off-the-book sites, all registered to different companies, I am constructing a search to find more details and, hopefully, blueprints of the buildings. That will run through the night and I have alarms set up if anything goes wrong with the search. I suggest we all get a good night's rest, as we may be in operation mode within the next twenty-four to forty-eight hours."

Chapter 16

As soon as Captain Vega turned off the seatbelt sign, Ryn left the plush seat to pace the carpeted floor of the Gulfstream G550. Clipping along toward Washington State, Captain Vega would assume she was going to meet with a music client, but the deceit was necessary.

The deceit wasn't what was making her pace, although she hated to play a part in deception of any kind. Some deception was more necessary than others. She knew that. Sometimes maybe more than any of them.

The pacing was due to Zane informing her that she would be working with a team again. And, of course, he chose to drop that little nugget on her as she was leaving.

"Domineering butthead." Her ire at Zane bubbled.

Not only did the Senator remained unaffected by justice, but Zane was immovable when it came to her working with a team for this reconnaissance op. Based on Kotan's surveillance of the facility, he was certain it currently was unmanned. However, Zane reasoned the team was still a necessary part.

"They have a crucial parallel op to get to the computers at a nearby legit Strada Indonesian office. And that needs to be done before you enter the black site facility. If something goes awry on your portion of the op, then we're into their system before Strada Indonesian can amp up their security."

"There can be parallel teams and ops, they don't have to be interwoven." She had stubbornly insisted.

"We're sneaking you into the facility with the cargo, so we can't rent a car, drive it out there, and leave it for you to get back. Until you learn how to space travel, you're stuck with them, kid."

Okay, that made sense. Dammit.

She jammed a piece of lemon into her glass of soda water and snatched a handful of cashews. It wasn't exactly like she could call an Uber to pick her up. That still didn't mean that she had to like the idea.

When she learned who the team was, she knew she shouldn't have been surprised. Zane and Kotan did employ several operatives on a contract basis, but only a few had earned their highest regard.

"You're sure there isn't anyone else?" She had pressed, to no avail.

"We're not going to entrust your safety to just anyone. No kissing on this op." Zane flicked her nose affectionately and left her to pack, her cheeks flaming.

Maari had sought her out, flopping across her bed, silently watching her pack.

"You hide it better than most, but I can tell you're steamed. But you need to stop being pissy and selfish."

Ryn arched an eyebrow at her, yanking open the trunk that housed Demetria's paraphilia.

"If a team is what the situation needs, is what you need to help you accomplish your mission, then why fight it? If it means you come back home unharmed and undead, then fuck yeah, take the team." Maari flipped onto her back, her midnight poker straight locks dangling over the edge of the bed. "And then there's the mega-hot chemistry factor."

Maari's jibe made her cheeks warm again. That kiss in the elevator had been an impromptu adjustment on an op, not because her and this Taggert were attracted to each other.

A bump of turbulence brought her back to the present. How does Lok do this almost every day, she wondered, clicking in her seatbelt.

Thinking of Lok, brought the reminder of her promise to him, that she would keep herself safe.

She sighed, closing her eyes.

Yeah, she'd work with a team this op. They could pick her up after she was done at the facility, but there was no need for her to go for beers to get to know them better afterwards.

Do the op, then done.

Chapter 17

The search worm Kotan programmed had infiltrated all sorts of places that Strada Indonesian worked very hard to keep dark. From what Kotan had pulled out, the black site facility in Washington state served as a transfer and hold location for cargo diverted from the nearby port. The type of cargo that came in and out, and the nature of the activities at the facility would soon be found out, if she was successful.

There was a chill in the air coming off the Pacific waters that one wouldn't expect for a mid-June night. With the dark cloud cover, a storm might be on its way.

Ryn was thankful for both. The cooler evening made the wig, skull cap, balaclava, and hood she wore more bearable. The dark clouds were a definite plus, providing many shadows for her to move silently within.

She looked up at the tower of shipping containers that rose on either side of her, thinking of a rat in a maze looking for its cheese reward.

"At the end of that row turn south." Zane's voice came over the tiny hidden earpiece.

Zane had a bird's eye view of the shipping yard thanks to drones, Kotan's nimble hacking skills to commandeer a private satellite, as well as the shipping yards' system.

"Halt."

She was nearing the end of the row and did as Zane instructed without hesitation, listening to Kotan mutter under his breath. Her breathing felt like it was singing out her location in the silence, until a loud clang, the sound of metal crashing together, echoed in the distance.

"All clear. Move now."

Ryn turned south until she found the container with the check digit she was looking for, slipping into the small nook of space between it and its neighbour.

"There are hazardous material labels all over the container. Are we sure about this?"

"It's a deterrent for snoopy people."

"If I come out glowing in the dark or with a third boob, there will be a whole lotta hell to pay."

Chuckling rang in her ear before Zane and Kotan resumed their seriousness.

"We're sure this little do-hickey is necessary?" She patted the device in her inner pocket of her black jacket. "The handle and lock isn't like all the rest of the cargo containers?"

"Positive." Zane's voice carried a slight insult by her questioning. "We still have eyes in the sky and aren't seeing anyone close to you. But we'll set off another distraction to give you time, and minimize the risk of anyone seeing you."

"I breached the last bit of resistance, but they have a roving code." Kotan's voice was tight. "We have a small window of ninety seconds. Two mins max. Is the device ready to attach?

"Ready."

"Three, two, one."

She moved like silent lightning to attach the round disc directly above the handle and locking mechanism. Lights around the edge of the disc blinked rapidly before moving around at dizzying speed, making the device look like it was actually spinning. A vibration started, exactly like the buzzer you get at some restaurants when waiting in line.

Chaotic yelling reached her ears. Whatever Kotan had done,

their distraction was working well to wreak havoc and hell.

The vibrations and spinning lights disappeared followed by a clicking noise to indicate the container door had successfully been breached. Once inside she flipped on her night vision, then reattached the disc to the inside of the door to re-engage the lock before she slipped the mechanism back into her jacket pocket.

Zane and Kotan had discovered there was one cargo container belonging to Strada Indonesian waiting to be delivered this evening. With opportunities like that, you hesitate only long enough to do your damnedest to ensure it isn't a trap. Then you jump on it.

The shipping manifest Kotan had secured showed a mixture of legitimate items. The destination listed on the manifest was some art gallery warehouse in the city. It felt off, especially given they knew there was an off-the-books Strada Indonesian facility nearby.

A facility that was owned publicly by a different company, was termed decommissioned, and was fenced off to prevent anyone accessing the grounds or the facility.

It was a golden opportunity they didn't pass up.

"Remember, leave the crates until the transport is complete," Zane instructed.

She had argued that if she was discovered before they arrived at the facility, or if the destination actually was the art gallery warehouse in the city, they would have missed the opportunity to discover what the actual contents of the crates were. Zane wouldn't risk it though, feeling that increased the risk to her.

"Are you in place?"

Ryn cautiously stepped around the crates toward the middle of the container, activating the other device she had with her, and pulling out a tightly folded package. It looked and felt like a thin pliable sheet of aluminum.

"Activated. How are we looking?" she asked, sitting low between the crates and pulling the aluminum sheet over her.

"Perfect. The heat of the container is increasing thanks to the device and the sheet is masking your heat signature. Our equipment doesn't detect you at all."

She pushed a few buttons on the device that looked like an old flip phone. "Temperature is set to hold here."

Kotan and Zane periodically fed her visual updates to what was transpiring in the area around her. After thirty long minutes, the cargo container was lifted and swung slowly toward the flatbed truck waiting to transport it. The swinging motion made her nauseous and brought forth flashes of memory of being on a boat caught in a raging storm, with waves crashing over the side.

"Your heart rate is increasing. What's wrong?" Zane asked tersely, while she focused on her breath and calmed her racing heart.

"Just some motion sickness."

The container landed with a jarring thud on the flatbed truck, and she kept her hands ready to grab her weapons, if the two men decided they needed to have a peek inside. Thankfully, they both hopped into the truck to depart for their destination.

The minutes dragged on and her legs were getting numb from the lack of movement. She sat flat and contracted and relaxed her limbs to get the blood moving more fluidly.

"Minute 37 since departure. On the road that leads directly to the facility now."

Another ten minutes and the truck slowed. She heard the whine of a large mechanical gate before her body rocked slightly with the motion of stopping and starting.

"Any security personnel are on site?" she asked quietly.

Kotan answered after a brief pause, "The site still appears to be empty. The only heat signatures I am getting are from the occupants in the truck."

"Could they have the same technology that you created that blocks the detection?"

"I don't see how."

Zane chuckled, but didn't dispute his long-time friend and

partner's statement. Kotan was a genius. Coupled with Maari, their devices were unrivalled. And Zane constantly had his ears open for developments in the security tech field, as well as the far-reaching tendrils of his network into the dark underworld, for any new developments.

Ryn's legs and butt vibrated as the truck entered the facility, reminding her of driving over the cattle guard in the road at her uncle's ranch. She carefully adjusted into a crouched position as the truck came to a halt. If the drivers decided to go poking around in the cargo container, she wasn't going to meet them flat on her ass.

She rotated her shoulder to pop the built-up tension, making sure she was limber enough, but tense and ready, for any required sudden movements.

The semi door slammed hard. Harder than she thought was truly necessary, as she could feel the vibration under her feet in the cargo container.

"I said no, Si. My job is only to pick up the container and drop it off. I don't give a rat's ass or flying fuck what's in it. And if you know what's good for you, you don't either."

"Shit, Oscar, I was just sayin'."

"Yeah? Well, you've been 'just sayin' since we picked this up. It's time to shut the fuck up about it. This gig is sweet for me. All I have to do is drive my truck when they call me, drop off the load, and I get paid real good. It's none of my business and sure as fuck none of yours. I've been doing these runs for four years now and it's been real sweet to me. Like hitting the G spot in some sweet ass pussy. You ain't gonna fuck this up for me."

Oscar kept yammering at his nosy sidekick, Si, but eventually their voices faded away under the loud hum that rumbled the cargo container. Metal on metal rang through the air and the container shook enough that Ryn braced herself to avoid fully crashing into the crate in front of her. The protruding edge of the night vision goggles painfully compressed the tender tissue under her eye.

"Come on, Oscar, more finesse and smoothness please," she muttered under her breath, and then cursed quietly when the container hit the ground with a hard thump.

"I am into the facility's system. The jammers for any communication, except ours, as well as their electronic and motion monitoring are in place now. So far there are no other security measures in place or personnel. Give your escort a few minutes to clear out."

She pulled her balaclava up onto her head, thankful for the cooler air on her face. She quickly readjusted the night vision goggles, folded and pocketed the heat detection prevention sheet. The facility may have cameras, and if by chance, they escaped falling prey to Kotan's jamming device, Maari's cream would distort her facial image enough that she would be indistinguishable on any video or photographic lens. Couple that with being currently disguised as Demetria Xeno, she was confident in her anonymity.

"You remember how I showed you to open the crates without leaving a trace that they've been tampered with?"

"Yes, but we don't know if they're booby trapped, now do we?"

"That is why you follow the instructions precisely."

She ground her teeth at Zane's placating tone, but his low chuckle indicated he was trying to get a rise out of her.

She carefully opened the crates one by one as Zane instructed before closing them again, perplexed.

"Why go to all the expense and trouble of shipping one container here that contains household items, jewellery, bolts of silk, and some artwork. There must be something hidden deeper in the contents of the crates. Maybe there are some false bottoms? Like that time you smuggled the woman and her children out of the country."

"You'll have to leave them be. To do that, someone would know that these have been tampered with or that we've been here." At her silence, Zane reminded her, "There is a bigger opportunity to explore the facility."

"Roger."

"Team Alpha has completed their task and are en route," Kotan reported.

"I'll get my butt in gear then, so my ride isn't kept waiting. Wouldn't want those pretty faces out there exposed too long."

Kotan would do his damnedest to jam any AV equipment on and around the grounds. The disruption would even affect any satellite imaging of the area, but still, one couldn't be too careful. And any fancy ass equipment Kotan could dream up wouldn't help if the team was encountered physically by in-the-flesh human beings while they sat there waiting for her.

She moved quickly to use the lock device to exit the cargo container. She may not be happy with the idea of a team being brought in for an assist, but she wouldn't needlessly increase their risk.

"Only heat signature in the building continues to be you." Zane nudged her to get her ass moving.

Ryn secured the device back in her pocket and smoothed the fabric of her snug fitting gear. The snugness allowed free movements and prevented anyone from gaining an advantage by grabbing hold of loose material.

One of the most comforting pieces of her gear was the black gloves that fit like a second skin. They shielded her from leaving any prints and permitted full dexterity.

She swung around, peering through the night vision, taking in the first level of the facility. One large cavernous room with huge doors at either end to allow large trucks to drive right in and through the facility.

"Convenient. Easy access and exit. Can fully unload inside, away from any prying eyes."

"Well-equipped with the track system that runs up high, with the magnets to unload full cargo containers," Zane added.

"There isn't any other cargo or containers here, except for the one Oscar and his pal delivered tonight. Wait," she paused walking toward the back wall, "are you getting this?"

"The image from your night vision goggles is what we're working with, as the facility cameras don't show much in the dark. Go a bit closer."

An area was railed in, with a grated floor. A few shower heads stuck out of the wall and hoses lay discarded.

"This wouldn't be for washing the trucks, no way to get them through the section. Hosing off cargo?"

"Maybe a wash station for workers in case of contamination? Facilities would need to have a wash site, but I haven't seen one set up like this before." Kotan grunted his agreeance with Zane's observation.

Bothered by the sight of the area, Ryn pushed it down and finished exploring the first level, but she found little else. An old-school cargo elevator travelled to all the floors of the facility, she chose the stairs instead, taking the hundred plus stairs two at a time. Not even breaking a sweat or breathing hard, thanks to Kotan's vigorous training, as well as the extra she demanded of herself.

"And behind the door to floor number two—" She paused for dramatic effect. "—some sort of living quarters."

Cots indicated the sleep area of the large open room, but no privacy or seclusion was provided to get a good or lengthy rest. The other part of the room included a small kitchen and lounge area.

"The bathroom area is at least somewhat private in that it has a door. Although they took out all the dividers to make it one big area with toilets."

"Maybe it is a safe house? That could explain the relative higher level of security features and it being off the grid. Your friend have a place in this neck of the woods?" Kotan asked Zane about Virginia Ruthley, Director of the CIA.

"I'll inquire, but it doesn't explain the lack of privacy."

Ryn went back up the stairwell and cleared the third floor opening before she proceeded. The building was deserted, but she still had a lingering feeling that made the hair on the back of her neck stand up.

The night vision goggles illuminated the dark space as she explored around.

"Storage area for mechanical parts, small equipment, tools and non-perishable food supplies."

The next two floors were similar to the one below.

"It appears to be a self-contained facility when it's being used. People can work, eat, sleep here. With parts readily on hand for repair and maintenance, they wouldn't have to leave for much of anything. But it appears as abandoned right now on the inside as it is on the outside."

"If Oscar is the norm, then they use select outsiders for deliveries," Zane added to her summation.

"And ones that do not ask questions, since they like money more than answers."

She had to agree with Kotan's thoughts.

Conscious of the time she was taking, she sprinted up the stairs, but the next two floors were easy to investigate since they were completely empty.

"Next will be the top floor. All dark in the building except you," Zane reassured her she was still alone in the big cavernous building.

"Team Alpha is now in place and still dark."

Meaning her taxi had arrived, and Kotan's genius jammers continued to be in place.

Reaching the top of the stairs, she was surprised to find a locked door.

"Interesting. Except for the second floor, the other floors didn't have a door coming from the stairwell, but this one has a door and it's locked."

"Give me one second to check if it is rigged."

Kotan had recognized the bare elements of the security and monitoring system as some of his earlier designs. Handy, as he knew the foundational aspects and back doors to navigate through their system.

"It is clear, use the lock device you have with you."

"Already ahead of you," she stood back as the disc lit up, the lights spinning as it vibrated. "One more time, you little restaurant buzzer."

"What?" Zane gave a small laugh.

"Never mind." She snatched the device off the door after the lock unlatched and swept the area. "Okay we have a single long hallway, with doors off each side, and one at the end."

She methodically worked her way down the hallway. "They aren't locked and appear to be offices of some sort."

Reaching the door at the end, she tried the handle, but it wouldn't budge. "This one must have something important behind it, it's the only one that's locked. A locked door behind a locked door. And no key lock."

"Is there a keypad? Scanner device?" Kotan asked.

"Not that I can see."

"Must need a fob then? An electronic lock?" Zane added.

"One minute." She could hear Kotan pecking away madly. "Yes, a fob is needed from what I can tell. A receiver plate for detecting the fob will be on the other side of the wall parallel with the handle of the door."

"Will the wonder disc work?"

"It should."

"Must be really something behind door number ten. Any heat signature behind the door?"

"It's clear," Zane confirmed.

The device took a bit longer to work this time, but finally the locked clicked open.

"What the hell? All this for paper? It's a file room."

Ryn looked around at the numerous filing cabinets that packed the room. A small wooden desk sat in the centre, with a lone chair that looked like it should be in the Guinness World Records for most uncomfortable wooden chair in existence. The crack in the seat would probably pinch a nasty chunk out of the ass of whoever sat there.

"There's not even a computer. Who doesn't have a computer?"

"It's a dark room. Not in the sense of developing pictures, but for keeping information off the grid," Zane mused.

"I have detected a jamming signal, but it cannot detect our communication devices." Kotan stated matter of fact, without any ego.

Ryn moved to the closest set of filing cabinets and worked the lock. She quickly flipped through the meticulously labelled files of shipping manifests, her black gloves making it easy to manipulate the paper without leaving any physical evidence behind.

"Risky that people can get their hands on physical documents. That risk must outweigh the risk of it being hacked electronically," she pondered.

"Add the layers of security and barriers to get to this room, plus the jammer, significantly diminishes that risk." Zane agreed.

"Doesn't stop people from snapping pictures though. Very kind of them to have everything labelled and organized so nicely." She moved to another cabinet. "This one is organized by product type. This must have taken forever to cross reference all the shipping manifests. Why wouldn't they just leave organizing it by the manifest?"

She moved quickly to the next cabinet. "Shit just got real people. This cabinet is organized by name. Let's see who some of the names are. Oh lookie-loo, here's our friend Senator William Hanelson. What do you have in your file?"

She pulled out his file and noted the last entry was marked with 'pending' but with no date or product entry. "Even though it's pending, it has paid written in the far column." She started to snap pictures of the Senator's file.

"You need to get out of there." Kotan's voice was calm, but urgent.

"What's wrong? Is there incoming? Where's Team Alpha?"

"You need to move. Now. It's not incoming, it's—it's the building."

She slammed the filing cabinet drawer shut and nearly crushed her finger in the process. "What the hell does that mean?"

"Heat signatures are showing up but not in the form of bodies. It is like the pipes and the infrastructure are heating up. There must have been a trigger. Maybe when we opened the lock without the fob, that might have been their failsafe."

"Whatever the hell the reason, it doesn't matter. Get out of there, now," Zane demanded.

She whirled around to race out of the room, but her eye was drawn to the filing cabinet that was right beside the wooden desk and wicked looking chair. The massive group of cabinets had seemed organized, even though the room was chaotically tight. One group of cabinets had been the manifests, others by product and individuals' names.

What about by location?

After a split second, she made a dash for the cabinets in the far corner by the table, frantically working the lock. The hairs rose on the back of her neck with the urgent orders of Kotan and Zane, but she deftly continued working on the lock.

The drawer sprung open. A quick scan confirmed these were files based on location. A flicker of doubt passed through her mind though as she scanned the location names, but she shoved it down as she ripped open the second drawer.

"Get out of there, now! The first four floors below you are entirely lit up like a fucking Christmas tree and there's pockets of fire that have started on the floor beneath you."

Zane rarely swore and she knew she was literally about to be playing with fire. Cursing at her delay for a fool's errand, she was about to slam the drawer of the cabinet when she saw a file shoved in the back. With a name that pierced her gut.

Monahague Bay.

She grabbed the file and ran.

"Back toward the door where you came in, there's a stairwell to the roof." Zane's voice was terse, but his relief was evident that she was finally getting out of there.

"First five floors completely engulfed and moving quickly on the others. Speed is your friend, get a move on it," Kotan urged.

"The fuckers rigged it so the escape routes would be cut off." Ryn ground out, bolting down the hallway.

"Real boy scouts, now move faster," Zane demanded. "What the hell are you carrying?"

Shit, the Monahague Bay file she grabbed must have swung into vision on his camera.

She yanked the stairwell door open, taking the stairs to the roof three at a time. A small explosion knocked her sideways into the wall, jamming her right shoulder.

"You can't bring that with you. If it's the only record they have, they aren't going to want to lose it." Zane's voice was tinged with apprehension.

"Well, they set the building on fire, so they can't be too attached to it." She gritted her teeth at the pain in her shoulder, pushed off the wall, and continued to sprint up the stairs.

"What I mean is they probably have some way of tracking it."

She still took the stairs three at a time, praying the door coming into view was not jammed. "It's a file on a very important location." She hesitated to say the name in case, somehow, their transmission was intercepted. "I can't leave it. If there is a trace on it somehow, there's got to be a way around it."

"The risk is too great," Kotan agreed with Zane. "There is no way to clean it until you get back here, by then it would be too late."

"God fucking damn it." She shouldered her frustration into the door, bursting through it into the open air of the roof. The large building shuddered under her feet as another explosion rocked the building. Flames shot high through a roof vent. Pain stabbed her eyes at the flash of light, and she pulled her night vision down around her neck.

"Okay, okay, I have an idea."

"There is no time," both men bellowed.

She sprinted toward a wooden structure, finding the side most sheltered from the wind. Thankfully, there were only two sheets in the file. Since she didn't have time to lose precious seconds taking off the black skin gloves, she quickly spread out the papers. She never loved Maari's brain and ingenuity more than at that moment.

Ryn snapped the pictures of the sheets with her encrypted phone. "I'm uploading the images to you right now. There's three, are they coming through?"

She wasn't chancing that she, or her phone, might not make it off this roof.

"It's coming through. Now get out of there right now!"

Ryn pulled her balaclava back down over her face, tossing the file into the flames leaping out of the roof vent, watching it light up. She looped the strap of the night vision under one armpit, so she didn't get strangled, and looked around her.

The nice thing about facilities like this were the numerous, secure footings that act as wonderful anchors. She gave the retracting cord a vicious tug after clipping it to one.

Flames burst through another vent twenty feet from her and the heat moved over her fully clad body. The balaclava reeked with a toxic, burnt smell, making her gag slightly with the unpleasant smell trapped in the cloth.

The building was making an eerie, odd noise, but she wasn't waiting one more second to figure out what it was trying to say to her.

Her feet flew across the asphalt covered roof in a full out sprint. Her breath came in rhythmic, deep surges, her powerful legs ate up the distance, the roof edge loomed closer and closer. Her left foot hit the edge squarely, every muscle working in perfect synchronicity to push away from the building as she flew over the edge.

Chapter 18

The nondescript black cargo van had waited until Kotan gave Team Alpha the green light to proceed. It was now backed tightly into the trees off the side of the road while they waited.

The fenced grounds were dark with the tall concrete structure black and massive beyond the gates.

Tag, Team Alpha's leader, leaned against the van, enjoying the cool night air brushing his uncovered face. Sharp, alert eyes scanned the surroundings to add to the surveillance by the van equipment as well as the bird's eye surveillance from Kotan's hacked satellite and overhead drones.

One of the convenient pieces of equipment they had with them was the jammers, which would prevent any audio or visual recording of their presence. The newest protection layer was a cream product that would distort any imaging of their faces just in case the jamming equipment failed. Or someone, somehow, bypassed their heat imaging detection and snapped pictures of them. The air felt nice, instead of keeping their faces covered, and he was grateful for the cutting-edge stuff that Zane and Kotan had at their disposal.

He felt the van move as Nexin's lean frame slid beside him.

"My face feels supple as a newborn's butt. It's a wonder cream, I tell ya." Nexin stared shrewdly at the blackened structure beyond the fence. "It's been a while. Think they ran into some dicey trouble?"

"It's been ten minutes," Tag replied blandly.

Former CIA, Nexin was no stranger to cloak and dagger

missions in the dark of night. But waiting was not one of Nexin's strong suits.

"Our eyes and ears will let us know if we need to move."

A large bear of a man joined his two teammates. His six-foot six-inch frame, packed solid with powerful muscle, seemed to swallow his colleagues, even though they were not small men themselves. "This shit on my face feels like I walked through a mist of oil." His large hands wiped his face to emphasize his point.

Tag grunted in amusement. It was common for Rolf and Nexin to have polar opposite viewpoints.

"That's what moisturizing your skin feels like, dear friend. Your parched, weathered skin doesn't know what the hell hit it." Nexin ignored the scowl of his teammate and friend.

"An extra layer of preventing identity detection is always helpful." Tag narrowed his eyes looking toward the trees around the side of the facility. "Even if spit would be instantly repelled."

"Shit, you two better start moisturizing those faces, so you stay pretty. Your bulging muscles and tight asses won't always be around and then what will the ladies like about you?"

Nexin, the smaller and leaner of the three, was still muscular, but next to his two companions, he joked he was a tree branch in comparison to medium and large trunks.

The device Nexin held in his hand gave a quiet beep and all three forgot about moisturizing skin instantly. Tag's earpiece signalled the incoming communication as Kotan or Zane switched to their frequency. On their ops, they were usually in constant contact with them, tonight was an exception. Definitely keeping their team separated from who or what was in that facility.

As a soldier in the army for years and then as a Ranger, Tag was used to compartmentalized information. However, it was not the norm of operations with Zane and Kotan since their team had come to work with them three years ago.

"Update," Tag demanded quietly.

Nexin adjusted the zoom of the overhead drone on his screen. "Too uneven heat distribution to be human. Deer maybe?"

"Affirmative. There is more wildlife within your set perimeter and are possibilities for getting within your range of detection," Kotan confirmed.

"Any updates on your end, Team Leader?" Zane chimed in.

"Nothing to report. We're standing by."

Tag continued his silent, alert scanning of the area, listening to the quiet chat of his two partners. Impatience was starting to nibble at his stalwart demeanour, and he quelled that instantly. Impatience led to decreased vigilance and increased risk of mistakes. Both of those things led to making you dead.

Zane had recruited him from his fast-track career in the Army. Tag had enlisted as soon as he was old enough, quickly making a name for himself with his sharpshooting and dead calm under pressure. A Ranger for two years, he was strongly being considered for Delta when Zane had sat across from him at a local Hawaiian bar when Tag was home for a visit. With Zane's negotiation skills, coupled with Tag's growing discontent with the military machine, he eventually left the army and joined Zane.

Tag' primary goal was, and still was, protecting those that needed it. That was his reason for joining the army. But he had begun to question the missions he was leading on behalf of Uncle Sam, of whose interests where really being protected.

He flicked a stone with the toe of his black boot. So far, Zane had delivered on his promise that their work would directly make a difference to people that needed it desperately. For those that had no one else to stand for them. But periodically, his patience and the waiting game was tested.

"I know I've said this before, but we're a hefty group to be acting as an Uber driver." Nexin pulled a blade of grass through his teeth.

"If you know that you've said it before, why repeat it?" Tag's eyes continued their vigilant scan.

"Just sayin' out loud. And wondering who's in that facility, and what they're doing."

Zane recruited Nexin from the CIA and Nexin was the pro espionage and undercover personas when needed. He was an attractive flirt, but had a cunning ability to blend in easily and had deadly efficiency when it came to hand-to-hand combat. That was one of Nexin's strongest suits - his ability to make people see and assume what he wanted them to about him. And then to strike like a cobra when the opponent least expected it.

Naturally, Nexin had a suspicious mind, but Nexin wasn't offside in his musings. Tag was asking himself the same thing.

The op was rated low risk but with potential for elevation. In their experience, Kotan and Zane were not prone for an overkill of resources, so the pick-up target must be highly valued or carrying precious cargo.

Tag's earpiece clicked on again, and, hearing the background noise, he snapped immediately to attention. He could tell from Rolf and Nexin's quick movements they received the message loud and clear.

"Be ready for rapid departure." Kotan's voice was tight. The rising urgency in Zane's voice yelling in the background spurred them to move faster.

"Get out of there, now! The first four floors below you are entirely lit up like a fucking Christmas tree and there's pockets of fire that have started on the floor beneath you."

"We will be ready." Knowing he didn't have to give instructions to his two fellow teammates, Tag calmly removed any evidence of his presence while continuing to monitor for incoming traffic to the facility. Whatever the hell had happened in that building didn't sound good and it would likely trigger an alarm for someone to come investigate.

Rolf maneuvered the van out of the shelter of the trees to

position for an expedited departure and Nexin readjusted the bush and ground.

Tag jumped onto the van's long seat, his body angled to bolt out the side sliding door if needed. Nexin settled his ass into the passenger seat and nabbed the monitoring device from him.

The night air was surprisingly quiet within the context of the shit show going down in the building. The wind gently rustled through the large ancient pines and brushed the fresh buds of leaves on the birch trees. The air was cool as it snuck in through the open door, carrying the periodic croak of a frog.

Tag used the night vision goggles to scan the dark grounds beyond the fence that surrounded the tall black facility. Nothing.

Having been in many warzones in his past career, the familiar sound of an explosion carried over the wind, fingers of flame leaped into the air looking small from the top of the building.

"Shit."

Tag leapt out the side door, the van shook as Rolf did the same.

"Continue to watch for incomings." Tag instructed Nexin. "Scan bottom and out to the grounds." Tag instructed when Rolf joined beside him. "I got the upper part and roof. Anything on those screens signalling anyone creeping up on us?"

"Only the same wildlife signatures as before," Nexin pecked feverishly at the screen to adjust the sensitivity and zoom on the drones that flew in the sky above them.

"Nothing on my level," Rolf's low voice, a rumble in his chest, as he continued to scan every possible exit and the ground between them.

"Same on my... holy fucking hell."

"Bloody Jesus." Rolf gaped.

Nexin, ass still planted in the passenger seat, cranked around to see what they were seeing, slamming the night vision on top of his nose.

A body flew from the top of the building quickly beginning its plummet to the ground. The building wasn't tall enough for a parachute to be snapped open to reduce the speed enough to prevent death at impact.

Three pairs of night vision goggles, still trained on the falling black figure, watched it jerk midair before it swung back toward the building wall.

"Was there a shot? Why did the body jerk?" Rolf instinctively took a step forward, straining against an innate urge to bolt toward the person. The physician, the life saver, his mind and body always ready to go where he was needed.

Astonished, Tag watched the body reposition itself to be parallel with the ground and run down the side of the building. "The jerk must have been a cable going taut to slow the free fall."

"I've seen some crazy shit, but never someone running down the side of the building that fast before. But get your ass going faster." Nexin urged wildly.

As if the black clad figure heard Nexin's urgings, it pushed off the building to land on the ground sprinting toward them, disconnecting the cable without breaking stride.

Feats like dropping down from an elevated height and absorbing the impact while immediately breaking into a sprint took some serious training. The green grainy image through the night vision didn't hide the speed the person was moving. The speed could easily challenge an Olympian sprinter, and the distance was quickly eaten up.

The sound of more explosions in the building spurred the racing figure on toward the towering chain link fence that separated them from the waiting team. Kotan had disrupted the electrical flow previously on the fence and it was obviously still disrupted, since the figure didn't get tossed backwards by a current.

"I'll be damned," Rolf muttered under his breath.

The black clad figure shimmied up to the top of the fence in the blink of an eye, reaching over the top and down to grab the fence on the other side. They flipped themselves over, dropping the rest of the way down.

"Must be part cat," Nexin agreed.

Absorbing the twelve-foot drop with a shoulder roll, the figure was back on their feet sprinting toward them.

"Incomings," Zane clicked in over their earpieces. "Two potentials traveling at high speeds. Rapidly approaching the road that leads to the facility. Get the package and get out now."

Rolf moved with fluid speed to resume his role as driver, Nexin secured the electronics.

Tag moved toward the figure sprinting toward him. "Potential incomings!"

The building rumbled as the foundation of it collapsed, followed by a rapid set of explosions. Tag watched in horror as the ground inside the parameter of the fence, where the sprinting figure had been just moments before, turned into balls of fire.

He had seen this before in combat with explosives that were triggered by some other event. They were timed to give the fleeing party just enough time to think they were getting to safety before a new set of explosives went off right where they would be.

The unusual speed of this particular person allowed them to be past the areas when the blasts went off.

But he strongly suspected something even bigger was about to happen.

"Move it!" He yelled running toward the racing figure when they turned to look backwards. "Move, move, move!"

Another blast threw Tag back on his ass. The impact knocked the wind out of him, but he was back on his feet instantly. Battling to regain control of his breath he watched the previously sprinting figure fly through the air to land with a deadening thud.

"Fuck, fuck, fuck." Tag scrambled over to the still lump on the ground. A swell of relief broke when he heard a groan from the crumpled figure as they rolled over.

Tag's observant gaze took in the flat raised rock and he grimaced in empathy for the ribs that would have landed right on it.

"Holy fuckballs," a woman grunted, her eyes, the only visible part of her body, filled with pain but were deadly alert. Her narrowed gaze locked with his, silently assessing him for a friend or foe. Tag forced himself not to take a step back, shocked by his body's immediate reaction to those eyes.

"Out of there. Now. All of you," Zane commanded.

"You heard the man. On your feet, soldier."

Chapter 19

"The two incomings are now on the road to the facility. Three, four minutes max, until you meet." Kotan reported in their earpieces.

"How the fuck do we know we aren't going to trigger some IED like those nice little treats inside the parameter?" The guy in the passenger seat scanned the monitor in his hands, trying in vain to see something that might illuminate where any pockets of danger lay.

Ryn's head throbbed with pain. Cyril, no, Nexin was his name, she remembered. Her ex-fiancé from the recent op in Miami.

Her left side hurt with the smallest of breaths and she shook her head to clear the fuzziness caused by its vicious contact with the ground. Even with the pulsating pain in her head and shearing ache in her ribs, she still felt a twinge of annoyance that Zane had sent them.

No time to dwell on her pissiness though, she knew she needed to pull her full attention to the situation she was in. She zeroed her gaze on the one named Tag, sitting beside her on the seat.

"We don't know." Tag looked grim and tapped his index finger against his thigh.

Her eyes were riveted to that moving finger. The finger that was attached to the hand that sent unexpected electricity through her arm and whole torso when he grasped her forearm to help her up after that stupid explosion. It wasn't covered in the white glove of the bellboy this time and the shocks were more intense tonight.

Maybe he had a zinger in his palm. Like those prankster ones that zap you when you shake someone's hand.

She wanted to laugh, but her pounding head told her this wasn't the time or the place.

"Deploying Exit Plan B," Tag updated Kotan and Zane, and instructed the immense man driving. She forgot how large he was from the first time she was in his presence at the hotel. The span of his shoulders was wider than the back of the driver's seat.

The seat under her sore ass absorbed most of the impact of the rough transition from the main road to the ditch, but she grunted in pain and worked to keep her breathing smooth.

Tag glanced sharply at her, prior to launching himself out the sliding door, before the van came to a complete stop. He was back inside seconds after the van pulled through the section of fence he had pulled back.

"You pre-cut that."

"Always know—"

"—your exit and have more than one open to you," Ryn finished Tag's sentence. Kotan had ruthlessly hammered that into her during her training.

In the dark, she could sense the intensity of Tag's gaze, but Zane's terse update cut off what he was about to say.

"T-minus forty-five seconds before they reach the spot where you left the road."

Three sets of weapons were immediately out as the big man, Rolf, she recalled his name now, maneuvered them through the trees as fast as he could.

"You armed?" Tag rechecked the clip on his Sig Sauer, but something told her he was a meticulous planner and it was unnecessary. "You okay?"

"I'm armed and I'm fine."

"Just wondering since you still have your balaclava on."

Shit. She must have clunked her head a good one.

"Maybe it's part of her mystique. Or maybe she doesn't want

your ugly mug to see hers. She is a beauty. I can tell by the sound of her voice." Nexin winked at her. The illumination from his monitor made his attractive face and blonde hair glow. Flashing those pearly whites, the blue eyes danced with excitement.

"You guys aren't disguised."

"And how would you know that?" Tag quipped.

Their bodies slammed to the right, throwing Ryn into Tag's side. She grunted at the white-hot stab of pain in the left side of her ribs.

"Sorry. Damn trees," Rolf apologized.

Tag glanced down at her, his eyes narrowed in contemplation.

"Your company is not pursuing; they're continuing toward the facility. The drones will continue to monitor their activity, but that leaves you with no over-watch on your path." Zane updated, but no concern rang in his voice about his belief the team couldn't proceed without that added layer of visual protection from above.

Nexin nodded in agreeance, continuing to watch the distance widen between them and the red dots on his screen. "Roger that. Proceeding to the drop off point."

Ryn straightened, sliding to the side of the seat as far away from Tag as the vehicle would allow. "I've worked with you before," she carefully pulled her balaclava off. The last thing she needed was her dark wig and facial prosthetics to come off with it.

"Demetria," Nexin exclaimed. "Nice to see my fiancé again."

"Ex. We broke it off remember?"

Nexin flashed her a pout.

She shoved the balaclava into the pocket of her black jacket and felt the broken edges of the unlocking device scrape her fingertips, still encased in Maari's miracle gloves. Her ribs weren't the only casualty of landing on that rock.

"And how do you know that we aren't wearing anything to change or disguise our appearance now or on that op?" Tag pressed.

"I don't." She decided to come clean. "I guess you could be, and you were wearing the same disguises when I chanced seeing you meet with a mutual acquaintance of ours, outside his hotel a year ago."

Tag gave her a nod of approval. "They would never use an amateur and unskilled operative. Your head seems to have cleared from its knock with the ground, but let's look at those ribs."

Rolf cut through the trees and quickly worked up the ditch to get back on the road before they needed to turn onto the Interstate.

"I am fine," she said through gritted teeth.

"Let him look." Concerned eyes stared at her in the rearview mirror. The deep rumble of Rolf's voice left no room for disagreement. The interior light flicked on in the back part of the cargo van.

Ryn eyed the path between the seat she sat on and the back door. One smooth flip over the back and she'd come within arm's reach of the back door handle. The roof was tall enough to accommodate it. She would have to tuck her legs and keep it tight, but it was doable.

Always have more than one exit.

"It's bruised ribs. They aren't broken," she insisted. With the light on, she felt a jolt travel through her again. Those eyes. Those lips.

Vivid memories of Tag's lips and hard body pressed against hers in the elevator coursed through her.

Fuck me.

His shoulders, although not as massive as Rolf's, were still broad. His face was clean shaven today. She pulled her eyes away from him. "I am fine."

Rolf merged them onto the Interstate, the city lights glimmering in front of them instantly.

Zane clicked on her earpiece. "I'm thankful you weren't seriously harmed." The relief was evident in his tone. "He, any of them really, won't take no for an answer though."

Tag, or her fellow van-mates, didn't react to Zane clicking in, so she surmised he must have used the frequency from when she was in the building.

True to what Zane said, she recognized the unyielding resolve in Tag's eyes along with the stubborn set to his jaw. She undid her gear jacket in annoyance and hefted up the side of her shirt.

"You have to turn more to me." A quiet tone had fallen into Tag's voice. His hands wrapped around her shoulders to turn her to face him squarely.

His hands were large and strong, but his fingers were ridiculously graceful when she watched them move down to inspect the damage the rock did on her side.

His quiet curse mingled with hers when she jumped at the physical contact of his fingertips on her bare skin, hissing out her breath.

His eyes flew to hers thinking he had hurt her further. Another spike of annoyance rammed through her at her physical reaction to him.

"See, all good. They aren't broken; just sore."

Rolf was watching her in the rearview mirror again. His light brown eyes were bright over the wide bridge of his nose. "It might be prudent to stop and check them," his German accent heavier now. "Broken ribs can puncture organs."

She pulled away from Tag's closeness, insisting, "They aren't broken," she added when Rolf arched his dark eyebrow, giving her a skeptical look. "I've broken ribs before. These aren't broken."

To prove her point, she palpated the tender area, gritting her teeth. "There's no movement of bone. Just soreness."

Rolf acquiesced. "My medical supplies, under your seat," Rolf instructed Tag. "The compression wrap will give some stability and help with swelling."

Not wanting to chance physical contact with Tag again, Ryn snatched the wrap out of his hands before he could wrap it around her. "I got it, thanks."

She secured a ten-inch-wide short tensor snugly around her ribcage. It had less elasticity than a regular tensor and the throbbing eased considerably.

"If you start feeling dizzy, trouble breathing, vomiting, especially blood, emergency help is needed immediately. Keep an eye on her for any signs of shock," Rolf instructed Tag.

The speed of traffic eased up slightly as they entered Tacoma's city limits and Rolf flicked off the interior lights, giving his full attention to navigating. Looking for their exit while avoiding them smashing into vehicles around them.

So, the big guy is more than a driver. Medic training maybe?

Calm under pressure or maybe he was unemotional and stoic? Didn't want the complication of someone dying when he was involved in an op? Either way, it made sense that Zane and Kotan would outfit their lead operative team with someone with medical knowledge.

Ryn settled back against the seat, relaxing, at least outwardly. Her head felt fully clear now and the incessant throb in her ribs had eased off.

The way that Tag handled himself, she would wager all her songwriting income that he had military training. The other guy, Nexin, she was less sure of. Flirty, comfortable with playing different personas and roles, along with the techie skills she observed while he worked the multiple screens on his handheld monitor, didn't really define an obvious career background. He was definitely fluent in the mumbo-jumbo techie language and easily conversed with Kotan as they sped toward the drop site.

"Any thoughts on what caused that explosion?" Tag turned toward her again with those intriguing eyes. She caught a glimpse of his gun he had returned to his shoulder holster after the threat of pursuit was removed. She felt hers press reassuringly in her back, as well as the thin knife that was sheathed on the inside of her jacket sleeve.

Zane's words echoed in her head, 'You can trust them."

But trust doesn't come easy to her.

"Well, you see, when a starter agent like heat comes into contact with a reactive substance, there can be big bangs."

"A smart ass I see. We already have one of those thanks." Tag unfazed stubbornly refused to accept her answer.

God, he's good looking. Goddammit, Severyn, stop it, she chided herself.

"You're always checking out my ass. But who can complain when my ass is supreme." Nexin swivelled and grinned at her. "And from what I've glimpsed of yours, it's smack-dab in that category as well." He winked, and mischief danced in his blue eyes.

She laughed, despite herself. The pain in her ribs not as strong with the wrap tightly compressing her ribcage.

"From what I understand, a room I went into triggered a silent alarm which started a cascade of events. One of them being the infrastructure of the building heating up."

She omitted any mention of what she found in that room, or of the file she risked her life to photograph and send to Kotan.

"Infrastructure heating up?" Tag sat a bit straighter.

Kotan chimed in, "The heat signatures that showed up rapidly spread through the heating and electrical systems. Strategically originating at the exit points on the lower level and quickly advanced to the upper floor. There would have been accelerants or flammables to trigger small explosions. Again, strategically placed."

Nexin's look was intrigue, mixed with concern. "You mean the building became the weapon?"

"It would seem so." Kotan agreed. "All exits were blocked in what I am assuming was meant to fully contain and destroy everything in the building. Including any occupants."

She was sickened by the thought of the planning and the intent that went into fortifying the building. The second floor filled with sleeping cots flashed in her mind.

Planning, without any regard to who was inside that building. Purposeful to prevent any evidence or knowledge from leaving that file room and beyond.

Tag slid a sidelong look at Ryn, his mouth set in a grim line. "Since there's no way to hide the fact that someone was in the building, what is the trace back risk?"

"Low," Zane quipped. "Any surveillance - either on site or remote - was jammed by us and you had the anti-detection cream on your faces. There was no heat imaging around you, therefore no human eyes on-site that could identify you."

"No tails?" Kotan asked.

"None," Rolf affirmed in a quiet rumble.

She glanced at Rolf and remembered her first impression of him from the hotel - he reminded her of a giant. Quiet, but she suspected, definitely not a gentle giant when he chose.

"The drones or satellite images didn't pick up anything of interest from the vehicles sent to investigate. We'll scrutinize the footage further though, do more facial recognition, deeper plate runs, but it looks like they used a local monitoring company. Any need for the drone to come to you, Team Leader, for eyes in the sky?" Zane inquired.

"Operating in city limits is risky, even with your anti-detection tech, and we have no reason to think we need it."

"Agreed," Zane said.

They moved slowly through the city streets, crowded with vehicles, pedestrians and nightlife.

"What were you looking for, or trying to accomplish, in that building?" Tag looked at her once again.

Rolf's gaze flicked up to the rearview mirror and Nexin glanced quickly back, slight shock on his features before he flashed her a grin. "Do tell."

"What were you guys doing before you came to be my personal

chauffeurs?"

"Compartmentalization. That's how we're playing it, I see."

"Something you're used to. Right, soldier?" She kept her features neutral, watching the corner of his mouth twitch slightly. Amused or pissed that she had guessed something about him?

"I know you've been read in that you can trust us."

The look of openness in Tag's eyes created the sudden need for her to stomp down the disastrous urge to not only share what she was doing tonight and what she had found but also, the full burden of her secrets. She was shocked to the tips of her toes by the feeling and the intensity it hit her.

And disgusted with herself that all it took was one look from him.

However, she refused to give any indication that the mere act of him looking at her, or the presence of his solid frame so close to her own, was starting to pull on her control.

Starting to pull it from her clutch one fraying fibre at a time.

"If you were to know those details, you would have been read in," she said, her tone quiet.

"If this is to work, there needs to be an element of trust."

"If what, exactly, is to work?"

Where the hell were Zane and Kotan? An intervention here would be nice.

"I'm certainly grateful for your assistance." She held up her hand when Tag was about to interject with a heated comment, if she read his body language right. "Without you three, I wouldn't be sitting here. Or anywhere actually. I'm truly grateful, but that doesn't mean we sing Kumbaya and exchange our darkest secrets."

She looked directly in his eyes, the streetlight flickering across his face. Those eyes and that face once again called her to unburden her secrets. Urged her that she didn't need to go at this alone. Asked her to depend on them.

The smack to her head wasn't letting her think straight.

Panic brewed in the pit of her stomach. She needed some distance. She needed to get the hell away from this guy, and all that he was asking her to do, without speaking a word.

"In this game, to survive, you need a bit of trust." Tag's voice was low, his eyes intent on hers, refusing to unlock his gaze.

The vehicle rolled to a stop, waiting for the light to change. To her left, the cars traveling in the opposite direction were already streaming past. Their line of traffic would start moving soon after the signal loop was completed.

"This is no game for me."

She arched back, her feet pushing off the back of Rolf's seat, and tucked her knees tight to her chest to roll over the seat. She used the momentum to shoulder roll out of range of Tag's lightning reflexes and bolted out the back door.

Nexin and Rolf, momentarily stunned, watched Tag burst out of the side door sprinting after her toward a dark alley. Rolf maneuvered the van out of traffic and Nexin chased Tag to provide backup if she meant to ambush or take him out, cursing while he rushed to catch up.

But when Nexin rounded the corner to the alley with his gun drawn, Tag was alone. The dim alley only ran half a block and ended in a dead end. Tag ran to each door, giving them each a vicious yank, to no avail. They were all locked and Tag's curses filled the empty space.

"She's gone."

Chapter 20

Lok pushed back from the music equipment console and propped his orange Puma runners on the lip. Larger than life, he pinched the bridge of his nose and closed his eyes.

"I think we got it. You happy with it?" Lok dropped his feet and leaned forward, looking at her from halfway around the world on the large screen they used for collaborating via video.

"It sits good with me." Ryn stretched like a cat reaching her fingertips toward the rafters of the large open room, careful not to let the pain in her left side play on her face. The loft area, on the second level, with its comfy hammock, beckoned her to have a siesta.

"Two people sounding like they're settling." Maari glided into the studio smartly dressed in a dark peach pencil skirt and white silk blouse that accentuated the exoticness of her colouring and features. A pair of death-defying Jimmy Choo stilettos swung casually from her slender finger.

"It was a rough afternoon." Lok laughed, making his crystal blue eyes ringed with dark blue, sparkle. His dark colouring matched Maari's in many ways. Raven black hair, darker skin tones - his a mix from Italy and India, hers from Japan and North America Chippewa-Cree.

Ryn, dressed in navy capri leggings and oversized white shirt, probably looked the sloth to Maari's sleek butterfly, but she didn't care. Working in the studio, she always opted for comfy rather than publicly presentable.

And who the hell was she kidding? She would rather walk across hot coals than wear the business posh ensembles that her friend did every day. But Maari's sleek attire matched her personality to a razor point that was as sharp as her cheekbones.

Maari gave her a quick hug of welcome, her dark sheet of hair brushing around her. "An air kiss will have to do, Lok. I must say, being on that monster screen does you justice. Not many people can say that."

"Well, thank you. It's a pleasure to be in your sparkling company, Maari. Ryn is always telling me my pores are too big and where I have a zit coming."

The accused laughed. "I most certainly do not. Now, if you two are done fanning each other's ego, Lok, you have a meeting to get to, do you not?"

"Giving me the boot. Very you, Severyn Andrews." Lok's eyes danced without any mirth or anger. "But yes, I do have a meeting, so that means you must give in now."

She pulled away from Maari's side to grab some water and growled. "Enough already."

Maari looked between her and Lok on the screen, perplexed. "What am I missing?"

"Our girl didn't tell you?"

"No, our girl is good at keeping things to herself."

"This girl is standing right here, thank you."

A pair of tongues stuck out in unison at Ryn.

"May Antel's upcoming fundraiser—" Lok began.

"May Antel? Her events are legendary."

May Antel was the daughter of the Massachusetts Senator and a philanthropic fundraising event planner extraordinaire.

The excitement rang in Maari's voice, and she did a little jig, when the realization quickly dawned on her sharp mind. "You're performing."

"I am not performing."

"Yet."

"Will you drop it already, Lok? You know I don't perform in public. I am a songwriter. I write songs, the music, I play that music. In private."

"That's not true, you've played with me. And you were and are amazing. You have a gift. Audiences connect with you almost immediately."

"That, that is—"

"Different? No, it's not," Lok pressed. He popped a hard, red candy in his mouth, puckering slightly at the sour and sweet burst of flavour.

"I was going to say, that is a random event. Only a few times. Not something I do regularly."

"Why the resistance?" Lok asked softly.

She kept neutral even though she could feel Maari's eyes boring into her back. "It's not me, who I am or want to be. I don't want the front stage or the public life that comes with it."

"Antonio won't take no for an answer. He and May are tight, and he wants you to step into the performing musician role even more than I do."

"And what about what I want?" she asked, sharper than she would have liked.

"Ryn—" Maari started but stopped.

She stalked over to the large windows showcasing the lazy, flowing river. The thought of being more in the public eye spiked panic in her and she worked to get it under control.

"I'll cut a cheque like I always do for these things. May would know already that I'm a supporter of Annelou's school since I mentor students in the music stream they started."

Annelou's School of Fine Arts was a growing school in Boston. It started with art and dance and most recently expanded to include music. The target demographic was at-risk youth, to give them an opportunity, or even just an outlet, to go down a different path.

May's fundraising efforts were to help expand the school geographically, as well as set up scholarship programs for the students to pursue post-secondary training, in the field of their choice.

"Your generosity is exemplary, however, there needs to be more, and deeper, pockets involved. You are an enigma, a puzzle. Someone people know about, but don't know. And they are interested. You will be a big draw to the event. This doesn't mean that you're committing to a career change, only that you're sharing a unique opportunity for these wealthy folks to experience."

"For the greater good."

"Pimping me out to the overprivileged to separate them from their godly money, more like it."

"Like I said, for the greater good." A smile tugged at Maari's mouth, making the two studs below her lip dance.

"Okay, I really do have to get going now for my meeting. Promise me you will think about it." Lok blew them both kisses before disconnecting.

Ryn powered down the video screen, quiet.

"There's been more and more things I've been hearing about, bugs that get embedded into your system, and when you disconnect from video calls the other people can still listen in. Like a backdoor thing." Maari ran her fingers over the dustless piano while Ryn finished powering down all the equipment.

"You think Lok is up to nefarious things and that's why he's working with me?"

"No." Maari gave a guilty smile.

"But one can never be too careful, I guess."

"That's a sour way to look at the world and those who are your friends."

"You brought it up." Ryn threw up her hands. "Zane and Kotan's life motto is, you can never be too careful, but they worry and take care of that for the both of us. Your father has installed a better than first rate system here and is constantly updating it. He's the only one with access to the system. No external company's fingers in any of it, for installation or updates." She shook out her wavy hair from the restriction of the ponytail. "But let's go upstairs to my apartment anyway. I need a change of scenery."

They climbed the stairs to the loft and made their way to the backstairs that led up to Ryn's private quarters on the next two floors.

"I haven't had a chance to talk to you about the Monahague Bay file that you found."

Ryn re-engaged the apartment lock after Maari stepped through. "The file that I got my ass kicked for? Your father doesn't forgive or forget easily. My body has paid for it numerous times over the last couple of days. You'd think that getting at least one picture of the Senator's file would have countered some of that."

Maari snorted. "His file entries were quite ambiguous and inconclusive unfortunately. For the Monahague file, there didn't seem to be much in there either. Some random dates, snapshots of items." Maari smoothed the rippling silk shirt over her flat stomach. "Got any food, or should we order in from Neara and Mason?"

"We can order in." Ryn cleaned up the counter of the breakfast dishes. "It might have been limited in details, but it wasn't a waste. The file existed so that means there's a connection between Strada Indonesian and that location. Which is close to where I lived, and Vlad had been seen coming from there before his murder. It was completely worth the risk in finding out."

"It seems the patriarchs deem otherwise," Maari said sarcastically.

She snorted in response, wiping the deep browns of the granite countertop.

"Zane was almost back to being in his normal mood today. I think he has burned off most of his pissiness at you for ditching your team the other night."

"They are not my team."

"Right, well you know what I mean." Maari swung open the fridge, cracked two beers, and shoved one into Ryn's hands. "The 'doesn't play well with others' helps keep people at a distance, but in some cases, it can come down to life or death."

She glared at Maari suspiciously. "Are you here of your own accord or because Zane sent you?"

Maari tossed her long tresses over one shoulder. The raven tattoos along her neck gave the illusion of the birds taking flight. "You know I don't do others' dirty work or play messenger."

That was one of the things she loved about Maari. The backbone ferocity of a T-Rex. She didn't do anything she didn't want to do and you always knew where you stood with her.

"But, listen, about this opportunity with May's fundraiser."

"I know you're a big fan, Maari, I can get you an invite to the event, don't worry."

"It's not that." Maari waved a graceful hand. "However, I am totally keeping you to that promise. But I think you should perform."

"You are one of the few people that know the full reason why I can't."

"Not can't. Won't."

"No, I *can't*, Maari." She tossed the cloth she felt like ripping in half into the stone sink. "I'm hiding in plain sight as it. And now I'm supposed to take an even larger spot in the public eye? That's asking for a world of trouble and it isn't just me to think about. I cannot do anything that will put my family in the crosshairs again."

"You said yourself that you lived more in disguise of your true self before all this happened than you do now. Back then you dyed your hair, changed the colour of your eyes to hide any uniqueness, hid your face as much as you could, and blended into the background and shadows. And—" Maari clasped her hands, a sign of her momentary discomfort. "—there's the facial alterations that were done after your *accident*."

Ryn touched her cheekbone and forehead but remained silent.

"Even without the reconstructive surgery, you were a late bloomer and your face changed considerably the past two years as you took on your adult features. You have grown two or three inches, and now have a ripped body like an Olympian. And you got a boob reduction to boot." Maari laughed and cupped her own. "Not as small as these puppies though."

Ryn laughed, shaking her head at the woman before her. A jokester golden thread ran through her, no matter the seriousness of the conversation.

"Daddy has run risk analysis and image comparisons out the ying yang. And who would equate the insanely talented and mysterious adult musician in the spotlight with a frumpy - your words not mine, by the way - timid, excessively shy young teen?"

Maari squeezed her shoulders, the two similar in height, staring eye to eye. "There is no risk of someone recognizing you as Raya."

Ryn hung her head. "It isn't only that. It's—" She tried to pull away but her friend held firm.

"This is a dream come true opportunity that so many want but never get. It's amazing. Surreal. But it's coming at the cost of a nightmare. A nightmare I'm putting my family through and at a cost that they're paying."

Ryn's breath hitched and she closed her eyes to settle herself. "How can I expect them to live out that nightmare and meanwhile I live a dream life?"

"I get it." Maari let her go to the living room window that looked out at the river. "But you have to live a life, Ryn. Not an *existence*. I don't know your family, but I know you. Those that loved you, and who raised such a compassionate individual, cannot want that for you either."

Maari's onyx eyes glistened with unshed tears. "Watching you play your music, there is something that happens within you. You connect to it. I think it's almost your lifeline that keeps the dark that haunts you from consuming you. You need it."

Ryn felt the connection with her friend. Understood that Maari also had, earlier in her life, struggled to stop her own darkness from consuming her.

"Just promise me you will really consider it. Please."

At Ryn's nod, Maari clasped her in a tight hug that belied the strength of the lithe young woman.

"Now—" She tugged Ryn's hand to come back to the island. "—tell me about the op."

Ryn perched on the stool and gave Maari a small grin. "Your gloves were a lifesaver; saved me critical seconds and allowed me to get pics of the Monahague Bay file."

A smile that balanced on the precipice of patience and annoyance flashed her way. "I'm glad. Of course, I'm please they worked well, but we knew that because you tried them out many times. I listened to the recording when daddy was reviewing it again. It sounds like it got dicey."

Ryn swallowed a swig of her beer. "A bit."

"A bit? Bullshit." Maari leaned her elbows on the swirling deep browns of the countertop that shone with the late afternoon sun. "You were lucky your non-team was there."

"I was."

Satisfied that she sounded authentic, Maari gave a mischievous grin making her look like a sly feline. "Tag didn't sound like the only one with a high hotness factor. Tell me all about them."

Ryn rolled her eyes, but laughed good naturedly. "One is a giant that appears to be the doc of the group, another is a flirt that uses his charm and good looks to hide his operating agenda, and the other…"

"Tag. Over the recording, he sounded like a hunk-a-hunk."

"If you mean intense and bossy, then yes."

"I just about choked on my muffin when he demanded to see

your ribs. So obvious that he just wanted to touch your bare skin. That elevator kiss affected both of you." Maari tipped her bottle in Ryn's direction.

Leave it to Maari to read sexual tension in any interaction. "Hardly."

"Double bullshit. You could hear it in his voice. That deep sexy voice. I bet he sings a deadly baritone; you should hook up with him for one of your songs." An onyx eye winked at her. "Double meaning intended."

"Gawd, you're excessive." Ryn couldn't help but laugh.

Her phone vibrated, and she paused slightly, before accepting the video call. A handsome face of Spanish descent with an angelic smile and devilish chocolate brown eyes filled the screen.

"*Mi amor. ¿Cómo Estás?*"

"I'm well. And you, Antonio?"

"Beautiful. I had a beautiful day that's being made even more beautiful now that I have feasted my eyes on you."

"Smooth talker. I had a feeling I would be hearing from you. Say hi to Maari." Ryn swung the phone to pull Maari into the screen.

Antonio's hand fluttered to his custom-made crisp white shirt. "Now my day has doubled in the pleasure department. I don't think I can take much more."

"Oh, you scamp. But I do love the love you give." Maari fluttered her eyelashes, waving her hand in front of her in the act to cool herself off.

Ryn rolled her eyes again. "Alright, scamp, get to it."

The fake surprise didn't last long under her bland stare.

"Okay, you caught me with my pants down, so to speak." The devilish grin was back. "We don't have much time until the event. You know May likes to plan these under a tight timeline. Gives less time for other socialite scavengers to try and hijack her event by scheduling one of their own."

"Lok already prepped me for your sales pitch."

Antonio flicked at an invisible fleck on his shirt, indignant. "Sales pitch? I'd hardly call it a sales pitch," he muttered. "But either way, he must have forgotten to call me with the good news."

"He didn't call because he had no such news."

"Ryn," Antonio called her every sweet name in Spanish before continuing, "please."

Maari smiled encouragingly at her.

"If I agree to this, it's under the condition that this is not a regular occurrence. It's not the direction I'm steering my work into. Nor will it give you a foothold to try and strong-arm me into other events if I do not desire to do them."

Antonio looked ready to levitate. "Yes, yes, and yes. Agreed, agreed, and agreed."

Ryn sighed, "Hook me up with May, then."

Chapter 21

True to Antonio's prediction, May Antel's fundraising gala for Annelou's School of Fine Arts was planned for less than a week from when she accepted the invitation to perform. The days sped by, and the evening before the event, she went out to the estate to help distract herself.

Her anger at Zane, and his at her for not following the plan one hundred percent, had abated over the ten days since the op. They were both stubborn and each felt they were on the right side of the argument, so she steered clear of him until emotions had settled. It made it much more pleasant for those around them.

The rain pelted the window and shrouded the trees beyond the field. She lay sprawled on the sofa facing the floor to ceiling windows in her studio, playing with the bronze dragonfly pendant, contemplating that she really needed to get up.

Sitting up made her groan though. Standing added another layer of complaining from her seizing limbs and joints.

Kotan had worked her ruthlessly again today. Her ribs were healing but it felt like fire was going to erupt from them at any moment. She snagged Rolf's compression wrap that she had chilling in her cold pack freezer. The pressure and cold provided instant relief to move the pain dial from burning-shear-hot to a more tolerable level.

Nessa had immediately done a thorough examination when she returned from the op, complete with x-rays, to make sure her ribs were intact. Nessa had hissed at Kotan, actually hissed at her husband, when he told Ryn to gear up and meet in the studio after Nessa's assessment.

"Her enemies aren't going to wait until she is healed and all better, Nessa. She needs to work through this, not be coddled."

He was right, of course. He knew it, Ryn knew it. And she went to the suffer-fest training sessions willingly. Not only to work through pain and weakness that her enemies would exploit but because the punishing sessions were an effective reprieve.

Nessa knocked softly and wriggled her nose at the lingering smell in the studio, her heels clicking across the blonde, knotted hardwood floor. "You really should separate your training area from your work studio. Lord knows there are enough rooms in this house to do so."

She placed the tray, with a pot of jasmine tea from the smell of it, on the island counter and Ryn opened a few windows. "Efficiency, you know, and all that."

Steam rose from the mug filled with the sweet and fragrant liquid. "Drink this, it helps with pain and stress. Since you, nor my husband, heed my medical advice."

"I have been doing so. About the other stuff. I have, I promise."

Nessa had given her strict instructions for no additional physical exertion beyond the training sessions with Kotan. No additional running, jumping, or climbing. Nothing.

Nessa's dark brown eyes narrowed over her sharp cheekbones.

"I swear. Walking, sitting, and wiping my arse, are the only additional things I've been doing." To emphasize her point, Ryn perched her butt on a stool at the counter, sipping the soothing liquid.

The scathing look smoothed from Nessa's face and she skimmed a hand over Ryn's cheek. "Supper was nice, I've missed you. It will be nice to have you and Zane back in the same room and setting aside your divergent views."

She sighed. "Like I told Zane when I got back from the op, maybe not in the nicest way or tone, but the op was over. I wasn't in danger. The op wasn't in danger. The mission wasn't in danger."

"He cares about you and knows how things can easily go sideways in the field."

"The plan was for me to break away from those guys at the bus station anyway. He was pissed because I thought for myself. Because that exact point, that exact time, wasn't what he meticulously planned. What he *told* me to do."

"It might be that way, yes. But he does have your best interests in mind. Everything he does is to serve you, your goal, but keep you as safe as possible in the process. That isn't an easy feat."

"I know it makes me sound ungrateful and I don't mean to. After all that he and you guys have done for me, for my family—" She bit her lip. "But I am not a robot. And I don't need babysitters."

Remorse and guilt swirled in her gut remembering exactly the tone and phrases she told Zane the same thing. Yeah, she definitely could've used more tact and diplomacy.

"Put the guilt aside. Do it right now, Severyn," Nessa ordered. "Zane knows all this and never sees you as ungrateful. Strong-willed and stubborn, absolutely. Also, incredibly wise beyond your young years, but never ungrateful. Or selfish."

Nessa's small hand turned her chin, so she faced the petite woman. "The mind makes different decisions when love is involved. Zane loves you as his own. Never forget that."

"Come on you slow shit, the girl is going to beat you."

She turned to look down the hill at her childhood friend, Vlad, as he struggled up the steep incline. His dark hair, normally stuck up in tufts, laid limp on his head from sweat and mist from the ocean.

"Shut up, Victor, no one invited you anyway. You have an unpleasant habit of showing up and sticking around. Like a piece of dog shit on the bottom of your shoe."

She laughed quietly and quickly hid her face, as Victor looked ready to push someone down the hill and she didn't want it to be her.

Her dyed black hair fell across her face to hide her smile. She was used to Victor's condescending and derisive tone and she only tolerated him because of Vlad. Not that she would take a stand against him though, if she decided she couldn't tolerate him anymore.

Weakling, she berated herself.

Good looking, and vain enough to know it and use to his advantage, Victor always made her uncomfortable. There wasn't anything that he had done. But there was something. Something that she couldn't pinpoint or explain.

Maybe it was that he never made any effort to hide his annoyance at her presence with Vlad. Or his leering looks at her breasts that made her skin crawl. The exact look he was giving her now, the wind pressing her t-shirt to her front.

"You really do have nice, big tits. Your only redeeming feature maybe."

"Screw you."

She cursed herself for taking off the sweatshirt she stole from one of her older brothers.

Vlad caught up, giving her a thankful grin for waiting. She returned it with a scowl. Surely, he'd get the message how displeased she was with Victor's presence and Vlad's lack of inaction for getting rid of him.

"Drop the sour looks," he pleaded.

"Maybe we can push him off the cliff?" she asked hopefully.

Vlad's laugh was cut short and he started to gurgle looking at her alarmed. Crimson blood seeped from the corner of his mouth, his hazel eyes wide in surprise and fear.

The landscape shifted, blurring. He reached for her, but his face was already vacant when he tumbled over the side of the cliff.

Ryn jerked upright, clutching desperately at the empty air in front of her. Realizing she was in her bedroom at the estate, she slammed her head back on her pillow, calming her breath.

"That was a new one."

Cletus climbed onto her chest to drag his face along her chin, purring in response.

The end events in the dream had never played out in real life. Which was sometimes how her dreams and mind found new ways to mess with her.

She hadn't thought of Victor in a long time. He was a bit older than her and Vlad. A drifter of sorts. He had come to their small community, but from where, she never knew. And he had left weeks before Vlad died, but to where, she didn't care.

Weird that the dream version of her suggested pushing Victor off a cliff, yet it was her friend that plummeted off.

She scratched Cletus's head to quiet her mind, hoping to get more sleep. She'd dissect that a different time.

The air was heavy and saturated with moisture. She tried to take a replenishing breath in, but the air was so water-logged, it was like she was breathing water deep into her lungs. Panic snaked up her spine as she coughed and sputtered, and the world spun around her.

Air, air. She must have air.

She could feel herself gasp, her stomach muscles trying in vain to help her lungs breath in air that didn't choke her. She clawed at her throat to open the airway, the pain of her tender flesh ripping open caused tears to stream down her face.

It was all a futile effort.

She was going to die.

Black spots dotted her vision, the world tilted around her and spun faster as she fell to her knees. Pain seared through her body as she crumpled to the ground, still clutching in vain at her neck.

Amid the enlarging black spots in her vision, the vague outline appeared of someone slowly approaching her. She concentrated all her dwindling energy on that outline, praying it was someone to help her.

Air began to flow freely into her lungs, her lungs no longer water-logged or burning.

Blessed air. She gasped, greedy for more.

"You left me. You left me to die," a voice hissed.

She took gulping breaths to refill her oxygen deprived lungs. "No, no. I, I didn't. I didn't know."

"Liar. Excuses. Where were you? I was all alone. Alone!" His hazel eyes seethed with rage and betrayal.

"Please, I didn't know. I didn't know you were in danger. Please forgive me. Vlad, please."

Saying his name tasted like bitter bile.

"You live while I'm rotting in the cold earth. You selfish, worthless bitch," he roared lunging to choke the life out of her once again.

Ryn, sweating and gasping for breath, ripped herself from the dream. Her long legs swung over the side of the bed, a bubbling need to get away from the horrors her mind unleashed in the vulnerable moments of sleep.

The sun was beginning to crest over the trees and her breath caught seeing the dull red blood on her hands. She frantically looked around but found no other signs of blood or anyone else. Only Cletus who paced anxiously at her feet.

The dream felt so real and her body reeled from the physical effects it had on her. She stumbled to her bathroom in the grey dawn light, her throat and chest burning. Shocked, she stared in the mirror at her terror-stricken, ghostly white face. And her neck.

"Oh my god." She whispered, gingerly touching her neck to feel what the mirror revealed. Where all the blood on her hands was from.

Her neck stung, her hands shook so hard, she nearly ripped the vanity drawer onto the floor.

Shaking uncontrollably, gasping for breath once more, finally giving in, she sunk to the cold bathroom floor and wept.

Chapter 22

Her throat was an angry red with clawed scratches down her slender neck. She hissed through clenched teeth while she cleaned it.

It was a good thing she kept her nails short and blunt otherwise she would have completely shredded her skin.

"How the hell am I going to cover this in July?" she muttered to the cat who sat on the vanity with watchful eyes.

Frustrated at herself for her actions while trapped in a nightmare. Frustrated at her mind and self-conscious that continually sabotaged her while she slept and the insanely, creative ways it came up with to further torment her.

Reliving the horror of finding Vlad dead was bad enough. She didn't need new fictional twists to compound her grief and guilt.

In the dream, Vlad accused her of being alive while he laid rotting beneath the ground. She shuddered at the memory of the rage that seethed in his eyes, the betrayal. She shuddered again realizing it was her own mind's creation.

Survivor's guilt, maybe.

She was alive. But was really living a half-life. One full of fabrication and lies. One full of hidden truth and secrets. Could that be called living? Or just surviving? Or existing as Maari suggested.

Maybe her guilt and doubt of having something in her life like music, and taking that deeper now with performing in public, was the culprit between the two new nightmares.

Or, she was a fucking sadist who lived to torment herself.

The splash of cold water on her face was a welcome shock.

Sleep was beyond her at this point. She could sneak out for a run and be back before Nessa was awake and got wise to her breaking the temporary no-extra-exertion rule. Last night she was able to convince Nessa to lift that in the next twenty-four hours, but the tiny woman wouldn't budge for any earlier.

Ryn decided to risk the chance of discovery and Nessa's wrath. The thought of racing through the silence among the trees to the spot overlooking the Atlantic Ocean, as it roared against the rock cliff was too powerful to ignore.

She made sure the compression wrap was snug around her ribs and slipped quietly into the hallway. And right into Zane. He put hands on her shoulders to steady her and they tightened as he observed the pallor of her face and the massacred skin on her throat.

"It's nothing," she said flatly.

"Nothing? Never have your nightmares caused you to physically harm yourself, Severyn."

She shrugged. As much to blow off his concern, as to try to dislodge his hands from her shoulders. But when she took in his appearance, she paused. He looked rumpled and tired. Zane never looked those things.

"I heard about May Antel's benefit, I'm glad you're doing it. It will be good for you. And it's an opportunity to infiltrate that circle in a legitimate way."

"I—" She paused. "I hadn't thought of that."

May loved planning fundraising events, the target invitees often those from the political circles she grew up in, being the daughter of a senator.

"I'm more than willing to be the opportunistic cad." Zane tried to dispel the doubt that flickered across her face. "You know that in order to right wrongs, I'm willing to colour the lines to accomplish that. You have a different stance though and I'm not asking you to blur any of your lines in this situation."

He scooped Cletus up and met her dark grey gaze. "You accepted an offer for an opportunity. You're using your music career and talents to help out a charitable cause and it also could benefit your other *career*. You did not lie, cheat or hurt anyone to get May to offer you this opportunity. She offered it on merit alone. You're very talented and many, many people connect with your music and your words. You're doing nothing wrong."

"I feel like a fraud in so many ways." She lowered her gaze away from his, as Vlad's accusing face and words flashed in her mind again.

"I understand how you feel like that. But believe me, it's not true."

"About last week, when I returned from the Strada op…" She paused as she felt him stiffen slightly, but she needed to get this cleared up between them. "I'm not sorry for my decision to extract myself when I felt it was the best time to do so. However, I am sorry for how I handled it. And I want to apologize for sounding ungrateful for the vital role you play in all this and all that continue to do for me."

She could feel the weight of his gaze, in the morning dimness of the hallway, as he contemplated his reply.

"I accept your apology. But not because I feel you're ungrateful. Please accept mine as well, however, I won't apologize for doing what is necessary to keep you safe."

They followed Cletus down the stairs to the brightening foyer, happily leading them toward the possibility of food. Ryn smiled at the bounce of his plump belly.

"So now that we know what we are and aren't sorry for, it can be water under the bridge?"

Zane nodded but stopped her at the bottom of the stairs. "I accept your decision to act. You're right, you didn't put yourself, others, or the op in jeopardy. You were acting as someone who is used to working solo in the field and as someone that does not trust others easily. I know those boys very well, and as I've said, I trust them with my life. But as Nessa so gently reminded me—"

Ryn snorted, knowing gently would not have been the method Nessa used.

Zane's laugh lines on his handsome face deepened. "Yes, well she reminded me those are my experiences that I've used to formulate my trust. They're not yours."

Her love for that tiny feisty woman deepened.

"They are a very capable team."

She thought of the calm and precision their team operated under. The strength and assurance that emitted from Team Alpha's leader.

Somehow, she suspected that was not the last she'd see of Tag, Nexin, or Rolf.

Chapter 23

The music hall boasted rooms in the back, to give performers an element of privacy as they readied themselves to perform for the masses. Ryn contemplated taking the ankle-breaking heels off and going barefoot, for the fourteenth time, but Maari made her solemnly swear she would not.

She had chased Maari out of her dressing room when she came backstage. She loved Maari, but she needed some alone time to prepare herself. Her reflection in the mirror reassured her that the high neck of the winter green sleeveless jumpsuit covered the markings on her neck. Make-up effectively covered up the redness and mild bruising that emerged today. Only prosthetic skin would cover the scratches, but she opted for the fashionable high neck ensemble instead.

Her rich caramel hair cascaded down her back in waves, tickling the bare skin exposed by the open back of the jumpsuit. The humidity in the early July heat made her tresses feel heavy and she resisted the urge to put her hair up in a ponytail.

A swift knock announced May's arrival, and Ryn's grey eyes met green ones in the mirror as the tall curvy blonde glided in, a shimmer of gold.

"There's the woman of the hour." May clapped her hands, her slight Boston accent still evident regardless of her world travel and education. "You nervous? If so, you certainly do not look it." She handed Ryn a bottle of sparkling water, but she politely declined, holding up her glass.

"No bubbles tonight, but thanks. And a little, this isn't exactly my comfort zone."

Ryn watched the golden hair beauty quietly. She hadn't formally met May before she'd agreed to play tonight, but she was familiar with who she was. So far, the woman had earned Ryn's respect. She wasn't anything like the privileged, airhead socialite that reporters tried to paint her as.

May propped a silk covered hip on the vanity, twisting to check on her hair, swept up in a knot, in the mirror. "You'll be amazing. Antonio says you have a way of forgetting about everyone and everything around you when you play. I can honestly say I think I'm the one that is most excited here. Inviting some of the students from Annelou's school to perform with you was a brilliant touch."

"They're extremely talented." Ryn felt a surge of pride for the three students willing to come onto the stage with her. "That's why we're all here, is it not?"

"Absolutely. Annelou is clucking like a mother duck protecting her ducklings tonight." May's delicate laugh filled the room, and Ryn smiled remembering seeing the devoted woman doing exactly that.

"Annelou's love for her students is second only to her belief in their potential."

"She is a commendable woman, as are you to donate your time and talent to help mentor those in the music stream. I love that jumpsuit and colour on you, by the way. It's stunning. Whose design is it?"

Ryn shrugged her shoulders. "I honestly don't know. Maari told me to put it on. If you know Maari, you do as you are told."

"Those are good friends to have in your corner." May grinned. "The students for the dance segment go on in five and then we will proceed with your segment. Good?"

"Good."

"The demand was so high for tonight; I could have sold double the tickets. But I love this old music hall." May's gaze swept up to the ornate ceiling, sighing in bliss. "Thank you once again for agreeing to this."

"It's for a cause I believe in."

May nodded and her green eyes narrowed. "I come from privilege and so many people think I'm a blonde airhead. But I truly do care about making a difference and giving children different experiences that could help their future."

"We never know what will help alter the course of someone's life or what can help people find their purpose. But providing opportunity and belief in someone's potential is a catalyst." The reality of the truth of her statement was not lost on her.

"I knew I would like you." May smiled in appreciation. "Now," she clapped her hands, heading to the door, "I have to run, but tag me or Raul if you need anything."

Ryn watched in awe, from the side curtains, at the group of Annelou's dance students performing. Gravity defying flips, pounding energy, moving in perfect synchronicity, hitting every transition flawlessly. She had seen them work at the school, but watching them on a scale like this, in a venue like this, they were on fire. Annelou was beside her counting out the rhythm, vibrating with electricity.

Short and curvy for someone from the dance world, Annelou never let that hold her back in the pursuit of her passion. She may not have ever danced in world renowned troupes, but her knowledge of dance and teaching skills were exemplary.

Lavender spiky hair matched the lavender eyeshadow and lipgloss she wore, along with cat eye spectacles perched on her button nose.

"They're doing so good. So good. Aren't they?"

Ryn knew Annelou well enough now to know that was a rhetorical question.

"Oh my goodness, hit the finale strong guys, hit it strong." Annelou held her breath, continuing to tap out the rhythm, and then went berserk at the end.

Ryn joined in, laughing at the jubilant woman beside her. Normally Annelou had a reserved demeanour, but tonight she let her pride and excitement shine through.

Each one of the students radiated as they ran off the stage. Three balls of energy zeroed in on Ryn, making Raul, May's short, tight-lipped efficient assistant, jump to the side.

"You watched it," Maysha gushed still catching her breath. "I thought you might still be warming up your voice." Maysha's dark skin glistened, making the teen look even more beautiful.

"Did you see my flips?" Thad, the angelic looking sixteen-year-old twin brother of Maysha, shoved in closer.

"I did. And noticed a lot of your hip hop and breakdancing choreography in there, Divya and Maysha. It was extraordinary." She glanced quickly at Raul's face, looking more pinched by the second. "But you three better get changed for your set with me."

A set of matching squeals pierced her ears as Divya and Maysha jumped, hugging each other. Thad pulled them along blowing her a kiss. "Knock 'em out."

Raul's dark eyebrows almost touched with his permanent scowl. "We are one minute thirty-seven seconds and counting behind."

"Well, what are you making me wait for, Raul?" She regretted the joke immediately. "It's all good, the crowd is still settling down after those kids' amazing performance."

The scowl eased somewhat but she only got a humph for a reply.

She watched the curtain pull aside for the piano to be wheeled to the middle of the stage and shuddered a breath.

Please God, don't let this be a mistake.

"Oh my God, oh my God, oh my God." Maari ran toward her through the crowd backstage like a seasoned running back. May finally disengaged Ryn from the crowd and she gave the blonde beauty a grateful smile just as Maari barrelled into her for a giant hug. Ryn grabbed her, fearing her friend would break her ankle, then her slender neck, on the skyscraper strappy sandals she towered on.

But it was like Maari had been born with high heels on and she didn't miss a beat. "Ho, lee, shit Ryn. You were so freaking incredible."

Happy tears flowed from Maari's eyes without shame. In the black sequin dress, with glistening black eyes, her silk black hair, raven birds tattooed up her shoulder and graceful neck, she was a vision.

"I could hardly breathe the whole first song. The crowd was struck silent at first, I don't think anyone had any idea of how good you are. Wasn't she unbelievable?" Maari asked May, but didn't pause for a response. "It was like you embodied every musical icon up there."

May led them down the narrow hallway to unlock Ryn's dressing room, and ushered them in. "How did it feel?"

Ryn sat heavily on the sofa, starting to feel a bit shaky. "Honestly, I remember walking to the piano, feeling the cool of it, seeing the white and black of the keys… And then nothing but the music until Thad, Maysha, and Divya came on. They were so good, weren't they?" Her breath caught, thinking of the three youth.

"That young man has a wide range of talent. Is there a musical instrument he can't play? And those girls. Their voices sounded like they'd been touched by angels." Maari poured Ryn some water.

"They were fabulous," May agreed. "It was a genius touch to have them up there with you. I think it will really drive the donations." May slyly winked.

"Daddy and Mama are going to be so sorry they had to miss

this, but May said she can send them a recording. Zane was here too, but I haven't seen him all night. I better go find him. Join us soon."

Maari's lithe frame shimmered under the sparkling black gown and she blew Ryn a kiss before disappearing.

"She is a force to be reckoned with, isn't she?" May asked good-naturedly.

"You should meet her mom. She's a hurricane, Maari is more of a tropical storm." Ryn joked, but the affection in her voice was evident.

"Thank you once again for stepping out of your comfort zone and performing tonight. It truly was amazing to be a part of and witness." May kissed her on the cheek. "I will let you get resettled. I suspect you would rather escape out the back door than face the lion crowd, but I would love if you came out to mingle. Even for a short while."

"I should be unnerved that my thoughts are so apparent."

May's green eyes twinkled. "I can't take credit for being that perceptive. Antonio gave me a heads up and strict instructions not to let you bolt right away. See you soon."

Socializing and chatting up the crowd was part of her job tonight. So rather than bitch and moan, she put on a smile to play the charming extrovert. When all she really wanted to do was head home, toss on some comfy pants and eat popcorn with Maari.

Ryn reached the grand staircase that descended into the beautiful music hall which had been restored to capture its history and retain its elegance. The decor and patrons made the room glitter like a sea of diamonds. The elite, highly connected political crowd mingled, networking, drinking and listening to soft music played by the Boston symphony.

She walked down the stairs as gracefully as she could in the blasted high heels, running her hand along the smooth, cold marble bannister. Her fingers gently touched the high, tight neck of her jumpsuit, making sure it was still in place to cover the nasty scratches. Her unsheathed arms and open back helped cool her in the heat of the room, as the AC worked overtime.

With the open back of the jumpsuit, she wasn't able to wear the compression wrap.

Maari claimed that fashion requires sacrifice.

No wonder she couldn't give a rat's ass about fashion.

The wrap was no longer medically necessary the majority of the time, but with her added run this morning, and extended time in the evening wear, her ribcage was getting sore. She wished again she could escape home.

Ryn spotted Zane halfway across the room. With an infinite amount of bodies to separate them. She promised herself once she made it through the crowd to Zane, her duty would be complete and then she could ghost. People smiled in greeting while she came down the stairs and she renewed her smile in return.

She glanced once more to where Zane was to map her path to him, and she would have stumbled on the stairs had her hand not gripped the marble bannister. Instead, thankfully, she continued smoothly down the stairs, carefully schooling her face with a pleasant smile.

Standing with Zane were three tall men. One in particular, with a pair of golden-brown eyes. Eyes that made her breath stutter, that appeared in many of her dreams this week, and that were staring intensely into hers.

Chapter 24

By training and natural tendency, Tag scanned the room noting details of the guests in the music hall and the exit routes. He also noted the points of potential threat where someone with ill-intent could gain advantage.

Given the high-ranking government officials in the room, and the collective wealth of the patrons, he wasn't surprised by the amount of security. This was a social outing and Team Alpha was traveling weapon-free tonight, but that didn't make them any less effective if the need for action arose.

"Would it kill you to smile? Your scowling face is scaring away Rolf's and my admirers."

Rolf gave a quiet grunt while Nexin flashed his pearly white smile and gave a provocative wink to a group of passing women. Nexin looked resplendent in his tuxedo, like a pro-surfer who donned stylish evening wear.

Tag looked blandly at Nexin shamelessly flirting with the giggling women. One in particular was doing her damnedest to physically attach herself to Nexin's tuxedo-clad, sinewy body.

Rolf moved out of range of the forward ladies, joining his side. Even with no words, it was near impossible not to feel the presence of the large man. He wore his long dark hair pulled back tonight, as he usually did. A darkly attractive man, his hair pulled back from his face accentuated the high arched eyebrows. Tag had to admit, the guy may be massive and quiet, but he sure had magnetism.

The two towering men wove their way through the crowd

toward the vicinity of where Zane stood socializing with political players and the wealthy in attendance tonight. The small white streaks in Zane's dark blonde hair, coupled with his tux, along with his social ease, showcased a refined gentleman that walked easily in this elite world. This was a strong contrast to the version of Zane they worked with.

Zane had invited them here tonight to meet his niece, Severyn Andrews. He didn't provide many more details other than with her growing popularity and fame, it would serve her well to have some security-minded people around her.

All three of the guys had reservations of playing babysitter to a potentially self-centred musician, but they agreed, out of respect for Zane, to come along to at least meet her. They would assess the situation, do a little 'get-to-know-you' before they made any commitments.

"That lady had a vise grip and was very creative to ensure I remain in her presence." Nexin's windswept hair looked even more mussed when he squeezed in between them.

"No sympathy here," Rolf's voice rumbled, his light brown eyes held a hint of humour.

Tag remained silent, watching the graceful figure walking to the piano. She smiled at the crowd and looked calm, but he was fixed on her eyes. A large screen showcased her, and Tag watched the flicker of nerves in eyes the same colour of the storm clouds that he loved to watch roll in from the ocean on the Hawaiian Islands.

None of the men spoke another word as she sat at the piano and began to play. Tag watched transfixed. Her hands fluttered and skimmed over the keys to elicit sounds only a magician could. Her voice as strong and mesmerizing as the night he watched her play with the DJ in New York.

Her body language visibly relaxed, lost in the music. She appeared serene and content while she played. When the students from Annelou's school came on the stage, her ability to blend with them and to draw out every ounce of their talent, was captivating.

Rolf sucked in a breath as the young man traded his guitar for a sax and played alongside Severyn. Rolf loved sax music and he stomped his large foot to their beat. Severyn had won herself a fierce fan and admirer.

Zane found them after the crowd had finished its raucous applause, delight on his face at the performance. Zane was not a short man, but beside Rolf and Tag, his height was not as noticeable. "Did you enjoy her set?"

"She is extremely talented." Rolf's rare smile still lingered.

"A very different experience watching her perform tonight than it was with that DJ in New York. She plays to a crowd well."

"I didn't sense any divaness about her. If she's as nice off stage as she appeared onstage, she should be a gem to be around." Nexin finished his drink and crushed a cube of ice. "Unless she's one of those devil-incarnates when she's out of the public eye. She isn't, is she?" he asked Zane suspiciously.

"She does have her moments," Zane said with a laugh.

Nexin's previous clingy friend was honing her radar on him, but Zane adeptly intercepted to talk about one of the woman's pet projects, her show dogs. She quickly forgot about her mission to clamp onto Nexin's ass.

"Oh, he is smooth." Nexin whispered, appreciatively.

"Your ass is quite skinny."

"I agree with Rolf and don't know what the appeal is," Tag ribbed his friend.

"It's part of this whole magnificent package boys."

Nexin stopped suddenly struck speechless as a tall, lithe young woman joined Zane's side. Poker straight black hair swung across the small of her back, the black gown looked custom-made for her, hugging every indent and curve of her body. Small tattoos marked the graceful curve of the side of her neck, disappearing under the mass of silky hair. Facial piercings, that would look out of place on any other woman in the room, suited her perfectly.

Her black eyes glanced their way, quickly masking her surprise. Her gaze cut back and lingered a bit longer on Nexin, as she talked quietly with Zane.

"Tag, Rolf, Nexin, may I introduce you to Maari," Zane offered finally. "Kotan's daughter."

More than a tad of warning accompanied that last simple statement. They hadn't met Maari before, but all understood the role Kotan's daughter played in their ops. Her creative genius coupled with her father's, to covertly engineer the devices that gave them an added advantage in the field.

"A pleasure," she replied demurely.

Tag could tell instantly there wasn't truly a demure bone in this ones' body. He smiled and nodded in greeting at the beautiful woman.

"A pleasure to finally meet." Rolf shook her hand, his large one swallowing her delicate one.

"Likewise."

"The pleasure is entirely mine, Maari." Nexin looked slightly flushed, his blue eyes had yet to leave her. "What inquiring eyes you have. Just like your fathers but much, much sexier if I might be so bold. May I buy you a drink?"

"Nexin—" Zane started with a warning tone.

Blue innocent eyes swung to Zane. "It's one drink. You are of age, aren't you?" he turned to Maari, who laughed.

"Of course." Maari gave Zane a peck on the cheek at his scowl.

Nexin extended his arm and Maari looped hers easily through his. Zane continued to scowl at their backs as they made their way to the bar. His paternalistic protection of his friend, and partner's daughter, evident.

Tag wondered if he should reassure Zane that Nexin would tread carefully where Maari Luo was concerned, but he felt Rolf nudge him firmly. He turned at Rolf's silent signal toward the stairs.

She hadn't changed her outfit, which inordinately pleased him to put another check in the non-diva column.

He appreciated, again, how the narrow cut of the dark green jumpsuit highlighted her lean frame as she came down the marble staircase. He admired the strong lines of her shoulders and toned arms. She smiled as she looked at the people milling around the stairs. He continued to study her. The radiant contentment she exuded while on stage was no longer present, the natural smile having been replaced with one a bit more forced.

Her eyes began to move over the crowd, searching, and she paused slightly on the stairs when her eyes met his. He felt a jolt to his very core.

He stood stock-still, contemplating, watching her resume her descent of the stairs.

In his twenty-eight years, he had only ever felt that connection, that reaction, two other times; on the Miami and Strada ops. The person may have appeared visually different, but he knew they were, in fact, one woman.

Keeping a smile pasted on her face was a challenge as she struggled to regain a normal breathing pattern coming down the stairs.

Worlds colliding was an understatement.

This was no accident. No happenstance. No coincidence.

What the fucking hell was Zane doing? Why would he bring them here? Why was he intersecting Severyn Andrew's life with her undercover one?

Well, in honesty, Severyn Andrew's whole life was an undercover life. But that was beside the point she reprimanded herself silently.

Her head swam as she contemplated the complexity of her life and what the hell Zane might be up to.

Her grey eyes assessed around her. She was struggling to keep control of her composure, but no one was giving her an odd or worried look. Even though it didn't feel like it internally, she must be doing an adequate job of keeping the anger and panic off her face.

She forced herself to be casual and unhurried, no longer quite as impatient to reach Zane. She would find out soon enough what the hell her benefactor and mentor was up to.

Or maybe she would be able to sneak out before reaching Zane and his entourage.

May touched her shoulder. "Severyn, I would like to introduce you to my mother and father, Ida and Bernard."

It was easy to see what traits May inherited from which parent. Tall and blonde from her mother, the sparkling green eyes from her father. Mr. Antel had a shock of white hair and was shorter than his wife.

Ryn watched May's parents hug closer to their daughter's side. Gentle, quiet love flowed from them as they pleasantly greeted her. A sharp pang of sadness washed over her for her own parents, but she pushed it aside quickly.

"It's a pleasure to meet you, Senator and Mr. Antel."

"Please, dear, call us Ida and Bernard." The Senator replied graciously. "That was a lovely performance you gave. And truly wonderful to have Annelou's students join you."

Ryn thought back to Thad, Maysha, and Divya. Three months ago, Annelou had introduced the four of them, all of them hesitant and a bit skeptical of what the other had to offer. Faced with so much adversity in their young lives, it would be easy to understand if the three students were cynical and derisive. But instead, they quickly blossomed, with a bit of support, to embrace new possibilities.

"They're so wonderfully talented, that should be what is experienced."

"That's a glorious idea," May exclaimed. "A full show solely featuring all the students and all the various streams of fine arts at the school."

"Easy, dear, you already have the next event to focus on." Her mother touched May's hand and her doting father kissed her cheek, his green eyes gleaming.

"That's an Annelou conversation." Ryn smiled at May's enthusiasm. "She's very sensitive to anything that might be exploitative and not in the best interests of the students."

"Oh, I know. Leave Annelou to me."

"You played beautifully, my dear. Very relaxed for not being a regular performer." Bernard looked at her with respect and appreciation.

"Yes," Ida agreed wholeheartedly. "May said you were hesitant to agree to this, but I am glad you were swayed to share your talent with us firsthand."

"It helps to have Antonio in your corner. He's very hard to say no to." May flashed her a grin.

"Is it like giving a speech and you are supposed to envision the crowd in their birthday suits?" Bernard winked at her. "That was always my suggestion to my wife when she started in politics and public speaking."

"Oh my God, Daddy."

They laughed heartily.

"I can't say that was my strategy. Does this strategy work, Senator?"

"I daresay, it does not. And please, it's Ida." She spoke between breaths.

"What is your strategy, my dear?" Bernard inquired.

"Nothing as racy as your recommendation. I block everything else out, just focus on the music and let it lead. It seems to work out, I guess."

"Overthinking can make things fall apart," Ida agreed. "Isn't that the truth of many things? We do not trust our instincts enough."

"Are you talking about music now dear, or politics?" Bernard kissed his wife's delicate hand, his authentic affection evident.

"Politics, how droll." May rolled her eyes. "But this crowd is my bread and butter for my fundraising efforts, so I will continue to tolerate that pesky topic." May smiled impishly at her mother. "The students are going to be so blessed, the dollars coming in tonight have already exceeded my expectations. Thank you, again, truly, for your part in this."

A lump lodged in her throat, so Ryn gave May a nod.

"It was a pleasure to meet you tonight, my dear. I do hope we will see you again at more of May's events."

"We, ourselves, attend as many as we can with my wife's work schedule, and I trust our paths will cross again soon."

Ryn shook their hands once again. "Your daughter goes above and beyond for a good cause; you should be very proud. It was wonderful to meet you. And thank you, May, for getting me out of my shell."

May made her promise twice before she left their company that she would be available for future events. Ryn made a mental note not to get cornered in the same room with both May and Antonio. They could charm the hair off a cat, she thought wryly with a smile.

Zane had confirmed that Senator William Hanelson wasn't on the attendee list of tonight's event and the multiple visual scans around the room confirmed he still wasn't in attendance. However, she did hear reference to him a few times as she made polite conversation, winding her way through the crowd.

A twinge of guilt bloomed at the thought that she may be able to use her meeting with May's mother to her advantage to gain closer access to Senator Hanelson. She would only explore, or exploit, that advantage if she absolutely needed to, she promised herself.

Coming closer as she wound through the people, a head with long dark hair pulled back towered over everyone. She knew his two companions wouldn't be far.

Zane's easy laugh reached her. Always comfortable with crowds. Always smile ready for networking opportunities. His keen mind, always gathering, assessing, strategizing. Always ready to make connections, to think of new ideas in his security technology world domination.

Always plotting.

Her anger was still brewing, mingled with dread, but it was tempered with curiosity. She wondered how Zane was going to play this.

Maari saw her first, flashed her a smile and pulled slightly away from Nexin's side.

Zane caught Maari's smile over his shoulder and turned to her. "Here's the lady of the hour." He kissed both of her cheeks; the lines around his eyes deepened with his smile. "It was a beautiful performance, you did wonderful. I'm glad you were finally able to make your way to us."

Zane turned to the group that crowded around them. "I would like to introduce you to a few new faces. Rolf Torkelson, Nexin Walsh, and Taggert Hale, this is Severyn Andrews."

New faces my ass.

She glanced at each of the introduced men's faces searching for any glimmer of recognition or realization they had all met twice before. Only then, they had met Demetria Xeno instead of Severyn Andrews.

Her hand disappeared in Rolf's large one. "A pleasure to meet you and to hear you play." Rolf's heavy German accent accompanied his serious smile.

Instead of a handshake, Nexin brought her hand to his lips, a devilish glint in his blue eyes. "In the presence of two incredibly striking young ladies, the pleasure is all mine, I assure you."

Maari rolled her eyes, which matched Rolf's, and Ryn worked to suppress a smile. Nexin's impish, flirt personality clearly wasn't an act he used when on an op, but a deeply embedded part of his personality.

She turned slightly to the right, tilting her head up and found a pair of intense eyes gazing down at her. Another jolt ran through her.

The memories of the elevator kiss, the light touch of his fingertips on her bare skin to inspect her ribs before she had jerked away from him, were all a bit too fresh.

"Taggert, is it?" she asked without offering her hand.

Those golden-brown eyes with flecks of green and a whisper of orange were starting to unnerve her.

"Just Tag. The rumours of your talent do not do you justice, Severyn."

She felt a blush heat her cheeks and was annoyed at her response to a basic compliment. The sight of him in a tuxedo added new dimensions to her growing discomfort of being so close to him

Maari quietly sipped her champagne, watching the exchange.

"I'm happy you three were able to take in the show for such a good cause." She stamped down the urge to jump away from Tag, to put some distance between them. The distance would be worth it, but it would raise more questions than she was ready to answer right now.

"Can I get you a drink, Ryn?" Maari motioned a server to come in their direction but Ryn waved them off.

"Ryn?" Tag asked curiously. "I like that."

Her gut leapt at his comment, raising her growing ire at her response to him and Zane's role in placing her in this predicament.

"Yes, in our family only us oldies call her Severyn." Zane smiled down at her.

She fought to mask the scowl she dearly wanted to give Zane right then. "I'm going to slip out quietly and head home. It was a pleasure meeting the three of you. Maari, I can give you a ride if you need."

"I'm staying in the city tonight, but I'll catch up with you tomorrow."

Zane put a fatherly arm around her shoulders, hugging her affectionately to his side. "Of course. I know crowds aren't really your thing. We will join you at the estate shortly."

Ryn froze, sure she had misunderstood.

"I would like the four of you to become better acquainted."

"Why would you like that?" She quietly clenched her teeth and felt her anger rear its head again, quickly surpassing the level of when she first spotted the three men with Zane.

"The lady was unaware of our meet and greet?" Nexin asked, put off.

"I hadn't had a chance to properly to discuss it with her."

Damn Zane and his plotting ways.

"Is that so? This morning —" She narrowed her eyes, successfully biting back a snarl.

"Didn't give us enough time. But with the growing fame you're accruing, Severyn, it would be wise to have a security presence."

Of course, he would wait to spring this on her here in front of them and when they were among hundreds of guests. In front of powerful and very gossipy circles. A blow-up scene would be just grand, wouldn't it? She was seething inside, and it took considerable effort to appear calm.

Tag watched her quietly, intently.

"A security presence?" She gave a small laugh. "My fame and notoriety has hardly reached the level of needing three men babysitting me. I'm sure you three have more interesting things to do."

"We do have some down time right now." Tag smiled sweetly down at her.

Bugger.

"Well, I imagine we could do this tomorrow. It's getting late." She returned his sweet smile.

"No worries, we'll discuss it further at the estate. The boys travelled with me in the limo tonight. Why don't you leave your vehicle with Maari and come back with us?"

"I see." Her chin elevated a few degrees, it was becoming harder to disguise her growing anger. Maari gave her a smile and mouthed, *I had no idea.*

"That's not necessary. I have early morning plans and need the vehicle." The tightness in her tone was starting to escalate. If she didn't get out of there soon, Zane was going to have a nasty scene on his manipulative little hands.

"I was not aware of any early morning plans."

Her grey eyes were hard, but she smiled innocently. "It's really hard to be aware of all the planning that happens around you, isn't it?" She turned on her heel and strode away.

Chapter 25

The moon glimmered on the soft Atlantic waves to make the water look like molten silver. Ryn blasted down the I-93 toward the estate and hugged the curve, the dark rocky embankment illuminated by the bright shining moon. She rolled down all the windows of the Range Rover; the swirling wind whipped the long, unbound mass of hair she held back with a thick headband.

Maari had called her almost immediately after she stomped off to assure her, she had no idea that Zane was planning to ambush her like that.

"What do you think he's up to? Maybe there have been threats toward you? Or maybe you are getting a stalker following? That's when you know that you really made it big, when you get your first stalker." Maari joked, trying to make her irate friend laugh.

"I have no idea. But I'm pissed that he blind-sided me yet again. And after he promised wouldn't."

The brief chat with Maari didn't calm her anger. She couldn't fathom Zane's play. *What was he trying to accomplish?*

And he had never been so sneaky and non-transparent before.

It didn't sit well with her. When they first met, it had taken a large effort on her part to trust and open up to Zane. He, along with Kotan, but especially Zane, had worked hard to get them to this point and this was so out of character for him.

Was there some threat she was not made aware of, like Maari suggested? Or why would Severyn Andrews need bodyguards all of a sudden?

Or had he already exposed her to Tag, Nexin, and Rolf and they already knew she was not only Severyn Andrews but also the operative known as Demetria Xeno?

And if that was the case, then why blindside her under the ruse that they were there to be bodyguards because of her work as a musician?

Probably because I would be vehemently opposed and throw a fit. Kinda like I'm doing now.

The thought made her snarl into the wind.

She fishtailed into the small parking lot, rocks spraying behind her. Slamming the vehicle door, she stomped to the water, kicking off her shoes as she went. She didn't care that the legs of her jumpsuit were getting wet. She didn't care that the cold water stung her skin. The shock was welcome and she splayed her toes on the rocky bottom, concentrating on the feel of the waves, the pull of the retreating water that headed back out to sea. Half wishing that the water would grab her and pull her out with the receding waves.

Eventually the water worked its magic. She knew it would, hence the dangerous stomp on the brakes to pull into the beach. She stood in the moonlight, feeling and listening to the waves with eyes closed. Allowing the water to calm her, ground her. The anger still simmered but she was more in control now.

Water, particularly the ocean, was her elixir. Her mother called her a *babi dwr*; Welsh for water baby.

With that thought, a stab of fear stole her breath.

What if Zane's actions were because whoever thought they had killed her, now knew she lived, and they were going after her family again?

She vigorously shook her head, refusing that logic. Zane wouldn't keep that from her. Of that, she was certain.

But the fear lingered as she drove toward the estate.

The dark blanket of trees greeted her along the long winding drive and the lights burned bright in welcome when the large, sprawling house came into view.

"Dammit, my timing is pure shit."

The limo was unloading its four passengers when she pulled around the drive that looped in front of the house. Lights danced in the gently flowing water of the fountain in the middle. She would have rather been at the estate before they arrived, but the stop at the beach was still a wise move, she decided.

She slowly got out of the Range Rover to hear Zane say thank you to Charles, his regular driver of the car service he used. Rolf and Nexin followed Zane up the front steps framed by pillars that supported the high balcony above. The fragrant scent of Nessa's roses carried on the late-night breeze. She caught another scent that mingled with the roses. One she smelled when talking in the small group with Zane. Citrus and sage.

Ryn slowly brought up the rear of the group and Tag paused as she neared the steps. She assumed he was playing the gentleman to wait for her and let her go first. But at the last second, he turned to press the bony protrusion of his elbow hard into the left side of her ribs.

Her vision swam slightly, and she sharply sucked in her breath through clenched teeth.

Simply moving her body no longer caused her pain but a sharp elbow pressing directly into the epicentre of where the soft flesh met the unforgiving rock not that long ago, was an entirely different story.

And he hit it dead on the spot. As if he knew what was hiding under the material of her jumpsuit. And how it had gotten there.

"A bit tender there I see," Tag said quietly.

She raised her eyes and there was no mistaking the recognition when hers met his. Or the curious, questioning look on his face.

Fuck.

"I don't like people invading my personal space."

A lame excuse for her reaction, even to her ears.

She pushed past Tag, needing to be away from him. She didn't give a hot-damn if it was rude to leave him at the bottom of the steps as she stalked into the house.

Kotan and Nessa were in the foyer welcoming Nexin and Rolf and Nessa bustled over, gushing how she heard the event was a smashing hit. "Maari let me know it was such a success and that there are all sorts of posts raving about it."

"Posts?" Ryn's addled brain struggled to regain its calm and some semblance of reason. "Oh, like social media?" She gave a dismissive wave of her hand.

"Not an Insta junkie or a Twit?" Tag looked amused, but pleased.

"Well, it sounds like you knocked their socks off. Speaking of socks, how did the legs of your pant legs get wet?"

"How the hell does that have to do with socks?"

Nessa gave her hand a small squeeze and smile of understanding, glancing at the group of males assembled in the foyer.

Ryn quietly sighed. "I need a drink."

"Are you old enough to drink, young lady?" Nexin's eyes belied the sternness of his tone.

Back at home, she would have been legal to drink for almost two years, but she often forgot about it in the States as she drank very little. And Severyn Andrews' ID stated she had turned twenty-one earlier this year even though her actual coming of age wasn't until November.

You can fight and die for your country when you are eighteen, but God forbid if you try to buy a case of beer. She gave an unladylike snort and pushed past Nexin into the library.

She preferred this room. She knew Zane would prefer his personal study to have the little meet-and-greet he had meticulously planned. She felt a spike of satisfaction for derailing that at least.

She could feel Tag's eyes studying her as she poured a vodka soda and lime but avoided his gaze and sat down beside Rolf on one of the sofas. She remained silent and waited for Zane to play host and lead the conversation. She may be a pawn in his little chess game. She certainly wasn't going to play game maker.

Normally this room, with the dark colours, plenty of comfortable options to relax amidst all the books and fireplace, brought her calm. Her short nails tapped the crystal tumbler in her hand.

Nexin sat across from her in a deep navy wing chair. "Ryn," he paused, his nod indicated he liked the nickname, "how *did* your pant legs get wet?"

"I helped a family of ducks back into the water." She replied blandly.

"A gentle, bleeding heart protectionist. I can see that." He smiled in approval, accepting a glass of cognac from Zane.

Nessa joined them and Kotan followed closely behind her. Zane finished passing out drinks then casually leaned on the desk to offer a round of introductions. She knew Kotan and the guys were well acquainted, but she wasn't sure about Nessa. Going by her response though this was the first time meeting them herself.

Assuming it was for her benefit, Zane gave a brief rundown of the bios of the three men that made up Team Alpha. Rolf was an emergency room doctor and was familiar with crisis medical situations. That very well could be the reason why Nessa had never met the team before.

Tag was ex-military and ranger. No surprise there, she had deduced army or something military from their past dealings.

And Nexin was ex-CIA. She hadn't suspected that one, but it did explain a few things.

"So, a doctor, a spy, and a super soldier. Quite a stellar line up. A bit of overkill for one budding, pretty tame, artist wouldn't you say?" She leaned back casually on the sofa and observed Rolf's giant frame out of the corner of her eye. His quiet nature only magnified his size.

"Pretty tame? Ah Severyn, my sweet, sweet Ryn, how boring. Good thing I'm on the job to spice things up." Nexin batted his eyes at her.

She smiled despite her mood. She could feel Tag's frequent gaze on her and she avoided meeting those intense eyes again.

Zane undid his bow tie and dragged a hand through his thick dark blonde hair. "Maybe a drink is the only thing we need tonight. Give you some time to process, Severyn. We can pick up in the morning."

Ryn did not move a muscle. Not to twitch. Not to blink. Not to breath.

That son of a bitch. He invited them to stay here.

Her anger red-lined and she stood, no longer able to contain herself. "Process things? You—"

Nessa quickly read her body language. "Come, boys, I will show you where the kitchen is for the morning, and up to your rooms."

Tag rose slowly, glancing at his teammates and arching an eyebrow at Ryn. He gave Zane a long, hard look but didn't say anything before he followed Nessa out.

The door clicked shut and Ryn whirled on the two men left in the room. She didn't bother to mask the fury, or the hurt, she was feeling.

"What in the fucking monkey-flying hell is going on here?" She pointed an accusing finger at Zane. "You promised you'd never ambush me again with this bullshit."

"You're not in the field."

"I'm not in the field? I am not in the field?" She yelled. "That is how you justify this?"

She wanted to throw the crystal glass she clutched in her hand at Zane's head. "So, *this* is the house that trust built?"

Both men winced at the accusatory tone in her voice, but Zane's face was stubbornly set. She had her suspicions Kotan wasn't fully behind the idea of springing this on her but by his body position, he stood with Zane.

"You know that we have your absolute best interests at heart, Severyn. That is why they are here."

Zane continued where his friend left off. "You're too close to this and to your desire not to let people in or close to you. That clouds things for you. We see the big picture."

"Of course, you know all, see all, don't you? You know what is best," she bit out sharply.

"Have I ever led you astray? Have I?" Zane pressed her silence.

"No."

"We wouldn't do anything that would jeopardize you."

"You introduced them to Severyn Andrews, Zane. You purposely blended the very separate and distinct parts of my life. With them."

"I didn't overstate the importance of the growing need for protection as your notoriety is dramatically increasing. We need your back covered on both levels and it's less complicated if it's with the same team." The look on Zane's face implored her to understand.

"There has been chatter that Ched is starting to look heavily into finding Demetria. The things we found so far, both through the Senator, and the fact the Strada facility was rigged to explode, is showing that this is a path more dark and dangerous than we expected. You cannot do this alone." Kotan added to the argument.

"As I said, it's less complicated to have both parts of your life covered by the same team but there's no need to blend them. Not yet. Not until you're ready for them to know you're also Demetria. It will be work, yes, but we've worked out the details to keep your cover intact, even from them." Zane squeezed her shoulder, trying to reassure her.

She shook his hand free to move over to the window and leaned her forehead against the cool glass. Exhaustion settled into her bones. "He knows. Tag knows that I'm not just Severyn, but also Demetria."

"How?" Zane's tone was incredulous. "We haven't disclosed that yet to them."

"Because of the kiss in the elevator? Somehow because of that?" Kotan wondered.

"Have you seen him and kissed him again since the elevator, as Severyn, I mean?" Parental suspicion seeped into Zane's question.

"No. And I don't know how, not really. It doesn't matter how he knows; he just does."

"It's okay. We can work with this." Zane walked closer to where she remained at the window. "You're upset, we understand that."

Ryn turned and looked Zane unflinching in the eye. "No, I don't think you do. Or maybe you do but you don't care. I'm only a pawn, another operative for you to run while you push the buttons behind the scenes."

"That is not fair, Severyn."

Her hair flew when she whirled to direct her wrath at Kotan. "Oh, we're concerned with being fair now? I guess that was an oversight on both your ends while you conspired with this game plan. Otherwise you would have talked to me about this."

"And you would have gone along?" Kotan challenged her quietly.

"Probably...not. I don't know." Ryn felt like stomping her feet in rage. "But what I do know, and what you both damn well know about me, is that I don't appreciate the autocratic and authoritarian bullshit when this is my life we are talking about."

"It's my job. No, sorry, it is our job," Zane corrected, looking at Kotan, "to protect you."

"No." She stalked toward her two mentors to stand defiant in front of them. "No, your job was never to protect me. It's to help me achieve my goals. To train me and give me the skills to accomplish that. With minimal risk. Not with no risk," she jabbed her finger at them to emphasize the point. "Your job is not to sideline me or to give me three fucking babysitters to keep me out of harm's way."

"We are not sidelining you and they are not babysitters, but rather, your team. Each with a set of skills to help you accomplish your goals." Kotan's eyes urged her to be reasonable.

The stubborn set to Zane's jaw increased. "It needs to progress this way, Severyn. Or the road ahead stops. That is not an ultimatum, but a fact. Without a team, you cannot accomplish your goals. Or, if I'm truthful, survive. But the choice is yours. I won't force or trick you into this decision."

"But you aren't above manipulation, are you?"

She felt an immature feeling of satisfaction when she slammed the door behind her.

Nessa quietly slipped into the library after showing the men to their rooms. She felt her anger subside somewhat when she noticed the slump in both Kotan and Zane's shoulders and the pained looks on their faces.

"We need to talk with her further. Make her see, to understand. If she wants to survive, this is the only way." Zane's eyes darted to the door which Ryn had slammed only moments before.

Nessa was a tiny woman, but she was an immovable wall as she held up her hand. The look on her face stopped both men in their tracks.

"You will do no such thing. Not tonight. That poor girl needs some space to process this after the antics you pulled."

"She would never have agreed to it otherwise." Kotan leaned heavily back onto the large dark wooden desk and Zane slumped into the chair behind it.

"You didn't give her a chance not to."

Nessa poured herself a drink, walked over to the wall filled with books and pulled out one of her favourites. Some reading because she didn't think she'd sleep well at all tonight.

"For being two brilliant men in your fields, and at strategizing, you both fell incredibly short with this."

"Thanks for sugar coating it, Nessa," Zane said dryly.

"You know that's not my way," Nessa retorted sharply. "It's a lot for her to take in. You have to appreciate that. She's not resisting because she's a spoiled entitled person or mad because she isn't getting her way. She has spent the last two years working on this in secret with only us. You're asking her to expand her circle of trust with people she didn't choose herself."

Nessa pressed the cool glass against her forehead and her dark, long lashes feathered her skin as she closed her eyes. Her voice was husky when she spoke again. "Her largest concern will be how this could increase the risk to her family."

"Those three men would never betray her that way," Zane vehemently stated.

"I've said this before but apparently it needs to be repeated - you two trust those three men because of your experiences. Those were not hers and she will wonder if she can trust them. Or if she does come to trust them, what if they fall into enemy hands and are forced to tell what they know. Both those increase the risk to her family in her eyes. Even if she doesn't disclose any of her secrets to them, the more people she allows into her circle, the more people to hide the truth from. And the closer you get to people, the harder it is. Look at how she struggles with Lok."

Nessa walked back to the door, taking their silence as a sign they were taking what she had to say to heart. "To work as a team, she will have to learn to rely on them. That makes her vulnerable in her eyes. And she has had years of training to hide or avoid making herself vulnerable. That started even before she met us, I suspect."

She gave them another firm look. "You both need to analyze how your fatherly feelings toward Severyn are clouding your judgement." She held up a hand to stop their justifications. "I know you love her. I do as well. Dearly. But she is right. At the foundation of this, the goal for this is to identify and remove the threat from her family's lives and hers so she can return to them. To train her to accomplish that. It was never to protect her as a victim. You need to determine if what you're offering her will achieve that goal. Or if somewhere along the way, your goals have changed from hers, and you're now serving your own."

Chapter 26

The gentle breeze brushed over the greenery that surrounded the house. A cloudless sky shone, beckoning all to enjoy the wonders under it. Bright morning sunshine covered everything in the room with an angelic halo. Loud purrs emanated from the grey tabby as Cletus lapped up his morning milk.

All signs of a peaceful, gentle day.

But the occupant in the room neither saw, or felt, those signs of tranquility.

Sleep did little to dampen Ryn's anger and the leather-hide punching bags felt every ounce of it. Her shoulders burned and the pain in her ribs threatened to steal her breath. But she pushed on. Every ounce of her emotion focused in her high roundhouse kicks. Any opponent would have a hard time walking away after getting the powerful, whipping kick to their head.

Normally, while training, she could blank her mind and focus on the skills that would save her life in the field. This morning she wasn't so lucky. Her relentless brain bantered back and forth in its analysis regarding Zane's actions and it was driving her mad.

She truly believed he had her best interests at heart. And he was right, he never had led her astray with his plans.

But that man could be so insufferable and domineering.

She punched up her left knee for a jump kick followed by a vicious elbow to the bag. A good amount of skin remained on the bag, but she hardly registered the sting.

If she removed any emotion from this situation, she knew in

her gut he was right.

But knowing that and accepting it were different beasts.

She delivered a series of vicious punches to the bags.

The ops had been getting riskier and more complicated to execute. She was at a crossroads.

One way led to her evolving from a solo act in the field, to team up with three hulking brutes.

The other, the path she was currently on, would probably lead to her death, as Zane direly predicted.

She knelt on the ground and absorbed the impact of the swinging bag. The rough leather scratched her forehead as she pressed against it. Cletus butted his head against her thigh and petting his soft fur calmed her raging internal debate.

Her greatest chance of finding the people and the reason behind all this lay with them. With agreeing to work with those three hulking brutes.

She squeezed her eyes shut to block the panic at the thought of trusting strangers. If anything went wrong, or it they betrayed her...She felt sick contemplating the deadly results to her loved ones.

"Is this a bad time?"

Ryn was on her feet to face the intruder in a flash. Lounging against the doorframe was Tag. For the early hour, he looked good. Fresh and ready for the day. She remembered his military background.

"No sleeping in for you." She grabbed a towel from the shelf by the island to mop the sweat from her face and neck. She looked like a sweaty fiend and he looked good enough to nibble on.

Dammit, stop it.

"You neither. From the look of it you're at the end of your workout, not the beginning."

He stepped into the room and she was acutely aware of how his t-shirt pulled across his broad chest and shoulders when he moved.

"This is an amazing room. Functional in lots of ways." His gaze ran from the variety of training equipment to the musical instruments and consoles. "You spend a lot of time here?"

"It is functional. And the view is exceptional." She shrugged. "What's not to love?"

She pulled her braid over her shoulder to undo it and let the fullness of her hair cover the side of her neck and the fiendish scratches.

She could feel Tag observing her remove Cletus from the island for the second time. She finally relented and gave the prince some cat treats.

"He has a mind of his own." Tag chuckled, walking further into the room.

He reminded her of a wild animal stalking confidently into new territory.

"His name is Cletus. Nessa said there's a name connection with a General in Alexander the Great's army. I think we shot ourselves in the foot."

Tag laughed and got a glass of water from the water cooler, but she refused to feel guilty for her lack of gracious hosting manners.

"He's a unique looking cat. Where did you find him?"

The clearing in the trees and cliff overlooking the Atlantic Ocean flashed in her mind. It was the day her memory had just returned and with it, the full realization of the situation she and her family were in. Racing through the trees, she had found the clearing and cliff overlooking the ocean. A vicious winter storm was starting to blow in off the Atlantic which matched the storm of her terror, guilt, and denial. Cletus had been there, huddled, hungry, and shaking.

"Do you ever really find a cat? I think they find you."

"You answer my questions with a casual one of your own."

"Does that bother you?"

Tag laughed again and his golden-brown eyes were less intense when he did.

"You answer without divulging much information of yourself but still give engaging responses to satisfy. A normal individual wouldn't pick up on the fact that they learned very little of you in their interaction until well after the fact, if at all. That's a subtle skill."

"All that in a few sentences of conversation. I never caught psychoanalyzing as part of your brief bio last night."

"No, we didn't exchange our various skill sets last night, did we? I'm an astute observer, but I didn't need those skills to know you didn't know ahead of time about our invitation here. Into either Severyn Andrew's life or—" He let it hang there without verbalizing he was well aware that she was Demetria. "But I want you to know, we were not aware, nor did we play any part, in that deception."

The sunlight fell over Tag's face, turning his eyes to liquid gold. The intensity of him was overpowering and she found herself resisting the urge to move toward him. Drawn to the power and strength that emanated from him. She swallowed and dragged her eyes away from his.

She needed space.

"You do believe me, don't you?"

She put the island between them and felt her control over her body return. "You ask a lot of questions, Taggert Hale."

"You offer few answers, Severyn Andrews. And it's Tag. Only my dad, late grandfather, and Zane call me Taggert."

"I would most definitely call you Taggert if it meant not getting shot in my sleep." Nexin sauntered in hair still wet from his shower. "And holy shit, what a room and one that comes complete with a sweaty, beautiful woman. You went all beast-mode already at this ungodly hour? Is there coffee in here?"

"Jesus, is he always like this?" Ryn turned to Tag's amused attractive face.

"Verbal diarrhea? I would love to say it's a symptom of waking up in the morning that dissipates, but sadly, I would be lying."

Ryn laughed lightly. "I only have tea up here."

"I'll take whatever caffeine I can get." Nexin gave her a thankful grin when she passed him the steaming mug.

"Not an early bird like this one?"

"Heavens no. Not if I can help it." Nexin closed his eyes after his first sip then propped his elbows on the island and set his chin on his knuckles. "There's so much for us to learn about each other, isn't there? This is where the magic happens? I'm hoping not just music." He gave her a conspiring wink.

This guy was impossible. Barely awake, flirty antics all geared up. But she was finding it hard not to like him.

The small video screen on the edge of the island signalled an incoming and Nessa's smiling face greeted them in the navy and white kitchen washed in morning sunlight.

"Sorry to use this technology but this house can be too darn big. Cletus, you get off the counter." Nessa admonished.

"Brat." Ryn grabbed the sneaky cat and received a loving grind of his face along her chin.

Nexin paused his mug midway to his mouth, complete shock on his face. "Holy lamb of God, Rolf, you're up already? It's only after seven, my man."

Rolf grunted in response. He sat perched on one of the stools and Nessa passed him a steaming cup of coffee. A groan of pleasure rumbled from the massive man as he took his first sip.

"This is worth getting up at this indecent hour," Rolf replied, his German accent heavy, his deep voice still croaky from sleep.

"She does brew a mean pot of coffee on the stove," Ryn agreed.

"It's not quite like brewing it on a wood stove or on the fire like I learned as a child, but it will do." Nessa flashed her a small smile before turning her attention to Tag and Nexin. "Now, come down and grab muffins, fruit, or toast. A larger breakfast will be made in a bit. After your discussion in the library."

Nessa's pointed look made her sigh. No use delaying the

inevitable longer than she had to.

Ryn showered, but not too quickly. She lingered to let the pounding jets and hot water work on the tightness in her neck and shoulders. Zane could wait a few extra minutes.

She donned a pair of plaid shorts and a maroon, high-neck, sleeveless shirt.

"Time to face the music," she muttered to her reflection.

The three guests were entering the library as she came down the stairs and Tag paused to let her go ahead of him. She was ready this time in case he tried to jab his elbow into her healing ribs. The faint, but definitive, scent of citrus and sage filled her nose.

"I'm very curious how you came to have those marks on your neck."

Her hair and body angle in the studio had apparently not been enough for his all-seeing eyes.

"Changing your tactics. Is that a question or a statement?"

Tag grunted and she settled down in one of the oversized olive-green armchairs.

Many nights she had curled up here reading when the nightmares robbed her of sleep. She deeply wished she was here to do that instead of this.

Kotan smiled quietly at her as he sipped his green tea. His gentle calm settled her growing twitchiness.

Tag leaned back into the corner of the sofa across from her, casually tossing his arms over the back and crossed his long legs out in front of him at the ankle. Nexin joined him and Rolf chose to stand behind them. The big guy still didn't look happy at being up at this hour. The mug clutched in his large hand, filled with Nessa's coffee, looked like it was making it bearable though.

"Morning, everyone. I trust our guests slept well?" Zane strolled into the room.

"Like the dead. In a good way, of course." Nexin winked at her. "Ryn that colour of top does wonders with your eyes."

She smiled despite the cold fingers of dread twisting in her gut.

Zane crossed his bare feet as he lounged against the front of the desk. He adjusted the collar of his polo shirt, the only sign that belied his slight nervousness. Ryn knew from their conversation last night, in his careful plotting, he hadn't planned to include her role of Demetria yet in their 'introductions' and was adjusting as needed.

He and Kotan would have discussed this at length after their late evening ambush. At least her night's sleep wasn't the only one disrupted by the ploy.

Tag caught her small smile and cocked his head slightly as he watched her. A growing familiar jolt travelled through her when their eyes met. She looked away, keeping a careful neutral expression pasted on her features.

"As you know, anyone in the public eye has elevated risks to their well-being and needs to take precautions. I've spoken at length with you three about the possibility of providing security protection for Severyn and you were to consider it."

Ryn arched an eyebrow at the 'spoken at length' but remained silent.

Tag caught her eye again, but his look was unreadable as he swung his eyes to Zane.

"Yes, having a capable group around a public figure, like Severyn, is important. As you are aware though we are often—" Tag paused briefly. "—unavailable for large chunks of time. Our other reservation, mirrors one that Ryn raised last night and that is we are no one's babysitter. So, unless there's more to the arrangement then was previously identified…"

Her assessment of Tag being pragmatic was right on the money. *The guy doesn't waste time getting to the point.*

Nexin cut his eyes over to Tag and back to Zane. Rolf quietly put down his mug and crossed his burly arms over the muscular girth of his chest, waiting.

By their questioning reaction, it was apparent Tag hadn't shared his knowledge of her being the operative they knew as Demetria Xeno. And weren't clear on where their team leader was taking this.

Zane stood to his full height, clasped his hands behind his back, and glanced at Kotan, who nodded slightly. "Yes, she did tell me that you had discerned the additional reason of our request for your services."

Nexin leaned forward; his normally relaxed face set seriously. "Discerned? Additional reasons? Oh, do tell." Nexin looked between Tag, Zane, and Ryn.

"This is not how we anticipated divulging this information, nor is it the timing we would have chosen." Zane looked pointedly at Tag, who met his look evenly. "Rolf, Nexin, in addition to Severyn Andrews, the songwriter and musician, I would like to introduce you to Demetria Xeno."

Rolf did little to hide his shock but stayed quiet and motionless. A mountain that remained sturdy regardless of the small quakes.

Nexin was struck momentarily silent. He dragged his hand through his blonde hair before bolting forward to grab her hands in his, searching her face. "Well aren't you a bombshell, in all sorts of ways. This deserves a righteous 'holy, what the fuck'. Demetria, my love, my betrothed? How could I not have seen?" Nexin joked, but his blue eyes were shrewd and assessing. "Actually, I still don't see."

"Behind every mask there is a face, and behind that a story." Rolf quoted quietly and her eyes flew to him.

"I'm still trying to determine why a songwriter-slash-musician, who is the niece of a successful businessman, is living a second life as a secretive operative," Tag inserted quietly.

She pulled her hands from Nexin's, swallowing hard but raising her chin. "That is not open for discussion."

Zane made a motion to speak.

"That—" She replied tightly. "—is not open for discussion."

Ryn stood and moved behind the armchair to face the five men. She looked from Rolf to Nexin and finally to Tag, her resolve hardening her grey eyes to steel.

"What you three need to decide, is if you will parade around as Severyn Andrew's security detail as well as team up with me on ops. Some ops," she corrected, "as needed."

She felt Kotan and Zane's eyes bore into her, but she kept her eyes trained on the three men who may potentially be part of her future. "You're right, Tag, I do not want, nor do I need, babysitters. But before all three of you agree to this, know that it's on the condition that there will be few, if any details, on the why. Either about my role, or the purpose of the ops, or the larger mission."

No longer relaxed, Tag shot her an incredulous look. "How can we accept the offer to work on a mission that we know nothing about? Don't know any details for?"

She stiffened, but remained calm. "You do that all the time, to some degree, do you not? Or do Zane and Kotan always give you a full synopsis of the why, who, and what for all your operations?"

"This is different."

"I don't see it that way. Besides, you were in the army. You know about compartmentalization. Need to know basis and all that."

Tag moved his long legs and was on his feet instantly. "I am no longer in the army and do not operate that way. There was a damn good reason why I chose to leave and join Zane."

"This is a non-negotiable item." She tilted her head back to maintain Tag's hard gaze and put up her hand to pause his vehement disagreement.

"But know this." Her eyes were dark; the three men now stood together, facing her. Seriousness etched on their faces, even the usual jovial, relaxed Nexin.

"The why is not illegal nor is it immoral. I will never ask you to put yourselves in any more danger than you naturally do by way of your current occupation. I will never withhold information that, if by doing so, will put you in harm's way. You are free to walk away at any time. And lastly, I will not lie to you from this moment forward. I may not be forthcoming in sharing details, but I will not lie to you."

She took advantage of the stunned silence as they absorbed the conditions she laid out and moved toward the door. Turning back, Kotan met her steadfast gaze and she could swear she saw a whisper of approval in his quiet onyx eyes.

"Rolf, Nexin, and Tag, if you're still here when I return at noon, I'll have my answer."

Chapter 27

Kenzo pressed his black face into her palm, nuzzling her affectionately. His strong head was a heavy weight and she relished his trust and the power of his body as he angled it to press against her.

"Make no mistake, I know your affection is tied to me having treats."

Kenzo snorted in response, as if indignant, but he threw back his powerful head when she started to brush him.

She couldn't make herself go to the big house quite yet. Coming back from the city she had veered off at the barns, purposefully averting her gaze from the house. She wasn't ready to see if the truck Tag, Rolf, and Nexin had brought was still here or not.

She wasn't ready to analyze the ramifications if they had chosen to leave.

The three horses had come thundering when she whistled, content to get out of the hot sun. And to get treats of course. Her visits and rides often included oats, apples, and brushing. She had developed a loyal following. Kenzo, the large, powerful, black and white paint was the most loyal of all.

Her phone buzzed again. Maari. Ryn put the phone back in her pocket, she needed more time to disconnect.

In her city studio, she had tried for an hour to work before finally abandoning the futile effort. Grabbing a late breakfast, Neara had taken one look at her in the bustling restaurant and led her to the back patio. She ordered Ryn to sit and was back with coffee, freshly squeezed juice, and a plate brimming with food.

"I cannot solve the heaviness I sense about you this morning, but I can ease an empty stomach. I'll ensure you're left in peace."

Tears burned the back of her eyes as she remembered Neara's intuition and thoughtful action.

She should be forsaken.

Instead she was blessed with people in her life to help her travel this difficult journey. Neara, Mason, Antonio, Lok, Maari, Nessa, Kotan. Even Zane with all his autocratic bullshit. Each one of them, regardless of how guarded she was, helped to heal a piece of her that was ripped open from being torn from her family.

They helped her, yet what did she offer them in return? Potential risk because of who she was.

Since her departure from the library earlier this morning, she had fully reconciled herself with the fact that she did indeed need Tag, Rolf, and Nexin. Needed their abilities and assistance if she wanted a chance to succeed, to keep those connected to her safe, and to survive her mission.

But that meant adding three more people that she had to figure out navigating her life of secrets with. To figure out how much truth to share.

Three more people who could be harmed because of her.

Ones she promised that she would not lie to. And yet, the very existence of Severyn Andrews was a lie.

If a promise was paired with a lie, was the promise immediately broken?

Kenzo nuzzled her, his breath hot on the bare skin of her shoulder, and she buried her face in his silky mane.

"Being a horse is way easier I suspect," she murmured, then louder, "I see you're still here."

Ryn turned to face the wall of three imposing men who had soundlessly entered the barn.

"She has eyes in the back of her head. Are you related to my mother?" Nexin took off his sunglasses, flashing his trademark smile.

"Straw may have dampened your steps but no amount of quiet matters with the horses. Their body language changes." She gave Kenzo's mane another two strokes before appeasing him with a chunk of apple.

"He fancies you. What's his name?" Tag slowly held out his hand to let the big horse get a sense of him. The other two mares, two sorrels, came to investigate as well, but Kenzo nipped at them.

She snorted. "He fancies treats. He's sniffing to see what you come to offer. A pig but a beauty. Kenzo, meet Tag, Rolf, and Nexin. The Japanese meaning of his name is strength and health, but he's still a pig."

The scent of Tag, citrus and sage, filled her senses. Close to her, enough for their shoulders to touch, his scent was stronger. The reaction of the horses to the approaching strangers wasn't the only thing that announced their arrival to her.

Distracted, but keenly aware of Rolf and Nexin silently watching them, she moved away from Tag and Kenzo to put the brush and materials away in the tack room.

"It isn't quite noon yet. If you stopped here on your way out, there's no need to give me any explanation." She stood, hands on hips, facing them, face neutral.

She figured it was Zane's problem to figure out the damage control of the three of them knowing that Severyn Andrews wasn't all that she appeared to be.

Rolf's dark hair was pulled back, the shadow of his stubble giving him a dark, attractive look. Dressed black on black he looked menacing yet was surprisingly gentle when he swiftly scooped up the grey tabby cat winding around his legs. Cletus instantly pressed his head along Rolf's rough stubble.

Traitor, she thought, but smiled at the loud purrs of Cletus' betrayal.

Nexin leaned lazily against the wooden beam chewing a piece of straw, giving her a slow drawl smile.

Tag's golden-brown eyes were dark in the shade of the barn but caught the glint of sunlight from outside. "We're here, not because we haven't left yet, but because we're staying. Welcome to the team."

Not one to waste time, Kotan was merciless and demanded they begin their training together immediately, regardless of the heat of the day. He ran them through endless drills to test endurance, strength, power, hand-to-hand fighting, knife-throwing, and sharpshooting at the secluded range on the property.

Kotan knew the physical abilities and limits of each one of them. The purpose was for him to assess how they worked together, as much as it was for Ryn to witness Team Alpha's skills and for them to witness hers.

Ryn held her own for the physical aspects and hand-to-hand fighting. Even against Rolf, who was the opponent to beat. For being such a large man, he was unbelievably agile and fast. She quickly realized he wasn't only on the team for his medical skills but was an accomplished mixed martial arts fighter.

She sat winded after her pairing with him, and Tag handed her some water. "You read your opponent well and are surprisingly strong."

"It's reassuring you three aren't here for your good looks and charm."

"She thinks we're cute." Nexin grabbed her hand, pulling her up. "But I'm the cutest, obviously."

Nexin and Ryn tied in the knife throwing and Tag, unsurprisingly, led in the shooting drills. Watching him work with a gun, like it was another limb, was slightly unnerving. Especially his deadly accuracy.

Lowering the binoculars after another bullseye, Nexin looked at her with a grin. "So, you're acro-cat-woman?"

"Acro-cat-woman?"

"My pet name for you after watching you free-fall from a building, land on your feet, scale and descend a fence within seconds. I thought it was a fitting name."

"Let's stick with Severyn, or Ryn," she said, biting back a smile.

"Ryn, I especially like. As well as your phrase of, how did that go last night guys—" Nexin paused, winking at her. "—ah yes, 'fucking, monkey-flying hell'." Nexin gave her a friendly push.

She groaned inwardly wondering how much they overheard of her heated outburst last night with Zane and Kotan. She wasn't proud of her loss of emotional control.

"Monkeys flying around would be hell." Rolf's large frame shuddered.

Tag popped to his feet and quickly decommissioned his gun. "It certainly was creative."

"Monkey's do that to your neck?" Rolf's physician healing eyes looked closely at the scratches she couldn't fully cover up in her training clothes.

Nexin sobered quickly, eyes on her marked neck. "Those look like they hurt like hell. Happen on an op?"

"Dangers of the game." She shrugged noncommittally. "Or maybe Cletus. He gets ornery, looking for treats." She joked lightly, hoping to subtly change the subject.

Nexin looped his arm over her shoulders. "Us three strapping, virile men are now here to stave off all sorts of depravity. And crazed monkeys in whatever hell we're bound to get ourselves into. Don't you worry, Rynnie, my pooh bear, we got your six."

"Don't you dare."

Rolf and Tag roared with laughter at her horrified expression and Kotan grinned while he strode up to join the group. Kotan was closest to Nexin in height but with a leaner build. Regardless of him being the male, Kotan commanded their full attention and respect.

"It was a good day. You all were able to see each other in action to learn each other's strengths and skills. You boys already know that about one another, but it is important to see how and where Severyn's attributes fit in. Of course, these were isolated executions of skills, in controlled settings. Tomorrow we expand that."

The wind tousled Kotan's dark hair, the breeze carried the scent of ocean air and a hint of a cooler evening. "I suggest you take advantage of the amenities we have. The pool, hot tubs, cold tubs, heating or cold packs. We reconvene for training tomorrow morning at eight."

Zane was grilling steaks when they returned to the house and they ascended like a pack of ravenous hounds. Nessa and Maari had plans in the city, although she had sensed her friend was reluctant to leave the presence of one flirty blue-eyed, blonde surfer look-alike.

Nexin picked at the last of the potatoes and grilled vegetables and considered Ryn out of the corner of his eye. "Where did you learn to fight like that?"

Tag paused wiping his hands on his napkin. "Breaking our agreement already?"

Them not prying was one of Ryn's conditions that she added when they decided to stay.

"It's an honest question after seeing you work today, Ryn."

"I've trained with Kotan." She said simply.

"According to the gossip mill, you've only come to live with your Uncle Zane in the past few years. By the level of your skill, I would assume you have trained much longer. Did you work with Kotan prior to coming here when you lived, where was it, in Switzerland?"

Nexin was treading a fine line and she knew he knew it. She rested her chin on interlaced fingers and remained casual. Here lies the trick of maintaining her cover story. Her life as Severyn Andrews was a lie, however, she would not compound that by speaking any further lies to her new teammates.

Zane and Kotan remained quiet, letting her decide how she wanted to address this.

"When I came here, I had—" Ryn rubbed her thumb over the dragonfly pendant tucked beneath her shirt, contemplating. "—time on my hands. Rather than sit idle, I turned to training. One could say, obsessively."

"Starve your distractions, feed your focus?" Rolf speared a juicy chunk of steak.

"She was a willing pupil and a quick learner. She had a good base of natural skill and instinct that was easy to hone further," Kotan added quietly.

"A strong purpose can lead to intense focus. Obsession doesn't always have to be bad. As I would say is the case in your situation." Nexin crunched a Brussel sprout.

She smiled and let it end there. Thankfully, so did Nexin. As they cleaned up supper, Tag joined her at the counter making her jump slightly.

"I'll wash, you dry."

"I prefer to wash, thank you very much."

"So do I. And as you can see, I'm the one in front of the sink so I beat you to it." Tag triumphantly snatched the dish cloth from her, sinking his hands into the water.

She laughed as he hissed at the heat. "You know what they say, if you can't take the heat...dry the dishes instead."

Tag turned on the cold water. "A good soldier knows how to improvise. And by the way, I grew up with three older sisters, so I know my way around getting bullied."

She relaxed slightly, realizing he was easy to joke around with if she let herself. "I'm a bully now, am I? Or are you teaching me some tricks of the trade for dealing with a bully?"

"Definitely a bully. You may appear all sweet and innocent, but I'm onto you."

They worked in silence as Tag washed the few larger dishes that didn't fit into the dishwasher while the others finished cleaning up. The guys made plans for their recovery evening and Zane gave them instructions to the pool area.

"Will you join us, Ryn?" Rolf rumbled quietly.

"I have some work that needs to be done. Thank you, though."

"Obsession doesn't only apply to your training. All work and no play makes for a very boring Ryn, you know." Nexin tried his best at a pout.

Ryn rolled her eyes as she walked out.

The pool area was a dream relaxation place and the guys took advantage of swimming a few laps to loosen tight muscles, then alternated between sitting in the therapeutic cold and hot tubs. To finish it off, they entered the hot pool area off to the end of the larger pool and Tag tipped his head back on the rock ledge.

"This isn't so bad after a day of training. The only thing we need now is a beer." Nexin looked hopeful that a beer would magically appear.

Rolf grunted and nodded his agreement.

"I, um, hate to bring this up. But I feel I would be remiss if I didn't."

Tag popped an eye open to glance at Nexin. Normally the guy spoke what was on his mind with no hesitation.

"Doubt is too strong of a word, but I have concerns about Ryn's youth and relative inexperience."

"We don't know of her experience or lack of," Rolf stated simply.

"Yes, that's true. But unless she was in the field since she was fourteen, I would say she's relatively inexperienced."

"True." Tag sat forward slightly, the water swirling around his broad chest. "But we've seen her in action somewhat in the field; she held her own."

"Yes, but not in hostile situations. The Strada op was an exception but there still weren't people opening fire. I do trust Zane and Kotan's assessment of her, but they truly don't know what she's fully capable of in situations like that either. That's why we're here, is it not? Because she is just now moving into those potential situations?"

"Are you concerned she'll freeze? She'll abandon her role and put us at risk?"

Nexin dragged his hand through his wet hair, a pained look on his face. "I don't know, Tag."

"I don't know how she'll handle herself in situations like that. None of us do. Even trained veterans in the field can be wild cards. I've seen highly trained soldiers freeze because of something in their environment, or in here." Tag tapped his head. "But I have a strong feeling that she would prioritize other's safety over her own."

Rolf looked them both square in the eye. "You would have had the same concerns about me. You must trust your gut. My gut is telling me I can count on her."

"The decision that I made this morning, to stay, hasn't changed. Seeing her in action today, she's really good but…" Nexin closed his eyes briefly. "It's a shitty world out there in the territory we wade in. I think my hesitation isn't for joining with her but rather that she shouldn't be touched by that world at all."

"Not our call," Rolf replied gruffly.

"No, no it isn't our call," Tag agreed quietly.

Ryn's ribs ached, her right shoulder burned, and her skin was irritable. She winced at the thought of how she probably smelled. She had yet to shower from the afternoon training and her evening run. The run, although it hadn't helped in the smell department, had burst the creative block she faced.

Tomorrow morning's deadline loomed since she'd only been

able to grab small chunks of time between the Strada mission, May's charity event, and now training with her new team. But she finally got a product she was pleased with and that fit the band's style.

She stretched her right shoulder but that did little to alleviate its displeasure after sitting at the piano for hours. The previous injury from her death scape made her think of Vlad and to be grateful she had survived the attempt on her life while her childhood friend did not.

"This song has elements of you in it, buddy." She closed her eyes, her heart aching with a wish that her friend was beside her.

"Holy shit, Ryn, you did more training?" Nexin walked in after a slight knock. "Or do you always have sweat stains from working on your music?" His blonde head was damp, and he looked comfortable in joggers and a t-shirt.

She schooled her face into a neutral mask, pushing thoughts of Vlad aside, and motioned to the treadmill. "A tool of my creativity."

Tag wandered in, beer in hand, jeans covering his long legs and an army t-shirt over his muscular torso. Her eyes took in the long length of him and she quickly turned away.

"Rolf ditch you?"

"He's in his element with Nessa in the medic suite. An impressive set up. Not really Tag's or my thing, but Rolf was a kid in a candy store."

Ryn stood, every muscle unhappy with the movement, but it helped chase off the melancholy. "Did he ever serve in the military?"

"No military medic training but the way he handles himself in the field, you wouldn't know otherwise. He has saved my and Nexin's ass more than we care to admit."

"Tag's more than mine." Nexin wandered over to the music equipment area, eyeing all the buttons and levers on the control consoles.

"No hacking skills needed there."

"But there's so many pretty things to push and pull."

The large screen at the end of the room started to flash and a loud ringing noise emitted from the console.

Shit.

She forgot Lok was connecting tonight. He was over in Europe and it was early morning for him. He had wanted her opinion on a song before he flew to a music festival.

"Don't press that," she yelled, but it was too late. Nexin's deft finger pressed the flashing button to make a life-size Lok appear on the screen.

Lok looked tired, but he smiled brightly at her. Seeing Tag and Nexin in the room with her, his smile faded, and he looked taken aback. "Good morning, I mean, evening, Ryn. I didn't mean to intrude." His shrewd eyes took in everything as he sized up Tag and Nexin.

"No, no, it's okay. They were just leaving."

"Aren't you going to introduce us, Ryn?"

Lok's brow arched at the familiarity Nexin used with her nickname.

She sighed. "Lok Bello. Nexin Walsh and Tag Hale. They are—"

"Her security detail," Tag completed for her.

Lok sat straight up, alarmed, and she shot Tag a dark look. "What has happened? You have always shut down the idea of security. Did something happen at the gala last night? Are you alright?"

She cursed silently at the concern etched on her friend's face.

"It's okay, it's not like that. Only Zane and Kotan being overly cautious and over-inflating my success as an artist."

"A musician." Lok insisted, but sat back down behind his console. His eyes continued assessing Tag and Nexin. "I don't think they're over-inflating it, especially after the coverage of you has exploded since May's event last night. You boys look capable enough." Lok's eyes widened. "And where you fall short, he will do fine, I'm sure."

Ryn turned to watch Rolf walk in, looking menacing in both size and his serious expression. Nexin and Tag bristled at Lok's comment about their falling short and she bit back a smile.

"Lok, I'll call you back in ten. That way we can work uninterrupted before you have to leave."

Lok gave the guys one more critical look and signed off.

The large screen went black and seeing the look on Tag's face, she snapped. "This isn't going to be a pissing match. There'll be no trouble with any of you with Lok. Got it? And please do not touch my equipment." She whirled on Nexin, anger all over her face.

"I'm sorry, Ryn. Me and shiny buttons." Nexin looked apologetic but shrugged. "However, to protect to you, we need to know the people in your life."

"He is unaware of your extracurricular activities," Tag surmised.

"Yes." She reclaimed control of her emotions. "I'm sorry I lost my temper, Nexin. I hadn't given thought to how I would explain you guys to Lok. And then you were all there."

Images of wolves circling each other trying to exert themselves as the dominant flashed in her mind.

She put her palms on the console and leaned toward them. "This is new to me. I need some space. Some time to get used to working in a team, to adjust to having this thrust into every aspect of my life."

"That's fair, Ryn. Right?" Rolf turned to his teammates.

"Understood," Tag said tersely and then more evenly. "Understood. It's getting late so we'll leave you be to finish with Lok so that doesn't impact on tomorrow's training."

At two in the morning Tag was still restless. He padded silently down the hallway in search of the kitchen and paused outside of

Ryn's studio. Light was poking out under the closed door, so he silently looked inside.

The room was quiet, the equipment turned off and the large screen that had featured the mega-DJ star Lok Bello was now black. He glanced toward the large wall of windows and saw a small foot perched on the back of the sofa that overlooked the black night beyond.

Ryn was asleep on her side with the grey tabby curled into the curve of her stomach. Carefully, he lifted the pack from her right shoulder while Cletus stoically watched him, guarding his human. Tag was unsure if it had been a cold or heat pack but, obviously, she had an injury that bothered her. Old or new—he would have to find out, as it could jeopardize them in the field.

Sensing no threat, Cletus snuggled back in and Tag looked down at Ryn while she slept. At the length of her, at the lines of her face relaxed in sleep. Images of watching her play weeks ago with Lok in New York ran through his mind. Zane and Kotan had deployed him to covertly watch and protect her should she need it. He went there as with any job, cool, detached, observant. Ready to deploy deadly force if needed to execute his role.

He noticed her quiet, shy nature when she had emerged onto the stage. But as she settled into the music, he watched her metamorphosis into a presence that commanded his complete attention. Sadness and pain had wisped across her face, but it was quickly gone. Replaced with an excited enthusiasm that portrayed the authentic contentment she felt behind the keyboard.

Looking at her tonight, he tried to reconcile that initially shy young woman with the fiery spirit of who they had met as Demetria Xeno and of the walled-off no-nonsense teammate they worked with today.

An enigma lay before him.

One that had no hesitation to take on someone who vastly outsized her, one that showed cunning and analytic skills to quickly assess her opponents and turn their weaknesses to her advantage.

A spitfire hell-bent on not fully trusting anyone and keeping her motivations and agenda all to herself. Someone who lived so secretively, yet, was in the public eye.

He gently placed a blanket over her and quietly shut the door.

Chapter 28

Ryn was in a foul mood. It matched the howling wind that swirled around her and the grey skies that blanketed the landscape.

She had woken up on the sofa in her studio with a wicked kink in her neck covered with a blanket she knew damn well she didn't cover herself with. She was pissed at herself for not waking to whoever had obviously come into the studio while she slept like the dead.

They could have stabbed her in the eye and killed her before she had a chance to twitch.

In all honesty, she didn't think for a second that would happen at the estate, even with the three relative unknowns that now slept there. And the safety she felt in the home did allow her to sleep so deeply. But she was still peeved at herself for not even stirring when someone was so close to her in the most vulnerable state.

On top of that, another nightmare came in the dark of night to steal her precious moments of sleep. This was not unusual but the intensity of them was startling. The ferociousness of the people's emotions and accusations in the dreams continued to escalate with each passing night.

The only reason she could attribute this to was the looming anniversary of Vlad's death, as well as her own death scape.

At least she didn't claw herself again or maim any other part of her body. That was a positive.

The other positive, she reminded herself as she trudged along, was that the band loved the song and only wanted to make minor changes. At least that didn't contribute further to her dark mood.

She scowled at the back of today's main thorn in her ass.

Kotan had left them to train alone together and Tag was one bossy piece of work. She kept pace behind him as he worked them through long fast-paced distances, short rapid sprints, and bursting through the trees while being as silent as possible.

"You sound like a herd of elephants, Ryn."

One branch snapped under her foot that she missed in her rapid dodging of them. One. "And you sound like a buzzing gnat that I'm going to squash soon."

Nexin's suppressed laugh came out as a half cough. Tag glared back at them over his shoulder.

Tag's powerful back muscles were evident through the shirt slick with sweat. His arms looked like bands of rigid steel as his powerful legs maneuvered him nimbly through the trees.

Regardless of the tight ass that was now level with her eyes as they powered up a hill, all she wanted to do was trip the bugger.

Her quads screamed as they raced up the hill, but she refused to falter her pace even slightly. They crested the hill and Ryn slammed into Tag who had come to a sudden stop, jarring her chin on his shoulder blade. She bit out a curse and moved quickly out of the way before she was steamrolled by Nexin and Rolf.

They were now on a part of the expansive estate property that Ryn didn't often go. Her long runs tended to loop by the cliff overlooking the ocean instead. A gully split through the trees at the top of the hill and a suspension bridge spanned the fifteen-foot-deep gap.

"That little gnat comment cost you. Give me twenty standard burpees. Fast or Nexin and Rolf will get too far ahead of us."

"Are you kidding me?"

Tag's rigid face brooked no argument.

She did as he demanded and sprinted to catch Rolf and Nexin as they were crossing the bridge. No longer wanting to trip Tag but to send his ass sailing over the side.

"You truly missed your calling, General Hale." She huffed derisively.

He stopped in the dead centre of the suspension bridge and turned to face her.

"You have a problem."

"I have a problem? Of course, I have a problem. What the hell is this?" Her eyes flared and her feet spread in a solid stance, signalling her anger. "From the looks that Nexin and Rolf have been exchanging this isn't how you guys normally train. So why the military rule? To show me who's boss? Who's in charge?"

Loose strands from her braid whipped her face, but she made no move to push them away. To do anything that would disrupt the stare down she was having with the very alpha male of Team Alpha.

"A team that trains together, comes home alive together. We change up our training methods."

"Bullshit. You claim you're no longer in the army and don't operate that way, but when it suits your purposes, you whip out that card. This is some sort of power game and you know it. You're trying to show me my place."

"I'm trying to show you to work with a unit, as a unit. Take this for example."

He stepped toward her, and in a blink, she dangled over the edge of the suspension bridge with Tag crouching down to clutch her arm under the bottom rung of the wires. She jerked her arm, thinking the drop would hurt but wouldn't damage anything vital. He held fast.

Her face red with anger, gritting her teeth at the pain in her ribs, she pulled up on his arm to do a one-arm pull up and swung her legs over the side, rolling quickly to her feet. She whirled on him with fire spitting out of her eyes. "Are you fucking mad?"

"This is something we do in ranger training when people are not falling in line. A reminder that we are to work as a unit, or it all falls apart."

"That stunt had nothing, nothing," she yelled, "to do with showing me how to work as a team. And everything to do with demonstrating yourself as the commander and I as your subordinate. All you're trying to prove is that you have power over me."

She whirled around and stomped off the bridge to the grassy area where Nexin and Rolf were watching, stunned.

"I am not a goddamn fucking Ranger and I did not ask for your help."

"We didn't ask for this either."

"And yet you took the assignment. You're getting paid to do a job, what the hell does it matter to you? This is just a job to you." She jabbed a finger at him. "This is my life. Other people are relying on me to—" She snapped her mouth shut. Her chest heaved with anger and unreleased emotion.

Tag's golden-brown eyes were hard and fierce as he stood toe to toe with her. "As team leader, it is my responsibility that everyone gets home safely and is competent to carry out their roles. And yes, it is a job, our job. Yet, here we are willing to risk our lives even when one team member does not truly want us here, does not want to trust us."

"Would you? Did you? Did you three immediately trust each other at the start? I don't know any of you from shit and yet you, Zane, and Kotan think I'm supposed to kiss your goddamn asses. Trust everything blindly. I'm still alive today, because a developed lack of trust has served me well."

She turned to leave and found an iron grip clamped around her arm. A blanket of eerie dead calm fell over her. "Let me go."

"I will not."

She moved like a rattlesnake, hiding in the grass, waiting to strike - fast and precise. She executed a few movements with her arm to loosen Tag's advantageous grip and flipped to spiral up his body like a corkscrew. Wrapping her legs around his neck, Ryn whipped him to the ground and rolled as soon as her body hit the hard surface.

She left her new teammates in the clearing with their jaws hanging open.

Nessa sought her out in her studio carrying a tray ladled with supper. The tray looked abnormally large compared to her small frame and Ryn hurried over to relieve her of it. Cursing her stubbornness and that Nessa felt the need to trudge the heavy thing all the way up there.

"Thank you, but you didn't have to do that Nessa. I would have gone to the kitchen when I was hungry."

Nessa was breaking her cardinal rule of people not eating on their own and off in their secluded areas of the house.

Ryn knew she was avoiding Tag, Nexin, and Rolf. She had secluded herself and pounded out her anger and frustration the rest of the afternoon.

After the anger and frustration ebbed, then guilt reared its nasty little head. And she did her best to pound that into oblivion as well.

Tag did have it coming.

Somewhat.

But still, she could have acted with a bit more grace.

There was something about him that made her flare up like dry kindling with sudden and, surprisingly, strong emotion. It frustrated her to no end.

She had become adept at masking her raging emotions, so others were unaware. And yet he had proven he could get under her skin to have her wanting to shriek like a banshee, within a minute.

Nessa's voice snapped her out of her brooding.

"You know that I know, you're avoiding them. But…" Nessa sat gracefully on the piano stool, her eyes kind and understanding. "I know this is a big adjustment for you. I heard there was some, er, challenges, this afternoon after Kotan left."

Ryn groaned and flopped herself over the back of the sofa. Staring out at the scenery, upside down, reminded her that she used to love doing this as a child. "I lost it. Basically told them, well, Tag anyway, to go screw himself."

Nessa's face appeared over the back of the sofa, her black hair gliding over the sharp bones of her jawline as she peered down at Ryn. "Do you accept them? Or better yet, do you want to work with them? You need to first decide - truly decide - if you're willing to work with a team. And then beyond that, moving forward, you have to accept them and all that comes with them. It's your choice, however, you have to fully commit to whatever you decide."

Nessa patted her leg. "He rattles you. That's not necessarily a bad thing."

Ryn continued to stare out at the darkening sky long after Nessa quietly left the room.

Ryn walked the hallway on the bottom level of the house, away from the pool area, and ran her fingertips along the wall covered with textured ivory wallpaper. She loved the suede feel of it and the ridges, some rough, some smooth.

The door loomed ahead but she forced her feet to keep moving, calmed her nerves, and readjusted the tray she carried. Beyond that door, she wasn't sure of the reception she'd receive. If they told her to go play on the interstate with razor blades, well, she kind of deserved it.

The fact that they were still here, said something though.

And she did come bearing gifts. A truce of sorts.

Three heads turned when she entered the entertainment and games room. One dark, one blonde, and one with colouring somewhere in between.

"You're heaven sent, my little Ryn-Ryn, the train that could." Nexin rushed over to help her with the tray of nachos and beer.

"Jesus, you keep getting better and better renditions." Sarcasm dripped from her voice.

"The true sign of a great name."

"Would you like to join us?" Tag pushed out of his chair and pulled out the one next to him. "Twenty gets you a buy in."

Taken aback by his welcome, Ryn shook her head. "No, thank you, I—"

Nexin passed the beer around and started devouring the cheesy mound of nachos. "You make these? Top notch. So much cheese. And come join us, you can spare to lose twenty bucks I'm sure."

"You assume I don't know how to play poker." Thanks to her three older brothers, she was actually a sharpshooter at poker, but they didn't need to know that.

"Sit." The single word was gentle but still a command. And coming from the man-giant in the chair on the other side of Tag, one tended to respond.

"Any chance your raven-haired friend is with you tonight?" Nexin asked innocently.

"If you mean Kotan or Nessa—" She gave him a small smirk.

"Brat."

"Is this one of yours?" Rolf asked, but she was perplexed. He pointed up at the speaker.

"Not every song Lok plays is one that I have written or played pieces in." She laughed easily.

"You do collaborate with him a lot. Have been tied to him publicly often."

"Tied to him publicly?" She was curious where Tag was going with this.

"Seen with him, mentioned with him." Tag shrugged.

"Is that a problem?"

"No problem. We need to know the nature of your

relationships and get to know who is in your circle better."

"If you want to ask me if I'm sleeping with Lok then get to it, Tag. But no, I'm not sleeping with, or romantically involved, with him in any way."

"Have you ever been?" Nexin peered at her innocently.

"That has little bearing to the current status of the issue."

She could of swore Tag's shoulders tightened again at her elusive answer. "I would like a full dossier of each of your relationships on my desk in the morning."

"Touché." Nexin winked.

"Well, I really am glad the little matter of my relationship status is settled." She glanced around the table at the three men assigned to be her team.

Out with it already, coward.

"As for today." She looked around the table again and ended with looking Tag square in the eye. He leaned back, crossing his arms over his chest, and she did her best to ignore how the movement made his pecs contract. "I want to apologize for the way I acted today. For my insolence."

"You told me that you've been doing this solo since you started. It can be hard to get over that hurdle."

She jarred slightly at Tag's recollection of a comment she said to him in the hotel elevator the first time they met. The memory of their kiss, his body close to hers, his forehead resting on hers, the acceleration of both their breaths, and his question if she would be okay on her own. Looking into his eyes now, she knew he was recalling the memory as vividly as she.

She swallowed hard. "But that doesn't excuse my lack of control." She paused, drawing a deep breath in. "Even as a child, I was independent and loathed having to rely on others to help me."

Three pairs of surprised eyes continued to look at her. Surprised by her willing admission to something of her past.

She ignored the myriad of feelings that caused and pressed on.

"I can accept authority. However, I need to know that I'm a valued member of the team and not some burden that you guys are saddled with."

"You clearly don't need a babysitter, Ryn. The way you got yourself back up on the bridge and how you took Tag down in under ten seconds…wowsa." Nexin whistled quietly before he crammed more nachos in his mouth.

"You did hold your temper for an inordinately long time. Kudos." Rolf tipped his beer in her direction.

Tag quietly assessed her while he took a long swig of his own beer.

"You did aim to insult our integrity. Well, my integrity. And if I was less of a man, I'd be embarrassed by being bested so quickly by you. But pride and ego be damned, I'm pleased. You handled yourself well."

She processed in stunned silence, then finally demanded, "That was a test?"

Tag grabbed the plate of nachos before they were completely demolished by Nexin and Rolf.

"Yes. I pushed and baited you to see what you were made of. How you responded to authoritarian instruction. Because believe me, it's imperative to have that in crisis situations. How much it took to get you supremely pissed." He shoved a nacho chip dripping with cheese into his mouth. "And how you handled yourself once you were supremely pissed."

Tag cracked one of the beers open and offered it to her, watching her closely to see how she was taking the news that he had played her. "I have to apologize myself though. I did take it a bit further than I anticipated. Responded with a bit more emotion than I normally am known for. For my loss of control of my temper, I apologize."

"So, you didn't intend to throw me off the side of a bridge?"

Rolf's laugh rumbled. "Oh no, he completely intended to do

that."

Tag gave her a devilish smile and an impish light danced in his eyes. "I admit it was an extreme example of how we cannot fight each other while we're in the field. And how we need to rely on one another. As a team."

"I can relate, Ryn. Not to getting thrown off the bridge, of course, but getting used to the team idea. The type of work I did in the CIA was very much solo work. There were no team members there on a day to day basis. When I made the choice to leave the CIA and accept Zane's offer to complete the dream team with Tag and Rolf, they took a big chance on me that I could be a functional team member too."

Nexin's normal joking demeanour was replaced with stark seriousness. "If I can do it, you can. We're willing to bet on you. Will you bet on us?"

"What made you three decide to leave your careers and work with Zane and Kotan?"

"She does avoid answering questions by asking more questions." Nexin whispered to Tag. "We're onto ya, sista." Nexin tossed popcorn at her which she snatched from the air.

"Our answer may influence her answer." Rolf shuffled the cards. "My path crossed with Zane's in a series of trauma victims that were the result of a vicious drug. Not one of them survived and I was powerless to stop it. I worked with Zane to help end it though. He helped me see I could still help people but could do more by eliminating the root of the problems, rather than always dealing with the aftermath."

Nexin sighed heavily and pushed his beer away. "I had to betray and kill an asset I had cultivated for the better part of five years. Not because of their actions or anything they did. But because my boss lady said it needed to go down in order to get a bigger fish. It was my last straw."

Ryn stared at Nexin's sombre face, his blue eyes lowered with self-loathing. "The Slaughterer of Lambs."

"What?" Nexin questioned with a tiny smile.

"Virginia Ruthley?"

"How dare you utter her name aloud." Nexin gasped theatrically.

Worry pinched Tag's brow. "You know Virginia? She knows of you and your role with Zane?"

"Very little. I steer clear when it comes to her. Whatever Zane's relationship is with her, he keeps me, as Severyn or Demetria, off her radar as much as possible."

"Good to have our little Ryn join us on the anti-VR team, wouldn't you say boys?"

"Agreed." Rolf replaced her empty beer with a fresh one.

"And you?"

Tag's eyes were lowered, and she watched his Adam's apple move a few times waiting for him to speak.

"I loved being a soldier. The order, the line of command. You knew what your job was, knew the person beside you did as well. I loved the team-ness of it, knowing that your squad had your back and you had theirs. We might have been in the shittiest shit holes on the planet, but I felt we were doing something good. To protect those that couldn't protect themselves. That made all the killing a bit easier to accept, to deal with."

No one spoke or moved when Tag paused, his eyes still lowered.

"But you start to question who you're protecting, and the why, when the innocents start to be the pawns. It wasn't always like that," he looked at her, his face filled with sadness. "Until it was. I was home in Hawaii on leave and Zane approached me, laid out the opportunity to work with him. I could still protect those that had no one else to stand for them, but I would be more in control with him. Know who I was protecting, know the why, the details and have some op control. But I turned him down and went back on another tour. My last one."

"What happened?" She asked, even though she was afraid to do so.

"There was a little girl. Only three or four. She lived in the house with a high-level target. I had met her the day before when she dropped her doll when she was out with her nanny. The nanny was working with us and was to get her and the girl out at my signal before the drone strike happened."

"They didn't let you give the signal." She whispered.

Tag shook his head.

Nexin finished for his friend. "Our boy here went a bit berserk on his commanding officers. Got his ass hauled back stateside immediately. He would have been court marshalled, but Zane stepped in somehow and they allowed Tag an Honourable Discharge."

"He didn't do it to manipulate me. It was a no-strings-attached sort of thing, but I eventually took him up on his offer."

"So, there you have it. Some of the dream team's dirty laundry." Nexin looked expectantly at her, finishing the last nacho chip.

Rolf leaned his elbows on the table, the table shifting slightly under the weight. "Will you bet on us?"

She slapped a twenty on the table. "May the flop be with us."

Chapter 29

Tag threw back the covers and flipped his legs over the side of the bed. Scrubbing his hands over his face, he looked around the spacious room. They usually had little face to face contact with Zane and Kotan, and certainly had never stayed at their personal residence before.

He was restless. Every time he closed his eyes to sleep, he saw a beautiful face, surrounded by a mass of wavy hair, swirling with browns, blondes, and streaks of red. A face with the most gloriously unique eyes he had ever seen. Light grey as the early morning sky or dark and hard as steel. Eyes she was careful to keep shielded. Eyes, that he caught glimpses of, that were haunted by her hidden secrets and demons from her past.

He wondered if she went back up to her studio, her sanctuary, after she robbed them blind playing poker.

Unable to resist any longer, he left his room, but was disappointed when there was no light shining underneath the door of her studio. Silently cursing himself, he turned to go back to his room. What would he have done if she was up, anyway? What would he have said to her as to why he came to seek her out?

Would he admit to her that he continually replayed their kiss in his mind? Remembering explicitly how she smelled, tasted. How her lips felt under his, how her body felt pressed tightly against his. How he very much wanted to repeat that experience with her.

He clenched his hands to stop his train of thoughts when he stopped dead, instantly alert. Straining, he listened to the quiet of the house.

There it was again.

He walked faster toward the noise; his heart accelerating when he recognized the faint voice was Ryn's. And heard the terror in it.

He sprinted the last short distance and shoved the door open, ready to smash whoever was hurting her, but he only saw Ryn's form on the bed, twisting in the moonlight. His training and instincts naturally took over and he quickly cleared the room to make sure no one was there before he turned back to the bed.

Ryn's long bare legs were twisted in the covers and her tank top rode up slightly. The bronze dragonfly pendant he spied earlier glittered in the moonlight against the sheen of her skin right above the swell of her breast. She gasped and her hands flew to her throat to clutch at her skin. He bolted to the bed and grabbed her hands, understanding now how she had gotten the previous marks on her slender neck.

He sat beside her to hold her flailing hands and spoke gently, trying to wake her. To get her to breathe.

"It's okay. Ryn, wake up. Breathe, you can breathe. Ryn, wake. Breathe." He shook her gently, holding both her hands in his to keep them away from her delicate skin. "Breathe and come back to me."

She bolted upright looking around wildly. Finally remembering she could breathe, she took great shuddering breaths and began to shake violently.

"Ryn, you're in your room. You're safe. You are safe. It's okay."

He wrapped his arms tightly around her. Her heart thudded against his chest as he held her, her body felt so small and fragile as the shaking wracked her frame.

He held onto her, letting her take from him what she needed. What he could give her to calm her, to remove the nightmare from her mind. Her hands clenched and relaxed against his chest; her face buried deep into his neck. Her breath hot against his skin as she inhaled and exhaled deeply. And with each breath she took, she relaxed in his arms until she was back in a deep sleep.

Tag whispered into her tangled hair as he smoothed it back and gently laid her on the bed. She murmured, but he couldn't make it out as he readjusted her covers. Her brow was pinched by whatever plagued her in sleep and the tension eased when he softly brushed his thumb over her forehead.

He watched her for a few moments before turning to leave. Even sleeping, the power of her tugged at him.

"Bug, I'm here. I didn't leave. Bug."

The restless agitated state returned, renewed in its fervour. The horror of her nightmare spiralled from the depths to grip her once again, pulling her back into its clutches.

"Ryn, it's just a nightmare. It's okay."

She turned toward him, responding to his voice, her eyes fathomless pools of pain. "I left her."

The anguish in those three words sucked the breath from him, pulling the strength from his knees.

Not sure if she was awake or still stuck in that nightmarish state, he sat on the bed to gather her close again. Holding her tight, he stroked her back, murmuring into her hair, hoping to ease her torment. As before, she breathed deeply, as if drawing in the scent of him was her lifeline to escape the ghosts that chased her. Tag continued to hold her tight, hand skimming over her hair, whispering until he felt the tension release from her completely once again.

Instead of re-adjusting the covers this time, he laid down, holding her close. He stroked her hair down her back while she buried her face into his chest breathing steady and calmly as sleep settled over them both.

The morning sunrise peeked through the opening of the burgundy brocade curtains and Tag blinked the sleep out of his eyes. Momentarily confused by his surroundings and the warm hand that curled lightly on his chest.

Shit. He only meant to stay until she had completely settled into a peaceful sleep. She hadn't stirred again throughout the night, so she must have slept more soundly.

Not wanting to have to awkwardly explain why he was in her bed half naked, he gently disentangled their legs and laid her hand on the pillow.

He also didn't need her to wake and see the evidence of her effect on him either. Praying she didn't suddenly wake to find him in her room, staring down at her with an erection, he silently left her room.

Saying another prayer of thanks that he didn't encounter anyone else in the hallway, he quickly went to his room for a long, cold shower.

The smell and sound of sausage sizzling on the grill greeted Ryn in the kitchen all awash with bright sunlight. The skies had cleared from yesterday's miserable overcast, and promised a beautiful, clear day.

Rolf worked competently at the counter, his long, dark hair pulled back to showcase his high, arched eyebrows. The lightness of his eyes stark in contrast to his otherwise dark colouring. His perpetual look of a five o'clock shadow lingered and he signalled her to sit.

"Good morning, my dear."

Ryn burst out laughing. "Nessa, I didn't even know you were behind Rolf."

Nessa looked up at Rolf, who was a good foot and a half taller than her. "A behemoth of a man, but not a monster." She patted his large arm. "And a master chef."

"I appreciate you making breakfast, Rolf. Can I help with anything?"

"You can sit." Rolf wore a content smile, multitasking with the food prep.

"Is Maari coming out today, or soon, Nessa? I haven't seen her much the last few days."

"She's burning the midnight and all-day oil. Had a brainwave with her father, so she won't rest until she flushes it out."

Rolf and Nessa finished laying breakfast out as the rest of the crew came in. Sausage, eggs, fried potatoes, fresh waffles, fruit. They were gearing up for a busy day from the looks of it.

"Did I hear mention of your beautiful daughter, Nessa? I had the pleasure of meeting her at the charity soiree."

Nessa's sly grin implied she had heard all about Nexin and Maari's meeting from Zane. And most likely, from Maari herself.

Ryn moved out of the way so the food procession could start and walked over to the coffee bar. Tag squeezed in beside her and grabbed a mug for each of them. She paused, inhaled briefly and contemplated Tag.

The smell of him.

The hint of citrus mixed with faint sage hit her senses again. Keenly aware of his arm pressed into hers while he waited for her to pour them coffee.

She watched his Adam's apple move as he swallowed, growing surprise spread through her when she raised her eyes to meet his.

"Good morning," his voice was quiet and husky.

Vague memories of his soothing voice over the roaring horror in her dream.

The feel of his hands as he stroked her hair, her face, her back.

The feel of his powerful body and arms holding her close as he whispered, she was safe.

The smell of him drawing deeply into her as she finally found peace and drifted away into a dreamless sleep.

"About last night…" He paused, looking unsure of his next words. "I'm not sure if you were aware...but I heard you. You were very agitated, and I couldn't get you to fully wake. I laid with you, as that seemed to be the only thing that calmed your nightmare. I tried to leave."

This close she could easily see the specks of green and the faint swirls of orange in his golden-brown eyes. Eyes the colour of autumn.

"I'm sorry if I invaded your privacy or if I offended you in any way." He continued to look down at her, unable to break her steady gaze.

She placed a hand on his chest, feeling it jump under her touch. "I didn't dream of you there."

"No." He replied hoarsely.

"I woke up feeling the most rested I have in a long time." She removed her hand and broke the spell wrapping around her. "Thank you."

She poured them coffee, succeeding in keeping her hand steady, but chose a seat away from Tag. However, having him sit across from her wasn't any easier than having his body physically close, and she struggled to keep her gaze away from his. If any others around the table noticed, they thankfully kept it to themselves.

After breakfast dishes were dispersed, they were to join Kotan and Zane in the battle room.

Nexin belched and patted his stomach, walking along the hallway. "Rolf, my man, you always cook a mean meal and know how to make a man comatose."

Rolf, in his usual quiet way, smiled and grunted his acknowledgement. His glance lingered on the medic suite as they passed by. He had a lot in common with Nessa and enjoyed being in that space. She couldn't say the same.

Kotan and Zane were ready for them when they arrived. They had blueprints spread out on the table and the computer screens ready to go.

They were heading into Boston today to get their feet wet working in a real-live field situation as a four-unit team. Ryn knew it was a test of her willingness to work as a unit and to work out any kinks that could later mean disastrous and deadly results.

Zane started speaking as Kotan pulled up the relevant information on the screen.

"Meet Henry Wormid. Real last name is Worm, but he legally changed it, understandably. He's a financial lawyer and partner at Powerstern and Associates. Lately, he has quite a track record of clients being financially ruined while he's their lawyer."

Seven different faces flashed onto the screen.

"A real bad luck charm." Nexin stepped closer to read more information on the clients. "None of the reasons for them seeking a lawyer indicate they were facing that severe of a financial crisis."

"No." Zane agreed. "The single common denominator between these clients is the lawyer."

"He's been investigated by the authorities? By his overseeing association that monitors lawyer ethics and conduct?" Tag asked Zane.

"He has. He has been cleared on both fronts."

"You believe otherwise."

"We do. Unfortunately, the authorities don't have the leeway we do, the technology nor the abilities of this man." Zane smiled over at his lifelong friend and partner.

Kotan was serious and intent as he brought up yet another screen.

Ryn sucked in a breath through clenched teeth. "He engineered their financial downfall. He used his access and knowledge of them to embezzle their money and secretly blackmail his own clients."

"Fits his last name." Rolf's face filled with disgust.

"But to what end? Besides padding his own pockets, this isn't a sustainable strategy. Eventually the finger would point to him or he would become a pariah and clients would avoid him since he would be a bad luck charm like Nexin said. I don't see the long game here."

Tag contemplated with his arms crossed over his muscular chest. "There is no long game, Ryn. This isn't an organized, methodical criminal. This is someone acting on impulse, driven by the thrill of his success. He has no plan."

"Just relishin' the moment isn't he, the twat. It's all about the power. And he's drunk with it."

Rolf nodded in agreement with Nexin. "He could be a wild card."

"Could become volatile with desperation." Tag continued the team's assessment of their target.

Zane and Kotan exchanged a look, pleased by the process unfolding in front of them.

"Why not just hand this over to the authorities on a silver platter? Even with their own investigation being a dud, could this information not be anonymously given for them to act on and build a case against him?" Nexin cleaned his fingernails as he leaned against the desk.

"We have no guarantee that they can or would use the information you see here to successfully prosecute him given the means it was collected." Kotan unfolded his frame from the stool and moved away from the computer console.

Zane regarded the four of them. "And it provides a low risk field training opportunity for you to work out your kinks as a team."

No eyes turned her way, but she knew the point was directed at her.

"As you know, you need to infallibly trust each other, know how each other works, before we ramp up deploying to the next phases of our lead mission."

"It is a good opportunity all around. Now, the target has a safe in his office and we suspect—"

"Suspect?" Ryn interrupted Kotan.

"Yes, suspect. I realize we are asking you to operate with a large unknown. But this is a white-collar crime category, one with low risk. As pointed out though, the target, if threatened, can be a wild card and unpredictable. You all need to act accordingly."

They ran through the details of executing the op and bantered back and forth to pick out the weaknesses and potential threats that needed to be mitigated. Everyone dispersed, comfortable with the plan, the roles they were to play, and had what they needed to disguise their identities.

Tag walked alongside her, back to their rooms, as Rolf and Nexin hustled ahead. The sage and citrus scent of him assaulted her senses again and she felt the magnitude of his presence. The quiet power in his stride as he strode beside her.

"You good?"

She nodded and felt her hair glide unbound along her cheek and neck. Soon the dreaded skull cap and wig would be planted on. "You worried about me falling into line soldier?"

He shrugged noncommittal. "It's not how you've operated in the past, but it needs to be."

"I'm not here to usurp your leadership position, Tag," she joked, but her face was serious. "Honestly. But I also cannot act under the pretense that I need to be directed for every one of my steps that I take out there."

"Agreed."

She didn't realize they had passed the room where Tag was staying until they stood outside her door. The hallway was deserted with Rolf and Nexin already inside their rooms readying for departure.

Tag leaned closer to her and she pushed back against her door to give more distance between them as he braced his palms on either side of her head.

"I worry about my team falling in the field. Not about falling in line. The same goes for you. You're one of mine now."

His eyes looked the colour of chestnuts in the hallway that was lit only by the light streaming in from the skylight above.

Those eyes dropped to her lips and trailed down the length of her neck. A touchless caress that sent waves of reaction through her. She squeezed her hands into fists to stop them from rising to roam over the powerful plane of his chest and through his close-cropped light brown hair.

His eyes snapped back to hers, slight shock settling in them. As if he woke from a trance to find himself so close to her, her pinned between him and the door. He smiled slightly but didn't move away from her. Instead, he pushed a tendril of her hair behind her ear, letting the soft length of it trail through his fingers.

The intimacy and tenderness of the action made her gasp quietly.

"Be ready in fifteen."

Chapter 30

The skull cap, wig, facial prosthetics and skin colouring, along with Maari's anti-detection facial cream, were all in place. With her height, she was satisfied she realistically looked to have Japanese heritage. The goal for every disguise was to have little in common with how Severyn Andrews looked.

They travelled in separate vehicles into the city. Normally they would never leave the estate in their disguises to avoid any connection of their op activities to their real lives. However, Kotan and Zane assured them it was a low risk, fairly uncomplicated op and were comfortable with them leaving from there.

They were to meet up with Tag and Rolf once they had secured a van to replicate it as one from the computer repair consulting firm. Since Ryn and Nexin were the ones executing their roles in public, there was no benefit in risking any cameras picking them up before the van was secured.

"You're quiet. Not that I've found you to be a chatterbox." Nexin looked over at her with a black faux hawk, neck and full arm sleeve of tattoos, and body padding to disguise his lean frame.

She shoved down the memory of Tag's closeness and his actions. She couldn't afford to analyze that now. "It isn't necessary when there's already one present. Your disguise is interesting. I would've thought you'd go for a bit more nerd."

"Oh, my dear, the technology field has become more sophisticated than that. It's a playground for all makes and models. An equal opportunity employer you could say."

She pulled up the blueprints for the building that Powerstern and Associates was in, as well as the two adjacent to it. She restudied them even though she had committed them to memory. And they would have Zane as the bird in the sky directing them if needed thanks to Kotan's hacking skills into the building's cameras.

Nexin rubbed his face. "So, Maari is the one who made this facial cream? I'd like to get to know her better."

Ryn snorted and cut her gaze quickly at Nexin before her brown-coloured eyes turned back to the blueprints.

"Smart and creative. Maybe you could put in a good word?"

"Not even gonna dip my baby toe into that shit pool. You're on your own to navigate that one."

"Some sort of friend you are."

Tag's voice came over their earpieces. "Ready. We didn't have to replicate, got the real deal."

Tag gave them the address of where they would pick them up in the 'borrowed' computer repair van. Once there, they hopped into the front seats and Tag communicated to Kotan they were ready.

"I am in and sending it now." Kotan hacked into Powerstern and Associates mainframe and sent a surge.

It wasn't an electrical surge that destroyed any part of the system but rather a surge of code that masked his presence and made it look like havoc was raging throughout with their system.

Within a few minutes, the phone rang, with the call diverted from the real computer repair company to them. Tag answered with a nasally, annoyed voice.

Ryn suppressed a smile.

"Of course, yes, we'll see about getting a team there soon."

The yelling on the other end of the line was loud and clear for them all to hear.

"Oh, very well, just give me a moment. Okay, I have a team fairly close that's finishing with a client. Yes, they can be there in ten minutes. No, they cannot get there any sooner. Yes, I will tell them without haste." Tag's nasally voice drawled sarcastically. "Have someone waiting in the lobby to expedite them through security and up to where they need to go."

Phase one. Create the crisis and control the urgency.

Exactly eleven minutes later, the van pulled up in front of the building where Powerstern and Associates resided and Nexin and Ryn grabbed their equipment bag. They strolled leisurely into the main entrance.

"Here to see about Powerstern's computer issues," Ryn stated to the front reception and security desk of the building. Nexin leaned against the desk, wearing a look of bored disdain. Both wore the second skin black gloves Maari created with no worry of sticking out, as it wasn't outlandish for repair techs to wear hand protection.

"Finally, you're here. You are late." A peckish, round woman huffed her way toward them and snapped at the security guards. "They're with me. No, no they're good I said. We need them upstairs stat. Everything is ground to a halt with our computers and people need documents and are waiting for court."

Ryn arched an eyebrow at Nexin and mouthed, *Super important things, you know.*

"I saw that missy," the lady slammed open the security arm and they sauntered slowly through. "Hurry," she hissed as she marched off.

The woman's demeanour didn't improve on the elevator ride up to the sixteenth floor. Nexin peppered her with questions to discern the problem.

The nasty woman finally left them in the server room and they quietly checked in with Kotan on the status of his hack and control over the system.

"Stable and steady."

"All clear outside," Tag reported.

"Eyes inside are up. Target is in the cafeteria. Route to target's office is clear," Zane reported.

Phase two. Execute the plan.

Nexin and Ryn quickly slipped out of the server room with their bag and made their way toward Wormid's office. Nexin spouted computer-ese and potential diagnoses of the problem for others in the vicinity to overhear. Although, many people were taking advantage of the no-computer access for an early lunch. It's amazing the amount of work that's now tied to a computer.

They slipped inside the thieving lawyer's office and took in the ornate furnishings.

"Spares no expense on surrounding himself with nice things." Nexin's look of disdain was back.

"Thrilled by the fact that his clients unknowingly paid for it all while he watches them crumble and fall apart before him." Rolf's low voice carried his disgust.

Her jaw hardened as she thought of the worm of a man who occupied this office. "Any additional security features in here?"

"None that I'm picking up on site," Nexin said.

"None I have picked up either," Kotan added.

Nexin pulled out a tablet and started the hack on the electronically protected safe. He moved closer to the safe as the signal was weak.

Ryn pulled out the lock device that was similar to the one destroyed on the Strada op, when the blast had sent her flying and she landed on that cursed rock. At least her ribs had stopped hurting for the most part. She realized she hadn't thanked Rolf yet for the compression wrap and made a mental note to do so.

"Ready."

She placed the device on the safe and keyed in the sequence Kotan rattled off. Nexin continued on his tablet, not looking up or breaking his concentration.

"Come on you dirty stud. Let go of the code."

A beep finally emitted from the safe and the door swung open.

Nexin slipped the tablet back into the bag and she added the contents from the safe - an external hard drive, ledgers, legal pads scribbled with notes of ideas and planning, and stacks of cash.

Zane clicked in over their earpieces. "Move. Now. Target is en route."

Phase three. Get the hell out of Dodge.

They slipped out of the office, Nexin talking nonchalantly to her. "The cable is fried. I think I have another one back in the van that we can use to repair the section. Hopefully that works, otherwise the whole cable length will have to be replaced."

"So, does that mean we could be down longer?" A short, thin lawyer with slicked hair whined from the door of his office.

Henry Wormid glanced at them as he appeared around the corner and went into his office.

"Possibly a day," Nexin replied and continued walking, pushing Ryn slightly ahead of him. He readjusted the bag on his shoulder.

"Are you effing kidding me?" the short lawyer huffed.

Henry was back in the hallway sputtering, his face as red as an overripe tomato. "Stop! Stop them! They've been in my office. It, it must have been them all this time. The ones that have been compromising my clients. Stop them!"

"Slimy fuck." Nexin threw the bag strap over his other shoulder so it would be more secure. "Run."

As chaos erupted behind them, they sprinted down the hallway and shoved people back into their offices as they whizzed by.

"We split up," Nexin said as they thundered down the stairwell, the sound of confused turmoil echoed in the cement structure as the stairwell door banged open.

"No, I don't like that." Ryn vehemently disagreed.

"Me either," Tag agreed.

The noise in the stairwell increased as Henry shrieked behind them, calling for security. More doors banged open further down below them.

"We divide their responses and attention. She can handle

herself." Nexin lumbered under the awkward weight of the bag.

"Okay." Tag relinquished his initial resistance and immediately explained each of their exit strategy plans.

"Go get 'em tiger." Nexin winked at her as he sprinted back up the stairs.

Zane's calm voice took over to direct her as she raced down the stairs and finally got out of the stairwell. Kotan worked his magic of opening doors that were for authorized personnel only, sending her back down the stairs and zigzagging through the floors while Zane directed her away from security by using the cameras. Tag was doing the same for Nexin, and Kotan worked double time to control the electronic doors for both of them.

She blazed through an empty floor that was being renovated and a debris shoot came into view. She sprinted like hell for it.

Pretend it's a water slide, she thought as her frame slide against the plastic tubing that encased her, praying it didn't detach from the top. Her boots pressed against the tube creating a bit of friction to slow her descent slightly. Thankfully her gloves and gear covered her fully, so no skin burned off on the hard plastic as she zipped down.

Rolf had scoped out the bin to ensure she wouldn't shatter her body on chunks of concrete or impale herself with rebar. However, the insulation-filled bin still packed a wallop and forced the air out of her body with the jarring impact.

Tag and Rolf's sigh of relief was audible when Ryn bound out of the bin. The van now sat at the entrance of the alley, watching the building exits from their vantage point, to signal and act upon any threats.

"Fuck." Nexin voice sounded pained. "Damn it."

"Status. Now." Tag's voice was terse.

"My foot fell through a board and debris fell around it. There's chunks of concrete and I can't reach down to them. I can't get my foot out."

"Where?"

"Across the way. Top floor of the parkade."

Tag's instruction to Nexin had been to go to that building via the duct work that was on top of the catwalk that connected the two buildings. The building housed a parking garage on the first six floors of the building and Nexin was supposed to exit from there. He had to get out of there quick before security realized he had gone over to that building and blocked those exits.

"Shit. Fuck. I'm screwed guys. Get out." A loud screeching beep sounded. "The gate is closing. They're securing the exits. The stairwell will be locked too."

"We'll have to devise a recovery plan for you."

"But he'll be found with all the evidence from the worm's safe," Ryn exclaimed, disagreeing with Tag's decision.

"It can't be helped. We will get you out," Zane promised Nexin.

"I know it. Don't worry, peanut, I've been in worse." Nexin avoided using her name just in case someone intercepted their transmission or had made their way to his area of the parkade.

"In the van. Now." Tag's voice tightened at her hesitation.

"Hack in and stop the gate." She urged Kotan while she looked at the buildings around her.

"No. The van. Now." Tag voice was curt.

She turned and sprinted away from the van and Tag's thundering curses rang in her ear. Zane's tried to reason with her, but he quickly realized the futility and directed Kotan to do as she asked.

She ran as hard as her legs would allow and with perfect timing pushed off the ground onto a tall crate and then immediately pushed off and up again. Her palms grabbed the lower rung of the fire ladder that was attached high up on the building. The grip from Maari's super gloves let her hold tight.

She swung her legs as much as the wall would allow, arching her back, and did a muscle up. Grabbing the higher rungs of the ladder she ascended it fast and agile like a monkey climbing a tree. She jumped from the ladder to the top of the catwalk, her boots gripping the steep curve of the roof. Moving quickly, she found a repairman hatch to slip inside the vents.

Tag's cursing might have quit but she could sense his seething anger.

Kotan cursed in Japanese as the beeping started briefly again but then stopped.

"Hurry," Zane instructed.

"I'm out. Where do I go now? Where?"

She sprinted following Zane's directions, the periodic beeping and Kotan's cursing fuelling her on.

"Is there a power box or control device for the gate that you can hit?" Tag asked Nexin.

"Not from the angle where I'm at. Fucking construction debris and piece of shit building. But at least the gate descends slowly."

As if on cue, the beeping started again, except this time the beeping didn't stop.

She burst through the door and saw the descending gate ahead of her.

So close.

"It's gonna be too late, don't risk it," Nexin yelled at her.

She sprinted the fastest she ever had in her life, her ribs screamed in protest, her breath came in short, powerful bursts.

"No, it's down too far, you'll get pinned. Don't do it!" Nexin thundered.

She blocked out his voice and dove headfirst under the gate. As soon as she cleared, she twisted onto her back, pulling the knife sheathed in her boot and whipped it, with perfect precision, into the control box of the gate.

"Holy fuck. Holy fuck, you did it. Okay, okay, help me get this debris off my foot. I can't reach around low enough to lift it."

She tossed boards and debris away to reach down into the hole that Nexin's leg had fallen through. Chunks of concrete surrounded his buried foot. She moved one away, but his foot was still pinned. Grunting, she lifted the largest one enough for him to shift and wiggle his foot out.

"Can you weight-bear on that foot?"

"I'd say that's the least I can do after what you just did." Nexin grunted as he rose. "There's another debris shoot."

"Given the space you're in and the type of material around there, I don't think we want to chance landing in a bucket of jagged concrete," Tag supplied.

"True."

"Fire escape, south side."

"Yes, that's good." Zane agreed with Rolf's suggestion.

They hurried back in the direction of the stalled gate. Ryn ripped her knife from the control box then crawled through the narrow opening. Nexin passed her the equipment bag and wiggled through.

Hearing voices coming up from the floors below and across the catwalk, Kotan continued to work his hacking magic to open the stairwell door and the subsequent door that opened out to the fire escape. They could take the fire escape stairwell down, but the straight ladder attached to the side of the building would be faster and offered less chance of them encountering pursuers from the lower levels.

Ryn gave Nexin a look to see how his foot was but he readjusted the equipment bag and gave her two thumbs up. They swung out from the landing to grab onto the ladder and quickly descended. Rolf had maneuvered the van to the alley on the south side of the building and it idled waiting for them.

Phase four. Face the music.

She yanked open the side door and met the fury in Tag's eyes.

"You did good, you little nut. Thank you," Nexin had said when they got in the van, pounding his fist lightly on top of hers. Tag had remained silent and stoic until they had dropped her and Nexin off at a busy mall eight blocks away where they changed out of the disguises, separated, and made it back to their vehicle.

Rolf and Tag would do the same process once they returned the computer repair van. And they would all reconvene at the estate.

For her to face the wrath of Team Alpha's leader.

Nexin turned the car onto the long drive that led to the house. His hair, now his natural blonde shaggy locks, blew in the open windows. "He's pissed right now, but he'll come around. You did what any one of us would have."

She nodded but remained silent.

"You saw an opportunity to save a team member and you acted without hesitation. Without fear. You proved you have your teammates' backs out there. That's the very crux, the very foundation of a successful team."

Somewhat comforted by his words, she pondered the confrontation that was sure to happen in a few minutes.

Tag was waiting for them on the step, his face was tight and unreadable. "Battle room for debrief." He turned on his heel and strode up the steps.

She bit back her retort and tried to calm her annoyance at the brisk order. His tone. The fucking stick up his ass.

Rolf paused her before they went into the house, gazing down at her quietly. "Well done out there. In there—" He thumbed toward the house. "—cool heads will prevail."

A man of few words. But she got the point.

In the battle room, Nexin dropped the bag on the table and spread out the contents. "Mother load."

Zane looked pleased. "Well done. We'll go through this carefully, but I think we'll find there is more than enough for the authorities to build an airtight case against Mr. Wormid. We'll make the evidence 'easily findable' for them to proceed to do so."

"And your foot?" Kotan asked Nexin. "Do you need Nessa or Rolf to look at it?"

"No, it's fine. It wasn't hurt badly; I just couldn't reach the chunks of concrete. I guess I need to work on my flexibility and contortion skills to be more like our girl Ryn."

Tag remained as he was - standing tall, arms crossed over his chest, face unreadable. "Our girl Ryn disobeyed a direct order out there."

Rolf sat with his elbows leaning on the table, Zane and Kotan continued to observe, while Nexin made a move to stand between Tag and Ryn. But Tag motioned him to stay put.

Tag strode over to where she stood, while she stamped down her anger and kept her features neutral. Her chin rose of its own accord, the only signal of her defiance.

"Should Nexin have been taken by the police, it would have added some complications. But no life-threatening danger."

She looked hard at Tag but kept her tongue. Tag arched an eyebrow at her, so maybe she wasn't looking as calm as she thought.

"However, being taken in by the police would not have been without its own risks and would have resulted in Zane needing to call in favours that would be better used elsewhere. Another time."

Tag's eyes softened while he looked at her, but his features remained serious. "You proved yourself today. In your skill, your rapid calm thinking under pressure as well as your commitment to a fellow team member. I'm glad we bet on you."

Being on duty for supper tonight, Ryn chopped basil and garlic to add to the butter for the potatoes and marinating chicken. She was still stunned by Tag's response during the debrief.

Her head snapped up, startled by Tag's quiet appearance in the doorway. "Been relegated to the kitchens, have you?"

"It would seem. What are you making?"

Ryn inclined her head to the kitchen door that led outside. "Nessa has an herb garden, thought a flavoured butter would be nice for supper."

Tag started to wash the vegetables for a salad and asked curiously, "You cook? More than boiling potatoes?"

She shrugged. "A bit. And you? Being the baby of three older sisters, I imagine you didn't do much and were doted on instead."

"Bullied, remember?" Tag laughed and she liked the relaxed sound of it. "And you?"

She quickly contemplated her response. Share something of her past or not? And if so, something innocuous, something safe.

"I found at a young age that I enjoyed being in the kitchen and helping cook. Not because I had a love for cooking but because I wanted to be part of the activity."

"That's where all the juiciest gossip and visiting gets done. In my family, whenever we're all home, we cluster in the kitchen. Not all of us are there to help of course," he snatched a carrot from the salad to prove his point, "and incessantly get under my mom's feet. But no one wants to be left out."

The way Tag's face softened when he talked about his family, the fondness she could hear in his voice, made a surge of longing for her own family run through her.

Tag watched her eyes and lowered his small paring knife to move toward her. She abruptly shook her head and turned away to ready the meat.

The wariness of missing her family and the torment of her guilt and regret weighed on her. Coupled with the growing attraction, and alarming urge to unburden her secrets to Tag, she couldn't risk letting him in. She wasn't ready to tell him or the others about her past. Couldn't add that additional risk to her family.

She could feel the unasked questions hanging like a weight between them, but he honoured her silence and refusal to open up.

For now.

She wondered how long he would be willing to do so. And how long she could keep her guard up around him.

Chapter 31

Tag's eyes snapped open, his body instantly awake, although he hadn't moved a muscle. A noise had woken him. Or so he thought. He listened intently but had yet to hear anything again.

It must have been something in his dream. Or his subconscious, wanting him to hear something.

His mind wandered to Ryn as it was doing often these last few days. Astonishingly often. He couldn't get her out of his head.

It had begun a month ago when Zane and Kotan sent him to keep a secretive eye on Severyn Andrews while she performed with Lok in New York.

Then the kiss happened in the elevator at the end of the op in Miami after Ched's party. Even though his mind had no way of knowing the operative was actually the musician he watched in New York, he hadn't been able to get the feel of that kiss, the feel of that person out of his head since it had happened.

His mind might not have known, but his body registered the connection. And reminded him on the Strada op and then again when he met her at May's gala.

As soon as he pieced together they were all the same person, and his body wasn't responding to separate women, his thoughts were amplified.

Being around her and working closely to establish their connection as a team was doing nothing to diminish it, at all.

Especially now that he discovered the nightmares she was plagued with were added into the mix.

Nightmares were one thing. But to see a nightmare have physical manifestations on her was another. The second he realized that she had clawed the skin of her neck while trapped in the throngs of a powerful nightmare, his gut had twisted.

Based on his own experiences of how powerful nightmares, coupled with ongoing sleep deprivation, can impact someone's actions, his concern for her rose.

Tag sighed and rolled over to crush a pillow to his chest.

Even if she had cried out in her sleep, would he have been able to hear her?

What demons haunted her?

And why? What happened in her past to warrant such a powerful impact?

He didn't buy the story of her being Zane's niece who had lived a secluded life in Switzerland. Rolf and Nexin didn't either regardless of how solid it stood up under their diligent fact checking. But they had quickly reached a consensus that they wouldn't press it and demand the full story. They wanted her to come to them. Trust them enough as her teammates to share whatever secrets she hid.

Contemplating his other teammates, he knew they both were forming a protective bond over Ryn after only a few days of working with her. It was surprising given Rolf's usual aloofness and Nexin's perpetual playful side that he used to prevent too close of connections. A remnant of CIA training and the lived experience of a spy.

And him…

Restless, Tag tossed the pillow aside and scrubbed his hands over his face. The attraction her felt for her was unlike anything he had ever experienced before. It was visceral, not tied to visual. How else could he explain his body, his very core's response to her on three different occasions when she looked like completely different people.

It wasn't only the attraction to her that he felt rapidly blooming.

It was the scale of protectiveness that was developing.

One of his biggest drivers in his career choices had been to protect people. However, that alone didn't fully explain the protectiveness he felt for her. The depth, as well as the rate and intensity it was developing, shocked him.

But how does someone protect another from the psychological horrors and harm of ghosts that haunt them in their sleep?

And I'm right back at ruminating about her sleep.

Realizing he wouldn't get back to sleep himself until he put his mind at ease that she indeed slept soundly, Tag left his room.

His feet sank soundlessly in the soft, plush carpet as he moved swiftly listening to the hush of the late night. The bright moonlight streamed in through the skylight above to illuminate her door and his hand paused on the doorknob.

Pushing aside his hesitancy, he silently opened the door to allow moonbeams to spill into her room, casting the bed, and her, in a silver glow.

Curled tight in a fetal position, the bulk of her mane of hair splayed across the pillow, except for a smaller chunk that fell across her cheek and her chest to rest on the bed.

Not perspiring in panic, gasping for breath or clawing at her throat like she had last night, the knot in his gut released.

But that was short lived when she began to whisper.

"Fi. Fi. Fi."

The sight of her face contorted in despair, the anguished whispers turning to a whimper, were like a sucker punch to his gut. The air left his chest and it was as if he could feel her emotional pain himself.

He was unsure what was worse. Her terror while she clutched at her throat gasping for breath, shaking violently in the aftermath. Or the soft tortured whispers of her pain.

Tag knelt beside the bed, running his hand over her brow, remembering how it soothed her last night. "Ryn. It's okay, it's only a dream."

Her eyes opened, focused on him kneeling beside her bed. Her chest rose and fell with her deep breaths. He remained motionless when her hand rose to touch his face, to run her fingertips delicately over his lips.

"I left her. I left her Tag." Tears overflowed her liquid grey eyes making her face shimmer under the glow of moonlight. "I left them all. They are gone from me now."

He didn't think. He didn't analyze his actions.

He gathered her close and laid beside her. Her tears wet his chest as she held him as tight as he held her. He didn't speak, for what words could he say to ease her pain?

He stroked her back, repeatedly, constantly until the rhythmic motions broke the tension in her to leave her completed relaxed in his arms. When the smooth breathing signalled her return to a restful sleep, he made a move to leave but her arm over his waist tightened in her sleep and her face tilted up to breathe deep. Whatever scent she breathed in relaxed her further.

Tag smoothed the hair back from her face, hugging her close again as she slumbered peacefully until dawn.

Ryn sat in the sunken room off the foyer in the sunlight, thankful Kotan was elsewhere this morning instead of there, enjoying his morning ritual of green tea. She sat up rigidly when Tag came down the stairs, his hair wet from his shower, and padded barefoot in jeans and a black t-shirt.

He noticed her sitting at the long table. "Mind if I join you?"

"You did it again, didn't you?"

"I've done lots of things more than once. Could you be a bit more specific?"

"You know exactly what I mean," she said through clenched teeth unfolding her legs to stand.

In beige shorts and a white t-shirt, hair still wet from her own shower, she looked beautiful and angelic in the sunlight. Except for the fire spitting from her eyes, the angry tilt of her chin for her steel grey eyes to meet his.

Tag was not taken aback by her anger and looked like he understood it, understood her, immediately. "I meant no offense or inappropriate actions, Ryn. I'm sorry you're upset. However, I'm not sorry that you slept more soundly the past two nights. Your colouring is good." His hand cupped her cheek, his thumbing grazing the skin under her eye.

She stood ramrod straight, shocked that he would be so forward. Shocked by her reaction to his touch.

Ryn jerked away to break physical contact but Tag placed a hand over her clenched one.

"Honestly. You were struggling and my presence calmed you. I was trying to help. That is all."

"What did I say to you last night?" She demanded ripping her hand away from his.

"No devastating secrets, Ryn." He stood still, watching her closely.

"What did I say to you, Tag?" She bit out, panic threatening to steal her breath.

"Someone's name, that you left them, and that they are gone."

"Oh my God." Her voice cracked and she turned from him.

"Ryn, what you said revealed nothing. Not really. And it isn't information I'm going to investigate or use against you in any way. I would never exploit your vulnerability."

She lowered her head, her hair shielding her face from him when he walked around in an effort to get her to look at him.

"How are you doing this? Why in a matter of days, are you—"

"—breaking through the walls you have mastered hiding behind?" Tag finished for her.

She straightened, finally looking at him. "You can't do that again. I don't have control of what I am saying in my sleep. It isn't fair." Her eyes hardened further with her resolve. "I don't need your help, Tag. Not with this."

The set of his strong jaw told her he disagreed, but he said quietly instead. "Is it so hard for you to let me in a small step?"

Ryn moved further into the sunken room to add distance between them. "This isn't a small step. Besides the invasion of my privacy—"

"You mean the invasion into your private tormenting hell."

She glared at him. "Besides the invasion of my privacy, it's...it's us sleeping in a bed together. It's—"

"Intimate."

"Goddammit, quit finishing my sentences." She flared.

"Intimate." Tag repeated. "And that is not my intention. I know there is something between us. A pull, an attraction. You can't deny it, and neither can I."

Her breath sucked in sharply at his open admission.

Undaunted, he continued. "But I swear I am not trying to take advantage of you, or to get into your bed for anything but to stop your nightmares."

Sudden images of them laying together, sheets tangled around them, the thought of his bare chest under her cheek, his hands running along the length of her back, stole her breath again.

Tag moved slowly to close the distance between them once more. His eyes darkened when he gently pushed the hair back from her cheek, letting his fingers run through the damp, heaviness of it.

"I will be honest with you. I would very much like to kiss you again and see where that takes us." He took advantage of her stunned silence. "But I swear on my integrity and honour, that is not the reason I calmed you the past two nights. I am not trying to take advantage of you. Or become privy to the secrets you hold with an iron fist. I only want you to have torment free sleep."

"Why? Why do you care so much?"

"I know firsthand what can happen if this goes on, unrectified."

"Tag," her voice softened at the look of remorse in his eyes.

Tag put some space and the table between them. "Answer this one question. Have you slept better?"

"It doesn't matter."

"I would say that is all that matters."

She sputtered, trying to find the right words in her frustration to make him understand. Without revealing too much. About the truth of her past, her secrets. But also, without admitting to him the depth of how he was beginning to affect her.

You are risk, Taggert Hale.
To my family's safety.
To me.
And I cannot afford you.

Grounding her jaw tightly shut, she wondered what the hell she had gotten herself into agreeing to work with him and the others.

He refused to accept silence as the answer to his question and he was also effectively blocking her exit. She sighed, "I did, yes. But this cannot continue."

"It's okay to depend on others, Ryn. To depend on me. I will not let you down, hurt or betray you."

"You make some pretty auspicious promises. For someone that has only met me, doesn't really know the first thing about me." Skepticism coated her words.

"I do."

"You can be my teammate, my team leader. Or whatever. But with this, Tag, you cannot be my solution."

She stood facing him, feet apart in a solid stance and he held her determined gaze.

"Sleep is vital. I cannot have a sleep-deprived member of the team when others are relying on them for their safety. For their lives."

"I've made do for two years."

"Why make do when there are other more appealing alternatives."

She barked out a laugh.

"Well, that's a much better sound than threats of combat." Nexin casually strolled down the stairs, Maari at his side.

"Ryn isn't much of a morning person I'm afraid until she has hit something or crushed an hour run. For most it's caffeine, for her it's physical exertion."

Ryn narrowed her eyes at her friend. "I didn't know you came out last night."

Thankful for the interruption but dread rose wondering how much Maari and Nexin may have overheard of their ridiculous argument. It was her bed for God's sake. If she told Tag to stay out of it, then goddammit he should listen to her.

The piercings on Maari brow, nose, and lower lip caught the sunlight and glittered as much as the ankle straps of her navy stiletto heels.

"I came out late last night. Mama and I are going over some items that she's taking with her on her next trip to her home community. I'll be back in the city at the lab in a bit, but can meet you for lunch if that works."

Ryn didn't miss the quick glance Maari gave Nexin before she continued. "Or I could meet you guys at the studio. Nexin is interested in some of the latest items I've been working on."

"They won't be with me." She quipped tightly.

"We would love to meet you, Maari. Gives us a chance to get to know the person behind all the gadgets that save our hides." Tag popped a piece of watermelon in his mouth.

Ryn's eyes cut sharply over to him, frustration pushing the threshold level. "There's no need for you to come with me. I'm working with a client."

"We're your security detail."

"No, we decided in public, for now, you're just my friends."

"Ouch, firmly put in the friend zone, Tag." Nexin quickly snatched two croissants tossing one to Maari.

"Shut it," Ryn and Tag said in unison.

"When I'm meeting with my clients, how do I explain I have my friends there for the meeting? Nobody does that." She threw her hands up in irritation. "And even if we say that you're my security, I'm not the Queen of England and need you to be an arm's length away from me at all times. I'm not in mortal danger, just mortal annoyance."

"Touché. Point for Ryn. Tag, any counter?"

Tag gave Nexin a dark look. Ryn snatched the last croissant before Nexin could.

"Fine. We'll go with I'm your boyfriend and cannot bear to have you too far from me at any time."

Ryn choked on the croissant as Tag strutted away, chuckling.

Chapter 32

The work with the band was quick and minimal. They had been ecstatic with the product she shared with them a few days ago and the process to finalize it went smooth.

Ambel, the singer of Ancient Highways, a pop band that was successfully crossing over into country music, clapped her on the back. "Let's work together again soon. You're a gem among gems."

She had been successful in convincing the guys they didn't have to be present and they spent the time at Neara and Mason's restaurant next door. Maari had joined them earlier and both Neara and Mason were laughing with the group when Ryn walked in.

Neara bustled over to her, the wispy curls escaped her tight bun to bounce around her face.

"My dear, come sit down, I'll get you your coffee and some soup and bread."

The short, portly woman clasped Ryn's hand leading her to the table. Mason kissed the top of his wife's head and gave Ryn's cheek an affectionate pat. "This young lady needs more than soup and bread, Neara. I'll prepare something for the table."

The table was already full of empty plates which Tag started to pile to clear but Neara swatted his hand. "Petro will do that. Come sit," she ordered Ryn. "They just finished a small appetizer. I'll get your coffee."

Tag slid over making room for her. "Small appetizer, my arse. You'll have to roll us out of here."

After the disconcerting and inconclusive conversation with Tag this morning, she was thankful he was relaxed. She didn't kid herself that was the last she had heard from him about the subject but for now, he was willing to let bygones be bygones.

Ryn smiled easily. "They do ensure you're well fed and taken care of."

Fresh baked rolls, soup, platters of meat and cheese, sautéed shrimp, Greek salad, and some sort of cheesy potato dish completed the eclectic spread on the table.

Neara looked pleased as they all dove in. "It's a pleasure having this young lady live beside us and we're so pleased that she sent you our way." Neara affectionately squeezed her shoulder. "Enjoy."

Rolf contemplated Ryn quietly. "You have something about you. People love to love you. You're real."

Ryn's cheeks warmed.

"It can't be because of her non-snarling demeanour." Tag quickly hid his smile, reaching across her for shrimp.

"I do not snarl." She snatched a dripping shrimp from Tag's plate, quick to avoid his stabbing fork. "Only when I have good reason."

"Before you three, Ryn here was the most affable of sweet young ladies." Maari bit a piece of smoked gouda cheese delicately.

Ryn snorted.

"We do seem to bring out the best in people, don't we boys? Where does sweet, affable, and agreeable get you anyway?" Nexin snagged Ryn's coffee and took a slug.

"Boundaries." She huffed, but not in anger. "Keep your filthy paws off my Neara specialty coffee."

"That's good." Nexin flagged Petro over to order one of his own. "But back to the snarling."

"I don't snarl." She insisted, laughing.

"Or when you do, it's mostly reserved for someone specifically around this table." Maari smiled wickedly at Tag.

"I do have an effect on her, don't I?" Tag stated slyly.

Discomfort spiked at Tag's comment and the possible turn the conversation could take and Ryn rallied quickly to smoothly divert it. Rolf tossed his burly arms over the back of the bench and gave her a quiet, small smile.

"You guys must have made a good impression for Mason to come out and see you. It's a rare occasion for him to come out of the kitchen." Ryn scooped more of the glorious potatoes onto her plate diverting her eyes from Rolf's knowing gaze.

"He's a gruff pussycat with no hiss. And I can't even take credit as he was out at the table when I arrived." Maari popped a black olive between her full lips.

Ryn watched Nexin drag his eyes away from her friend's lips, flashing his big grin. "It was all due to me, of course. What's not to love about this guy?"

His two comrades made impolite noises.

The atmosphere during their meal continued to be laid back and Ryn found herself enjoying getting to know her new teammates in a relaxed way. She even surprised herself to realize that she hadn't felt guilty that she should be doing something other than laughing with these four people during lunch.

Tag, Rolf, and Nexin were so different, but they had an easy candour with one another. And they wove both Ryn and Maari easily into their circle, regaling them with some of their colourful antics together.

"I shit you not. That's a true story." Nexin's blue eyes danced with glee.

"Rolf?" Maari turned to the quiet man, looking for him to confirm.

"It is." He rumbled. "It takes a lot for me to get drunk, but Tag's dad's home brew was something else."

"Scoot still won't leave his side whenever they come home with me." Tag's shoulders shook. "And the last time, Rolf didn't have much facial hair and you could see the dog's extreme disappointment."

"No beard treats to steal while he is sleeping it off in the backyard. Do your nieces still call him Tower of Rolf?" Ryn asked.

"If there is anyone more excited than Scoot to see Rolf, it's my youngest nieces."

"License plate to read 'Kid and Pooch Magnet'?" Nexin joked.

There was a uniform round of winces.

"Yeah that sounds bad, scratch that."

Maari's phone went off and she slid smoothly out of the booth, excusing herself. Ryn watched Nexin's eyes subtly track Maari's movements and contemplated the attractive, former spy.

Ryn had caught more than one hidden glance between Nexin and Maari during the meal. They would make an interesting couple. His light hair, blue eyed surfer look. Her striking beauty of dark hair and eyes, razor sharp cheekbones with tattoos and piercings making her look like she just stepped off the cover of Rolling Stone magazine. Ryn's impression of Nexin so far was that he was a flirty, womanizer type though. She made a mental note to warn Nexin not to mess with her friend when she could corner him alone.

"Sorry to dine and dash, but something's up at the lab and I have to jet. We'll get together soon to go over some of what I've been working on." Maari kissed her cheek and swung her oversized bag gracefully over a narrow shoulder. "Have fun going to see the new digs, wish I could come."

Ryn squinted in the bright sun after they forced the waiter to take money for their bill while Neara was preoccupied with the busy lunch crowd. The daunting ominous look of a serious Rolf finally convinced the new waiter to risk the wrath of Neara.

"Any way I can beg out of the home-and-show tour?"

Three firm "no's" settled that.

The guys had insisted they travel together into the city so she was stuck for transportation but there was no reason why she couldn't stay at her studio to work while they got settled into their new homes.

"It won't kill you to take a break from work or training." Tag held open the truck door and gave her a small push into the back seat.

She was quiet as Tag navigated the vehicle along the river, waiting for a mom and young child to safely pass on their bikes, before turning onto the short bridge.

On the other side of the river, Ryn watched the trees rise high, arching at the top to encase the street in a beautiful, lush canopy.

"You okay?"

Tag's questioning eyes met hers in the rearview mirror.

His ability to read her was beginning to unnerve her. She furrowed her brow and wrapped her arms around her torso but then relaxed, deciding to say what was weighing on her. "I'm sorry that you guys are having to relocate for this mission. It's a lot to ask."

"You have a habit of not wanting help from people." Tag replied quietly.

"Or expecting anything from others." Rolf twisted from the passenger seat to look at her.

She looked out the window to avoid their eyes, even if she couldn't avoid their words.

"You all had, have," she corrected, "lives outside of this. I'm intruding on that."

"Is your vexation with this because you wholeheartedly embody the principles of selflessness? Or are you fantastically and stubbornly self-reliant? Either way," Nexin leaned over from beside her in the back seat and bumped her shoulder with his, "you're worth it."

His characteristic easy smile tugged at the corners of her own lips. Clean shaven today, she realized how it was hard to discern the age of his angular face. He claimed to be a 'recovering-spy' but she was reminded how well he easily donned disguises and personas.

"We can't stay at the estate forever. The place is large, but everyone needs their space." Tag caught her gaze in the rearview mirror as he navigated through the narrow streets. They had crossed the river from where her studio was and were approaching a row of brownstones. "It isn't a hardship really. None of us have deep roots in our current locations and change is good."

"As long as I have a local health clinic where I can volunteer, I'm happy. And there's one very close to here." Rolf pointed north.

She realized how little she knew about each of them. Their families, their stories, their likes, what they choose to do outside of ops for Zane and Kotan.

Tag maneuvered the truck expertly into a tight spot outside three brownstones. Beautifully redone three storey homes that towered high.

"There's parking underneath each but street parking will do for now." Tag hopped out of the vehicle and was quick to get her door.

The road they had taken there had looped around a bit and she noticed the brownstones happened to be in close proximity to the river. And her studio and apartment building were conveniently in view from them.

"Zane owns these, doesn't he?" Ryn stepped onto the sidewalk, not surprised, but annoyance brewed quietly. Zane's plan for having these three men infiltrate her life, had been underway for some time now.

Tag watched her closely. "He does."

"He's giving us a hell of a deal on rent too." Nexin bound up the steps. "And they're outfitted with all the latest security specs of course. After you, my sweet." Nexin swept his arm in welcome.

The double wood doors opened into a small entrance separated from the sun-filled foyer by a glass door inset with beautiful stained glass. In the foyer, the beams of light reflected off the hardwood floors.

"Each place is relatively the same, but we decorate very different." Nexin pushed her into the living room to the left of the foyer. "We aren't really parlour type of guys so thankfully the main level has been opened up. The flow of the space spills back to the kitchen. That's where Rolf is going to make us supper tonight."

Ryn groaned at the thought of more food.

Characteristic of brownstones, the home was not wide but made up for it in length as well as the square footage of multiple floors.

After guiding her through the main floor, Nexin bounded up the stairs, trusting his entourage would follow. Tag lightly grasped her arm, turning her toward him before she went up after Rolf. The touch rippled through her and she watched Tag's throat move as he swallowed hard. *Does he experience the same electric reaction?* she wondered.

The urge to lean into him, to touch him, washed over her like a cresting wave. Powerful. And dangerous.

She stepped back to put space between them.

Tag's eyes met hers, his square jawline hard and serious. When he smiled, she thought, it softened his jawline, showed his perfect white teeth, made his golden-brown eyes dance.

She shook her head, trying to break her line of thinking.

Tag's eyebrows pulled together with his frown. "I want you to know, I'm not a fan of how Zane springs things on you, or on us, when it comes to you. In our dealings with him, he has always been transparent."

She relaxed, thankful she wasn't as transparent in her thoughts with him as she had been earlier.

"As you can guess, I'm not a fan either. And for what it's worth, I know this is all Zane's masterminding manipulation, not yours. It isn't how he normally operates with me either."

As annoyed and pissed off at Zane as she had been recently, she still felt compelled to defend her benefactor and mentor.

"Are you coming, Ryn?" Nexin yelled down from the third level. "I want to show you how you'll have perfect sight lines into our bedroom suites and where you can watch me do naked pull-ups before bed."

She laughed going up the stairs. "There's an easy fix for that, poser. It's called blinds."

After the grand tour of their places, she got rooked into unpacking a few boxes. The units came fully furnished thanks to Zane and each of the guys had already been in their places, so all the heavy lifting was mostly done.

Finished now, they sat enjoying the late afternoon July sun on the roof level of Rolf's brownstone while he grilled salmon for supper. The sun felt nice on the bare skin of her legs, as did the breeze from the river flowing over the treetops.

Ryn offered more than once to help Rolf and wasn't sure if she should be offended by his insistent refusal.

"Sit. Enjoy." Rolf ordered and topped up her wine.

"Yes, sit and enjoy. I certainly am. I'm always happy to watch while Rolf does all the hard stuff and I reap the benefits." Nexin kicked up his feet on the stone table with the fire bowl in the middle. "Now that we're all settled into our humble abodes, tell me your impressions of our places."

"This feels like a trap." She eyed Nexin with suspicion.

"It illuminates how you think. What you think of us."

"This definitely sounds like a trap. Or another test."

Tag grinned at her, before snagging a piece of broccoli while Rolf's back was turned. "Knowing how to avoid all the landmines is a critical part of the job, Ryn."

The wind played in Nexin's sun-kissed hair, the bright, lime-green board shorts and multicoloured shirt he had changed into, provided a full brightness assault on the eyes. Tag had remained in his jeans and black t-shirt and Rolf wore his characteristic black on black, only cargo shorts this afternoon, with his black boots.

So different, but elements of similarities ran through these three like golden threads. She sipped her wine, contemplative.

"You understand, this is a superficial assessment. You haven't exactly lived in the spaces yet. *That* is more illuminating."

"Quit dodging, chicken shit." Nexin slugged back the rest of his beer.

"Fine. Let's see...Rolf's place here is, very orderly, but that isn't really a surprise."

Nexin yawned, patting his mouth.

Rolf joined them on the sofas to hear her assessment. His presence, as always, was powerful but quiet.

"I'm not finished." Ryn scowled in mock anger. "His kitchen is the best outfitted for cooking so that implies to me, that he loves to cook. And that you two love him to cook for you."

"A keen observation." Tag nodded.

"It's also quite spiritual, I didn't expect that. Especially with all the medical texts and your observant, analytical nature, Rolf."

"An enigma, our Rolf is. Science to the bone but with philosophy as his marrow."

She couldn't agree more with Nexin's assessment. She continued, a bit quieter, "I felt surrounded by the love and honour you have for your parents. Do either of them still live?"

Rolf shook his head no but offered no more explanation.

"The memories of them are there." She added gently. "And finally," she continued with a grin, "I would say Rolf is the most sensual out of you three."

Rolf choked lightly on his wine and Nexin looked outraged while Tag chuckled.

"What?" Nexin croaked.

"Sensual, not sexual, Nexin." She patted his knee in reassurance. "It's the colours and textures of his accessorizing throughout his home. Very surprising, given your characteristic choice of wardrobe colours." She added, looking at Rolf's black on black ensemble.

"Okay, do me."

"For Christ's sake, Nexin." She laughed at his insistence for him, or his sexuality, not to be forgotten. "Okay. Your home is very feng shui. You maximize the use of the light in your space, especially in how you arranged key pieces of furniture. And your place is non-cluttered, balanced, and relaxed, like you. But there is an oxymoron to the feng shui. I can tell you could have a tendency to be...um, messy isn't the right word."

"Are you sure?" Tag sat back, enjoying himself at his teammate's indignant look.

Rolf snorted.

"Organized chaos. That would be a better way to put it. You could have the tendency to run that way. Am I right?"

"Yes." Nexin admitted, impressed. Even if it was begrudgingly so.

"There were no pictures of you, family, or friends."

Nexin shrugged slightly. "Remnants of my CIA days. Still re-acclimatizing, I guess." Nexin leaned forward toward her. "Ryn, you haven't ever asked us about our families."

She glanced quickly down before meeting his blue eyes. "I haven't known you guys that long. Been focusing on getting to know you as teammates."

"And if you don't ask us questions, it doesn't provide the opportunity for us to do the same with you." Tag stated matter of fact.

She struggled to keep the startled look off her face at Tag's accurate assessment.

"We will get there." Rolf said simply.

"Okay, your turn buddy." Nexin tossed the wine cork at Tag's head which Tag's lightning fast reflexes caught before it smacked him in the eye.

Ryn shifted to look more squarely at Tag at the other end of the sofa he shared with her. "I would describe it more along the lines of minimalist and efficient, which isn't a surprise given your military background and pragmatic nature."

"Another word for pragmatic is commonsensical. Aka boring."

Tag's eyebrow arched up and she responded quickly to Nexin's gleeful retort, "Not at all. It's balanced and practical. Okay maybe I'm digging myself a hole here." She laughed at Tag's pinched look.

"Your weapon safe and cache wasn't out in the open, none of your guys' were, but Tag's was the most accessible. You're used to moving around a lot. Don't place a lot of attachment on possessions. That's what I mean." She smiled at Tag, continuing. "But your place isn't cold or off-putting. The pictures of your family, the few souvenirs you've collected, and handmade crafts, which I'm assuming you didn't make, give it a warm and welcoming feel."

"Gifts from my nieces. They send me many." Tag supplied, affection for his nieces evident on his face.

"I get messy, Tag gets the award for best ready to protect you, and Rolf basically gets an opening to invite you to move into his sensual digs." Nexin pouted comically.

The other two men howled in laughter.

Her phone, thankfully, went off. "You're the one that asked for this Nexin." She reminded him with a laugh, rising to take the call. She stretched her stiff legs, catching Tag's eyes traveling from her muscular quads to slowly meet her eyes. Her cheeks warmed under his appraising gaze.

Rolf sidestepped her to check on the salmon, smiling quietly down at her.

"Hello, May."

After pleasantries, May got right down to business. "I have another gala. This one has the potential to be dreadfully boring and uninspiring. But don't get me wrong, the cause is *not* lacking inspiration. Politicians of all sorts will be there, including most of my mom's colleagues as well as those that like to hob-nob with them. So naturally, I'm working for this event not to be as drab as it sounds. I would like to invite you to attend. Not to perform, but as a guest."

Ryn looked perplexed. "I don't run in those circles and I don't think I've ever given the indication that I'd like to hob-nob. I'm confused May, why you'd want me there as a guest. If it's a donation you want, it's yours."

"No, no. But yes, I will take a donation." May added quickly. "What I want is for your presence to be part of the non-drab component of the evening. Hearing that a celebrity like you—"

"I think that's stretching it."

"We can agree to disagree." May laughed pleasantly in her ear. "But I believe a presence such as yours, and others of course, will be a positive draw for attendance. These things have the reputation to be the same old events and I want to maximize the attendance. Not just for the donations, but for the message. The foundation we are focusing on is about advocating for education resources and reform."

Ryn's memory pulled up the information they had discovered about Senator Hanelson and his backdoor dealings with Pallium that threatened the education of millions of students. She silently wondered if this was the result of Virginia's quiet heads up to rally support for the vote that would defeat Senator Hanelson's plans and felt a stab of satisfaction.

And couple that with the fact that most of Senator Antel's colleagues would be in attendance. Well, a gift horse was figuratively staring her in the face.

"Pimping me and others out again."

Three sets of eyebrows piqued in interest at her comment.

"Well, don't put it that way...but I guess so." May stammered.

Ryn laughed. "Don't worry, I'm only half joking. Count me in."

"Oh, I'm so glad. Thank you, thank you. I'll get the invite to you right away. You have a bit more time to prepare for this one."

After she hung up with May, she gave the rundown to the guys, and they quickly deciphered the opportunity that she had identified herself while talking with May.

"So, our senator will most likely be there." Nexin steepled his fingers together in thought.

"Will Maari's skin device be ready?" Tag asked quietly.

Maari had been working on an alternative version of the mole device that capture auditory communications in addition to electronic, as well as improving the adhesive. Being they weren't in a fully secure setting, they kept the specifics out of their conversation as much as possible.

"Just working out the kinks for the adhesive."

Ryn fixed Nexin with a steely stare and he quickly defended his statement. "I'm interested in the devices and electronic, computery things are my wheelhouse too."

"Computery?" Tag bite back his grin at his friend's discomfort under Ryn's searing look while Rolf clapped a big hand on Nexin's back.

Ryn made a mental note that the chat with Nexin regarding her friend needed to happen sooner than later. "So, we have a rough plan?"

Use the opportunity to get close to Senator Hanelson, without any alarms being raised. Plant the device on him, hoping that the adhesive lasts a few days so they could get as much information out of him as possible to add to what they had previously collected with the mole device planted in his home office.

Nexin gave her a conspiratorial wink. "And who, my dear, will be your plus one?"

Chapter 33

Ryn stifled a yawn. The sun was beginning its slow descent to cast a glorious blend of red, orange, and yellow. "I'm off. Eating and sitting takes a toll on a person."

"A strange day for you. No three training sessions along with working on music or mentoring students. No wonder you're exhausted." Nexin joked sarcastically.

"A day with you is equally exhausting." She kicked his foot playfully. "Thank you, Rolf, supper was delicious. I've joined the camp of 'You can cook for me.'"

"Anytime." Rolf slung a heavy arm over her shoulder and hugged her to his side.

"I'll take you home." Tag rose and she was trapped between two tall towering peaks of masculinity.

"You will not, you've been drinking."

"As have you. And I'll walk you home. Or you can call an Uber."

"I can walk there in under ten minutes. Quit being a protective pain in my ass."

Tag stared resolutely at her, refusing to budge.

"Fine. This is not the hill I want to die on." She stomped toward the stairs off the roof. "Wipe that self-satisfied smirk off your face, Taggert Hale."

The street was filled with young kids, ranging from five to ten years old, playing street hockey and she smiled at the competitive revelry. The youngest of the group was a small tyke of a girl, right in there, not intimidated by the age or size of the other kids.

"Reminds me a bit of you." Tag smiled down at her.

"The big one over there, pushing his weight around? That one reminds me of you."

Tag gave her a friendly shove when he caught up to her. "That bad, am I?"

She shrugged, noncommittal.

They walked in silence, taking in the evening sounds of the quiet, pleasant neighbourhood.

"I know you can take care of yourself. I don't see you as a damsel in distress."

She looked sidelong at him, doubt clearly evident.

"I don't. I wanted a few moments alone with you. Is that a crime?"

Surprise registered on her face at his open statement. "Playing favourites doesn't bode well for team morale."

He chuckled, the sound of it vibrated in his broad chest. She liked the sound of it but shoved that thought away.

"I didn't want to get into it again in front of the guys." He pulled her to a stop, turning her to look at him. "We aren't staying in the same place tonight. I'm worried about you, your sleep."

She watched him warily. "I'm fine, Tag, and I will be fine."

"It's not only that...I know what..." He lowered his gaze away from hers and she watched Tag's face change from his regular confident look to one filled with disconcertion.

"Tag?"

He slowly raised troubled eyes to hers. Eyes filled with something she knew often echoed in her own.

Memories that haunted the soul.

"I've been where you are, Ryn. After I left the military," he paused, "before I came to work with Zane." Tag resumed walking, breaking eye contact with her. She walked alongside him and waited for him to continue.

"No one comes home from tours over there unaffected. I was no different. But the last one," Tag's voice shook slightly.

A lump pressed hard in her throat recalling Tag's story of the young girl and nanny dying in the blast he was supposed to have gotten them safely away from. Except the powers that be decided otherwise, and for the innocents to be deemed as necessary collateral damage.

"When I returned stateside and was Honourably Discharged, my parents would not let me stay anywhere but home. I spent weeks withdrawing into myself, struggling to sleep. Telling them, telling myself I was okay. Until—"

They were at the short bridge over the river now, her building visible across the water. The gulls dipped low to catch a late supper; people strolled along the river path, embracing the twilight of the evening. But she didn't notice any of it. Only Tag.

She took his hand in hers, a sheen of wetness glimmered in her eyes. "It's okay, Tag. Until what?"

He leaned back heavily against the cement wall of the bridge, kept his hands in hers but closed his eyes.

"My dad came one night because he heard me having a nightmare. It was a particularly bad one. All my self-loathing and rage at my superiors boiled in that dream. It was all around me. It was me. It was all I felt, and it was consuming me. My dad tried to wake me."

Tag opened his eyes but was not seeing her. "I was caught between my nightmare and reality. He was only trying to help me. His son. I attacked him. I woke up sitting on him, my knees pinning his shoulders and arms, so I could choke the life out of my father, and my mom screaming and hitting me, trying to get me to stop."

He suddenly became aware of her and the full gravity of what he shared. Horror and doubt flashed in his eyes and he tried to pull from her, turning away.

She clasped his face in her hands, urging him to stay. "Tag, please. Please, it's okay." She pulled his head down to hers to press their foreheads tightly together. "It wasn't your fault."

Two tears fell from Tag's cheeks onto hers when he pressed his eyes shut. She continued to cup his head, holding it to her own.

Time seemed suspended as they stood on the bridge, heads pressed together, the evening fully enveloped around them.

Tag finally pulled his head away but pulled her tightly to his chest, his hand buried in the loose hair of her bun at the crown of her head. The familiarity and intimate nature of the embrace felt right, and she didn't question it. Didn't resist. Just let her presence bring him comfort like he had brought her comfort and peace with her nightmares.

"I finally admitted I needed help addressing my demons. My parents never blamed me or looked at me in fear but...It took me a long time."

He pulled away far enough to look her in the eye. "Ryn, I know what nightmares that torment you relentlessly, being sleep-deprived and not dealing with the mental traumas, can do to a person. It's a deadly cocktail."

"I—"

"I don't want you to suffer as I did. Not when there's something that can help you. Not if I can help you."

She pulled away and pressed her fingertips to her eyes.

"I'm not asking you to confide in me. Not yet. I want you to come to that decision yourself. If, and when, you're ready to trust me with it."

"Tag, I can't," she whispered, shaking her head. Sadness filled her at the lost connection she temporarily allowed herself to share with him.

"Why?" he implored her.

"I can't risk it."

"You can't risk what? Letting me or anyone in? Can't risk us if that is where this was to go?"

His forwardness and candour of speaking of the rapidly growing pull that was developing between them rippled through her.

"There's too much at stake. You don't understand." Her eyes begged him to at least try though.

"You're worried about what you may reveal. I would never exploit a vulnerability. Especially not yours."

She shook her head. "I'm sorry, Tag, this is how it has to be."

Chapter 34

"It's very James Bondish." Nexin turned over a pair of cufflinks, the latest signal jammer and listening device, which was completely undetectable. Kotan had upgraded the technology to beat what was currently on the market to detect such devices, and Maari had improved the device casing and coating.

They were in the battle room the next evening and Maari, true to her promise, had come out to the estate to walk them through the latest creations. Maari had put in an extra long day today after finding out about the upcoming opportunity to plant the device on Senator Hanelson. She looked stressed when she arrived due to the adhesive continuing to give her grief, but she was relaxed now, thankfully.

"This patch, when applied to the target's skin, renders them unconscious. The patch dissolves and there is no evidence of its presence. We also have an antidote patch that you can wear in case someone else tries to use this on you."

"And this?" Tag held up a spray can. "With a push of the nozzle a fully functioning car comes out?"

Maari's dark eyes looked like glittering obsidian as she laughed. "Not quite. Daddy and Zane haven't shared or used this with you yet? May I?" she asked Ryn.

Maari sprayed a section of Ryn's caramel hair and it turned jet black. She grabbed a small, slender tube and dumped a few drops on the top section of the jet-black hair. Three pairs of eyes widened in surprise as the jet-black hair turned a vibrant red.

"It works on clothes as well."

"Very handy without having to take the precious time to change clothes or wigs." Tag felt the section of Ryn's hair, his hand grazing her cheek as he did so. She kept her face neutral, however Maari's interested look told Ryn that her friend didn't miss the exchange.

"Plus, you don't have to worry about carrying the extras or for them to be discovered if you throw them away. What else do you have? I'd like to see it all," Nexin said earnestly.

Ryn was sure there was a double meaning to his last statement. She had cornered Nexin earlier this afternoon to read him the riot act when it came to her friend.

"Honestly, I'm not interested in playing her or playing with her." Nexin had looked desperate for Ryn to believe him. "I know I come across that way, but that's not how I want it with her."

"She's fierce and strong. But there's a vulnerability to her, Nexin." Ryn didn't want to go into Maari's past history of self-esteem and self-destructive tendencies. That was for her friend to share with him, if she chose to.

"I know. I see it. I swear to you, Ryn, I wouldn't do anything to hurt her."

Ryn quietly observed Nexin with Maari now and believed him.

"I'm going to leave you guys to it." Ryn headed to the door, Nexin and Rolf's heads nodded, fully engrossed in Maari's demo. Tag moved quickly to intercept her path to the door, using his muscular frame to partially block her exit. The white t-shirt he wore hugged his bicep when he braced his arm across the doorway. The day's growth of stubble framed his lips and square jaw.

Neither of them mentioned anything about last night's walk to her place, what Tag disclosed, or her insistent refusal to let him stay with her during the night. She, of course, had slept like shit, but she kept that to herself. With Tag's keen powers of observation, she knew she wasn't hiding much though.

"Look, about earlier with Lok," Tag paused, but didn't break his gaze with hers. "I think it's a good idea."

Ire spiked. "I'm glad I have your blessing."

She made a move to duck under his arm, but he blocked her.

"Giving permission is not what I meant. I think it's a good idea for you to go see him, but also for us guys to go as well, to get to know him. He's important to you, an important part of your life."

She had been working with Lok via videoconferencing in her city studio when the guys arrived unexpectedly. Lok and Tag were like oil and water. Add a match and there was some high explosion potential there.

"Like I told the both of you, I don't need a pissing match between you. He's my friend, a good friend. And you," she shifted her gaze away, "are you."

Tag rubbed the nape of his neck, glancing at the group, still immersed in the devices, and back at Ryn. "I think getting to know each other will set everyone at ease. He's protective over you. He wants to know that we're capable and are one hundred percent committed to the job."

She narrowed her eyes at him. "I realize Lok's side of this. But what do you want out of this, Tag? Why would you want to play nice with him?"

"He's not going away anytime soon. Honestly, I want to assess him, the threat he may play, the vulnerability he could add to you." The stoic, pragmatic leader of Team Alpha stared hard down at the defiant tilt to her chin.

"He's not some asset to cultivate and use to advance your agenda," she flared, her eyes a hard, steel grey.

"Our agenda."

Maari, Rolf, and Nexin stopped going over the devices, cued into the rising heat of their conversation.

"I will play no part in placing him in a position where he can be used. Or discarded because you or Zane deem him a risk." She gritted through clenched teeth.

She pushed by him into the hallway, but Tag stopped her from leaving. No longer the stoic mask of the leader, his face softened, regret clouding his eyes. "This isn't how I wanted this conversation to go. Listen, please."

He held her arms tighter when she jerked to get away from him. "As the leader of this team, it's my duty to look at everyone each one of us interacts with through that jaded lens. Like it or not, it's necessary. But I do want to get to know Lok. We all do. He's important to you and you're an important part of this team."

He released her, sensing that she wouldn't stomp away.

She let out a hard breath, the stiffness of her shoulders diminished somewhat. "You must promise you will not use him as an asset. A pawn."

"You have my word."

She looked hard into his eyes before giving him a curt nod. "I'm trusting you."

"See, that isn't so hard, is it?" A light smile danced on his lips.

Hers tugged back in response. "We'll see. Don't make me regret it."

"Since we're doing the full disclosure thing, I would be remiss in not telling you my other motivation for agreeing."

"Agreeing." She pounced immediately. "Like you're the one that holds all the power. You might want to tread carefully for the truce we just reached."

"I'll choose my words more carefully in the future."

"Please see that you do."

Tag took a step closer and she mirrored taking one back until her back was pinned against the wall. The look on his face and in his eyes no longer had anything to do with being the leader of Team Alpha.

"I want to know how he plays into your life." He said softly, his eyes scanning hers. "What effect he has on you. Can he ease the burden you insist on carrying alone? Does he soothe your torment?

How intimate your relationship is?"

Her breath sucked in sharply in response to his words as well as his searing, searching look. Unable to move, she stood rooted to the spot between the hard walls of the hallway and Tag.

"Do you turn to him for comfort, Ryn?"

The unspoken question hung between them. Was that one of the reasons she refused to let him stay with her to keep the nightmares at bay.

It might have been easier to lie and say, yes, her and Lok were involved in a passionate romance. She could tell Tag's integrity would put a stop to his pestering her about staying with her at night. Stop him from acting on this growing attraction between them.

But she couldn't, wouldn't outright lie to him.

"No. Not that way. I told you that before. He's like my brother." Her voice cracked saying the last word.

His eyes saw the pain she kept hidden from them all. "Like the one you lost."

"Don't. Please don't." Her chest heaved, repressing her growing emotion. Coupled with the ever-increasing pull of him and the overwhelming urge to confide in Tag and to let him comfort her, she needed to get away from him.

"I'm only surmising."

"Tag," she warned.

"Okay." He moved his hand to push her hair back from her face but lowered it before touching her. "Okay."

He stepped away from her, slower than he had advanced on her, and she warily watched him.

"We're in agreeance that Lok's brilliant idea for us guys to go with you to New York is a good one?"

"It's an idea alright."

A smile tugged at the corner of Tag's lips. Damn that small crooked smile. She ripped her eyes from his lips.

Meeting his golden-brown eyes wasn't much better.

The need to get away from him spiked higher.

"Can I go now boss?"

The alpha of Team Alpha looked down intently at her and finally stepped fully out of the way to let her by.

She cursed him, then herself, all the way down to the lower level of the house as she stalked toward the pool.

The crappy night of sleep, the constant battling of her attraction to Tag, along with managing the spike in emotions he caused in her, were starting to unravel her. Add in another day of being surrounded by people, and she was mentally drained. She needed some time alone to recharge.

The tension in her neck and back released seeing the water, breathing the humid air and hearing the tropical noises and water cascading down the wall. She grabbed a suit from the drawer, mentally making note to bring more one-piece swim suits down here. She quickly donned the two-piece and adjusted the cross-back sport top. It was lower cut than she was comfortable with, but it would do.

Diving into the cool water, she loved the shock it brought to her warm body. She was beginning to notice she felt warm whenever Tag was nearby. Annoyed by the thought, she kicked hard and deliberately banished thoughts of Tag, his hotness, and his growing effect on her.

An hour later, with smooth, relaxed strokes and Tag-free thoughts, the mental drain of the past twenty-four hours was washed away. She dove deep under the water and popped up on the ledge, feeling refreshed. Ryn stepped backwards when she stood up and Tag was right there.

He reached out to steady her, but she jerked without thinking at the contact of his strong, warm hands on her bare skin. Instead of letting her fall back, Tag clasped her tightly to him, his sturdy core stabilizing them, so they didn't topple into the water.

His broad chest rumbled under her cheek, pressed fully against it, one hand embedded in her hair and the other splayed across her lower back. His laugh died quickly as he processed what he was feeling across a section of her lower back.

She stiffened and pushed away from him, but he didn't fully let her go. His hands lingered on her arms. "Sorry I startled you. You weren't in your studio, so I took a chance you were here."

He let her go when she tried to step away from him again.

"Did I forget about a training session?" She made a move to go around him, turning her body to keep her right side out of view, but he sidestepped around her to stand behind her. His sharp intake of breath told her exactly what he was looking at.

Damn, why wasn't there a fucking one-piece suit down here?

A large jagged scar started at the base of her right underarm, ran the length of her side, and at the crest of her hip, it wrapped around her back, stopping just before the midline of her spine.

She normally didn't wear anything that revealed so much of her torso, but she didn't expect to have company. It wasn't vanity. She didn't want the questions that would inevitably follow when people saw a scar like that.

Nessa had offered to find a surgeon to help remove it or reduce it after Ryn had physically recovered from her death scape that brought her and Zane's paths together. But she declined. There were probably more to follow before this was over.

"Ryn."

"I'm sure you have many scars as well." She quickly wrapped the towel around her, not ready to turn around and face him.

He was quiet for too long. She could feel, rather than see, the intensity of his gaze, knew the muscle at the back of his jaw bulged as he clenched it tightly shut.

"I do. Every one of them with a story of how it came to be."

He left it at that.

Giving her an opening. An opening to share something of her with him.

She didn't bite.

"Why are you here, Tag?" She turned to grab her clothes.

"Ryn."

"No."

"It's okay. I—"

"I can't do this right now." She said hoarsely.

"Okay. Fuck. Okay." Tag clenched and unclenched his fists. "Is that how you hurt your right shoulder too?"

She whirled on him in anger at his insistence on not dropping the subject, but realized slowly what he asked. She narrowed her eyes.

"I noticed there was a tightness in your stroke on that side when I came in. And on our second night here, you were asleep in your studio with a pack on your right shoulder."

"That was you." She sat heavily on the lounger and he sat on the one across from her. His white shirt, wet from her, clung to his chest and stomach, his long legs relaxed in front of him.

"Was that part of the reason you were so pissed off the next day?"

She couldn't help but give a reluctant smile.

"I made a mental note to ask you about your shoulder in case it was a liability in the field. It's good to know what our limitations are and where our weaknesses lie."

"It doesn't impede movements or strength, normally. Only gives me grief when I overdo it."

Tag nodded, confident in her answer.

"Why are you down here, Tag?"

"Shit, sorry. There's been some quasi-relevant information starting to come in through the device we placed on the Strada computer server."

Their parallel op to hers the night the Strada site exploded. The night she found the file on Monahague Bay. The bay that was close to where she grew up and where her family still lived. Safe for now because they, along with her would-be murderers, believed she was dead. Safe because of her hidden truth and secrets.

"Nothing urgent or completely revealing at this point, but we wanted you to be aware."

"Give me ten and I'll be right there."

"Ryn, about last night and what I shared with you." He brought his knees in to lean his elbows on and interlinked his fingers before pulling them apart again. Nervousness was not a regularity for him. "We haven't had a chance to talk about it."

She wasn't sure where he was going with this and didn't want to say the wrong thing, so she waited.

"I hope it doesn't affect how you think of me or make you perceive me as a security risk to you or anyone else on the team."

She leaned forward. "Tag, look at me."

He looked at her through lowered eyes.

"I have no concerns about you or my safety or the safety of others around you. You didn't have to share that with me, but I'm glad you did." She smiled softly. "It explains why you're such a pain in my ass about the sleep issue."

"Don't let it bite you in the ass, Ryn. Promise?"

"Cross my heart."

"See you upstairs in ten."

Ryn continued watching the door after Tag left through it, startled by the ringing of her phone.

"Lok, what's up? Aren't you supposed to be on stage soon?" She quickly calculated the time difference in Auckland, New Zealand. It would be close to midnight the next day there.

"Ryn, so glad I caught you. I'm due onstage in five but...gah. I hated how things went down earlier with me and the guys. I needed to talk to you before I went on. It's been bothering me all night."

"Lok, it ended fine. You played nice and invited them to come up to New York when you're there next."

"I know, and I meant it. But it wasn't sitting well how I initially reacted to that Tag guy and put you in the middle of crossfire."

"Well, the first thing you can do to make this better is stop calling him 'That Tag Guy'."

"You're right." Lok chuckled guiltily.

"We're good. If you guys keep the aggressive and belligerent versions of yourselves out of the picture, we'll be fine."

"Peaches and cream are more my style than nails and pitchforks."

She laughed. "An interesting pairing and comparison, but I get your meaning."

The noise level in the background rose to a roar then cut off again.

"Doyle find you and is there to drag your ass onto the stage?"

"One more minute," Lok said before returning his attention back to her. "Sorry, and yes."

"Lok, we're good. I swear. Now get your ass out there before Doyle strings mine up the next time she sees me."

"If you can take a guy named Tank, I don't think so. But you sure? We good?"

"We good. Go blast the body paint off the crowd."

Chapter 35

Days later, Ryn stood in her bedroom in her underwear, trying on dresses Maari brought for May's gala that was in two hours. She was nervous. Not because it was an op, but because of who her plus one was for the event. She had made a case for Rolf or Nexin but everyone kiboshed that, for the 'chemistry' factor, and she was stuck with Tag.

She snatched the sheath dress Maari tossed at her, drawing her attention back to the task at hand. She threw it over the chair.

"Not gonna happen."

"It's designed by Toovan. He's the latest hot upcomer and he's to die for."

"I don't care if it was handcrafted by the big guy himself."

"All your private bits would be covered."

"Pass me the maroon glitter one."

"Christ, Ryn, it's burgundy and sequin. You're officially banned from training clothes, jeans and t-shirts." Maari, huffed, still dressed in her dress-to-kill work cloths, a thin cut ivory skirt, matching silk blouse with a navy paisley pattern and navy stiletto heels.

"Quit giving me the stink eye." Ryn shimmied into the dress and smoothed the material into place over her hips.

"Holy shit, you do have some fashion sense. That one is soul-sucking perfect." Maari turned her toward the mirror to do up the back.

The high choker style covered the residual faint scratches on her neck. The material hugged her left shoulder and arm like a second skin, leaving her right shoulder and arm bare. The sequin was embedded into the burgundy material to leave the fabric smooth over her curves.

"That colour makes your eyes look like charcoal. Like the colour of shirts Tag looks deadly in."

"Stop." Ryn groaned.

Maari's impish grin flashed in the mirror. "He's going to shit kittens."

Tag waited in the living room of Ryn's apartment with Nexin and Rolf, double checking the earpieces.

"I like the choice of a dark grey dress shirt instead of a white one. You look sharp man." Nexin set the tablet on the counter.

"Speaking of sharp, you have your blade?" Rolf repacked the equipment bag, sliding his gun into a secure pocket.

Everything had been packed at the estate, but they were all on edge. It was their first official op of Ryn's mission. It wasn't high risk, but they were prepared for any possibilities.

"We're sure the coating Maari applied to the knives makes them undetectable?"

"I went through four different metal detectors today and no blips. Maari's product is solid."

Tag smiled at the quiet pride in his friend's last statement. Working together the past couple of years, he had never known Nexin to be like this with anyone.

A movement on the stairs caught his eye and the air disappeared from his lungs. Ryn glided down, statuesque, and the dress shimmered with her every movement. Her tall, lean frame moved gracefully, and his eyes devoured the muscular curve of her bare shoulder and arm, the tight tone of her thigh that peaked through the high slit of the gown.

Her caramel hair was swept up in an elegant twist and Tag was taken aback by the open appraisal when he met her dark grey eyes.

"You are stunning."

"You clean up pretty good, Taggert Hale."

Nexin let out a long, low whistle. "Exquisite. You have your blade?"

Ryn patted her thigh.

"A functional dress. Good pick."

Rolf loomed tall over her even with the added height from her heels and pressed a tiny earpiece into her palm. "Steel wrapped in beauty. Ready?"

Maari looked proud as a mother watching her daughter leave for the prom. "The device for the Senator is on her earring."

"Rolf and I will take up position nearby in case you need back-up. We'll turn on communication in ten minutes."

"Let's go see what the asshat can tell us." The raucous laughter of her team settled her nerves.

Zane's regular limo service driver, Charles, smiled and opened the door for them. Tag pressed close against her on the seat. His citrus and sage scent, the hard press of his thigh and shoulder made his presence overpowering. She scooted away.

Ryn pulled a tube of lipgloss, a gift from Maari, and triple tapped the end to activate the sensor to detect any recording or transmitting devices that were not theirs. They didn't expect the limo to be bugged, however, caution was mandatory.

"Smart to put the device on your earring."

"Maari isn't completely satisfied with the adhesive yet. Less skin oils are better."

They determined the best place to put the device would be behind one of the Senator's ears. The trick would be to get that close to him and the area without drawing attention.

Tag's golden-brown eyes studied her and her skin tingled in response.

"You look amazing."

Ryn shifted under his intense gaze. "Surprised? Maari threatened to ban my entire wardrobe."

Tag chuckled and gave her chin a gentle flick.

The intimate gesture sent shivers of electricity through her.

"The colour of your shirt—"

"Matches your eyes."

"Most couples coordinate their outfits, not their shirt with their partner's eye colour." Ryn sucked in a breath, realizing what she implied.

Tag brought his thumb to her chin again to tilt up her face. "I'd say we aren't like most."

Tag's eyes were riveted to her mouth and his hand cupped the curve of her jaw. His fingertips grazed the sensitive skin at the back of her neck, sending another round of energy jolting through her.

The past week, she had worked diligently to keep a physical distance from him. After the encounter in the pool area - his hands on her bare, wet skin and being pressed tight against him - it was wise to do so.

Her mind told her to break contact now, but her body would not obey.

"You smell like cinnamon and vanilla."

"You smell like citrus and sage."

Surprised liquid gold eyes met hers. "I do?"

Ryn's eyes dropped to his lower full lip, the firm line of his square jaw. "You do."

He had left the scruff on his face, rather than going clean shaven. She ached to trace his lips with her fingertips, to wrap her hands around his head, pull those lips to hers and feel the scruff against her skin.

"We are en route now." Rolf's voice rumbled over their earpieces.

Shock ran through her and she pulled away quickly.

"It's been ten minutes already." Tag sighed leaning back into the seat.

"Time flies when you're having fun, right?" Nexin's mischievous grin carried through the tiny device embedded in her ear.

"We're ready if needed from our end." Zane confirmed. Kotan would hack into the hotel's system to trigger alarms if the situation with the Senator got too risky.

"It's your first date; it brings a tear to my eye." Nexin sniffed, but then gave a wicked chuckle. "Remember, this is your first public appearance as a couple, make sure you at least appear to be enjoying each other's company."

Tag gave her a long look. "We can manage."

The opulent lobby of the luxury hotel had additional security personnel and protocol for the esteemed gathering of political leaders and those in their elite circle. The elegant ivory marble floor gleamed and the people waiting to go through security looked as lavish and ornate as the lobby.

Tag tucked her hand securely in the crock of his arm and leaned closer. "Smile at me like I'm the most witty, charming man you have ever breathed on."

"Breathed on?" She laughed and returned Senator Antel's wave of welcome.

"That's better."

They passed through the metal detectors with no event and found the Grand Ballroom. Even more opulent and lavish than the lobby, the light brown floor glistened surrounded by ivory and bronze furnishings.

A string quartet played near the front of the room and Tag passed her a glass of champagne. His eyes only leaving hers to scan and observe the room for any hidden threats.

"My dear, it is lovely to see you again." A regal, blonde woman leaned in to kiss Ryn on the cheek.

"Senator and Mr. Antel, it's great to see you both as well."

"Please my sweet girl, it is Ida and Bernard. And who is this handsome young man?"

"This is Taggert Hale. Tag, this is Ida and Bernard Antel, May's parents."

Tag shook their hands while Ida looked closer at him. "I have seen you before. Ah yes, at May's earlier gala event. You were there with Zane Andrews."

Sharp and observant. *I wonder what she could provide on Senator Hanelson?* Guilt shot through Ryn and she shoved the thought away.

"I am pleased to see you at such a stuffy event." Bernard's green eyes softened when he gazed at his wife. "It is nice to breath new energy and life into these parties and this shrewish crowd."

Ida gently slapped her husband on the arm but looked at him affectionately. "It is true. But duty beckons and I must make my rounds with the shrewish crowd." Ida leaned in to kiss Ryn's cheek again. "Enjoy your evening."

"They're down to earth people." Tag finished his champagne as they walked away.

"I'd agree with that assessment."

"It pleases me that you concur."

She snorted lightly. "It pleases you that I don't disagree with you."

"It's all a matter of framing the message." He set her champagne down and his breath quickened along with hers when he pulled her close. "Dance with me."

He took her hand in his and wrapped his other snuggly around the small of her waist.

"Tag, people are starting to stare." She tried to create some space between their bodies.

"That's the point, is it not? And how can they not stare with you in that dress."

Tag was a smooth dancer, expertly moving them around the dance floor. For a tall, broad man, he moved gracefully with a quiet, sure strength. The taut muscles of his back rippled under her hand.

"Behind and to your left is Senator Asshat." Tag whispered in her ear. His scruff sent a tingle down the side of her neck.

"His eyes keep darting over to you." There was a firm displeasure in Tag's tone.

She took note of Senator Hanelson as her Tag spun her. He resembled his son, Ched, with golden hair, blue eyes, and tanned skin. But where Ched was attractive, the Senator's pampered lifestyle wasn't kind to him. His tanned skin was leathery and puffed and his large paunch strained the buttons of his tuxedo jacket.

He stood beside his ever-faithful wife, a short woman with black, curly hair that would be attractive except for her sour look. In public, the Senator honed the image of a doting family man, but she knew better. Judging by the look of disdain in his eyes when he looked at his wife, that confirmed it was a ruse for votes and power.

Tag spun her again.

"You won't be going far from my side given the look he just gave you." His hand tightened around her waist.

"To accomplish what we came here for tonight, that can play in our favour."

Tag gave a small growl and pulled her off the dance floor toward the food table.

"All this dainty finger food. Where's the steak?"

Tag laughed at her disappointment, passing her a plate.

"Mi amor! You are radiant. So ravishing."

Chocolate brown eyes and a devilish grin greeted her. Antonio, never one to blend in, was resplendent in a bronze silk martini jacket rather than the standard tux.

Antonio pressed a kiss on each cheek and offered his hand to Tag. "You're Tag. I've heard of you from Lok. You are a strapping guy, aren't you?"

Tag smiled and Ryn rolled her eyes. "Tag, this is Antonio Demeanus. I work with him at Classic Vibe Recordings."

"Work with me? Please, what we do is not work. Has she told you how Lok and I stumbled upon her?"

"No, she hasn't regaled me with that story." Tag grinned at her discomfort.

"It really is movie worthy. It involved a piano in a park, me innocently eating lunch, and then hearing the most glorious piece of music to ever grace my ears. It. Was. Breathtaking."

"Antonio has what many call a dramatic flair. I call it overinflating bullshit."

"Lies." Antonio growled.

"May, it's great to see you." Ryn diverted the attention from her to welcome the tall, curvy blonde. Draped in a black, flowing gown, her blonde hair bundled loosely on her head, she was a vision.

"I'm so pleased you made it. And with a gorgeous plus one." May flashed Tag an appreciative smile.

"One who does not compare with his present company."

"A charmer also. How delightful."

"How delightful indeed." Antonio contemplated Tag closer, and flashed Ryn a grin. "Miguel sends his hello."

"Couldn't convince him to come?"

"Ryn, the man would rather poke hot needles in his eyes. No offense, May, but you know how he is."

"No offense taken; these events are not for everyone." She leaned into the group to whisper. "But I do love swindling money out of this crowd."

"You're naughty and I love it." Antonio kissed May's hand lavishly.

"Seriously though, my drive comes from the causes and helping people."

"It's refreshing for people to use their influence to help others instead of themselves."

"I couldn't agree more, Tag." May turned her serious green eyes to Ryn. "I noticed when I was coming out of the side wing entrance from the kitchen that you had caught Senator Hanelson's attention. Be wary of that one."

"He seems to be a family man." Ryn hoped her innocent tone sounded sincere.

May scoffed. "Not even close. I have to run. Antonio, will you mingle with me, or would you rather stay and visit?"

"My dear, I'm your plus one. And I would never want to cramp the style of these two." Antonio gave Tag a conspiring wink and kissed Ryn's nose.

Tag contemplated May's back as the pair walked away.

"She's a possible source for information." Nexin clicked on over the earpiece.

"I'm not sure how we'd get it without raising any questions." Ryn was reluctant to pull any of the Antels into this.

Tag and Ryn continued to dance, mingle, and drink small amounts of champagne. The Senator on the other hand, drank copious amounts and the more he drank, the more openly he watched Ryn.

Her skin crawled and the tension in Tag's rigid back did little to alleviate the anxious pit growing in her stomach.

She excused herself to go to the washroom, but Tag followed closely.

"What are you doing?" she hissed.

"I'm not giving that lecher any chances."

She smiled sweetly up at him as a couple passed them in the narrow hallway. "Need I remind you, that is what we are here to do? Now please, I really do have to go. And unless you have the bladder of a whale, I imagine you do too."

Tag patted his toned stomach. "The first thing they teach you in the army is to hold your piss."

"Jesus." She couldn't help laughing.

"Do not leave without me."

The line in the women's restroom was shockingly short, and Tag wasn't out yet when she emerged. A hand darted out from an alcove. She resisted striking the figure and instead allowed herself to be pulled face to face with bloodshot blue eyes that leered at her.

"And who do we have here? I'm Senator Hanelson but you, my sweet juicy mint, can call me William."

Amazing how a look can make a person feel violated. The small knife strapped to her thigh pressed against her skin. She took a step back to widen the space between them, but he held fast.

"Nice to meet you Senator, I'm Severyn And—"

"Oh, I know who you are. You're a lovely peach." His sweaty hand rose to stroke her cheek but was caught midair by fingers that wrapped around his fleshy wrist like an iron-shackle.

She glanced over her shoulder at Tag staring at the Senator with cold, flat eyes and didn't hold her breath for a second chance. She gently removed the device off her earring while the drunk Senator stiffened his spine, trying in vain to look more dominant than the alpha male in front of him. He really was an asshat.

"Tag, this is Senator Hanelson."

"Senator. My apologies." Tag sounded genuinely verklempt. He released the Senator's wrist and gave her a slight nudge as he moved to shake the slimeball's hand. She stumbled slightly forward.

"Oh my goodness, I'm so sorry." Her finger grazed the skin behind his right ear while her other hand braced against his soft chest.

"No problem at all, my dear." He purred and rested his hands on her waist.

She fought the urge to break every one of his fat fingers.

Tag pulled her away from the lecherous grip, casually wrapping his arm around her shoulders. "A pleasure to meet you, Senator."

"The pleasure was all mine."

Tag pushed her ahead of him to shield her as they walked

through the narrow hallway.

"Success." She whispered.

"Good work you two." Zane let out a sigh of relief.

Tag took her hand. "Let's get the hell out of here."

Chapter 36

"Our first op was a smashing success, Rynnie, little moo moo. The big guy and I did jack shit but we were still there if you needed us. We need to celebrate."

Nexin poured her another shot of scotch as part of their celebration at her apartment. He had had more than his share and was oblivious when she dumped hers into his tumbler.

"We have been celebrating. For the past two hours. Your bed is calling."

"Do you think a certain raven-haired beauty might want to join me?"

Ryn snorted and Rolf prodded his resistant teammate toward the door, giving her a fond smile. "You were smooth tonight."

She gave him a grateful look. "Thank you, I'm leaving them in your care for safe delivery home. Now, Tag, get your ass moving."

Her shove did little to displace Tag's ass from the tall stool at the island.

"I'm not ready."

"Get."

"You may need help with the zipper on your dress. I am here to serve." He bowed, still seated on the stool.

Damn scotch. But her skin tingled at the thought of his fingers trailing down her spine.

"Surprisingly, I've been able to dress myself for many years and I'm certain I can manage. Now go."

Tag tilted her chin, standing to look down at her. His closeness was more intoxicating than the scotch.

"I can stay in case you need anything."

"We've covered this." She took a step back from his hard frame and the overpowering openness in his golden-brown eyes.

Rolf grabbed Tag, while pushing Nexin toward the door. "Like herding rabid cats."

She burst out laughing at Nexin and Tag's indignant looks but closed the door. She engaged the locks quickly before Tag changed his mind about being a willing passivist, led away by the giant man.

She leaned heavily on the door, fighting the disastrous urge to open it and ask Tag to stay.

Closing her eyes, she remembered the limo ride to the gala, the feel of him moving on the dance floor, the protective wrap of his arm around her shoulders. The desire she felt, then and now, wanting to be in his arms. To be his.

He filled her mind. Strong and honest. Integrity behind every one of his actions.

He deserved more. More than she could give him. More than she was.

She slid to the floor pulling her knees to her chest. The Grand Canyon of secrets, untold truths, and lies lay between them.

Severyn Andrews was a lie.

Taggert Hale was risk.

To her grandma, who was her third parent who enabled her secret talent for music. To her mom, who would work herself to the bone to give her children what they needed. To her dad, who would drop everything to help anyone in need. To her brothers - Reg, Hugh and Wilson - one wise, one adventure-seeking, and one yearning to live outside of the conventional box - family beat through their veins as much as blood. And to her young sister Fiala, sweet little Fi, whose innocence brought Ryn to her knees.

Ryn hung her head in her hands. Even if she thought there was no risk to her family by revealing the truth of who she was to Tag, how would he feel about her once he knew her truth and secrets?

Disgusted?

Full of contempt and loathing?

Would he despise her for what she was willingly putting her family through?

No, she must keep her secrets hidden. At all costs.

But she was not sure who, in the end, would pay the price.

I hope you enjoyed reading about Ryn as much I loved writing her. To read an excerpt from Hidden Carnage (Hidden, #2), continue reading.

Remember, you can grab The Hidden Dossier, the companion document for the Hidden Series, for FREE. This provides readers with some unique insight into the characters, the books, along with other interesting tidbits to illuminate bringing the story to life.

Please consider taking a moment to post an honest review of Hidden Truth & Secrets anywhere you choose (example: Amazon, Goodreads or elsewhere). Reviews are always appreciated and help authors out tremendously.

Download your FREE Hidden Dossier www.corajanzenwrites.com

Instagram @corajanzenwrites
Facebook @corajanzenwrites
Join Cora's Hidden Readers Facebook Group

Read on for an excerpt from Hidden Carnage (Hidden, #2)

Available Fall 2020

Her feet pounded the hard earth, the jarring action shooting spikes of sharp pain through her shins and knees as tree branches whipped her face. But still, she pushed on.

It was a well-trodden path in the woods, beyond the sprawling estate house, that she had walked many times the last few weeks. During those times, the path, surrounded by the raw beauty of nature and the hush of trees, was able to bring her a small measure of peace. Peace that resolutely alluded her everywhere else.

Peace that was nowhere in sight now.

Peace that she didn't think she'd ever feel again.

No, today was not a peaceful walk where she sought solace observing the wonders of nature. Today she was running. Running from the hell that opened like a swirling black hole, pulling her into its empty vortex.

The hell that came with the sudden, and full onslaught, of the return of her memories.

Memories that had been locked away, maybe as her mind's way of knowing to protect her while she physically recovered from her many injuries.

Because her mind, her heart, her soul, couldn't handle her memories and the horrifying reality that came with them. Couldn't handle the pain that she unintentionally caused to her loved ones. Couldn't accept the pain that she intentionally needed to cause them, in order to keep them safe.

She stumbled but kept running as if the demons had escaped from hell and were hard on her heels.

Her breath came in hard, ragged bursts as her lungs gasped and her legs burned. Yet she didn't give in. She pushed on.

Faster.

If she could go faster, maybe she could outrun the demons. Outrace the terror and horror of what her memories brought with them.

For weeks she had desperately fought to get her memories back. To remember who she was. Who her family were. Where she came from. And how she came to be at the estate so broken and battered.

And now that they finally returned…

She stumbled again on a tree root and slammed onto her hands and knees. Pain shot through every cell in her body and a sob jumped from her throat.

Tears streamed hot down her face, as she hung her head in despair.

Oh my god. Fi. Mom. How can I do this?

"Don't think. Stop fucking thinking!" She screamed into the silence of the trees.

A surge of rage flooded her entire being. Rage at herself. Rage at the trees and the silence. How dare they be there, surrounding her. How dare they exist, when everything that she had ever known had ceased to exist.

Now to be replaced with lies, deceit, pain, and regret.

She bolted to her feet, to resume her race away from the torrent of overwhelming memories and reality that came to consume her. To torment and haunt her.

Her right shoulder screamed with pain. Her ribs burned as if a hot poker skewered through them, the tight wrap around them only providing a small measure of protection. Her head and face ached in agony, yet she still pushed on.

She relished the pain. Focused on it. Drew strength from it.

It fuelled her on, as she struggled through the trees, to keep her legs running underneath her. The pain helped push down the guilt that threatened to wrap her in its iron-clutch.

Guilt for what had been done. Guilt for the lie that she needed to continue to let happen.

She was stumbling, barely on her feet now, her body and untrained system could no longer provide sufficient oxygen to meet the demand of her muscles and to clear out the build-up of lactic acid.

Crisp sea salted air hit her and she fell into the clearing where the woods ended. A rocky spot filled with tufts of wild grass ended abruptly with a cliff overlooking the wild Atlantic sea.

It was Fall on the Massachuets coast, and a storm brewed out over the waters, making the air chilled with warning of what was to come.

The cold, the whipping wind. She didn't care. Let the storm come and carry her away.

She pushed off the ground, only to collapse to her knees once again and cry into the wind. An anguished sound filled with sorrow and defeat.

Finally, no longer physically able to outrun her memories, her guilt, her demons, she let them overtake her. No fight left in her. No will to resist. Gasping for air, she let it come.

Sobs wracked her body and memories ravaged her soul.

Vlad, her friend since childhood, lying dead in her arms, her father's near death as his work truck exploded, her tiny little sister lying beaten and bruised in the hospital bed. All because of her. All because of something that she knew or had. And had no idea what in blazing hell it was, or who wanted it bad enough, to threaten, hurt, and kill people for.

She remembered the sheer terror she felt moments before she plunged to her certain death. She was only alive because of a narrow stroke of luck, that Zane and Kotan secretly intervened to pull off her 'death scape.'

Her sobs subsided, but her memories remained, along with the reality of what she must do.

Her family believed her dead. And she needed to keep it that way to keep them safe.

But the thought of the heartache and sadness her family would be feeling, and that she could take away their pain, almost undid her once again.

"How can I do this?" The violent winds coming off the ocean carried her question away.

"With a bit of help from your friends."

A tall, lithe young woman jumped down from the brown sorel she rode and tied the reins of her horse, as well as the large black and white paint she led, to the tree. Her sheet of razor straight black hair whipped in the wind and matched her onyx eyes. A striking beauty strode confidently towards her crumpled body on the ground.

"They sent you to retrieve me, Maari?" She sat up and roughly wiped the last of her tears from her face.

Maari gracefully sat down on a felled log and patted the rough surface beside her. "You are not a prisoner here, Severyn."

"That's not my name."

"I know it wasn't, but it has to be now." Kindness shone in Maari's eyes. "Severyn is nice though, even though it's characteristically a male name. Daddy says its meaning is linked with visionaries who are willing to change the world. Maybe that's a glimpse into your future?"

Severyn sat on the log beside Maari watching the ocean. The waves roiled with the growing storm, turbulent and harsh, yet they brought a measure of calm to her.

"Severyn is a good name but I do like Ryn. May I call you Ryn?"

"Whatever floats your boat."

A long piece of raven hair caught on Maari's two studs beneath her lip. "Ryn it is."

About the Author

Cora Janzen was born and raised in Saskatchewan, Canada and loves the beauty of the prairies as well as the rich diverse landscape of Canada.

Happily married with two teenage children, Cora made the leap to begin her author journey in late 2017 after realizing a 'daydream story' that had played, developed, and evolved in her mind is actually a novel. After this realization and a few more years of overcoming self-doubt and fear of putting herself out there, she took the plunge to capture the story on paper and to share it with the world.

She is blessed to be able to share the story of Severyn's journey that has blossomed in her mind for over 25 years.

Author's Note

The stories in the novel series, and the dossier information, is fictional. Any information regarding persons, places, various professions, and their roles, is used for fictional purposes, and with creative literary license, therefore discrepancies between fiction and reality may appear. In an effort for allyship, there was a desire to incorporate various cultures and identities into the story. The author acknowledges her lack of lived insight as well as the complex, diverse, and often layered experiences of people from all ethnic and cultural backgrounds, gender identities, sexual and romantic identities indicated with the novel series and the dossier.

Made in the USA
Columbia, SC
31 December 2020